RESURFACE

Tony Batton

A Chief Executive in jail,

a company in tatters

A hidden facility pushing

the boundaries of scientific research

A deadly assassin on a mission for revenge

An item of unstable technology

stolen from a CIA black site

A plot to make us more than human,

whatever the risks

A young man

that connects them all

RESURFACE
First UK Edition v.001

First published in 2016 by Twenty-First Century Thrillers

Find out more about the author at:
www.tonybatton.com

And to get a FREE short techno-thriller, go to:
http://www.tonybatton.com/free-story-from-interface

for Mum and Dad

ONE

TWENTY-SIX YEARS AGO

A bell jangled angrily as Amelia Fourier opened the restaurant door. She inhaled the sharp tang of fried onions and felt her stomach lurch – she had planned for so many things, but the odour had not been one of them. Adjusting the bag on her shoulder, she held her breath and stepped through the doorway.

Outside a steady stream of traffic droned past, headlights blurry in the drizzling rain, but few vehicles pulled over. The car park was nearly empty, as was the restaurant, with no other buildings for nearly a mile in either direction. Isolation had been one of her primary selection criteria: part of the detailed planning and preparation that had gone into this meeting, which was not surprising given the stakes.

The man sat in a booth next to a condensation-smeared window. He wore an unremarkable grey suit, his hair cut militarily short, although she thought she could see the first signs of baldness. His eyes did not even flicker her way, yet Amelia had no doubt he had seen her. She ignored the waitress, tucked the heavy bag under her arm, and slid onto the seat opposite him.

He glanced up from the plastic-coated menu. "French fries for breakfast, what's not to like?"

She swung her head around the room, counting four other patrons. "It hasn't drawn much business. I assume they're all your people, Mr...?"

He placed the menu down and spread his hands on the table. "Fine. Everyone in here, including the waitress, is part of my team. And you don't need to know my name."

"Behind that Ivy League accent, I can hear the edge of something else. Spanish or Italian, maybe?"

The man shrugged. "We're all from somewhere. And sometimes we want to leave that somewhere behind. Isn't that why you're here?" He produced a large, crisp white envelope, and placed it on the table.

Amelia held herself still, fighting the urge to grab the envelope and run. Although she wouldn't get too far in her present condition. She opened her black sports holdall and withdrew a thick card folder. She placed it on the table and slid it towards him. "That's everything I could access: schematics, test results, design parameters. CERUS Biotech's finest work."

He picked it up and started to flick through the pages. "You're sure you weren't detected?"

"If I wasn't sure, I wouldn't be here. You do with it what you will, but I don't want to know."

"We won't be able to do anything if we can't make it work."

"Not my concern." Amelia reached into the bag a second time and lifted out a cube-shaped object, wrapped in brown paper and tape.

The man frowned. "What is that?"

"I couldn't very well leave it unattended."

He coughed and shrank back. "I wasn't expecting... Is it safe?"

"The case is shielded. And of course it's just a prototype – not fully functional: I've been clear about that."

"I don't have the arrangements in place--"

"You want me to take it away?" She watched him think it over, knowing there was only one possible outcome.

He turned away, holding a finger to his ear, and muttered a few words that Amelia couldn't make out. He listened, nodded, then turned back. "We're arranging a secure transport. Our deal can proceed."

"I'm glad to hear it. And I'm sure this is doing no harm to your career prospects."

"That's of no consequence, Ma'am. I'm just doing my duty."

"Rationalise it how you wish." She looked pointedly at the envelope. "Now it's your turn."

He slid it slowly across the table. "My superiors would probably shoot me for asking, but I have to know--"

"Why didn't I ask for more? Because this isn't about money." She gave a half laugh, then carefully opened the envelope. A passport. Drivers licence. A selection of other identification documents. Two credit cards. "They look authentic."

"They should." The man cleared his throat. "You didn't want to change your first name?"

"No, I like it." She placed the documents in the holdall, closed it and rose to her feet, grimacing at the aches in her legs.

He stood and shook her hand. "Goodbye Amelia *Faraday*. I wish you both," he glanced at her belly, "the very best."

TWO

PRESENT DAY

DEPUTY DIRECTOR CONNOR Truman marched down the corridor of the Langley office building. He knocked once on the door at the end then entered, nodding to the man who sat at the long meeting table: CIA Director Lazlo Banetti was a squat, grizzled man with ominous eyebrows and an unreadable expression.

"What was wrong with my office?" Banetti said, rubbing a hand over his shaven head.

"We generally assume the NSA has it bugged. This needs to be for your ears only." Truman set his tablet computer on the table and began playing a video recording. On screen was a view of the side entrance of a metal-clad building. Stencilled on a small door were the words 'Government Facility - Strictly Private Property'. Below that was an eight-digit number. Two government security guards walked through the field of view. As soon as they passed out of sight, a figure clad in black sprinted from the shadows and straight up to the camera. For a moment, the man's face was framed in the shot. Then the image went blank.

"No other cameras?" Banetti asked.

"Already disabled. Within seconds of that last camera going out, all systems at the building went off-line - only for a couple of minutes, but it was long enough for them to get inside the warehouse and take something. It raised a flag and you were contacted directly; you were in a national security council meeting, so the call diverted to me. The item taken is described as a Level Seven storage pod, but I've been unable to learn what was in it," Truman coughed. "Or anything else about the facility. Classified above my level of clearance, apparently."

"Level Seven?" Banetti appeared to freeze. "What was the number on that door?"

Truman glanced at his notes. "8543-0009."

"Tell me that isn't Warehouse 102."

"I wasn't aware you took such a great interest in our storage facilities."

"It's an off-grid federal black site. It goes three storeys below ground."

"With only a few guards?"

"We try not to draw too much attention to what it really is, so we rely rather heavily on security systems. The face of the intruder - bring it up again."

Truman tapped his tablet and the image appeared on screen. "I had it enhanced but the resolution isn't great: the face looks a little flat. Male, Caucasian. I've already run him through the joint agencies criminal database. No hits."

Banetti stared at the screen. "He won't be in them. He's someone we've been trying to locate for more than twelve months. A British national named Thomas Faraday. Until this point we've found no trace of him."

"Isn't it odd then that he let his face be recorded?"

"Maybe. My more immediate concern is that Mr Faraday has taken a very valuable, very dangerous piece of technology. What do you know about CERUS Biotech?"

"Beyond what was in the news, very little. I never gave the rumours much credence."

Banetti raised an eyebrow. "Maybe you should have. Go home and pack. You're on a flight to London in..." Banetti glanced at his watch, "four hours. By then your clearance will have been upgraded and you can read the full brief. You'll need to be up to date when you land."

Truman gave a snort. "I can't just leave. Quite apart from my executive responsibilities, I'm working two dozen active cases."

"I'll reassign all of it. This is more important."

"I see. Why London?"

"So you can meet with an old friend of mine."

THREE

THE BOAT WAS A DULL grey: at first glance, quite unremarkable. It looked a little like one of the twenty-metre-long motor launches operated by the Metropolitan Police. But what was beneath the exterior was entirely different. It sat too low in the water, and moved with a nimbleness that belied its considerable weight, the result of its strengthened armour plating and the high-tech equipment woven into its structure. Its two 400-horsepower engines delivered a cruising speed of sixty knots, though it was considerably faster over shorter distances. It was one of a few special craft operated by the Security Service, MI5. Today, it was being used for a special purpose, not recorded in any official log.

On the top deck a woman in a smart grey suit stood looking out across the Thames. Here in London's Docklands the river was wide and slow, sweeping a great languorous arc, and the boat was holding station with almost no thrust. It was positioned in the shadow of a tall, glass-fronted office tower. She turned to a crewman standing behind her. "Bring him up."

The man spoke into his earpiece. A door at the foot of a flight of stairs down into the belly of the craft opened. Two heavily built guards steered an older man upwards. He was handcuffed and wore orange prison overalls. The man held up the handcuffs. "Are these really necessary, Stephanie?"

Stephanie Reems glanced at the steel bracelets. "I hear you're a good swimmer, Mr Bern, so I prefer not to take any chances."

William Bern looked up at the office building towering above them. "It's not like you to be so theatrical."

"Just reminding you what you've lost."

"*Lost* isn't the word I would use." He paused. "*Had stolen* would better describe the situation."

Reems bit her lower lip. "When we arrested you, you sang like a bird. Then you got your lawyers involved and your approach changed completely. It was like you were ready to atone and then..."

"Perhaps I just came to my senses."

"Perhaps you just wanted to spend some time with that attractive young lawyer you hired." Reems leaned towards him. "Or were you affected by your own nano agents? Perhaps those in the truth nano you were developing."

Bern shrugged. "I'm not responsible for everything that happened at CERUS. As I've said before, it seems that some of my team continued their work on that discontinued project despite my express orders to the contrary."

"You really threw Marron under the bus there, didn't you?" Reems' expression hardened. "*You* were in charge, and *you* are responsible. I know you didn't tell us everything. I know you had more than we found."

Bern looked at her. "Fallen under the spell of conspiracy theorists, Director?"

Reems looked up at the CERUS Tower. "We know you had another site."

"We had lots of other sites, but we were in the process of migrating everyone to this building. That's hardly a secret."

"I don't mean a site listed in your brochure. Tell me about the beta site. Where you ran the more legally-questionable tests. We've run detailed analysis of every project in your inventory. There are too many gaps in the technology map: things that must have been achieved elsewhere."

"Perhaps the gaps are simply where the data was deleted when my... *son* hacked the building systems?"

"There truly is no love lost there, is there?"

"Don't romanticise this. I never knew about him."

"Is that right? Or perhaps you just didn't want your late wife to know about your affair."

"Adultery isn't a crime." Bern leant on the rail of the boat and looked up at CERUS Tower. "Why are we here, Stephanie? To trade insults? To run over the same old arguments? I'm not some monster. I'm a revolutionary. A ground-breaker, an innovator. Maybe the world isn't quite ready for my ideas, but that's not my fault. I won't let idiocy stand in the way of progress."

"Incarceration is your more immediate problem."

Bern sighed. "What do you want?"

"I just told you what I want." She glared at him. "The problem is trying to work out what *you* want."

"What I want is to change the world." His hands tightened on the railing. "It is so frustrating when people try to derail the plan because of their own mis-guided agendas."

"Based on something trivial like safety?"

"If safety was an absolute we'd never have invented aeroplanes or cars."

"Not even a hint of contrition. Why did Marron react so differently?"

"I can't speak for Peter. How is he doing, by the way?"

"He accepted responsibility."

"Well he did kill my wife. Did they ever find his daughter?"

Reems shook her head. "They certainly looked."

"Quite a piece of work, that one."

Reems' phone buzzed and she stepped away from Bern to answer it. She listened carefully then clicked it off and signalled to the guards.

"Are we done?" asked Bern. "How disappointing. I presumed you'd brought a picnic."

"I have a meeting."

"Must be important for you to let it interrupt our quality time together."

"Given that you are telling me nothing that I didn't know already, I'd say I've overestimated your importance."

"Given the questions you've asked, I'd say you've underestimated it. You do realise you're not the only government that would like to get hold of my tech. Perhaps some of them might be more pleasant to do business with."

"You're in no position to do business with anyone except me."

"Say it, if it helps you believe it."

Reems gave a nod. The two guards walked over and gripped Bern's arms.

"I'm going back to my office," Reems said. "And you are going back to your tiny room with the tiny window."

FOUR

CERUS TOWER STOOD ELEVEN-HUNDRED feet, and ninety stories high, but while it still glittered in the spotlights surrounding it, the organisation that gave it its name was now more than a little tarnished. CERUS Biotech had seen many changes in the twelve months since Bern's arrest. There was a new CEO, a new corporate direction for its thirty thousand employees. Yet the press continued to hound the company and anyone who had even the remotest connection to its work.

High on the ninetieth floor, a woman dressed in jeans and a t-shirt stood, hands clasped behind her back, gazing out at the view. Twelve months ago she had been, to all purposes, dead.

A lot could change in a year.

Now Dominique Lentz was the Chief Executive Officer of a globally renowned technology company. She controlled a hi-tech colossus that had been teetering on the brink. And she had brought it back. But she was under no illusions as to who really owned the company: the British government.

They could not afford the embarrassment of CERUS failing. And, of course, there was considerable value in CERUS' assets. What government wouldn't want to explore their possibilities? Now they had unfettered access - at least to what was left.

Because between Bern and Marron's conspiracy, and Tom's sabotage, much of CERUS' intellectual property was missing. And its greatest triumph had been lost in the fracas. Project Tantalus 2.0 had cost the lives of so many. Now it was gone: the files deleted, the scientists dead. All that remained was the project's one success. And Lentz had been instrumental in his disappearance.

"Not tired of the view yet?" said a familiar voice.

Lentz turned to see her director of communications, Kate Turner, with a tablet computer and a questioning look. "Not yet."

"Are we good to catch up now?"

Lentz shrugged. "I have the Board in half an hour, but sure."

"And you're wearing jeans and a t-shirt?"

"I've chosen to resist the corporate power-dressing." She walked over and closed the door. "I wish I didn't have to waste my time on the Board at all. Bern was onto something when he decided to run this operation like a dictatorship." She gestured to one of two leather sofas.

"Perhaps. Although I wouldn't dip into his playbook too often." Kate pointed at dust sheets that were draped across the entrance to a doorway in one corner of the large office as she sat down. "Got the builders in?"

Lentz nodded. "Felicia Hallstein, my new team member, has been nagging me to have Bern's old private apartment redecorated. She says it's making a break with the past. Not sure why it matters, given that I'm the only one who would ever use it. And I've never wanted to. I'd rather go home. If I work late, I'd rather be there."

"You know, you don't look entirely like you're having fun."

"I always wanted to be in control of what CERUS was doing, but I didn't actually want to be skipper. I'd rather be rolling up my sleeves and creating stuff in the lab. I want to solve problems," Lentz sat opposite her, "just not the kind Reems brings me. All this time toadying to our shareholders – it's paralysing."

"It's what we need to do to be legal. Given how things have gone in the past, it's no bad thing. Speaking of CERUS' legal advisers, any word from Tom?"

Lentz hesitated for just a moment, then shook her head. "Not since I wired him the money - the settlement for what 'we' did to him. Which he said he didn't want."

"Did he say how he was doing?"

"Not really. Didn't say where he was either. Just said he'd come and find us when he was ready. It's a pity, because I could really use his analysis. We've found other holes in the finances. Big holes."

"I thought the funds got returned?"

"Some, but Bern had been syphoning systematically for years, with almost no oversight. It's not been easy to track. I'd love to ask him directly, but my favourite contact at MI5 is not proving cooperative."

Kate smiled. "Stephanie Reems not being helpful? You surprise me. Although wouldn't our interests be aligned here?"

"I'm not sure what's going on. She's been distracted by claims Bern's legal team have been making that his confession was coerced. The trial should have been months back. It keeps getting postponed as they call for more expert witnesses."

"Bern doesn't know when to give up."

"Not in his vocabulary. I thought the same was true of Peter Marron, but it seems I was wrong."

Kate nodded. "The loss of his daughter hit him hard."

"Best not to assume someone's dead until you see a body," Lentz said, raising an eyebrow.

"Well I guess you're proof of that." Kate picked up her tablet.

There was a sharp knock at the door and Lentz's PA stuck her head inside. "You just had a call: Stephanie Reems."

Lentz gave a sigh. "Put her through."

The PA adjusted her glasses. "She's not holding. She needs you over at her office. Now, she said. If not sooner. She's cancelled your Board meeting."

"Has she now? Did she say anything else, like what the new meeting is about?"

The PA rolled her eyes. "Just that it was classified. I've had your driver bring the car out front. Ms Reems did say one other thing." She paused, looking uncomfortable. "She said 'sorry'."

"*Sorry*?"

"She said you'd know why when you got there."

FIVE

LENTZ ENTERED STEPHANIE REEMS' SECURE Whitehall suite; one of a number of offices the Head of MI5 operated, it was buried underground away from prying eyes and ears – and hopefully any other form of eavesdropping. Lentz met Reems in the corridor outside her private conference room.

The MI5 Director gave a brief frown as her eyes flickered over Lentz's jeans and t-shirt. "Thanks for coming so quickly."

Lentz shrugged. "Thanks for rescheduling my Board meeting."

"I think you might actually mean that. Now there's someone I need you to meet."

They walked into a large, windowless room. Two powerfully built men in suits stood at the rear, doing their best to reveal no expression. An older man stood, hands in pockets, reading from a file on the table in front of him. He looked up and smiled.

"Dominique Lentz, I presume." He extended a hand, gripping hers with force.

Reems moved to the far side of the table. "Dominique, this is Connor Truman. He is--"

"Deputy Director of the CIA," replied Lentz, removing her hand from his grasp. "I've heard your name before." Lentz looked at Reems, then back at Truman. "You'll pardon my bluntness, but *why* am I here?"

Reems cleared her throat. "Mr Truman is leading the US Government's investigations into what they have labelled the 'Tantalus Incident'."

Lentz reached for a bottle of water in the middle of the table and poured herself a glass. "I'm a civilian. Surely this is an intelligence matter."

Reems extended her palms. "It's OK to speak, Dominique. We've been cooperating fully with our US friends."

Truman coughed. "I'm here as part of an operation lead by CIA Director Lazlo Banetti. Stephanie said I should speak to you in person, because of our interest in your developments in nanotechnology."

Lentz sipped from her glass. "The British Government banned nanotechnology in the UK, under the 2013 Nanotech Act. You have similar legislation in the US, I believe."

"Yes. But you did it anyway. At least that's what the rumours say."

"Rumours are usually just that. I only took over at CERUS after the *incident*, as you call it. And our records from before that day were severely compromised during the events that you appear to know so much about."

"But you were at CERUS in the early days. Let me be frank, we are worried this could be a whole new arms race. One where we're left behind at the start. And we do not want that."

"So what *do* you want?"

"To speak with Thomas Faraday."

Lentz glared at Reems. "I thought Tom's involvement was classified?"

"I'm sorry, Dominique. There were too many witnesses. It was impossible to keep a lid on it."

"Well, it's all irrelevant. We don't know where he is. Believe me, I wish we did."

Truman nodded. "Is it true, what they say about him? That he is the successful outcome of Project Tantalus? That he can interface with the control systems of a suitably sophisticated helicopter?"

Lentz hesitated. "Tom was an innocent caught up in a conspiracy. He didn't ask to get involved, and he deserves to be left alone."

"I wish it were that simple. Mr Faraday is of immense interest not just to us, but to any state or organisation with any interest in developing an advanced neural interface. The type of operational or combat advantage that such a system would bring would be significant."

"I imagine that's true. But why *now*?" Lentz asked. "This happened a year ago. Has something changed recently?"

Truman's brow furrowed. "We have no guarantees that this dangerous technology did not leak out of CERUS: that it is not out there, being used. Being weaponised. It remains a clear and present danger, and we need to understand it – and how it can be countered."

"If it helps, Deputy Director," said Lentz, "the technology that was developed was both incredibly complex and randomly lucky. And the lead scientists who developed it are all now dead. The few successes they had resulted from unforeseen and opportune circumstances that are unlikely to be repeated. Not to mention the research was incredibly expensive, and illegal almost everywhere."

"So you're telling me that I shouldn't worry unless someone with lots of money and the resources to do this somewhere in secret comes along?" Truman growled. "Because obviously, that's never going to happen."

"Well, I--"

"So why don't you cut the--" Truman's phone rang and he glanced at it. "Pardon me." He turned away, whispered, listened, whispered again, then put it back in his pocket. "I have to go."

*

Lentz watched Reems close the door. "Something I said?"

Reems raised a hand, then picked up a small handheld device and waved it over herself and Lentz, then around the area where Truman had been sitting.

"Don't trust him?"

"I'm naturally wary of anyone who can get a phone signal in this room. That said, I've no strong opinions about Truman. But his boss, Lazlo Banetti - I've known him a long time, and I trust him to do what he deems necessary to achieve his goals. Which means Tom is in danger."

"But they don't even seem to understand what Tom can do? They think it's just a helicopter control system."

"That was the stated goal of the recent project. Let's just be glad they don't know more, or they would be far *more* interested."

Lentz shrugged. "It doesn't really matter. Tom knows how to hide. I'm sure he's on the other side of the world."

"I wanted him to hear it from you direct. That you don't know where he is. And that you don't know how to find him."

"I don't."

Reems puffed out her cheeks. "Dominique, I'm under a lot of pressure here."

"From whom?"

"Our military. Other divisions of government. It's not just the Interface. They want to know about nanotech weapons, nano viruses, nano bombs, carbon nanotubes, tailored nanotech drugs

- all projects that are missing from the CERUS archives."

"Did you ask Bern?"

"He was not cooperative."

"If you want something from him, then you need to find out what *he* wants."

"I know what he wants: freedom. And it's not going to happen."

"You really think Tom can help?"

"We're not the only ones looking for him. And we're the good guys. We could protect him."

"Oh sure. Of course we could."

"You don't trust me?"

"To a point. But in this case--"

Reems' phone rang and she answered it, her expression becoming one of shock. "When? Why wasn't I told?" She clicked it off, her face pale. "It's Bern. He's been released on bail."

Lentz nearly dropped her glass. "What? Why?"

"His legal team are challenging his confession. Saying he was coerced."

"When is he being released?"

"Already happened. Some emergency sitting with a cooperative judge. Two hundred million bail. And he has agreed to remain under house arrest. With electronic tagging."

"Isn't letting him out at all a huge risk?"

Reems scowled. "I'm going to supervise a team to monitor his house. He might be out, but he's not going anywhere else."

SIX

KATE LOOKED AT HER WATCH as she emerged from the lift into the underground car park. Lentz had not returned from her meeting with Reems, and eventually Kate had given up waiting. She walked to her car, a compact grey Audi, and saw to her irritation that a leaflet had been placed under the windscreen wipers. She was about to throw it in the nearest bin when she noticed what it was for: Brocca, an Italian restaurant she'd once been to. They were offering a special deal, tonight only. The last two words were underlined.

She glanced around. There were no leaflets on the other cars. And of course the car park was secure: only CERUS staff could get in. She ran her fingers over the paper, thinking about the last evening she had spent at the restaurant.

*

The traffic was surprisingly light, and Kate was soon pulling up across the road from Brocca. As she got out, she saw her parking meter was out of order, but as she swore, the electronic display reset to show two hours' credit. She shook her head, put her purse back in her bag, and was about to cross the road when something made her hesitate: the feeling that somebody was watching her, a sensation she'd had more than once recently. Looking around she saw nobody paying her particular attention. Then she noticed several street cameras. Muttering, she marched towards the restaurant.

The Maitre d' smiled as she entered. "Ms Turner, your table is ready."

"My table?" She hesitated. She'd not been here in a year, and had never seen the man before. "How did you know my name?"

"Your host is already here. May I take your coat?" He signalled to a waiter, who walked over and nodded. She was shown to a booth at the back, almost invisible to the rest of the room. She held her breath as she approached. But the booth was empty. Confused she looked around the restaurant. Nobody was looking at her. What was going on?

"I can recommend the lamb," said the waiter, returning to place a basket of bread on the table. "And perhaps Signora would like to choose some wine. The Dolcetto is excellent."

The voice sounded familiar. "I was told my host was already here."

"That's correct," he replied. "Is the disguise that good?"

Kate blinked and looked up into the waiter's face. It was more creased than she remembered, and she suspected the eyebrows were false; she hoped the moustache was. It was *Tom*. She felt the air drawn from her lungs as she watched him take the seat opposite.

"I'll take that as a 'yes'," he continued.

She'd thought about this moment quite a bit over the last several months: planned various things to say, all crafted to sum up how she felt about him, her concern, her confusion. Had he been thinking about her, though? For twelve months she'd heard nothing. "You're not dead then."

He flinched at her words. As he did so, she saw the sallowness in his eyes, the pallor to his skin. "Not yet."

"So... the leaflet?" You could have just called me. Or do you think someone is monitoring you?"

"I have no doubt they're trying."

"Aren't the bad guys all dead or locked up?"

"Not all of them."

Kate shook her head. "How did you get into the car park to put the leaflet there?"

Tom smiled. "I bribed an employee. It wasn't hard."

"I thought you could just walk in anywhere, control the security system like some kind of digital superman?"

"It's not always that simple. More and more things are encrypted, and they're hard to break." He frowned. "Is something wrong?"

"It's just I'm wondering why we're meeting."

"Aren't we friends? Is it strange for friends to have dinner?"

"A *friend* would have been in touch more than..." She glared. "I haven't heard from you once in twelve months. After what we went through, I just can't believe it, really."

"You know that--"

"I don't know anything. Dominique has been worried too. It's been hard for all of us. You could have confided in me. You know you can trust me. I didn't go public with the story."

"That was your choice."

"Whatever. I didn't mean you owed me or anything."

"You don't know what I've been through." He rubbed his temples with both forefingers. "You really have no idea what it's like."

"I have a bit of an idea."

Tom looked at her and appeared to stifle a laugh. "You mean the truth nano? Seriously, you think that's the same? Those nanites were in you for a few minutes. I've had them in my head for over a year, and they're still there. For you they changed a moment. For me they changed my life, and that change hasn't stopped."

Kate stared at him. "At least you still have your life. Not everyone made it out of the events last year."

"You don't need to remind me: I think about Jo every day, about her pointless death... "

A few people looked their way. Kate took a deep breath and reached out her hand towards him. "I'm sorry, Tom. I really didn't mean to--" There was a spark between them. A jolt of static. "What the...?" she began, pulling her hand back.

He jerked back too. "Wearing nylon?"

She frowned at her fingers. "Not even close. My clothing budget has improved in the last twelve months."

He gave a strained smile. "I didn't ask you here to argue. Look I'm sorry. There are things about the last year that I would change if I could. Can we try and start over?"

Kate sucked in her top lip. "Perhaps. And maybe this time we can actually finish our meal." A real waiter appeared and they ordered. Kate noted that Tom ordered three main dishes. "Not watching the waistline?" she asked.

He tapped his head. "Using the Interface consumes a great deal of energy, so I still need a lot of calories. If anything, it's got worse."

"A problem many people would happily trade with you."

"I'll admit it's not the worst of the side effects."

"So where have you been hiding yourself, the last year?"

"I spent some time in New York and Paris. I did mean to go travelling - Jo and I were always going to do South America: Peru, Bolivia, Argentina - but I haven't got round to it. Mostly I've been in London. Easy to lose yourself in a city if you know your way around. And it was the last place anybody expected me to be."

"You didn't think to make contact, all that time? Even when you were right here?"

"I thought we were starting again?"

She raised an eyebrow. "Just answer my question, Mr Robot."

"As I said, it's complicated."

Kate folded her arms. "So why *are* we meeting?"

"Because I need your help."

Kate looked around to check nobody was listening. She leaned forward and lowered her voice. "Can't you just do anything you like? Given that everything is connected, can't you control everything?"

"If only." Tom lowered his voice. "I was able to... take over, if you will, the helicopters, because that's what the Interface was designed to do. I was inside the system, equipped with the right tools. Same thing with CERUS Tower: it was based on a shared technology architecture. What I can do elsewhere is more subtle and more variable. Publicly available information, sure that's easy, but then you can do that on your phone. Other bespoke systems, well that quickly becomes exhausting." He rubbed his temples again. "And despite what the media says, there's plenty of stuff that isn't networked at all. Or it's networked in a way that I cannot navigate. You've heard of the dark web. If Google can't find it, I certainly have difficulties."

"So how can I help?"

Tom removed a photograph from his pocket and slid it across the table. It showed a woman in her forties. "This is Amelia Faraday. My mother. I want to find out about her."

Kate's brow creased. "But she's--"

"Gone, yes, four years now. But she never told me about Bern. She said my father was dead."

"Perhaps she just wished he was."

"I'm not saying I blame her. But if she was hiding that from me, was she hiding anything else? I have to know. Last year, Marron told me she was a contact of Bern's. And CERUS had a file about her, but its contents were deleted. I've exhausted every digital avenue I can pursue and I've found nothing. I need someone who can look deeper, and you're a reporter--"

"Not any more. I'm in PR now, darling."

Tom folded his arms. "So you've lost all your contacts? Your skills?"

Kate leaned back in her seat. "You don't want a reporter. You want a private investigator."

"I want someone with the wit and grit to pursue this: someone I can trust. Bern wasn't just anyone, even twenty-five years ago. Whatever he did must have left a trail. Find it for me."

She shook her head. "I'm not supposed to have any involvement with matters relating to Bern. It's a corporate edict. We're trying to distance ourselves from him: prove that CERUS has moved beyond its founder."

"Maybe there's something on the CERUS systems. Old email records. They might be kept on tape, off-site."

"I don't know. It was such a long time ago. I don't think it's a good idea."

"So you won't help?" Tom's expression darkened. "I ask you one thing, and you won't do it for me."

"Maybe there comes a time when you need to stop looking back, trying to find answers in the past. Maybe you should do us all a favour and work out what you're going to do next, Tom."

He stood up. "Thanks for nothing."

Something made her reach out and grab his hand. "You said you wouldn't run off--" There was another spark, more intense than the last. With a shriek of surprise, she let go.

"Don't touch me," he glowered. "I'll manage without your help."

Kate sighed. "We're never going to get to finish a meal here, are we?"

He shrugged and walked away.

SEVEN

CARL BRODY GUIDED RATHER THAN steered the Toyota Land Cruiser as it bounced along the rutted icy tracks, its headlights fighting a losing battle with the flurries of snow that had been a constant presence for several days now. But there wasn't much chance of getting lost; high drifts framed the track on either side, and a powerful locator beacon ensured he stayed on course. The beacon was positioned on the top of the only sign of civilisation in this isolated spot. Brody was soon pulling up alongside it.

The building was more than two hundred metres in diameter, with a high arching dome of silver and grey-white, geodesic in form, the coating rendering it almost invisible from the air. It housed a substantial facility, although much of the volume of the structure was in the many sub-ground levels. The whole thing had been constructed and outfitted in considerable secrecy a decade previously, but had only been brought on-line in the last two years. At full capacity, with all the surrounding accommodation blocks, the facility could house over five thousand, although it was currently running at a mere six-percent occupancy. Yet, Brody had noted in his regular reports, they were a very productive six percent. The isolation was motivational: all they had to think about out here was their work and the triple pay they were earning. Away from prying eyes and distractions, they had excelled. A couple of key matters, however, remained stubbornly unresolved.

He pulled the flight case from the passenger seat then moved quickly from the vehicle to the nearby entrance, the first of the pairs of heavy sealed doors hissing apart to welcome him. A minute later he emerged from the airlock, kicked the snow from his boots and removed his gloves and coat. The interior was maintained at a balmy twenty-two degrees centigrade, but he knew it would take many minutes for the biting cold to leave his bones. He made his way around the perimeter corridor and then took a lift down three storeys to the control level and his office. Five minutes later Brody was sipping a cup of mint tea and starting to feel a little warmer inside.

He put the flight case on his desk and ran his fingers over the metal exterior. It was dented and scratched from regular use. Brody placed his thumb on the keypad; there was a soft beep and the lock clicked open. Inside were documents, a secure hard drive, and, within foam padding, a small metal box. All bore the logo of CERUS Biotech.

He flicked through the paperwork. It was a detailed set of specifications, including a system breakdown, along with a proposed testing regime. It covered responses and suggestions to his last report, and further access codes. The hard drive held operating-system updates and detailed simulation data. He turned to the metal box and flipped open the clasps. Inside, held in a further protective layer of padding, were five slender crystal tubes, a dark black liquid glistening within.

His phone rang. He looked at it with a start: it did not ring often. Staff at the Dome sent internal messages or came in person. Nobody from the outside rang in: nobody except the woman he knew only by the name of Fox. He swallowed and slipped on his headset. "You're watching me, aren't you?"

"It's a security measure, Mr Brody," Fox replied, with her soft French accent. "It applies to everyone, even you as General Manager. And I'm pleased to see the case has arrived. I need you to validate those samples immediately."

"What about the suits? I haven't made any progress there."

"It's not unexpected. Fortunately for you, we have an alternative plan, so you are free to focus on those samples. I'll be there in person in a few days."

"I presume that's related to the other item. It arrived yesterday."

"You kept its arrival on a need-to-know basis?"

"Of course. But I'm uncomfortable having it here, in the facility."

"It's quite safe if you don't poke it."

"Yet I'm sure that's exactly what you're about to ask me to do."

"None of us ever thought this would be a hazard-free venture. I'll see you soon."

The call cut off abruptly, and Brody slipped off his headset. He knew, when he took on this role, that he would have to accept unusual ways of working, odd procedures and protocols, along with risk. For the chance to work with the kind of cutting-edge science he was getting to experience, with an almost unlimited budget, he was willing to put up with that.

EIGHT

TOM EMERGED FROM THE RESTAURANT, glancing at his watch, then he flicked his eyes left and right. Nobody seemed to be watching. To be sure, he needed a better view.

He closed his eyes.

The buzz was there, as it always was, the networks around him, humming with data, with energy. He opened his mind to them and, this deep inside a megacity, it was a cacophony: electromagnetic radiation saturating the air, cables running beneath his feet and up into every building around him – too much for him to grasp properly. Yet within the masses he could feel patterns and concentrations. Many lines of data were encrypted, but if communications were localising on this particular spot in an organised manner, it might mean someone was moving against him.

There was nothing.

He didn't need to hurry away; instead he could walk and think. With no specific plan, he ducked into the nearest Tube station. He would see where the flow took him.

A half hour later he was moving through unfamiliar East London streets, weaving between traffic, feeling pangs for his missed dinner, but more in need of answers than sustenance.

What had made him come here?

And then he smelled the salt water in the air, and he knew. He put his hands in his pockets and walked towards London's first highway: the Thames was wide and slow east of the City, preparing for its final few miles before the open sea. He came to a boardwalk, bounded by a metal railing, ten metres above the river's rippling surface. He stared out, inhaling the salt and fumes, hearing the strangled choke of seagulls. South across the water was London's Docklands. And CERUS Tower.

He had wanted to meet up with Kate many times over the last twelve months, but had not followed through until now. Something had kept him back. A year ago he had felt the kindling of... something... between them. But everything had got crazy, and Project Tantalus had changed him forever. So he had stayed away, avoided her, until he needed her. From her perspective it must have seemed inconsiderate, rude even. It wasn't a mistake he would have made before all this happened.

Was he a little less human? Or a little more? He could connect to computers, to networks: he could often make them do what he wanted. But, as the meeting with Kate had just proven, with people, he seemed to be losing the ability to interface.

When he was just a lawyer, he could always go home and be somebody else at the end of a bad day. But now he was always 'Tom, the subject of the Interface'. Either people wanted to study him, or they were scared of him. Nobody took any kind of middle ground. Well, almost nobody.

He felt the watch on his wrist, the keepsake his mother had given him just a month before she had died. If she was still here, she would have offered counsel, even in these most unforeseeable of circumstances. But she was not.

There was one other person he could speak to: one who might actually have the capability to help. He pulled out a disposable mobile and sent a short text-message.

Slipping the phone back into his pocket, Tom looked back across the Thames, at the rise of office buildings, and the foreboding form of CERUS Tower. It was a constant reminder, as if he needed one, of everything that had happened: of the death of his career, of his old life. And yet the events leading to it had been preordained almost from the moment of his birth.

There was a soft ringing in his pocket. He tapped the earpiece in his ear to answer the call.

"Tom," Lentz said. "I'm so glad you messaged me. I just came back from a late meeting. With Reems."

"Wonderful. How is Stephanie?"

"Same as always. But I was introduced to Connor Truman. You know who he is?"

Tom closed his eyes momentarily, his mind making a connection, pulling the answer from a search. "I do now. What did he want?"

"To talk to you. My first thought was to tell him to join the queue. But I settled for explaining that I had no idea where you were. And that I had no way of contacting you."

"You think it's wise to lie to the Deputy Director of the CIA?"

"I'm sure he was lying to me. And I've lied to more important people for less important reasons. Besides, technically you have to ping me first."

"And I thought I was the lawyer," he laughed.

"Try being a CEO: everything I do is mired in protocol. Sometimes I'd trade places with you in a second."

"You're the scientist. Find a way to make that happen and I'm *on board*."

"For now, you might want to take extra care. Truman made a special trip over here so I'm thinking there's a good reason behind it. He also wanted to speak to Bern and Marron.

Marron's obviously out of the question, but... look I'm sorry to be the one telling you this, but you'll hear it soon enough: Bern has been released on bail."

"What? After what he did?" Tom felt an itch in the back of his neck. "How is that possible?"

"His lawyers persuaded the judge. Get hold of the papers, I'm sure you'll understand it better than I will."

"This is ridiculous. I thought we'd closed that chapter." Tom swallowed. "Perhaps I should go see him?"

"At his home? With a special forces team of a hundred stationed outside, I wouldn't recommend it. In fact, with the CIA involved I hope you are far, far away on some beach in a country without an extradition treaty."

Tom looked up at CERUS Tower. "You wouldn't believe how far away."

"So why did you call me? We haven't spoken in months."

"I was going to ask you about my mother. I want to know why she and Bern got together. And then why they split up. I feel there's a story there that I don't know. Even if I could get to Bern without flagging who I am, I couldn't trust anything he told me. I need a more reliable source. And I haven't found anything electronic. But someone like Bern always leaves ripples."

"More like horrible waves that sink those around him. It might be best to leave this all alone."

"Maybe you met her? Or saw her, when they were together?"

"I didn't really move in Bern's social circles. Look, making waves, trying to delve into old records, you're only going to draw attention to yourself. Right now's really not the time for that."

"You're right. Actually there's a trip I've been meaning to make; somewhere I can really unplug, so I'll be out of touch for a bit. You just make sure you stay out of trouble. I'd hate to lose the only person I can be candid with. Presuming that's still true."

"What do you mean?"

"Can you track me? Don't lie to me, Dominique. I have to know I can trust you – I'll know if you're lying."

She laughed. "I have no location data. All I can do is poll your Interface, and see if it responds. It confirms if you are alive, but I can't initiate any type of comms."

"Thank you. Take care, Dominique."

The call ended. Tom closed his eyes, connected to the net, and booked an airline ticket.

*

The woman emerged from the lift on Level 33 of CERUS Tower and adjusted her black-framed glasses. It was nearly 11pm and there were few people still in the office – which was exactly why she worked this late.

The phone in her pocket vibrated angrily for the third time: her contractor was certainly keen, although he was usually keen simply because it meant he could justify billing another few hours; as yet his efforts had proved fruitless. She made her way to a rarely used conference room near the middle of the floor – it was cramped and obviously had no external window – slotted into a small section of the floor plan that might have been better used as a storage room. Tonight it was perfect for her purpose.

She opened up the special app on her phone and connected. "This is Fox."

A man's voice, heavily digitised, replied: "You took your time. I said it was urgent."

"I have to take precautions. What's happened?"

"There's been a development. I followed the girl. She went back to that Italian restaurant, Brocca."

"Remind me."

"They were both there a year ago: it was in my original report. Look, my point is that it felt like too much of a coincidence. And I was right. Guess who was waiting for her?"

"Just tell me."

"Tom Faraday."

Fox hesitated. "Are you absolutely certain?"

"He didn't look in the best health, but it was him."

"Did he spot you?"

"I don't believe so. Obviously I used no tech whatsoever. I followed him after he left. He drifted all over the place. Made a stop in East London, then took a taxi out to Heathrow. Terminal Five."

"Did you go inside?"

"I watched him check-in with British Airways. Then I followed him as far as security. A contact I have there confirmed he boarded a BA flight to Lima, Peru. In South America."

"I know where it is. Peru was actually one of our priority targets. We know he'd planned a trip there, so we have third-party teams in place."

"You have teams in Peru? Just how extensive is your set-up? Look, I don't care: that's your business. But he lands in about twelve hours."

"You've done well."

"I know. So I'd like to talk about—"

She disconnected the call. After so much preparation, after so much waiting, things were finally starting to happen. And that meant she had a great deal to do.

NINE

THE FACILITY WAS NOT MARKED on any public map, and satellite images just showed a fuzzy grey building. The fading sign read 'GB Logistics, Northwell A Site, PRIVATE PROPERTY' but gave no further clues. There was a phone number, although it went straight to an automated message-service.

Nothing suggested there was anything of interest within. The worn metal gates were secured with a heavy locking mechanism. Beyond, a dusty road led down a steep hedged gully and round a corner, to a much larger, much heavier gate. From here there was a succession of three further gates, interspersed with short stretches of dusty road. At the end was a large warehouse, out of sight from any prying eyes. Hidden under the high, wide warehouse roof was a cluster of buildings surrounded by a six-metre high, hardened-glass wall that enclosed a space as large as four football pitches. The glass was a recently-developed material. Harder than stone, it provided perfect visibility for guards monitoring the exterior of the compound. Nobody could sneak up unseen.

It was quite a sight, but the driver of the generic grey van that had just negotiated the various gates and dusty roads had seen it before and did not spare it a second glance. He stepped out of the vehicle and approached the glass wall. Two armed men stepped from a guard post on the outside of the wall and asked to see his identification. He produced his ID and handed it over.

"Good to see you again, Agent Croft," said the first guard. "How are the family?"

"Well, thanks," Croft said, because that was what they wanted to hear. "How is our *guest*?"

The guard handed back the card. "No more effusive this week. Your phone, please."

Croft placed his mobile on the offered tray.

The guard pulled an electronic device from his pocket. "OK to be scanned?"

Croft stood, legs apart, arms extended, while the scanner was waved around his silhouette.

The guard looked at the display. It glowed green and the device chimed a soft, friendly tone. "No weapons or electronics," he confirmed. "You're good to proceed." The guard nodded to his colleague and together they lifted up the glass beam barring the door. Croft forced a smile.

Time to pay a visit to a special guest.

*

Northwell A was the very latest word in design for maximum security prisons, its very existence and location classified Top Secret. It was the first British facility designed for incarceration of prisoners classified 'above Category A', colloquially an 'ACA' prison, where Category A meant those whose escape would be highly dangerous to the public or those who represented a serious risk to national security.

It wasn't really ready for use, but a test case had presented: a prisoner the authorities were not sure what else to do with and who, without doubt, met the criteria. The prisoner was currently in his cell, drinking a cup of green tea and reading a book. Both items had been thoroughly scanned for active foreign bodies before being allowed into the cell. The floor of the cell was a highly polished granite, as was the table he sat at, and the chair he sat on. Both were fixed to the floor.

Agent Croft stepped in as the glass door slid open. "Hello, Peter."

Peter Marron did not look up from his book. "You again? Don't you get bored of asking me the same questions?"

Croft watched the door slide closed. "It's my job. I brought you the *Times*." Croft threw the folded newspaper onto the table.

Marron glanced at it. "I would like access to the internet. And a television. Or do you really think I'll manage to hack my way out of here?"

"I'm just following protocol."

"Like a good company man. Commendable. I also asked for a chess set. A good old-fashioned wooden one would have been fine."

"The pieces would be choking hazards. For you or the guards."

"Oh, come on. But I guess I'd struggle to find a worthy opponent in this place." Marron put down his book. "So what are you offering me this time?"

"That would depend on the value of the information you provide."

"Do you really think I would offer something up on a prayer?"

Croft shrugged. "If Bern decides to talk first then we may not need to speak to you at all."

Marron smiled. "Bern isn't going to talk. Ever."

"He blamed you for everything. And he had a lot of evidence

to back it up."

"Yes, how convenient for him. Anyway, there's still only one thing I want: news of my daughter."

"You're going to have to accept that she won't be found."

Marron reached forward and unfolded the newspaper, flattening it on the stone table in an exaggerated manner. "At least you still have your daughter. Although I was sorry to hear about her... condition." Marron looked up, his eyes unblinking. "I wish there was something that could be done."

Croft's cheek twitched. "How would you know about that?"

"We're not so different, you and I. The question is, are we men who are powerless, or men who have hope?"

Croft started to reply but the phone on the wall rang loudly.

"I'm guessing that will be for you," Marron said. "I don't get too many calls."

Croft picked it up. He listened to the quick words and put the receiver down. "I have to go."

"Until next time, Agent Croft. Oh, and do close the door on your way out."

TEN

IT WAS A COLD DAY in Moscow. But then it was always cold in Moscow in winter. Around the great stone house were high walls, heavy gates, and grim men with guns. Inside, huge fires blazed, not because the heating systems needed the help, but because the owner liked the effect.

That was to say, the *new* owner. Andrei Leskov's father, Viktor, had died a year ago. Now his son paced the huge wooden-floored chamber, glaring at the fire, glaring at the walls, glaring at the group of men who waited patiently for his next instruction. He was young and he had not expected to be in charge of his father's business empire for many years. Yet here he was.

It was a unique opportunity, but to take advantage of it the younger Leskov had quickly realised he was going to need a great deal of information. He had spent the last twelve months conducting an audit of his father's holdings and interests. He had studied reports, interviewed witnesses and, finally, he was ready to move.

The Leskov family business was in good shape. Diversification meant there were interests in many industries. There had been some losses, of course: mineral rights forcibly divested in a dispute with a Gulf state, the failure to win a large factory-maintenance contract that should have been a certainty. And a decommissioned aircraft-carrier stolen while on its way to be delivered into his hands. He would be investigating that in due course.

But one thing continued to taunt him: the web of lies and deception around his father's death. He had to be *seen* to deal with it or he would look weak. Then others would challenge him, and the empire that his father had built would crumble. Andrei Leskov would not allow that, and the necessary expression of authority needed to start with his inner sanctum. He turned to his elder cousin, Yuri, not hiding his irritation. "Summarise your findings for me, cousin, one more time."

Yuri adjusted his suit, which Leskov noted was certainly not from Saville Row. "The official position is that the two helicopters collided mid-air," Yuri said. "It was logged as an unexplained accident."

"And unofficially?"

"A British military helicopter shot down your father, after his craft shot down one of theirs."

Leskov shook his head. "He would never have opened fire. He would have landed and negotiated."

"Perhaps there was a system fault. Or someone tampered with the helicopter."

Leskov walked over to the fire, picked up a large dry log and threw it on top of the flames. "Why not finish the deal? Why not simply let him fly away? It makes no sense. And our money?"

Yuri shook his head. "Whoever moved it was good. Very good."

Leskov stared at one of the logs hissing and spitting in the great fireplace. "What about Bern?"

"He maintains his innocence. The evidence all points to Marron."

"Faking your own death is not the act of an innocent man."

"This is true. And the received wisdom is that Bern will end up in jail for many years. Unless he can buy his way out of the situation."

Leskov nodded. "A great deal of money can solve a great deal of problems." He interlaced his fingers. "If we could just get both of them in a room, we could find out the truth."

"Neither of them are likely to be accessible to us. Marron, in particular."

"Where is he being held?"

"Some new supermax detention facility, away from any other prisoners."

"For his safety?"

Yuri flashed gleaming white teeth. "For theirs."

Leskov gave a snort. "And what about the asset? The subject of the CERUS research?"

"Tom Faraday? Officially he was on-board the helicopter with your father. There are rumours that he survived, but he has not been seen since. By anyone."

"So where does that leave us?"

Yuri looked at his hands. "I want to give you good news, Andrei."

"There must be more we can do. There must be records at CERUS."

"They suffered a computer failure shortly after the incident: a large amount of files were lost. In any event, we cannot get inside that building."

Leskov walked over and leaned very close to his cousin. "Then we're not trying hard enough."

"I wish effort was the solution, but the building already had state of the art security systems and the British government has augmented them with measures of their own. It may be the most secure facility in the UK."

"I think we can do better. I think we can find the answers. Directly or indirectly. With enough money we can get to anyone. And we will. You will return to England. There's someone I need you to meet with. An old contact of the family." Leskov paused. "I will not let this insult go unanswered. I am going to send a message to everyone. And you are going to help me."

ELEVEN

OUTSIDE THE SHACK IT WAS dark. The night air was cooling fast, to the irritation of the mosquitos. A single fizzing electric light illuminated a printed notice. Inside, behind the corrugated iron and barbed wire, the atmosphere was heavy with sweat, smoke and tequila. A heaving throng, clutching local bottled beers, surrounded a roped-off area as they cheered the two fighters.

It was not a fair fight. The larger figure, whose name was Rodriguez, swung an ugly, ungloved fist. He struck his opponent glancingly on the shoulder, but it was still enough to knock the smaller figure back. Nobody could remember the other man's name. Nobody cared. He was just the 'challenger'. Soon he would not even be that.

Rodriguez knew what it was like to be forgotten. Nobody had beaten him in his five years in this dark corner of Ecuador. He stood two metres tall, had the balance of an elite athlete, muscles hardened by years in the gym and in the professional ring. And he would have been there still, but for that failed drugs test. One mistake and it had all been over. He had lost his licence, then lost his way. He had fallen far and fast, and had scraped bottom for more than a year. Finally someone had told him about this place:

somewhere that didn't care about a fighter's past, only what he did in the ring. Here, he could still do what he did best. And earn a living while he did it.

Not that it was much of a challenge these days. Nobody any good wanted to come and fight and, of those who did, many saw him and turned away. Most days he faced a succession of cannon fodder, like the unfortunate figure in front of him now.

The opening minutes of any fight were a warm-up. The owner didn't like it if things finished too quickly: less time for the crowd to drink. But even keeping things slow, the smaller man was clearly tiring; he could not be humoured much longer. Best to finish things with a crowd-pleaser or two. So Rodriguez ducked under his opponent's flailing arms and planted a right deep into his stomach. As the little man doubled over, Rodriguez rose up and head-butted him like a bull.

There was the sound of teeth splintering, and the victim fell back.

"*Get up!*" screamed the crowd.

The little man blinked, trying to wipe sweat and blood from his eyes, perhaps hoping the bell would sound and save him. The fight was scheduled for ten minutes, but often the bell ringer would get caught up in the action and forget his duties. And, until the bell sounded, the fight was not over.

Rodriguez glanced to his left and right. There was no referee: nobody to bring any sanity to the proceedings. Other than the time limit, there were no rules. Only the law of the crowd. And they were shouting his name, and holding out their hands, thumbs down. Wherever you were in the world, that meant only one thing.

The little man was still blinking as he staggered to his feet, and didn't even see it coming. The blow broke his nose, then he fell back with a sickening crunch, his head banging against the sawdust-covered floor. He went still.

Rodriguez paused a moment, making the sign of the cross. A brief moment of guilt.

But only a moment.

The crowd had no such reticence and roared its approval. The corrugated iron roof shook as they began chanting 'Rodriguez' and 'Champion', and money began changing hands. The betting had not been about who would win, but on how quickly Rodriguez would bring matters to an end. As the roars faded, the owner of the establishment stepped into the ring a little warily, as if making sure that the big man knew he was not the next opponent.

He pointed at Rodriguez and bellowed, "Another win for our champion!"

Cheers erupted again. Rodriguez raised his fists high, flexed his muscles. He needed to put on a show or the owner might take a percentage off his fee.

"Now who's next?" The owner looked around the room. "No one?" He held up his hand to his ear. "Because that's all for tonight, unless..." he looked around theatrically, "one of you *morons* would like to add a final bout to the card."

There were laughs from around the room. Only a fool would take it on.

"Come now. Ten thousand pesos if you can last ten minutes with the *beast*. You don't even have to knock him down."

More laughs. It was time to buy another drink.

"How much if I do knock him down?" said a voice that seemed to rise above the crowd.

It was as if all noise was sucked from the room. Startled men looked at each other. The voice did not belong in this place. Had they imagined it?

A *woman's* voice.

"Who said that?" The owner peered through the crowd.

"I did," said a slender figure, strolling forwards. She wore plain black overalls.

The owner looked around the bar uncertainly. "It costs a thousand pesos to fight."

She reached into her pocket, pulling out a roll of banknotes. Casually she flipped it to him. He caught it and riffled the notes, but did not smile. There were mutterings in the crowd.

"I will not fight her," said Rodriguez quietly. "Give her back her money."

The owner looked at the roll of notes and reluctantly held it out to her. "He's right."

She laughed and took a step forwards, placing her hands on the rope. "Anyone can fight. It says so on the notice outside." She raised an eyebrow then ducked under the rope and pushed the owner away, refusing the return of her money. "Perhaps I should fight your mother, then?" she said, tying her long dark hair up.

Rodriguez glowered at her. "My mother, may the Lord have mercy on her soul, would have taught you some respect."

"Your father then?" She tipped her head. "If you know who he is."

The crowd started shouting now. The owner looked around him and stepped out of the ring.

Rodriguez's brow furrowed. "You should go back to your husband and let him teach you a lesson. If he hasn't run off and left you." He paused. "And who could blame him."

She raised an eyebrow. "Don't tell me you've never hit a woman." There were jeers from the crowd. She turned and bared her teeth at them. "Stay out of this, you motherless sons of whores."

There was the sound of glass breaking.

The big man looked at the crowd then lowered his voice. "If I don't fight you, they will probably kill you."

She smiled. "Then we have an accord?"

"It's your funeral."

She pulled off her jacket to reveal a sleeveless shirt. "We'll see."

The crowd began chanting for Rodriguez. Bets began changing hands. The huge man loomed over the woman. He looked down at her, his eyes hard. "Ten minutes. We fight from bell to bell. We stop for nothing."

"Yes, I saw the notice." She shifted from foot to foot. "But then I can read. Can you?"

"You think insults will help you?"

She raised her fists. "Just trying to get you motivated."

He raised his own fists. "Stop talking and fight."

She threw the first punch. Rodriguez caught it on his arms, and countered with a left. But she moved easily aside. She hit his guard again. And, surprisingly, the blow hurt. She fought with technique, with balance. Like a professional.

He blinked and went on the attack. She floated backwards, dancing on the balls of her feet. He advanced on her, throwing a couple of tester jabs. She dodged with ease and circled away. The crowd did not like that, and shouted loudly. Betting slips exchanged hands. The majority of the money was on her lasting two minutes, if only because the champ might not want to hit her very hard.

"Think you can run away for ten minutes?" he said. "It's a very small ring."

"I just want you to show me what you've got. I came here to learn."

He blinked. "Learn?"

"I heard you were good. Before you screwed your life up."

He flexed his huge shoulders. "I *am* good."

"Then show me."

He glared then lunged forwards with a sharp one-two.

She dodged with ease, shaking her head. "I'm not seeing it."

Rodriguez growled and threw a disguised jab, his whole body weight behind it. It struck her in the stomach and she staggered back, falling to the floor. The crowd roared. But as she sat on the floor, Rodriguez was puzzled. It was almost like she had been watching the attack, smiling. As if she was more fascinated by the move than she was concerned at avoiding it.

"Nice," she said. "Do I get a count?"

The crowd roared with laughter.

"No counts here," he said. "Get up."

"As you wish." She bounced up and raised her fists. "Shall we dispense with the warm-up now?"

The big man flew at her. A four-punch combination. She moved within his attack, like she knew where every fist would fly. He hit only air.

"Come on," she said. "I'm questioning your motivation."

He grunted and threw a long right that went round her guard and glanced the side of her head. She stepped back, blinking, looking like she was trying to focus. The crowd roared, sensing it might be all but over. He moved forwards again but she glided sideways and they circled.

She moved so fast he almost didn't see it. She launched a fist into his side, which he got nowhere near blocking. Her hand seemed to be made of iron. He felt the rib break, and he wheezed in pain. There was a sudden hush.

"Not used to getting hit?" she asked, tilting her head on one side.

Inside Rodriguez something snapped. He exploded at the woman, ignoring her fists, her arms. His first blow lifted deep into her ribcage, his second caught the side of her head, full force. There was a crack of bone and she flew through the air, blood arcing from her mouth. She crumpled onto the sawdust. Everything went still.

Then the crowd exploded.

The owner looked at the slumped figure, stepped through the ropes and lifted up Rodriguez's arm. "A bit of a light entertainment to finish. Now if you..." He trailed off at the sound of gasps.

A woman's voice spoke. "*Get. Out.*"

The bar-owner span around.

"Get out of my ring," the woman said, her eyes almost glowing as she pulled herself upright, wiping the blood from her lips, then pausing to taste it.

The owner's face went white and he climbed back through the ropes.

"The fight is done," Rodriguez said, shaking his head. "This is madness."

"I will say when it's done." She stepped towards him.

Rodriguez looked at her face. No bruising. Even the blood was fading. A chill went down his spine. "Who are you? What are you?"

"I am the last person you will ever fight. Have you shown me everything you know?"

"You don't even look like you've been hit."

"I'll take that as a yes." And then she moved. With perfect economy, she struck him. Not with a fist, but with an open palm, square in his chest, directly over his heart.

Rodriguez barely knew what had happened. His heart ruptured as he flew back through the ropes, knocking over several patrons. He lay on the floor, coughing blood. As he breathed his last, all he could think was that he had just faced the devil.

Around the room there were gasps. The woman did not even

look at her fallen opponent. She was staring around the crowd. Then she turned to the owner and cleared her throat. "Ten thousand pesos, was it?"

The owner tugged at his collar, clearly not sure whether to be more worried about himself or the money. "I don't keep that much on me..."

Some of the patrons started muttering. No weapons were allowed in the bar, but that did not mean there were no weapons in the bar.

The woman shrugged. "Then drinks for all these good people." She waved around the room. "On me." She nodded to the owner. "Ten thousand pesos' worth should keep everyone merry."

There was a moment of hesitation, then the owner shrugged and nodded at his bar staff. The crowd cheered.

The woman nodded at the owner. "Smart move."

"I like to keep the fighting in the ring. Speaking of which", he looked at her hopefully, "I seem to have a vacancy for the role of house champion."

She adjusted her necklace. "Sorry. I'm just passing through. I heard Rodriguez had some moves and wanted to see them for myself."

"Where did you learn to fight like that?"

"I learn from anyone who has something to teach me. Then I move on."

The owner shook his head. "You are most unique."

Alex Marron smiled. "Very nearly."

TWELVE

THE BLACK MERCEDES LIMOUSINE DROVE through the automatic gates between the high walls. Bern glanced briefly at the police escort, which had stopped outside the gates, and permitted himself a small smile. His lawyers had fought hard to keep them off the property – and Bern could afford to hire very capable lawyers. So far they had failed in only one respect - he flexed his ankle, feeling the weight of the GPS tracking band that he had to wear as a condition of his release. It was a temporary setback: something he would deal with in due course.

The car rolled slowly up the curving gravel driveway, past immaculately coifed privet hedges, and finally he saw the classic Edwardian house he had not been back to in nearly a year. Of course he had not expected to ever be back here, but then very little had gone to plan. He should have escaped on his yacht, the Phoenix, with money and technology to deploy to take him on to bigger things. Now his plans were more than twelve months behind and deeply compromised. Before, he had meant to slip quietly into the shadows. Now the world, more than ever, was watching his every move.

The car came to a stop outside the house and he stepped out. Eli Quinn, his estate manager, was waiting. "William, welcome home. The house is ready for you."

Bern nodded. "I appreciate you keeping things running."

Quinn opened the front door and led Bern inside. The floors gleamed and the furniture looked freshly polished. They strode through the long hall, past a line of oil paintings, and into the lounge looking across the main lawn.

Bern walked over to the window and drank in the view. "So, what's new? They've refused to tell me anything about Marron. Did he make some kind of deal?"

"Not that we're aware of. Why, did you expect that?"

"Not really. If he wants to get out, he'll do it on his own terms. Any developments with his daughter?"

"No body. No trace."

"Pity." He rubbed his brow. "And my... *son*?"

Quinn picked up a file from the coffee table. "Have a look through this if you fancy reading the collected guesswork."

"Maybe later. I'm more interested in what's happening with my company."

"Best you speak to your lawyers. Fiona Farrow called. She wants a meeting here tomorrow."

"Get her cleared with our friends outside."

Quinn nodded. "If it's any comfort, Lentz is doing a competent job. She's steadied the ship."

"Better than sinking it, I guess." Bern poured himself a coffee from the waiting pot. "So, who has wanted to know about me?"

"There've been, at the last count, nine unauthorised books about you since the incident. Everyone wants to know the truth about what happened. We've heard that the Leskov family has been conducting investigations. Viktor's son, Andrei, is in charge now."

"An inevitable consequence of our carefully constructed house of cards falling down. We should watch them carefully.

They might have hesitated to reach me in prison, but here they may feel I'm more accessible."

"I'll review security. But it's going to be difficult getting any proper weaponry in with the police taking such a close interest." Quinn picked up a computer tablet and scrolled through a list. "Oh yes, your bank manager also wants to speak. Something about liquidity problems after paying the £200 million bail."

"More work for my lawyers, no doubt. If I have to get them involved any more I won't have any money left to pay them."

"Which brings me to the Americans. Specifically, the CIA. They've been trying, and failing, to get access to you in prison. Now you're out, they're hoping a meeting can be arranged."

"Why would I want to talk to them?"

"Perhaps they can make you an offer you won't want to refuse."

"I'd almost do it just to see the expression on Reems' face. But I'm sure I can trust them even less than her. Tell them to go screw themselves." Bern smiled. "Now, I'm going to enjoy my first day back under my own roof. Tomorrow, there'll be a surprise or two for everyone."

THIRTEEN

IT WAS A GREY DAY at King's College Hospital in central London, the clouds surly and low. George Croft pushed through the door and strode into the car park, his hands clenching and unclenching. His daughter had deteriorated and, although the doctors weren't agreed on why her leukaemia was advancing beyond their worst predictions, advancing it was. There were no more treatment options available. She had a few months at most.

Croft stared long and hard at the pavement. She was only nine.

His ex-wife had been there too, making the impossible even more so. He'd said he had to get back to work, but the truth was he just couldn't stand to be there another moment with the woman he could no longer talk to, and the daughter he could not save. The feeling of powerlessness gave him nausea. Swearing at the air, he walked back to his car and climbed in. He adjusted the rear view mirror and froze. There was someone sitting in the back.

The woman, who wore a grey coat and dark glasses, nodded. "Take a breath, George. I just want to talk."

Croft's hand strayed to his gun, concealed in his shoulder holster. "We agreed not to meet in public."

She smiled. Her teeth were perfect. "Sometimes we are not in control of the timetable. You do still want that miracle, yes?"

"That is a stupid question."

"Then shut up and let me explain the problem." She held up a large brown envelope and passed it to him. "Read the contents."

He took it and removed three neatly printed pages, which he quickly scanned. "How are you getting this?"

"All that matters is that Reems is a concern. She's going to need some assistance if she's to make the right choice."

"She's not one to listen to counsel."

"We just need you to stay close to her in case she makes any bad decisions. Be there to pick up the pieces." She adjusted her dark glasses. "Remember, she's the one breaking the rules. You're duty-bound to do something."

Croft slid the documents back into the envelope. "But is it the right thing?"

The woman looked towards the hospital building and smiled. "I think you know the answer to that."

FOURTEEN

KATE PARKED SMOOTHLY IN HER dedicated space, the Audi coupe lined up next to a number of other nearly-new vehicles. She grabbed her attaché case and strode into the express executive lift, her make-up already perfectly applied, clutching no take-out coffee because she had cut down to one a day. As she spoke the command for her floor, she glanced at her watch and saw she was early. She almost laughed: so much had changed in a year.

On Level 87 Kate stepped from the lift and glided through the open-plan area, past the smiling face of her personal assistant, and into her corner office. The door swung closed and she hung her coat up. As she did, a piece of paper fell from one pocket: the leaflet from Brocca.

Sighing, she thought again about the previous evening. So much for her idea that there had been a connection between her and Tom. Clearly that was all in her head – and she didn't even want to think about what was in *his* head: all he was able to connect with was computers.

The desk-screen bleeped softly and a message from her assistant flashed up; her nine o'clock was here. She tapped to confirm she was ready, and there was a knock at her door.

"Come in."

Geraldine, her former boss from *Business Week News*, appeared, a fixed smile on her face. They hugged awkwardly, and Kate ordered tea. It arrived in moments and she poured for them both as they took seats in matching armchairs around a glass coffee table.

Geraldine gestured at the room. "It has to be said, you were never going to get an office like this at BWN."

Kate waved her hands. "You kind of forget it after the first couple of weeks."

"Caught up in the work, I'm sure. How are you enjoying things?"

"It's been quite a ride, no secret. But the company is pulling together. A number of new product lines are about to--"

Geraldine leaned forwards. "I hear MI5 are still buzzing around."

"I can't really comment." Kate paused. "It's a lot less exciting than it sounds."

"I'm sure that isn't true."

"You probably know more than I do," she said with a particularly broad smile. "Your contacts were always better than mine."

"Oh come on." Geraldine flickered an eyebrow. "I heard that nanotechnology is back on the agenda, and you're going to be pushing for a review of the legislation."

"We have no plans in the realm of nano--"

"Sure, sure. And are you in contact with Tom?"

Kate felt her eyelid twitch. "You may have unrealistic expectations of what we can talk about."

"Unrealistic? A year ago you decided to kill the best story we've ever had. You said you'd get me a different scoop. Twelve months later, I'm still waiting."

"You know why I made that decision. You *said* you supported it."

"Yeah, well you said some things too at the time, but since then you've said *nothing*. What is CERUS's position on the release of William Bern?"

"He was bailed, not released. And my personal view is that it shouldn't have happened. Stephanie Reems must be furious."

"Oh I don't know," replied Geraldine. "I have a source that says Reems personally approved it."

"That's impossible. She'd sooner die."

"Which makes it all the more interesting that she did it. And what about this beta site?"

Kate folded her arms. "That's a myth. There's no way Bern could have hidden such a facility from all company records, let alone government surveillance."

"Given enough time, enough money, and enough motivation, do you really think that's true? Stories have come out that his late wife was plotting against him, and he knew. He had good reason to be hiding things of value." Geraldine slurped some of her tea. "If you were still a reporter, you'd be crawling all over this."

"Yes, well, I'm not."

"Don't you miss it? I'm doing a piece on Glifzenko, the Pharma giant, and their aim to drive CERUS Biotech into the ground. It could be career defining. That's the kind of mark I want to leave behind: I don't plan on selling out."

"You think that's what I've done?"

Geraldine gestured at Kate's office with a shrug. "How does it feel being the one killing the story, instead of writing it?"

Kate sucked in her top lip. "There comes a point when you have to move forwards, not backwards."

"Even if it means being economical with the truth?"

"Oh, come on. It's not like you to be so... unsubtle. What's going on?"

Geraldine cleared her throat. "You're right. My apologies." She stood up and held out her hand. "No hard feelings?"

Kate stood and shook the proffered hand. "Of course not."

"Good. And, really, I'm pleased for you. Proud even."

Kate felt the palm of her hand tingle slightly. Then the back of her head. "You know, I think you mean that."

"Well, I'm not some completely heartless monster." She turned to leave. "You know, if I were you, even if I didn't plan on using the information, I'd want answers to these questions. And I'd use whatever methods I could to get to them." She shrugged. "But of course I don't tell you what to do any more. It's up to you."

FIFTEEN

ON THE EDGE OF THE tiny village in the Atacama Desert in Northern Chile, in a crumbling brick temple that served as a Dojo, the old man stood poised. He ignored the dry, scratching heat. Instead he shifted his balance and breathed deeply, his worn robes flowing as he moved gently forwards. It was a complex sequence, but it was his creation, and he had been teaching it for nearly fifty years. Precision, grace and power articulated in what most would see as a form of dance, but which was, in fact, an expression of one of the oldest forms of unarmed combat. The old man brought his hands together, completing the movement. Then he waited.

The young woman echoed his moves, although to use the word 'echo' was to denigrate her achievement. He had never seen such a student. She recalled every nuance, every motion, with absolute perfection. Her body moved with a grace and control that was almost poetic. It was impressive enough and yet, by her own admission, she had had no formal training in any form of Kung Fu. After only a single day he had taken her through each of the fundamental disciplines of his art. She had grasped everything with but a single demonstration. There was little more he could teach her.

He bowed formally, indicating they should sit and take tea. They moved to a low, crude table and he poured the hot bitter liquid from a crude clay pot. They raised their cups to each other and enjoyed the moment of calm. He let it linger before speaking, "May I ask you a question?"

She bowed her head and replied in Spanish so good she could have passed as Chilean. "It is your Dojo, Master."

"I have been in this village for fifty years. I have seen thousands pass through. But I have never met one such as you." He looked deep into her eyes. "What is your secret?"

"That you are a great teacher."

He smiled and sipped from his tea. "If only that were true."

"I could have learned what you have taught me from no other." Her eyes flickered. "And believe me when I say I have looked."

"You have not told me what you are looking for. You have not even told me your name."

"It is safest if I don't."

"Safest for whom?"

She broke a slight smile. "Your brain is as sharp as a man in his twenties."

He gave a snort. "If that is right, why are you still such an enigma to me?"

"I'm not someone easily understood. Now I have one request, before I leave."

"Ask, my child."

"I should like us to duel."

He laughed. "Perhaps thirty years ago. Alas now my heart and bones would not honour my craft." Then he saw her expression and frowned. "You were serious?"

"I was. I am."

"But what would be the purpose?"

"I would give you that final moment." She exhaled slowly. "That you may die with honour."

The old man blinked slowly, but he did not move. "Why should I die without honour?" He paused. "Of course the better question is, why should I die at all?"

"It comes to us all, Master. And there will be those that seek me. I cannot leave one behind who knows so much."

"I knew you were trouble. Yet, something told me not to refuse your request." He stood up and straightened his robes. "Why are you doing this? What is it that you seek?"

Her response was immediate. "Perfection. I'm sure that's why you went to China. As a young man."

He narrowed his eyes. "What do you know of that?"

"I know you trained with true masters – one of very few Westerners to do so. I know you rose to greatness. And I know you left at great speed, and in disgrace."

"That was a lifetime ago." He shook his head slowly. "It took me years to be accepted - then in a moment of madness, of anger - and with the skills I had learned - I killed a man. After that, everything was lost. I learned so much, but I did not learn everything. Here," he gestured to the crumbling walls of the temple, "I've endeavoured to share what I could."

"For that I am grateful. But now the lesson has ended."

He looked at her and breathed out. "I have long wondered what this moment would feel like. I sensed it might be unexpected."

She looked at her right hand, rippling the fingers. "You think this is destiny?"

"Perhaps just justice catching up with me." He shrugged. " I am ready."

He saw her close her eyes. He saw again the unique quality that he noted when she first came to him: the impossible intensity. The heart of stone. Even in his prime he knew he could not have challenged her. He watched as she breathed deeply then opened her eyes.

"Thank you," she said. And then she moved.

In his eighty years he had never seen anyone move even half as fast.

*

Three hours later, Alex sat in a bar, having caught a bus to the next village. The venue was jammed with international backpackers, all exchanging stories about recent adventures in loud, inebriated, voices. Alex ignored them all. Instead, staring at the distant mountains, she quietly raised a cold beer in a silent toast to the old man. A thank you for what he had taught her.

She had buried him in the shade of a small pimento tree, covering the grave with the largest boulders she could carry. Had he deserved this fate? Perhaps not. Or perhaps he should have already paid the price for a crime committed many years ago. Destiny, fate, or just the toss of a many-sided coin? Others would have to make that call.

Then something else did catch her attention. Someone had flicked the bar's widescreen television onto CNN. In a moment she had crossed the room, sliding between some of the patrons, shoving others painfully aside. A sharp twist of an inconsequential wrist, and the remote control was in her hand. She turned the sound up, although the images made it clear what was happening: William Bern had been released. Only on bail, but she knew that with him out of custody anything could happen. Perhaps she had less time than she'd thought.

She adjusted her belt and straightened, feeling the blood pulse in her veins. She wanted to go to her father: to tell him she had survived, that she had never been more alive. She wanted to make those who had imprisoned him suffer. But recovering him would be impossible without assistance. No, she needed to pay a visit to an old friend.

And possibly alone on the planet, she knew exactly where to go.

SIXTEEN

HIGH IN THE PERUVIAN ANDES it was the last minutes before dawn. In the near darkness, tired but over-excited tourists stumbled along the last kilometre of the Inca Trail, up the final rise to the Sun Gate and the view of the Lost City of Machu Picchu. Phones, SLRs and video cameras were primed ready to capture every moment for posterity.

Tom kept himself separate from the others. He wasn't here to be with other people, although this brief moment of arrival was as crowded as a town centre. The other hikers had, for the most part, made a three-day trip of the forty kilometres of aggressive climbs and descents, all at considerable altitude. But Tom didn't like the idea of sharing a small campsite, so he had walked through the night, completing the entire trail in a little over eight hours, though he'd waited for the sunrise to complete the final climb. Even the locals might have been impressed, although the record was around three and a half hours, so he had room to improve.

He followed the excited group up the rocky trail to the ruins of the Sun Gate just as the sun broke through scattered clouds, and he saw Machu Picchu, on its famous saddleback mountain, spread out below. There were gasps from those around him, and they were justified. It must have been a city of incomparable beauty, and yet designed with a mathematical elegance, all without the aid of computers. If only he could live in an age like that. A simpler life, where he was not being pursued for what was in him.

Still, he was safe for the moment, and he would make the most of it. He gazed down at the ancient ruins. Soon it would fill up with other tourists shipped in by train and bus. But for the next hour it was only open to those who had walked off the trail. He would make the most of that hour. He started to bound down the path, but someone called after him.

"Hey! Stop!"

He slowed, an icy feeling in his blood. Had someone actually been following him? He had done nothing to draw attention to himself. Yet someone was running after him.

What should he do? Where could he run? Down through the ruins? What then? It was five hundred metres vertically down to the only town and, while he had a map, he did not know the terrain. Forcing a smile he turned around.

It was a young woman, waving at him. "Stop running off."

He held his breath.

"You dropped this." She held out his woollen hat.

He took it and blinked, letting the breath go. "Er... thank you."

"Amazing isn't it."

He looked at the hat. "Just something I bought at an army surplus--"

She laughed and pointed behind him at the ruins.

"Of course." He tucked the hat back in his pocket. "Yes, amazing."

"Who are you here with?" she asked, moving closer. She had a Peruvian *chullo* on her head: a knitted hat complete with ear flaps.

"Which tour?"

"On my own actually. Keeping my own company," he said, widening the gap between them. She seemed to get the message, shrugging and turning back to her group. Tom hurried down towards the ruins, wondering if perhaps he was being a little too cautious. But then he hadn't managed to stay hidden in a major city for a year to end up being discovered here, on the far side of the world. Still, it seemed the girl was harmless.

He tagged on to one of the groups touring the ruins, immersing himself in history, surrounded by endless views so beautiful he was glad he would be able to remember them perfectly.

SEVENTEEN

DEPUTY DIRECTOR TRUMAN ENTERED THE secure conferencing facility at the US Embassy in London. A technician dialled in the video call then left the room, sealing the door. Truman poured himself a glass of water, wishing something stronger was available, then took a seat facing the camera. Director Banetti's face appeared on screen, his eyebrows somehow accentuated by the slightly blurred image. As usual he spared no time on pleasantries.

"You met with Reems?"

"I did." Truman took a deep breath, wishing he had more to pass on. "She told me nothing about Bern, Marron or Faraday. Then she wheeled in Dominique Lentz, who told me even less." Truman shook his head. "We could just share with them what happened. That would get their attention."

"I don't have the clearance. If we told her that we're trying to recover *something*, it would only pique her interest. Which would make her even less likely to cooperate. You read the file on Faraday and the Tantalus Project?"

"A neural interface designed to operate an advanced helicopter. I'm not surprised they've kept quiet about losing him."

Banetti showed a faint smile. "I'm glad I'm not in charge of

MI5."

"I also read the brief on the stolen item, although it was so heavily redacted it was difficult to follow."

"I gave you what I could. The Accumulator is one of our most classified projects."

Truman took a sip of water. "It's a nuclear battery, so not exactly surprising."

Banetti grimaced. "A gross over-simplification, but I guess it sums it up. I've no doubt Bern would love to have a look."

"But why would Faraday take it?"

"When we find him we can ask him."

Truman nodded. "Speaking of Bern, you've been briefed on his release?"

"The timing is uncanny. We would never have allowed it if he'd been our prisoner."

"They do have him locked up in his private estate. He's not going anywhere."

"Not without help."

Truman hesitated. "What do you mean by that?"

"We don't know where Faraday is, and he may be very difficult to locate. Marron is locked away beyond anyone's reach. So," Banetti said, "that really only leaves us with one person we know the location of, who is accessible, and who may be motivated to assist us."

"You want to make a deal with Bern? Why would he trust us?"

"We just need to ask him in the right kind of way."

"And what about the Brits?"

"They had their chance. It's our show now."

"I doubt we can just drive up to the estate and ask for an appointment."

"I think we both know that's not what I'm suggesting."

Truman looked down at the table. "If things go wrong this could badly strain our *strategic friendship*."

"I have every confidence in you, Connor."

Truman sighed. "Am I being thrown under a bus here?"

"Just make sure you avoid the wheels." Banetti flexed his eyebrows. "Call me when it's done."

The screen went dark. Truman sat staring at the table. What he hadn't shared with Banetti was that he'd been doing his own research and he'd discovered that the CIA Director had taken a personal interest in the Accumulator Project since its inception more than two decades ago. For whatever reason, this was personal for Banetti: he wasn't going to let it fail, and he wasn't going to care who he burned in the process of securing its success.

Truman swallowed hard. Right now he was feeling decidedly flammable.

EIGHTEEN

FOR TWO HOURS TOM HAD truly forgotten about the modern world, immersing himself in the history and serenity of the ancient city. Thick cloud would sweep over then clear, the mood changing by the minute. But every corner turned brought a new item of interest, or a new vista. He wished it would never end.

But all too soon he was climbing onto a waiting bus. It descended fourteen aggressive, hair-pin bends: sharp switchbacks that the bus only just made. The newly built town below lay in the vicious channel between the mountains, where the wind never seemed to stop blowing.

Now, sitting by a swollen river, he was eating pasta and drinking bottled beer in a large, roughly-furnished restaurant. The place was heaving, two thirds full of backpackers, one third of locals. Tom had somehow found a table on his own. But as he shovelled in another mouthful of pasta, the young woman who had given him back his hat appeared from nowhere and sat opposite.

"So, where are you from?" she said brightly.

"Er... England."

"Duh, yeah. Where in England? London?"

Tom narrowed his eyes. "Sure. Why?"

She laughed. "Another wary Brit. I'm from California. San Francisco." She held out her hand in a way that was hard to refuse. "Mandy."

"Tom," he replied, feeling the warmth in her hand. "Nice to meet you."

She took a deep draught of her beer. "I've always wanted to come to this place. Can't believe I finally made it."

Tom nodded. "It certainly was something."

"I just wish I could remember it all perfectly forever."

"Wouldn't that be a thing?"

Mandy placed her bottle firmly back on the table. "So where are you off to next? Another trek? Or maybe into the jungle? You should do Ecuador. It has a bit of everything, and as for the Galapagos, they are quite..."

Tom nodded politely, but his eyes caught a newspaper on the next table. It was folded open, and one of the story titles leapt off the page:

FORMER CERUS CEO, WILLIAM BERN, RELEASED: LATEST DEVELOPMENTS

Tom stood up sharply and grabbed the paper, scanning the story. Bern's legal team had raised doubts about the validity of his confession, and were planning further submissions that might lead to the charges being thrown out.

"Something wrong?" Mandy asked.

He looked around. He had to know more, but there was no network near enough to access. This paper was a day old. "Is there internet in this place?"

She laughed. "No internet cafes until we get back to Cuzco. Why?"

"I need to check something." He hesitated. "I'm expecting an email."

"Then you should get the next train out of here. I have a timetable..." She started patting hands around her body, her face taking on a look of alarm. "Oh no! I've dropped my purse. It had my notebook and cash in it."

"When did you last have it?"

She closed her eyes. "Up on the trail."

"Won't be easy to go back. We could try--"

"*We?*" she said coyly. "Didn't want to speak to me earlier, and now you want to help me?"

"Yes, well..." Tom swallowed. "It's crappy when you lose something like that. I'd want someone to help me."

"I still have my credit cards and passport." She reached into her backpack and pulled them out. "And I think there's a Western Union down the street. They should be able to provide me with an advance." She stood up. "I don't suppose you'd come with me. Like a security escort."

A Western Union would have a network connection, which was what he needed: something he could tap into quietly. "Sure."

"Wonderful." She shouldered her backpack then walked towards the exit. Tom rose and followed her. In the corner of his eye he saw two men who looked like porters stand up.

Out on the street, cars and vans negotiated the muddy cobbles, trying to avoid the mules and handcarts. Tom and Mandy made their way parallel to the roaring rain-swollen river. The wind still blew almost continuously. The pavement was missing in places, showing a half-finished drainage system, and they were forced to step into the road to avoid falling a metre and a half into a small stream. Behind them Tom saw the two men appear at the door of the restaurant, then turn their way. He hurried to catch up with Mandy.

"Staying in town tonight? Or shipping back to Cuzco?" she asked, stepping around a couple of chickens.

"Haven't decided." Out of the corner of his eye he saw the two men maintaining their distance.

"Something wrong?"

"Don't look, but I think two men from that restaurant might be following us."

She immediately turned round. "Where?"

"Never mind, just keep walking."

"Why would they be following us?"

"Who knows? Are you somebody famous?" Then he immediately wished he hadn't raised the idea.

"No." She narrowed her eyes. "Are you?"

He glanced back again and saw one of the men talking into a mobile phone. Was it really unusual behaviour? What was triggering his suspicion?

"Maybe you read too many thrillers?" She pointed to a narrow side street. "Let's go up here and see if they follow." They stepped sharply sideways and vanished from the main thoroughfare. "If we go along here, then left, we can head back in the direction of the Western Union." Mandy turned left. They were halfway down an even tighter alleyway, lined with three storey apartments either side, when two new men stepped into view at the far end. They held ugly-looking clubs.

Mandy screamed, but the sound was all but drowned out by the background rush of the nearby river and the wind swirling above them. Tom grabbed her arm and began reversing back up the alleyway. Then the first two men appeared behind them.

"What do they want?" she asked.

Tom was pretty sure he knew: Mandy's credit cards and passport, and anything else they might have on them. Tom had been the victim of an attempted mugging once before. But that was a world away, in a different time and place. There had been just one attacker. And a friendly guardian angel to rescue him. It seemed unlikely that anybody would step in to save them today.

Of course, he wasn't the same person now. A moment ago he had wondered whether he could risk using his talents. Now he knew he had no choice.

He closed his eyes and concentrated. Quickly he felt a nearby satellite dish - it would take a considerable effort to connect to it, but right now that was not his biggest concern. At least it had only the most basic encryption. He was through it in seconds, and then he was online. There was a lot of latency, but the bandwidth wasn't bad. Part of him inside sighed at the feeling.

"Are you carrying any kind of weapon?" asked Mandy.

"Of course not," Tom said, opening his eyes. The two pairs of men strode slowly towards them. They were in no hurry. Where could their quarry go?

Mandy turned to him. "Any ideas?"

Tom blinked. Data streamed. In his head a street map appeared, overlaid with a recent satellite photograph. He knew where they were, and that was always a start. He turned and pointed to a door to their right. "Through here." With a fluid motion he lunged out, his foot landing square centre: a practiced motion, one that he had used before. It had saved his life.

The door buckled and collapsed inwards.

He pulled Mandy through with him, hearing shouts from the alleyway as the four men reacted. Inside, the ground floor apartment was dark and dirty, unoccupied, but he knew where he was going. He had the plan of the building in his head, downloaded from the construction company. He ran down a short hallway, through a kitchen, then to a back door. And escape.

Except it wasn't there.

He looked at the solid wall and swore.

"What?" shouted Mandy. "What's going on?"

"There's supposed to be a door here."

"How would you know that?"

He looked around. The plans must be inaccurate. In fact the room looked too large. Perhaps two rooms had been knocked together, and a door closed up. He looked to the side and saw an internal door. If there was still a back way out, then it must be through there.

And it was, leading off a small storage room.

He pushed Mandy through it. Behind floated the sound of the pursuers entering the apartment. Tom and Mandy slid out into the street, which was slightly wider, but lined with parked cars. Then they sprinted in the direction of the main road, and more people. But, as they did, there was a loud crack, the sound ricocheting off the close buildings.

A gunshot.

"Stop!" shouted a voice in broken English.

Tom and Mandy stopped, turning in frustration. The tallest of the four men held a hand gun pointing at them. "Wallets, passports." The man waved the gun at them.

Tom looked at the firearm. It was a revolver. No electronics. Nothing he could interface with. He had no weapon of his own. But perhaps he didn't need one. He looked at the car next to him. Even cars ten years old had some electronics. Most in this street were much newer than that. And many had alarms.

He reached out and connected, setting one off. The shrill sound bounced around them.

The man with the gun looked about, then back at them. "Your wallets. Quickly!"

Tom closed his eyes and reached out again.

Almost every car in the street erupted in shrill protest. The four men looked around them in confusion. Tom and Mandy sprinted round the corner, back onto the main street.

"What just happened?" shouted Mandy, gasping for breath. "Why did all those alarms go off?"

"Maybe one went, and triggered the next, like dominos."

She didn't look convinced, but from behind them came the shouts of the men, clearly not bothered about following them into a busier area.

"We can't outrun them," Tom said. "Not at this altitude." He swept his eyes left and right, and settled on a relatively modern 4x4, a Subaru Legacy. "We'll borrow this car." He ran over to it.

"You mean steal it?"

"Needs must. And we'll give it back when we're done." He queried the car's control system and popped the locks. "Look! It's open."

She stared at him.

"Get in." He scrambled into the driver's seat and made a show of scrabbling around for a key.

"Know how to hot wire a car, do you?" she asked, climbing into the passenger seat. "Because we've got about twenty seconds before they catch us."

Tom closed his eyes, muttering. The car's ignition system was encrypted.

"Now would be good," Mandy said, her voice rising.

Tom could feel the car's central computer. He opened his mind to it. He told it what he needed. And it broke open. The engine roared into life. Tom's eyes shot open and he forced the car into drive, jamming his foot onto the accelerator. With a scrabble of dirt and stones, they pulled away into the traffic.

Mandy sat, her head in her hands, panting. Tom looked in the mirror. There was no sign of the men. He steered the car smoothly onto the main road to Cuzco. Six hours' drive and they'd be back in civilisation.

NINETEEN

YURI WAS NOT HAPPY. HE bounced uncomfortably in the Range Rover as it made its way down the unmade road, the suspension managing to transmit the large majority of its bumps and potholes. He glanced at the satellite-navigation system; at least they were nearly there. The man they sought lived alone at the end of this road, on a small farm, miles from anywhere and anyone. If their information was correct, he could connect them to someone of tremendous importance.

There was one positive to coming out to England again: he had finally been able to get away from Andrei. It was madness that his little cousin now headed the family, inheriting the role without any thought as to whether it was right. He was young and impetuous, with little experience or training. And the two of them had never got along. Now Yuri was being blamed for a lack of progress in the London investigation. And blame was not something you lived with for long in their family's organisation. He had at least managed to get two of his own people out here with him: men who had been with him for years. The car pulled up on a gravel area near a small stone cottage. Behind, the ground dropped away steeply to the Atlantic Ocean. Yuri and the bodyguards stepped out, all wearing dark suits and black overcoats. A man, probably in his fifties, looked up from where he was kneeling, trimming a low hedge. "Can I help you?" He spoke with a clear, educated accent He was slim in build, but physically unremarkable.

"I hope so," Yuri said. "We're looking for a Mr. Porter." Behind him the two bodyguards looked around, making sure the area was secure.

The man put down his clippers and stood up. He was probably less than five foot six. "I'm Porter. Now what do you and," he pointed at the bodyguards, "your two rather serious-looking friends want?"

"We were told you could connect us with Sharp."

Porter blinked. He wiped his hands on a rag, staining it green. "And what exactly do you want this *Sharp* to do?"

"Deal with some friends of ours."

Porter tipped his head. "I'd hazard a guess that they are no longer your friends. I'm not sure who you are, but you are clearly mistaken as to who I am." He looked at the bodyguards again. "You come here, with two thugs, probably armed, to intimidate an old man. Perhaps I should call the police."

Yuri nodded. "I imagine they would be here within the hour." He raised an eyebrow. "Do you think that would be fast enough?"

Porter folded his arms. "Are you threatening me? Given who you suggest I work with, do you think that is wise?"

"I respect your caution, but I need you to take me seriously." He stood up straight, adjusting his jacket. "My name is Yuri. I'm here on behalf of my cousin, Andrei Leskov."

Porter's eyes narrowed. "I heard about his father. A most unfortunate business." He unfolded his arms. "Although knowing a name hardly verifies your approach."

Yuri pulled a phone from his pocket, pressed a speed dial button, and handed it to Porter. "My cousin."

Porter frowned and held the phone to his ear. "Mr Leskov?" He listened intently then looked at Yuri. "He says you have a list, and an item of equipment, for me."

Yuri removed a document from his pocket and held it out. Porter took it from him. Then Yuri snapped his fingers at one of his men, who produced a small hard case, marked with warning symbols, and set it on the floor.

Porter blinked and flipped open the case, examining the contents, then he read the list. "I see," he said into the phone. "Your terms are acceptable. You are certain about the last part?" Another pause. "I'll be sure to tell him." He clicked the phone off and threw it back.

Yuri caught it. "So how long will it take you to contact Sharp?"

"I'll take care of that right now." He reached behind him and pulled an item from his belt. Something about the movement looked too practised, too fluid, for a man of his age. Then Yuri saw what was in his hand.

An automatic pistol.

With unhurried precision Porter fired a single shot into the forehead of each bodyguard, before either of them had managed to unholster their own weapons. They collapsed as the gunshots echoed across the landscape.

Yuri gasped and took a step back. He was not armed. Why would he need to be, when his bodyguards were always with him? And then the realisation hit him. "You are Sharp," he said, trembling.

The assassin checked the gun, then aimed at Yuri's chest.

"You're signing your own death warrant, double-crossing my cousin."

Sharp looked surprised. "I don't double-cross my clients."

Yuri swore. "*Andrei* told you to do this? But why?"

"He told me that you would say you don't understand. And that I should tell you that you should."

"He thinks I'm plotting to oust him?"

"It doesn't matter what he thinks. It only matters what he tells me."

The pistol fired a third time.

TWENTY

NIGHT HAD FALLEN FAST AND hard in the high mountains as Tom drove, the windows up and the climate control on full blast. He took things slowly because the road was unsealed and littered with potholes, plus it was dark here in a way that it was never dark in London. They had passed a handful of other vehicles, but none in the last hour. It was still another three or four hours to Cuzco.

While they were leaving the town, Mandy had made a quick call on her mobile phone and told her group that she was OK, that she had hitched a ride back to Cuzco, and that she would see them back at the hotel there. "How do you know where you're going?" Mandy asked, curled up on the front seat, her arms wrapped around her knees. "I'd be completely lost."

"There aren't too many choices," Tom replied. "Plus there have been a few road signs." He didn't mention that he still had a map in his head or, of course, that he was making the occasional GPS trace.

"Thanks for what you did back in the village. Saving me and everything."

"I think we just got very lucky."

"I suppose. Where did you learn to hot-wire a car?"

Tom glanced in her direction. "Misspent youth."

"I'm grateful you were with me."

Tom gave a smile, then re-focused on the road ahead. A light appeared, then another: headlights. Something was parked in the middle of the road. He slowed the car.

"What's the matter?" Mandy asked.

"Up ahead." He pointed.

"Perhaps it's just broken down?"

He couldn't say: not because he didn't want to, but because he couldn't define it. There was just something *wrong*. "Maybe, but I don't think we should stop." He pulled wide to the left as they reached the other vehicle – it appeared to be empty. Suddenly, there was a sharp jolt under the car, followed immediately by four tight bangs, like the tyres had hit something: the scream of air told him it was something sharp. They ground to a juddering halt.

Tom spoke low and clear, his eyes flicking around. "We have to move."

"What? Move where?"

"This way. Keep low and--"

"Stay where you are," said a voice from outside, muffled by the vehicle's windows. The accent was not local.

Tom hissed. "I'm sorry, Mandy. I think this is my fault. Just do what they say. It's me they want."

"Yes, it is," said the same voice. "Please step out of the car, Mr Faraday."

Tom barely had time to realise his fears had been confirmed – that he'd been right all along and someone did know where he was – when he felt a sharp sting in his neck. He turned to Mandy, trying to tell her that everything would be OK. She didn't look afraid. That was good, he thought.

Then darkness took him.

TWENTY-ONE

LENTZ DROVE HER CITROEN 2CV into London slowly, partly because she was thinking, partly because the tiny engine wouldn't go much faster, but mostly because of the sheer volume of traffic, even at 10pm. She had received an obtuse message from Felicia Hallstein, her Head of Technology Development: *you need to come back here tonight.* Dr Hallstein was not one prone to dramatics. In her nine months at CERUS, she had proved to be a steady, effective, pair of hands: someone who could be relied on to do exactly what was asked - something that was, in a scientist, not always the case. Lentz was still trying to process the news of Bern's release, and she wondered if this summons was related. Eventually she drove into the underground car park at CERUS Tower and pulled into her personal space, frowning as she noticed the digital plaque flickering and alternating her name with that of *William Bern, CEO.* Technicians had been fiddling with it for days but had been unable to identify the fault. It was almost like Bern was taunting her. She stepped out of the car, feeling like taking a hammer to the plaque. A familiar, bespectacled woman stood waiting.

"Evening, boss," Hallstein said. "The system told me you'd arrived."

Lentz nodded. "I just need to swing by my office, then I'm yours."

"Actually your office is where we need to go. Best if I show you why."

*

Five minutes later, they stood in the private apartment attached to the CEO's penthouse office, amid the detritus left by the workmen refurbishing it.

"I got a call just over an hour ago," Hallstein said. "I was the most senior employee on site. The workmen found something when they removed the wall panels. I had them replace it for effect."

Lentz stifled a yawn. "We scanned these walls."

"If we did, we didn't do it properly." Hallstein adjusted her black-framed glasses, then removed the remaining wall panel with a flourish.

Lentz blinked. Then swore. There was a small, reinforced steel door, with a keypad and a fingerprint scanner. It was a second safe. The original safe in this room, in which she had discovered crucial documents a year back, had been removed. There'd been no indication there was another.

"I said you had to come in."

"I suppose you also found a note giving the combination?"

Hallstein put her hands on her hips. "It's the same model as the first one. Maybe it has the same combination?"

"That was overridden by Tom. I don't think even he knew about this one."

"Maybe what he did affected all safes in the building? Look, we can always get a security systems expert in, but why don't you try it?"

Lentz shrugged and typed in the twelve-digit sequence. She still remembered it by heart, but then she'd always been good at remembering important numbers. There was a soft beep.

"Is that good?" Hallstein asked.

"Half-good. Now for part two." Lentz placed her thumb on the scanner. There was a second beep, then a click.

"Almost too easy."

"I agree." Lentz reached out to turn the chrome handle.

"Wait," Hallstein said, adjusting her glasses again. "What if it has some sort of anti-tamper device?"

Lentz raised an eyebrow then pulled the handle firmly. The door swung smoothly backwards and they both peered inside. There was a single slim book in the safe, and next to it three plastic capsules, each the size of a large drink can. Lentz removed the book and looked at the cover. Sharply printed typescript read *PROJECT RESURFACE*. She carefully opened the book and skimmed the first few pages. Slotted into the back was a high-capacity data card.

"What have we found?" Hallstein asked.

Lentz shook her head and removed one of the plastic capsules. Embossed lettering read 'SUIT'. "I think the question should be: *what have we missed?*"

TWENTY-TWO

THE WALL WAS THREE METRES high at its lowest point, clad in brick but with a core of concrete and iron. There was no way to go through it, not without an unacceptable amount of disturbance. Along its top was a continuous line of razor wire and, every fifty metres, cameras, constantly rotating.

The senior operative was not deterred. Heavily armed, like all his team, he stood under the cover of a nearby tree, checking his scanner. The cameras now neatly missed this spot: the programming would be reversed once they had departed, which, if the mission went to plan, would be in less than fifteen minutes. That left only the physical barrier to deal with. He sent a message on his encrypted link: a moment later, he received confirmation that they had a green light. He huffed a laugh; with his night vision goggles on, everything looked green. He turned to his team of five and gave a hand signal.

They sprinted at the wall, threw up micro-fibre rope ladders and, in seconds, were scaling the bricks. Suddenly three metres did not look such a barrier. A deft hop over the razor wire, a tumble-roll to break their fall, and they were on the other side.

As a group they moved amongst the bushes, past a small outbuilding and in sight of the main house. At three in the morning it was almost completely in darkness, as expected. The leader paused to run a scan. The signal was immediately detected, on the first floor, confirming its location to within a few metres.

They moved quickly and efficiently, reaching the back door in less than a minute. A female operative stepped forward with a high-powered jamming device. The house was expensive, but it only had a domestic security system. In less than thirty seconds the female operative gave a nod and pushed the door open.

They were in.

The senior operative stepped inside and signalled for his team to fan out and secure the ground floor. Low wattage night lights caused their night vision goggles to flare and distort, but there were no pets, which made things considerably simpler. The bigger risk was that someone – perhaps MI5 – had bugged the place, but nothing had shown, even on a deep scan. His five team-members quickly signalled back that all was in order. They moved upstairs.

The master bedroom was to the left. The tech operative raised her scanner and showed it to the leader, whispering, "Signal is off. It's reading as five metres to the right, which is not in the bedroom. And it's too faint."

"Fault in the scanner?"

Before she could answer, the main lights came on, briefly blinding the entire team.

"Who the hell are you?" A man stood in the doorway of a room behind them, looking shocked and angry. He was not their target.

One of the operatives began to raise his weapon, but the leader shook his head.

"Abort." He turned to the man. "We'll be leaving now, Sir. No need for anybody to do anything stupid."

The man glared back. "My name is Eli Quinn, Mr Bern's estate manager, and nobody is going anywhere until I find out who the hell you are." And he planted his hand on a red button on the wall.

Then all hell broke loose.

*

William Bern's mansion had an elaborate panic alarm. When the red button was pressed a broad-frequency siren sounded across the estate. Lights came on everywhere and a distress flare fired into the night sky.

There was no question that people would notice something was amiss, even if they might normally leave the often reclusive billionaire to his own devices. The police delegation stationed outside did not hesitate for a moment. They forced open the front gates and, within a minute, a team of twenty armed officers were surrounding the house. They found all doors and windows locked down. It took several more minutes to override them, by which time another twenty officers had arrived.

Twenty minutes later Stephanie Reems marched into the hall, where the tactical team had been rounded up. "There had better be a bloody good explanation for this."

The six operatives stood quietly, looking somewhere between stoic and embarrassed.

"Lost your tongues?" she said, walking right up to them.

"I'm sorry, Ma'am," said the team leader. "We're not authorised to speak to you."

She swore. "I'm going to place a call to Connor Truman. If anyone here thinks I should call somebody else, then please cough."

Nobody coughed.

"That's what I thought." She turned to a police sergeant. "Nobody leaves until I say so." She looked around. "Now where is Bern?"

From the hallway a voice called out "I can answer that question, Ms Reems."

Reems saw Eli Quinn in a dressing gown, looking tired. "He's in the panic room."

"Bern has a panic room? Why was I not notified?" Nobody answered. "I want to speak to him now."

"It's not like he's going anywhere," Quinn said. "Not with that ankle bracelet on."

"I wish I shared your confidence. Now show me."

They pushed through the crowd of uniformed and plain-clothes officers, up the stairs to the master bedroom. Quinn walked over to a large, heavy bookcase. "Behind here."

"Open it."

"It can only be opened from the inside." He raised an eyebrow. "It wouldn't be much use if an intruder could simply access it."

"Can he hear us out here?"

"It has external microphones. They should be functional."

"Then why hasn't he come out?"

"I don't know. Perhaps he was injured."

"Or perhaps he's just messing with us. Either way, we need that thing open."

The sergeant reappeared. "Truman is on his way here, by helicopter."

Reems shook her head. "Such a risk to take. Why?" She looked again at the heavy bookcase, then turned back to the black ops team. "I look forward to asking Deputy Director Truman when he gets here."

TWENTY-THREE

THE WOODEN PLANK SNAPPED IN a protest of splinters, the two halves clattering to the concrete floor. Kate looked at them with satisfaction, feeling the heat on her knuckles. With everything going on at CERUS she had missed her karate class earlier, but breaking a few boards was helping temper her frustration. She took another piece of wood from the stack and placed it atop the two blocks. Her strike was just a small sharp movement, but focused on exactly the right point, it caused something to be transformed. If only her other problems could be solved in the same way.

Bern's release continued to swamp every news and social media channel: it was the *only* thing the press wanted to discuss. Her job had been reduced to fire-fighting. Lentz had been locked up in internal meetings and had barely spared her a word. And then there was what Geraldine had told her. Could there be any truth in Reems having authorised Bern's release? It made no sense.

Kate took a slow breath then punched sharply. Again the plank broke.

Bern was still locked up, just in a more comfortable prison, but meeting with Geraldine had upset her, tapping into an anxiety she hadn't fully been able to shake for a year. Had she been right not to publish the Tantalus story: to instead accept the unique opportunity within CERUS? Or had she forgotten what had set her on the path to becoming a journalist in the first place? For years, whenever anyone asked, she said, with no small measure of pomp, that she 'wanted to seek the truth': to hold big business and governments accountable. To help people understand what was going on.

Somehow that had been lost. She might not have been actively lying this last year, but she couldn't deny she had been promoting a narrow, partial view of the truth. That was what PR had turned out to be, at least at CERUS. So what should she do? What *could* she do?

Kate picked up another wooden board, the last one from the stack. A last opportunity, at least for this evening, to focus her rage. She drew back her fist then stopped. Tom's words echoed in her mind.

I want to find out about my mother.

She knew from her previous investigations into Bern that he was an only child whose parents had both died before he was twenty. His past was locked up tighter than a vice. Very little was known about him that was not in the official biographies. Sure there were rumours, always plenty of those, but they contradicted each other more than they agreed. What Kate needed was a way in. Maybe Tom's mother was it.

The fact that Tom was Bern's son was not public. Could Amelia Faraday be a way to get inside Bern's secrets and pull apart the web of deceit he had spun? And, after all, Tom had actually asked her to find out more. Of course if she did this, she could not ignore the very real risk she was taking. If Lentz found out she was using company resources and records for her own purposes, her situation could get tricky. If Reems found out, she could get arrested. But wasn't the greater risk not doing anything?

First she could try and find out the truth. Then she could decide what to do with it.

Kate looked down at the board. Her sensei had told her to 'visualise the broken board, and it is already broken. Apply not your fist, but your will'. She blew out hard and let the punch fly.

TWENTY-FOUR

LENTZ TYPED A LONG ACCESS code into the door control panel. The room had been closed off a year ago, and multiple protocols needed to be reversed before it became accessible. It was one of the unused laboratory facilities within the building, taking up half of Level 61. Mothballed to cut costs.

Not any more.

Lentz carried the book, data card and plastic capsules almost reverentially to one of the network terminals, an access point to the main building servers. She slotted the data card in a reader and watched files start to stream across the screen. She briefly wondered why the card had not been more heavily encrypted, but was distracted by the information.

Project Resurface.

This had been *her* project - more than any other. Tantalus she had provided support on. Resurface she had *led*. It was her biggest disappointment about having to live a different life. She thought perhaps CERUS had given up - she had tried to access the files during her exile, without success. Since her return to CERUS she had tried everything. She had searched the company's systems from top to bottom, and found no reference to Resurface. It was as if it had never existed.

And yet here it was, in her hands. Lentz was a scientist, of course, so her delight was naturally tempered with caution. Why, of all things, had it been in Bern's safe? She started reviewing the files. There were recent reports, schematics, as recent as just a year old. They had made great advances - inevitable given that nano manufacture had become a reality. But still they were having problems.

At its simplest level, Resurface was about a 'coating', although that new coating was a paradigm shift; by coating an object with a new 'surface', the material's properties could be fundamentally changed. It could be made harder; it could conduct or insulate heat; it could alter its appearance, in colour and brightness; it could become adhesive or slippery. And those were just the simple applications they were exploring, as part of which they had developed the all-in-one nano suits. As with Tantalus, there were many more exotic applications being dreamed up, and that was where they were having fundamental technical problems.

Because they didn't have me, thought Lentz with a sly smile. Her phone buzzed. It was Hallstein. "What are you doing?" she asked.

"Like you don't know." Lentz replied.

"Can I help? I'd really like to."

"Perhaps best you don't. Best that both of us don't get fired."

"Why would we get... oh. You don't plan on telling Reems?"

"Not until I have it working," Lentz said. "I'd rather surprise her with the outcome."

"Not counting chickens?"

"Something like that."

"Fine. Well let me know if anything changes. And I'll let you know if Reems suddenly turns up."

Lentz clicked the phone off and stared again at the screen. It was the most recent report. They really were 90% of the way there. And the final barrier was one she had been thinking about for more than twenty years - she had made extensive notes about possible paths to resolution. With the level of current processing power it might just prove...

And then it hit her. She almost did a dance on the spot. She could fix this. Sliding across to another computer terminal she called up the building requisition tool and started ordering equipment. She was going to need quite a lot.

TWENTY-FIVE

"I IMAGINE," STEPHANIE REEMS SAID, "that this operation didn't go quite as you'd planned."

Connor Truman sat at the table, arms folded, his coffee cup already empty. "Could we at least go somewhere secure for this conversation?"

"The entire building has been swept."

"No offence, but was it effective?"

"It detected the recording device you have in your jacket pocket. A pen, probably?"

Truman stared back for a few seconds, then reached into his pocket and placed a silver biro on the table. Reems smiled, picked it up and dropped it with a splash into a nearby vase of flowers. Truman scowled. "Do you have any idea how expensive that was?"

"Less costly than continuing to pull in opposite directions."

"And I should trust that *you* are not recording this conversation?"

"You're on my turf, Mr Truman, so my rules." Her expression darkened. "Why were your team even here without any form of authorisation or notification, carrying out a mission on British soil? An *armed* mission?"

"Do you want cooperation or do you want an argument?"

"Don't think you can just bluster your way out of this."

Truman looked around the room, sucked in his lip, then said, "We wanted to talk with Bern. Believe me when I say we would not have done this without good reason."

"You're going to have to do considerably better than that."

Truman looked at his empty coffee mug, then poured more from the jug in the middle of the table. "What I am about to tell you is strictly off the record. And I, myself, am not aware of all the details." He took a small sip from his mug. "We want to speak with Bern in connection with the theft of classified technology from one of our federal installations."

"Why not just go through regular channels?"

"If you'll recall, you turned us down."

"You didn't explain anything!"

"Because we're embarrassed. And," he paused, "because we don't want to share the technology."

"But why would Bern talk to you? What can you offer him?" Reems' eyes narrowed. "Unless you were going to smuggle him out of the country, offer him some deal in the US?" Her eyes almost became slits. "That's it, isn't it."

"I have no comment."

"And of course you're hoping that he will talk to you about Tantalus. Well, I have a deal for you. It's a non-negotiable one-time offer. You can interview Bern, as long as I can sit in."

Truman rubbed a hand over his eyes. "How am I supposed to sell that to my superiors?"

"Tell them it's the price to get what you want." Her phone buzzed and she looked at the screen. "And it seems we have worked out how to override the door to his panic room, so the moment of opportunity is now."

Truman groaned. "Someday you'll need my help and I will

remember this moment."

"Of that I have no doubt."

*

Reems gave the tech sergeant the order and an overlay lock was mounted on the sealed access panel of the panic room door. From a nearby laptop the override codes were fed in. Reems and Truman watched as the door hissed and swung outwards. They stepped forward. The room was perhaps three metres square and contained a small bed and a refrigerator. One wall was lined with shelves stacked with tinned food and bottled water. A selection of electronics was mounted in a rack unit on another wall.

But Bern was not there.

Truman walked in. "How is this possible? His locator is..." He stopped and picked up a blue band lying on the floor. "It's still working."

"Except," Reems said, "for the fact that it shouldn't have been possible to remove it without triggering an alarm. Still he can't have left the site." Reems turned to the tech sergeant. "I want the entire estate searched. And get Dominique Lentz out here. At once."

TWENTY-SIX

TOM AWOKE FEELING LIKE HE had been sleeping forever. He couldn't recall where he was or how he had got there. It felt like he was experiencing the after-effects of an evening of extraordinary excess. But as he looked around the room he knew that wasn't the reason.

No, he felt this way because he had been drugged. He tried to roll over, but found he was strapped to a metal-framed hospital bed. Sensors were taped to his chest and from them wires led to an archaic-looking medical computer; an IV drip ran into one of his arms. He moved his head and saw he was in a plain, concrete-walled room. A CCTV camera was staring at him. He tried to call out, but with a ferociously dry throat all he could manage was a croak. There were footsteps outside, then an old man, wearing a doctor's white coat and a tired expression, walked in.

"You're awake. Surprisingly quickly."

"Who are you? Where am I?" Tom asked. "And where is Mandy?"

"I'm the doctor, and that's all I can tell you. Sorry, strict instructions."

"How long have I been out?"

"Forty-eight hours, give or take. You're in good health." He looked at the screen. "In fact, better than excellent health."

"I don't know what to tell you," Tom said with a glare.

"Whatever it is, you can tell me," said a large man as he walked in. He had a shaved head and what looked like an ingrained scowl. "Although I should warn you, I know a great deal already, Thomas Faraday." He stared at the doctor, tapping what looked like the vein in his wrist. The man nodded and scurried out.

"So are you going to tell me what is going on?"

"We're somewhere no friend of yours is going to find you, if they were even looking."

Tom shrugged as best he could in the restraints. "Not surprising. I don't have many friends."

The large man paced to the end of the bed and stared down at him. "We know who you are. We know about CERUS. We know you stole technology from them a year ago. And we know that a lot of people are looking for you."

"And how is it you found me?"

"Someone put a bounty on you. And that means a lot of people were highly motivated. We were the ones that got lucky."

Tom closed his eyes. He could feel computers nearby. And networks. But he was still groggy, his mind felt like a wet sponge.

The man folded his arms. "We couldn't find any trace of the stolen tech on you - some sort of computer hardware, we were told - so we need to know where you've hidden it. Either hand *it* over or we hand *you* over. It's up to you."

"So you don't actually know what you're looking for? Didn't it seem odd that they didn't tell you?"

"Not really. The whole thing is highly confidential."

Tom opened his eyes. "You don't have a clue what you're talking about. Believe me when I say there is *nothing* I can hand over."

"Then you leave us with no alternative but to trade you."

"You think you're going to be allowed to walk away with your money?"

The man shrugged. "This isn't my first rodeo."

"What about Mandy?"

"The girl? Why do you care about her?"

"It's not her fault she got caught up with this. Just let her leave."

"You should worry about yourself."

The doctor reappeared, holding a large glass syringe. He looked nervously at Tom. "We need a sample for a DNA analysis to confirm your identity."

"You guys are way out of your depth. This might not be your first rodeo, but they're running it."

"Just take his blood and let's get on with things." The large man glared at Tom. "Don't cause us any trouble and we won't have to hurt you."

Tom growled. "Whoever comes is probably going to kill you, you realise that right? Once they have me, you become disposable."

The large man shook his head and walked out.

The doctor looked at him, somewhat reluctantly. "I'm sorry about this."

"Then do something to help me."

"But not *that* sorry." He stepped forward with the syringe.

TWENTY-SEVEN

LENTZ STOOD LOOKING AT THE interior of the panic room. Something was not right, but she could not place what. She had examined every inch of the walls, floor and ceiling, expecting to find a concealed panel, but there was nothing.

Reems folded her arms. "How did he get out?"

Lentz shook her head. "Are there any cameras in here?"

"None upstairs. Apparently Bern is not an exhibitionist. Downstairs there are several but nothing has shown up on them, besides lots of special forces and police in uniform."

"Then, much as I hate to admit it, I'm at a loss. Are we absolutely certain he went inside this room?"

"The log shows the room was activated. There was nobody else in the house and the bracelet signal confirmed it."

"So we just assumed? Did we really look? I mean, with the tracer showing where he was, did we actually look elsewhere in the building?"

Reems hesitated. "He had to be inside. That's where the bracelet was."

"Yet he has, unarguably, taken the thing off. And we have no idea when he did it." Lentz walked over and picked up the ID bracelet. "Did you use a second-hand one?"

"We did not."

Lentz held it up, pointing out scuff and scratch marks.

Reems snatched it off her. "This isn't the one we gave him. But we already confirmed it is the correct frequency."

"So perhaps he *didn't* take the other one off. These have anti-tamper alarms, which would have made it risky. Instead he set up this one," she waved the worn bracelet, "with the old frequency, and either masked or changed the settings of the one he was wearing. Then, while we looked for the original frequency, he left with the other still on."

"We've had a team watching the estate perimeter ever since he arrived home. There's no way he would have passed unnoticed."

"He's confused us somehow." Lentz suddenly frowned. "Do you have tracker dogs?"

"I already requisitioned a team," Reems said. "They'll be here shortly."

*

The dogs very quickly found a trace. Bern had left through the front door, then made his way across the lawn and along the driveway. From there he had walked straight through the main gates, and into a shallow stream that ran past the estate. The dogs chased about, barking enthusiastically but without further direction.

"They seem pretty sure," Lentz said. "Even if it hasn't helped us actually find him."

"I had several men stationed just outside," Reems replied. "Bern could not have simply walked past them."

"Even at night?"

"We have full floodlights. This would be the most difficult

place to try and pass by."

"Do you have the relevant camera footage?" Lentz asked.

"Why? What are you looking for?"

"Humour me."

They scanned through the CCTV recording. Several police officers walked back and forth. There was no sign of Bern.

"See, I told you," Reems said.

Lentz crossed her arms. "Then I'm out of explanations. But we still have the undeniable fact that Bern has vanished.

Truman walked up. "So, did you find him?"

"No. No thanks to you," Reems said. "Now I have to report back to the Home Secretary. I will be sure to point out your contribution to events."

"And here I was hoping we'd buried the hatchet."

"Now there's an image," Reems said. "Don't tempt me."

TWENTY-EIGHT

AFTER THE DOCTOR HAD FILLED two large vials with blood, Tom was unstrapped from the hospital bed and carried to a different room. It was small and stale, furnished with two grubby camp beds, a single strip light, and a window that had been enthusiastically but inelegantly boarded up. There were two power sockets but nothing plugged into them.

At least he wasn't strapped down any more, but otherwise his situation looked bleak. And, with the tranquilliser in his system, he couldn't make himself focus enough to work out what he might do about it. Everything around him was so basic, so purely mechanical. And the door looked solid. As he watched, it swung in, and a slim figure was pushed inside.

Mandy.

He sat up on the bed as the door was slammed, his head still foggy. "Are you OK?"

She glided over and knelt next to his bed, placing a hand on his arm. "I've been better."

"Why are they keeping you?"

"They keep asking me questions." She paused. "About who you are, and something you stole." She squeezed his arm. "You don't look like a thief."

"Because I'm not."

"Then what are they talking about? If you know anything, just tell them. Maybe they'll let us go."

"Believe me when I say that nothing I can tell them will help me."

"You don't trust me?"

He blinked. "You probably shouldn't trust me either. And it *is* complicated."

She sat on the bed next to him. "Did they drug you too?"

"*Lots* of tranquilliser."

"Then you're not thinking clearly." Her expression darkened. "They're not going to let me go unless you cooperate. We're both in danger here and it's not fair." She brushed her fingertips over his wrist.

As she did, Tom noticed something in her skin: a shift, like a tiny electric current. It wasn't static, rather he could feel the shifting patterns of electromagnetic flows in her body. Something was wrong. Something he should have noticed sooner, but the drugs were dulling his edge. And suddenly he knew what it was. "Back on the road, how did they tranq me?"

"What do you mean?"

"It was some type of tranquilliser gun. But all the windows were rolled up. Which meant whoever fired it was *inside* the car."

"That makes no sense."

"No. Not unless you're one of them," he said. She flinched, and he knew he was right. "You wanted to attach yourself to me from the start."

She stood up. "That's absurd."

But he knew that it wasn't. "Mandy, you have no idea what you've got into."

She looked at him, her lip curling, then she swore and shouted. "Get in here! He's not buying it."

The door opened and the large, shaven-headed man walked in. "Why is this proving so difficult? He's just some office worker. Maybe if your acting was better--"

"Bite me," she said. "And this room smells. Didn't I tell you to clean it up."

The large man shrugged.

Tom shook his head, still feeling the tranquillisers. "What are you, a bunch of backpackers with a laptop? Your weapons look like they were made in World War 2."

Mandy pulled a pistol from the large man's belt and pointed it at Tom. "Maybe. But they still work."

"You're hardly going to shoot me when you need me to cooperate."

She pointed the gun lower. "Maybe I'll just shoot you in the leg. But if that's the way you want to play it, then you've made the decision for us." She turned to the large man. "Contact the buyer. Tell him he can come inspect the merchandise."

TWENTY-NINE

THE MINUTE REEMS WAS CALLED back to central London, Lentz had taken the opportunity to slip away. Now she was back in her lab on Level 61, CERUS Tower. She gripped the pair of carbon tongs and lifted the opaque polymer panel out of the bath of fluorescing liquid. She propped it carefully on a display stand then turned to the nearest computer terminal, where she called up a pre-prepared software routine. She was about to run a test when the door opened and Hallstein walked in.

"Are you nuts?" Hallstein pointed at the panel. "You're already in fabrication?"

Lentz raised an eyebrow. "I know I encourage free speech, but I am still in charge here."

"Not for much longer if you're manufacturing nanites again."

"These aren't intelligent nanites. The panel is merely coated with nano-particles – we're talking a far lower level of capability and risk. Besides, I can hardly mention this to Reems if I don't know it works."

"You still haven't told her?"

"She's had bigger things on her mind. Now watch this." Lentz pressed a key and there was a soft hum. The panel changed colour, from black to red.

"How... underwhelming. You needed nanites for that?"

"They're not... never mind. Keep watching." Lentz pressed another key. The panel changed to give the appearance of polished wood.

Hallstein shrugged. "It's just a display. Why not just use a hi-grade LED panel or something?"

"I suppose you could think of it like that. When I did the original work we had to make each material from scratch. We'd created specific particles that could be changed to render an image. Nanotech has made this far simpler: now it's all in the coating. In theory it could be applied to anything, no other mechanism required."

"OK, so I suppose that is a little neat."

"You could say that. And I think this is how Bern escaped."

"He hid behind a sheet of plastic that looked like a plank of wood?"

"No, but he might have been wearing something like one of these." Lentz turned around and picked up one of the three plastic capsules, the lid of which was lying next to it. She reached inside and pulled out what looked like an object made from thin, dull-grey material. She unfolded it to reveal a one-piece suit.

"Fetching," said Hallstein. "If you've got the figure for it."

"Very funny. The suit material is designed to be coated with the Resurface particles. We actually made the suits many years ago, as part of a number of alternatives for Tantalus. But they would work for Resurface, and now I'm thinking Bern's people got there, at least with the basic stuff. Wearing one of these, Bern could have looked like someone else. Perhaps a generic policeman."

"So a chameleon suit presenting a static change of appearance? Impressive, but not game-changing. Wait, how would he have hidden his face? Because if he hadn't, they would have picked him up on facial recognition."

Lentz slid her hands along the fabric then held up what looked like a hood with a face cover. "Credit us with realising having a suit like this would be less than totally useful if it didn't cover your face."

Hallstein peered closer. "Is that a special layer on the inside of the mask?"

"The plan was that the nanites on the outside of the mask would have a camera function and those inside would act like a display panel, so that the suit would show the wearer what everything looked like on the other side."

"Or the user would be blind?"

"Exactly," Lentz said. "You know, we could have used you on this project - you grasp things quickly. Why couldn't you have been born thirty years earlier?"

Hallstein smiled. "Let's agree to research time travel options once we've understood the current project fully."

"Fair enough. But there's more, and it is at least part way to being as extraordinary."

"Do tell."

"The key development we were working on back when I was originally at CERUS was a more sophisticated manipulation of light flows. The goal was not to make the coated item look like something else. It was to make it look like *nothing else*."

"I don't follow."

"Imagine the perfect stealth tool."

Hallstein frowned. "Surely you don't mean..."

"Invisibility," Lentz said with a smile. "It's basically just a trick of the light." Lentz tapped away on the keyboard. "I've been having some issues with the process – unplanned resonance occurring in the material." She pressed a key and stood back.

The panel started to vibrate. The wood-grain pattern vanished and the surface seemed to ripple. Then the panel cracked loudly and fell into several pieces.

"*Some* issues?" Hallstein said.

"Yes, well, still some kinks to work out: part of the problem is the amount of power required to sustain the effect. Either you don't have enough, or..." she pointed at the fragments, "it can't be contained. But I think it is *possible*."

"To go from a suit with pre-programmed camouflage settings - or even faces - to dynamic camouflage or invisibility? That's a huge leap. A percentage of the nanoparticles would have to serve as cameras for the signals to go to the rest of the nanites to replicate."

"That's exactly right. And we would use the same tech that works for the face mask. In order to permit the suits to move while "invisible," the Resurface nanites have to dynamically evaluate and track light sources in the area to bend the light around the suit. They bounce light's constituent waves around, adding up here and cancelling out there in such a way that rays in effect curve around the suit. They precisely undo the light-scattering and absorption of the object they are hiding: taken together the suit looks like empty space. And the wearer is invisible."

"And are CERUS the only one's to develop this?"

"It's been done elsewhere, but it's only been made to work under lamentably limited conditions."

Hallstein scratched her chin. "Perhaps you should tell Reems about this. Given what Bern has been able to do."

"It would only help show how he got away. I think we'll have to rely on other methods to find out where he is now."

"But why not tell her anyway?"

"I'd rather not have my project taken away from me. There

were some other aspects to this that I always felt I could solve."

"Other aspects?"

"Changing surface properties other than light. For example, increasing surface tension, adjusting or reducing adhesion, varying the electromagnetic field, even boosting mechanics. Of course all of it is pretty speculative, but with the new nano particles, who knows?"

"You never could resist a challenge."

Lentz smiled. "This is what brought me to CERUS. Bern said it was the reason he hired me."

"You said that the suits were designed as an alternative for Tantalus. What did you mean?"

"Before we settled on more invasive procedures, we wondered if we could create the interface by full contact with skin. It is the body's largest organ. We didn't really know what we were doing, and it never reached anything like the right level of connectivity."

"But could it work now?"

"I don't know. So much about nanotech has transpired unexpectedly. So much has happened by chance. It would be wrong of me to make predictions."

Hallstein nodded. "OK, let's stick to what we do know. And see where that leads us."

THIRTY

TOM WAS NOW TIED SECURELY to a chair. The doctor had set up his laptop on a table opposite, but it seemed the laptop wasn't connected to any network.

"So you're the brains of the operation?" Tom asked. "But if that's the case, why not decide to get out of this situation? Not exactly intelligent."

"We were intelligent enough to find you."

Tom shrugged, idly testing his bonds. They were tight and strong. "So who exactly is coming to see us?"

"He gave his name as Temple: a consultant representing the actual buyer, as I understand it."

"I presume you checked him out."

"We're taking a number of security precautions. We have three armed guards watching the street."

"And you're OK with being involved with this?"

"One corporation stealing from another? It's a victimless crime."

Tom coughed loudly. "Apart from me, of course."

The doctor hesitated. "You decided to get involved."

"No, I didn't."

"Why don't you just tell us where you've hidden it? Then we

can take you out of the loop."

"How much is this Temple guy going to pay you?"

"Five million dollars."

"The rule is that when something looks too good to be true, it usually is."

The doctor shrugged and did not reply.

Tom frowned and looked at the computer. Could he connect to it? Would it help? He had to try, even through the fog of the drugs. Perhaps if he could get closer. He leaned forwards. "Have you asked yourself exactly what type of stolen property would be valuable enough for someone to pay five million on the black market?"

"Technology of some sort. Who cares?"

"Maybe you should. Maybe it's worth a lot more." Tom looked around conspiratorially. "Why don't I show *you*? It's complicated, so you're probably the only one who'd understand it, anyway."

"The buyer will be here any minute."

"Bring the laptop over here. I've got details stored on a private server."

The doctor picked up the laptop. "I'm not supposed to use the net."

"It'll only take a second. I thought you wanted to see it?"

"OK, but we need to be quick."

The man walked over and crouched next to him, pulling out a small hand-sized device that looked like a wireless modem. At least Tom hoped it was, and that he would have long enough to use it. Down the corridor he could hear voices. A surge of adrenalin hit him. He felt the tranquilliser in his blood. And he told himself it needed to be gone.

"So?" asked the doctor, a browser open on the computer.

Tom lost the feeling. He tried to shrug his shoulders. "I can't type with my hands tied."

"Nice try. Tell me the address."

Tom could feel the nanites doing something. Filtering the drug. Cleaning his blood. His mind started to sharpen. He reached out to the modem...

"The address?"

"It's..."

Heavy footsteps thumped down the corridor. The doctor flinched back, moving the laptop away. Tom's connection with the modem slipped out of reach. Mandy and the large man walked in, followed by an older, heavy-set man, dressed in rough street clothes. His eyes lit up as he saw Tom. "My, my. It's really him."

Mandy nodded. "We have the samples for you to test, Mr Temple."

"Excellent."

Tom looked at Temple. He didn't need any extra abilities to know that the man was not who he seemed to be.

Mandy cleared her throat. "You can *see* he's the right guy. We talked about a payment, if you're going to get the samples."

Temple shrugged. "We talked about it, but my people aren't going to incur any expenditure unless they know they have the real thing."

"That's not our problem. We had a deal."

Temple nodded. "We did. I'm changing it."

There was an explosion from down the corridor. Then two gunshots.

Everyone turned in the direction of the fracas, then noticed Temple raising a pistol. "On the ground," he said calmly. The large shaven-headed man glared and did so.

"Nice work," Tom said with a growl.

Mandy lowered herself to the floor. "I searched you! Used a

metal detector."

"Ceramic pistol, carbon ammunition," Temple said. He touched his ear. "Are they taken care of? Good." He looked back at Tom. "You're coming with me." Two similarly dressed figures, carrying identical pistols, appeared behind Temple, their expressions like granite. Temple gestured to Mandy. "Untie Faraday."

She muttered and pulled herself up, then over to Tom, and began fiddling with the ropes.

Tom lowered his chin and whispered. "Believe me now?"

"I hate you."

"Quit the chatter," Temple said.

Mandy finished removing Tom's bonds, and Tom stood up, a little unsteadily. "You don't need to hurt them," he said.

Temple gave a slight sneer. "What I don't need is to listen to you."

Tom knew that the crew of kidnappers were as good as dead. And for him it was worse. "Did they tell you about me?" he asked.

The man raised an eyebrow. "A little."

"Clearly not enough." Tom closed his eyes and let his mind unleash. He reached out into the room for the advanced electronics he knew would be there. He felt the encrypted earpieces in their ears. He started to weave his mind into their protocols...

A hard hand slapped his face. Tom's eyes flew open, his head reverberating.

"No, no. None of that crap," Temple said. "Now I have a present for you." He pulled a syringe gun from a pocket. In the chamber, a dark, flecked liquid, churned. "You're going to enjoy this." Then he reached forward, pressed it against Tom's neck and fired.

THIRTY-ONE

IT WAS LIKE ICE HAD been poured into Tom's veins. A feeling of cold malice raced around his body, and he almost fainted. Within his blood he felt a million tiny voices scream out in pain and desperation. Something was attacking him. Attacking his nanites.

"What the heck was that?" he wheezed.

"A little something the boys in the lab cooked up," Temple said with a smile, then he glared at Mandy. "You were supposed to have him sedated."

"Go to hell."

Two large men appeared in the doorway. Temple nodded to them. Tom tried to concentrate, reaching out for the earpieces. He could still feel them, but everything else was different. They were like fizzing, angry hornets. It was like breathing electricity. He couldn't do this. Then he saw the two men advancing on the kidnappers, lethal intent in their eyes.

So he did it anyway. The three men screamed. They each clutched their ears, tearing at them, their eyes bulging as their earpieces overloaded. Their guns clattered to the floor, forgotten. They jerked and then lay inert.

On the table the laptop was hissing and emitting steam.

"What just happened?" Mandy picked up two of the guns, the large man grabbed the other. "Who the hell are you, Tom?"

Tom stared at them all, feeling the pain surge in his head. "You really don't want to know."

Mandy pulled a knife from her belt. She stepped towards Tom, flashing the blade. "Some things need to be dealt with." She looked into Tom's eyes, seemed to shudder then stepped behind him. "Thank you for saving us."

Tom felt his bonds being cut. "This wasn't your fight. I suggest you stay out of it."

"What did they inject you with?"

"Another thing that I don't know. But what I do know is they won't have come alone." He knelt down and pulled one of the earpieces out.

The doctor whistled. "Government issue?"

Tom grimaced. "Probably."

"Which government?" asked Mandy. "Mine? Yours?"

"Might be a private operation. Does it matter?"

The doctor shook his head. "We thought it was just one company stealing from another. Now we might have governments getting involved. What exactly did you take?"

"Nothing by choice." Tom looked around. "Have you got a street map?"

Mandy pulled one out of her backpack.

"Open it up. I'm going to tell you the way out of here." Tom placed the earpiece in his own ear and listened. The voices had cut off. Clearly the others had realised that these three had been compromised, but he could still feel activity. He reached out. And he knew where they were.

"At least we have some decent guns now," the large shaven-headed man said, examining the pistol, hefting it in his hand.

"Except you won't get to use them," said Tom. "They'll have

snipers. Probably drones." He stabbed his finger on the map and traced a line north. "You need to go this way. It's masked from their line of sight."

"How could you know that?" asked the doctor.

Tom hesitated. "Did you really think I was just an office worker?"

"You're not coming with us?" asked Mandy.

"I think it's best if I go my own way. Unless you guys have a problem with that?"

THIRTY-TWO

THE WHITE VAN WAS PARKED a mere three miles from William Bern's estate in a small side road overlooking a lake, not another soul in sight. The driver had parked where he had been told to wait, half-watching the road, half-reading the paper, having given up on the crossword. It was a beautiful still evening, not a breath of wind, barely a cloud in the sky. It didn't seem like the type of place where something important would happen, yet that was precisely what he had been told in his briefing - this was not a task in which failure would be accepted. However, on most of the details they had been irritatingly vague. All he knew was that he had to wait--

There was a knock on the window. With a start the driver looked up and saw a man standing there, wearing what looked like a dark blue boiler-suit. The man bore an odd, flat expression, but he had been told not to ask questions, just to follow instructions.

The man in blue inclined his head. "Ready to go?" There was only the faintest suggestion that it was a question.

The driver nodded and unlocked the side door, sliding it open. It revealed a hidden row of rear seats in a compartment clad in special panelling. The man in blue climbed in and closed the door. The driver watched his passenger strap himself in, then pulled smoothly away. His instructions were to drive steadily and carefully. His only objective was to get his passenger to the destination in one piece, having attracted no attention.

*

Four hours later, after following a circuitous route, the van arrived on the Dorset coast at a small inlet. The man in blue climbed out and the white van drove off.

The man walked down to the pebbly beach, chose three small stones and threw them one after the other in quick succession. The pre-arranged signal.

From around the headland a dinghy with a powerful outboard motor appeared. It bumped and crashed towards the man, then cut its power, gliding the last few metres.

The driver of the boat touched his cap.

"You have your instructions?" asked the man in blue.

"Yes," said the driver, who had also been told not to ask questions. "Although they don't make any sense."

"I imagine not," said the man. "Just do as you've been told."

"You're the boss."

Behind the face-mask of his suit, William Bern smiled.

THIRTY-THREE

KATE PLACED THE ARCHIVE BOX on the conference room table. She'd chosen a discrete room on Level 32 of CERUS Tower and had a colleague make the booking; she knew the risks she was taking and wasn't yet ready to draw her activities to Lentz's attention. Even though her activities had started to bear fruit.

Her initial plan had been to investigate Bern's records to see if anything still existed about the time when he and Tom's mother had had their affair, but everything about Bern had been seized by the government and any searches she made would immediately flag on the system. So she had started by learning a little more about Amelia from the public record. Kate had the photo Tom had given her in the restaurant. It looked like it was taken for a passport application. Plain, unsmiling, it told her little about the woman. After only minimal investigations, it had become apparent that 'Amelia Faraday' was not who she appeared to be.

The details were perfect: the birth certificate, the tax records. But beyond that the illusion fell apart. Her parents had only been fabricated in the most cursory manner. It would fool the average civilian, but not a determined researcher.

Perhaps it was not surprising. Tom's mother had clearly tried to have nothing to do with Bern after Tom was born, and changing your identity was one obvious step in making a clean break. Now I know who she wasn't, thought Kate. How does that help me work out who she *was*?

Tom had said she was a physicist, not a high-level executive. How would she and Bern have met? They likely moved in very different social circles. What about at work? Could it be that Amelia had worked at CERUS? But presumably under the name she had changed from. Photo records from that time period were not digitised on the system, so facial recognition was out of the question. There had to be a more deductive way to the answer.

What if she kept the same first name? Kate had conducted a few investigations into corporate criminals who had sought to change their identities, and in many cases they had kept the same first name: to change it would have been too much of an adjustment. So Kate checked CERUS' records for someone called Amelia, of the same approximate age, and immediately found an Amelia Fourier, who had worked at CERUS at the right time, then left shortly afterwards. Could it be that easy? The actual employee records were old and in hard copy only. She'd called up the relevant files from offsite storage. And now they were in the box in front of her.

Kate used scissors to break the tape sealing the box then opened it. The documents were old and musty, crackling as she picked them up. There were five files; the first was for a lab technician, Edna Kim - the photo showed a woman wearing heavy-framed glasses, whose smile looked a little forced. Kate knew she'd given a smile or two like that in the last 12 months.

The second file made her stop: it was Richard Armstrong. The scientist who had been murdered a year ago - her original contact at CERUS. Was it coincidence he was in the same box?

Kate gave a heavy sigh. Delving into the past would likely uncover more questions than answers. She turned to the next file and smiled.

It was labelled Amelia Fourier. Kate withdrew it and flipped it open. Just a few short documents. Formal employee records. She looked at the photo clipped to the front page and let out a sigh.

It was Tom's mother.

She glanced through the other papers - mostly banal, standard stuff. But one item caught her attention: a record of a formal interview. Amelia had been questioned in regard to a security breach at one of the company's facilities, linked with a project she had been working on. The last page of the document was missing.

Kate's phone rang, jarring her from her thoughts. Her eyes widened as she saw it was Lentz. She pressed to answer. "I've been trying to get hold of you for--"

"Have you heard the news?" Lentz asked in a quiet voice.

"What?"

"This is for your ears only right now, but I want you to get your head round it. Bern has escaped - he removed his tracker and left his mansion."

"What? How?"

"That's not clear, but it obviously involved a lot of planning. Although I don't think Reems is telling me everything. What did you want to speak to me about?"

Kate hesitated. She could mention her meeting with Tom, but decided not to. "I heard something from a source. If I share it, you have to promise not to ask who that is."

"What did you hear?"

"That Reems authorised Bern's release."

"A *source* you say? Are you being a journalist again?

"I still have my contacts."

"OK, I'll accept that for now. If you're right... just get ready for the repercussions."

Kate glanced at the personnel file on the table. "Why? What are you going to do?"

"Bern rarely leaves clues behind, except those he wants to. But maybe Reems knows more than she is saying. So I'm going to go ask her."

THIRTY-FOUR

TOM COULD FEEL THE BUZZ in his brain, the echoing surge of adrenalin, but while he could sense the danger around him, he did not panic. The icy feeling from the injection still lingered, but, free from the effect of the tranquilliser and being tied up, he felt energised. Which was good, because he needed to get away.

He descended two flights of stairs and pushed through a fire exit. He stood in dusty sunshine, slammed with a cacophony of sounds and smells. This was not a small town: this was a city. And a city was connected, plugged into the rest of the world. He stopped and extended his senses, searching for a network. He found several.

This was no time to think about the consequences. He had to get away and for that he needed information. Within moments the nanites in his blood, hungry for connection, were interfacing. Protocols were forming and exchanging, channels of communication were establishing and broadening. Data flowed into him.

Tom's eyes widened at the rush. For a moment it threatened to overwhelm him. After so long away, he was a parched man in the desert, desperate to slake his thirst. He had to slow down, to take things steadily. Then he might be able to use the information, to absorb it. As he throttled back, he began to pluck useful data points from it all.

He knew where he was: Lima, the capital of Peru. A sprawling, eclectic metropolis of over seven million people, a mix of the modern and the degraded. He was west of the centre, near a business district. There were street cameras, although nowhere near as many as in London or New York. But it was enough to gather an idea of where people and things were, particularly when combined with other data from cell phone towers and GPS devices.

From one camera he saw his former captors heading east, away from the ocean. They should be safe, at least today. He could do nothing for them in the longer term. But for now he was pretty sure the others would be focusing on him.

He turned north-west, feeling for his enemies. He still had the earpiece and planted it in his ear. Breaking the encryption to listen in was not proving possible, but he could feel where the signals were coming from. There were three of them and they were closing in on him fast. He knew they would be armed. They might hesitate to use their weapons in public. Or they might not.

He needed to make sure they didn't have a target. It shouldn't be too hard: he had a whole city to lose himself in. He looked at the street map in his head and began plotting a path.

Of course, he had to be careful not to ask too much of his body. But that thought was pushed from his mind as he overlaid the signals from the team members closing on his position, with the map in his head. He started running.

He quickly realised the mere fact of running in this heat drew attention from everyone around him, so he slowed to a brisk walk, then quietly grabbed a cap from a street vendor who wasn't paying attention, and pulled it low over his head. He took a side street, threaded his way amongst a crowd of people in a chaotic street bazaar, then emerged in a large plaza.

The three signals continued to move towards where he had been held captive. He kept trying to decrypt the earpieces, but to no avail. Still, every moment was putting distance between him and them. They weren't going to find him now. His thoughts started to shift to where he would go next.

But then something changed.

There was a sudden increase in activity from the three communicators. Three more signals appeared on the map in his head, west of the building – closer to where he was now. All six signals began moving towards him.

He closed his eyes. As he did, three more signals appeared.

Closer to him again.

Now he had nine pursuers. He wasn't quite surrounded. Not yet. It was like some type of cell structure. New resources were activated when they were needed, cascading as required. He had considerably underestimated the team following him.

And how did they know where he was, which, given their trajectory, surely they must? He looked up, wondering if a satellite was overhead. But it would never provide the kind of detail needed to follow him in an environment this busy.

He pushed ahead, the crowd growing around him, a mass of figures going about their business. As he made his way through, someone bumped into him, although the contact was less than fleeting. But he had an odd sensation. Something in his blood almost fizzed, a feeling both strange and strangely familiar.

He spun around. Was it one of them? Someone he hadn't even detected? But nobody seemed to be watching him. Nobody cared who he was. Then he felt a vibration in his pocket. To his surprise he removed an old mobile phone. He had never seen it before. On its screen was a text message.

They're tracking you.

He blinked and tapped back. *Who is this?*

The reply was almost instantaneous. *Someone who knows they're tracking you.*

How do YOU know? There was no reply. Tom kept walking and typed again. *How are they tracking me? If you want to help, then help.*

I'd say 'search me'. But it should be 'search you'.

Tom rubbed his forehead. He broke into a run again, heading for the container port.

The phone buzzed. *You can run, but you can't hide. They will find you.*

Another three dots had lit up on the map in his head. Now twelve people were converging on his location from every direction except out to sea. He swore and began sprinting. Then three more dots lit up. That made fifteen. Two were directly in front of him.

He saw them immediately: large, strong, holding odd-looking pistols, that Tom quickly realised were taser-guns. They probably didn't mean to kill him, but apparently had no concerns with making him suffer a little. He reached out, feeling for their earpieces. But as he did so, he saw, with a howl of internal frustration, that the wired devices were hanging loose around their necks. Clearly they'd worked out what he had done to the other team members. His enemy wasn't stupid. Tom looked at the two huge figures advancing on him. He turned and ran.

The phone buzzed again. *You need to learn some new tricks.*

Tom's head pounded as he searched for a way out. He could not keep interfacing like this. It was too draining, even without running at full speed. If he didn't stop soon, he was going to collapse. He felt the map in his head flicker. And then another dot appeared in front of him. He ground to a halt and looked left and right, but there was nowhere for him to go.

The man waved his removed earpiece and advanced slowly, a grim expression on his face. Behind him the two other men caught up. "We don't *want* to hurt you," said the man in front. "But nothing in our instructions says we *can't*."

Tom thought fast. He wasn't helpless in a fight, but he wasn't equipped or trained to deal with three highly-skilled assailants, each with a fifty per-cent bodyweight advantage. And yet if he didn't fight them, then soon he'd be contending with – he checked his map – sixteen. The men closed in on him. Tom prepared to move, wishing he'd spent more time during the past year learning self-defence. He heard the sharp sound of a rifle firing three times in quick succession.

The three men collapsed, each with a bullet hole in their head. People nearby started screaming and pointing fingers. Tom realised he needed to make himself scarce. He ran on, until the waterfront was in sight. The remaining thirteen dots continued to follow.

The phone vibrated again. *You're welcome.*

THX, he replied, sending the message with a quick thought.

I said they were tracking you. You're smart, I'm sure you can work it out.

Tom hesitated. How were they doing it? He thought back to when the 'buyer' had arrived. He had patted Tom on the... He swore and reached for his shoulder. And there it was: a tiny metal stud, stuck like velcro to his t-shirt.

He glared at it, then connected to it and forced every ounce of his hatred into its receiver. Somewhere else he sensed something exploding. Then he threw the stud on the ground and walked on. He had so many questions - including who was the mystery shooter who had just helped him - but first he needed to put some distance between himself and the remaining pursuers.

*

An hour later, he had covered another five miles and had reached a small plaza on the city outskirts. Intermittent glances at the map in his head showed him his pursuers had lost any sense of where he was. His mobile phone had buzzed no more and, not knowing the motives of whoever had given it to him, he had left it in a waste bin. Perhaps the mystery of who had helped him would remain just that.

He had won, at least for now. He needed to get back home, back on his own territory. This whole trip had been a bad idea. The game had changed and he could no longer assume he was safe anywhere. But before he could do anything he had to eat: he was desperately hungry, close to collapse. He had used the Interface far too much and it had taken from him: resources his body could not afford.

He stopped at a cafe and ordered most of what they had on the menu. Then he pulled out the two vials of blood he had liberated from his captors and stared at them. So much effort for something so small. He placed them on the table and shook his head.

It was something he hadn't asked for, but now it was part of him. Was there any way for him to be rid of it? If he could even be rid of it, would these people believe him? They might keep pursuing him anyway, and he would have no abilities to defend himself. Thinking about it just made his head hurt. Perhaps after he ate he would think more clearly. Perhaps something would come to him, to show him the way.

He was tucking into his second plate of paella when a slim figure walked up to his table, dressed in jeans, a sleeveless t-shirt, dark glasses and a broad-rimmed sun-hat. She smiled and placed her hands on the back of the chair opposite. "Of all the cafes in all the world, I happen to find you stuffing your face in this one."

He studied her face and felt the same fizz from earlier. It was the woman who had tried to kill him, on more than one occasion. It was the person he held responsible for the death of his best friend. It was the daughter of Bern's despicable henchman, Peter Marron.

It was Alex.

THIRTY-FIVE

IT WAS THE MIDDLE OF the night and Eli Quinn sat in his quarters in Bern's mansion, cursing his employer. He nursed a large measure of Bern's fifty-year-old single malt – specifically not to be drunk by anyone but Bern, least of all any staff. It was a small act of defiance. But it did help his mood.

Months of Quinn's life had gone into positioning himself within Bern's organisation. While his friends had said he was crazy to jump onto a sinking ship, he had seen an opportunity. In demonstrating that he could be trusted when others had deserted, he had been given a position close to the great man. The billionaire, he knew without doubt, was a phoenix. He would rise again and Quinn would be there to ride on his coat-tails. At least that was his plan. Yesterday, everything had seemed perfectly on track. Bern had arrived home, having taken the first step on the road to freedom. He was a man reasserting control.

And then he had vanished.

Quinn had no idea what had actually happened, but clearly it had involved significant preparation. And none of it had been shared with him. Bern might indeed be a phoenix, but he would rise somewhere else. So much for being one of his trusted inner circle. Now, Quinn knew, he might face arrest on a conspiracy charge. It would have been better if Bern had simply fired him: things couldn't get any worse.

There was a knock at his half-open door. He looked up to see a policeman staring at him with cold eyes. "What?" he snapped. He was exhausted and long past politeness.

"Mr Quinn?" asked the man, who looked very short for a police officer. "I have a couple of questions."

"I've already been interviewed three times. Speak to your colleagues downstairs." He turned back to contemplating the single malt.

The man didn't seem to hear him and stepped into the room, swinging the door closed.

"I don't know who you think you are..." He stopped as the man pressed a button on his belt. His features seemed to melt and warp, along with his uniform. And then a different man stood there, clad in black. "What just happened? Who the hell are you?" Quinn leapt to his feet, trying to think where he'd put his phone.

The man strode towards him, drawing a silenced pistol and pointing it directly at his head. "Sit, Mr Quinn. And please keep your voice down."

The tone was calm and polite, the eyes like washed granite. Quinn sat quietly. "What is going on? How did you change your appearance?"

"My name is Sharp and I work for Andrei Leskov. I presume you know who that is."

Quinn's eyes widened. "Bern's not here. If I knew where he was I'd tell you. You don't need to threaten me."

The man looked at the gun, as if puzzled. "I'm not here to threaten you. And I'm not here for Mr Bern either. His future has not been placed in my hands. Unlike yours."

"But I don't know anything."

"That doesn't change what I have to do."

"What?"

"Wipe the decks clean."

Quinn's hand tightened on the glass. "I didn't even work for Bern a year ago. I had nothing to do with what happened to Mr Leskov's father."

"I'm sure that's true, but you are a part of Bern's infrastructure, and my orders are to eliminate it. A message must be sent." He raised the gun. "Any last words?"

Before Quinn could reply, the weapon fired twice.

THIRTY-SIX

TOM COULD FEEL THE CHARGE in the air. He held the bridge of his nose, trying to breathe slowly. Feeling both sick and overwhelmed with curiosity as to why she was here. As to how she was even alive.

"You're not here to kill me," he said.

"If that was the case, don't you think you'd be dead already?" She pointed at the chair. "Mind if I join you?"

"It's not like I could stop you." Tom glanced around, then shrugged. "Everyone said you were dead."

She flashed gleaming white teeth as she sat down. "You never really believed that though, did you?"

"You always struck me as a survivor." He paused. "So it was you helping me? With the phone? With the bug? With the sniper rifle?"

She tapped her temple in a mock salute. "Couldn't have you being carted off again. It's very important that we speak."

"Why? What..." Tom stumbled over his words as he felt a subtle fizzing in his bloodstream. His eyes flickered.

She watched him and smiled. "You feel it too."

He took a deep breath, his pupils dilating. "*What* am I feeling?"

She reached over and grabbed one of the two bottles of beer in front of him, pushing the lime down the neck. "*Me.*"

He thought about what she was saying. There was only one thing that made sense. "You used my blood. My nanites."

Alex pointed at the two vials Tom had placed on the table. "Is that more?" Her hand shot out and she picked them up, holding them up to the sunlight. "You should be careful with this. It's not a gift for just anyone. Who knows what the wrong hands might make of it."

"You need more?"

"No, I'm good." She tucked the vials into a compartment on her belt. "I'll make sure these are destroyed securely."

"So explain. What happened to you? How are you here?"

She reached across and took a large spoonful from his plate. "I swam for nearly twenty-four hours. Throughout that crazy, impossible time the only thing that kept me going was the fact that I held in my pocket something that could transform me. If I gave up, I knew I would miss out on a true quantum-leap moment. To come so close and come up short was something I could not accept."

"You swam for twenty-four hours?"

"That water was dark and cold. Impossibly cold. Really I just managed to stay afloat. In the end the current washed me up somewhere in France: I was more dead than alive, although I have few memories of that. I was in and out for three days. It was pure luck they didn't throw away the vial of blood in that time, but they just bagged up my stuff and didn't examine it. After I recovered... it took me a while to persuade a doctor to perform the procedure."

"What procedure?"

"An injection into the base of my skull. Same as the other Tantalus subjects." She paused. "Same as you."

"It could have killed you."

"You *do* care," she said with a smile. "And, yes, it very nearly did kill me. It was pain like I've never experienced." She shook her head. "I thought I'd been tested before, in my training, but nothing had prepared me for it." She took a deep breath. "I came through."

"Well you *chose* to take it. I had rather less choice in the matter." Tom cleared his throat and looked at her pointedly. "Something you had a lot to do with."

She took a sip of her beer. "At some point you're going to have to let go of the past." She banged the empty bottle down on the table. "Things have changed. *We* have changed." She smiled. "It is so *good* to see you again. I have been longing to compare notes."

Tom shook his head and stuck a fork unenthusiastically into another plate of paella.

"You must want to talk about it. To share what you've gone through. I am the only other person in the world who can understand."

"Why would I want you to understand?"

Alex sat back in her chair, casting an eye cursorily around the restaurant. "I remember everything I do. Every nuance of every motion. *Everything* about every movement." She paused. "And then I'm able to repeat them."

"And I imagine that you've been learning origami or flower arranging."

"I have been honing my preferred craft, making a grand world tour of acknowledged experts."

"And you've found a string of tutors, ready to share their knowledge?"

"Some more willing than others. I've learned from all of them."

"And after you learned everything?"

"I killed them."

"You... what?"

"I couldn't let them live."

Tom shook his head, unable to find words.

"I only killed them when it was necessary. Of course, it usually was necessary."

Tom glared at her. "Why can't you just leave people alone? That's what I want. But I don't have the luxury of people thinking that I'm dead."

"You have this amazing gift and you're just hiding? Why?"

"I can't protect myself – as today has shown."

"But you can! You can interface with computers and technology – the original purpose behind Tantalus. You can fight on your own terms."

"It's not without its complications." He loaded his fork with rice. "Wait, are you saying you can't?"

She stared at him. "That's why I'm here."

"I don't follow."

"I want you to teach me."

Tom snorted. "You want me to teach you, a highly-trained psychopath, to visit your talents more broadly upon the world?"

She reached into her backpack and pulled out a slim laptop, setting it before him. "Let's start with something basic. Show me how you talk to it."

He raised an eyebrow. "What makes you think you'll be able to do what I do?"

"I have your nanites."

"They've evolved to work for you. Perhaps that means a different outcome."

She shook her head. "From what I know of the science, anything is possible if the nanites make the right connections. We just need to show them how."

"So you want to steer your own evolution? Why would I help you do that?"

"Apart from the fact that I saved your life today?"

"Tomorrow you may take the opposite view."

"Tom, you need an ally."

"Maybe the cost is too high." He sighed. "If I show you, will you let me go?"

"Why not. Although I think it's a mistake, I give you my word."

He looked at her. "We'll shake on it." He spat on his palm then extended his hand.

She took his hand dubiously. "Was that really necessary?"

Tom nodded. "Most definitely." He felt the nanites in the saliva. His nanites.

And he told them what to do.

THIRTY-SEVEN

TOM SHOOK ALEX'S HAND. AND closed his eyes.

For a moment he was distracted by the feel of her skin: soft, delicate, sparking with life. He shook his head and concentrated. And he felt the nanites in his saliva transfer through to her bloodstream. As he had done with his father, he would take over. All he needed was to paralyse her for a few moments: just long enough to get away.

He felt her hiss, then gasp. Her grip flinched then lessened. He smiled inwardly and began to stand up. Then something went wrong.

The cold rush in his veins, that he had felt when the man called Temple had injected him, came back, intensified. The moment of control slipped from his grasp. Her hand tightened on his like a clamp and she dragged him back down, bringing his face close to hers. He could smell her, feel the energy vibrating from her. And, in a burst of electricity that was almost like anguish, the nanites he had transferred simply died.

"What did you just try?" she hissed.

His head span. All through him, he could feel tiny flashes of dark, specks of confusion, diffusing his thoughts. "I'm not feeling very well. Must be the sedatives they had me on." Tom grimaced as she twisted his arm. She was strong. Almost impossibly strong. Her face turned dark and she pushed him back, knocking him from his chair.

"You think this is a game?"

Around them several patrons edged away. A large, heavyset man, probably the owner, appeared from the back. Alex scowled at Tom then stepped towards the man, her hands clenching and unclenching. Flowing like a cat, she shifted her balance, ready to attack.

Tom spoke low and clear. "Stop. I'll show you what you want."

She held the owner's gaze. "This is not your business," she said in Spanish.

Around her a couple of solid-looking customers stood up and took a step towards her. Alex twitched and, in a blur, a large automatic pistol appeared in her hand. She breathed and pointed it at the owner's forehead. The man swallowed, his eyes flickering to the customers, who stared back in blank terror.

"You don't need to hurt him," Tom said. "All he wants is to get on with his day. Let him do that."

Alex held the gun motionless. After several long moments, she took a step back, raising an eyebrow. Tom slid the laptop back into her backpack, shouldered it, then held up his palms in what he hoped would be understood as a gesture to stay calm. Then they backed away. Alex grabbed his arm and steered him away from the plaza, down a narrow side street.

THIRTY-EIGHT

THE F33 NIGHTHAWK STEALTH HELICOPTER touched down on the dusty soil at Las Palmas military base just outside of Lima, its dampened rotors eerily quiet for such a craft. Connor Truman, wearing a plain unmarked flight suit and dark glasses, climbed into a waiting military transport. The vehicle accelerated away towards a collection of low buildings separate from the main infrastructure. It slowed and turned into a drab warehouse, and Truman saw the US team waiting to brief him. From their body language, they did not have good news to share.

"Could we not have landed somewhere more discrete?" Truman asked as he climbed down from the transport vehicle. "Half the country probably knows I'm here."

"The locals frown on us landing off-grid, Sir," said Colonel Duane Jeffers: the man assigned to be his liaison while in Lima. A square jawed, grim-looking man, Jeffers had seen service in more active regions than this.

"What's the latest?" Truman asked.

Jeffers turned and led him over to a cluster of portable screens and charts arrayed around a large table. "We've been monitoring the city for four full days now: ever since sources suggested Faraday was here. We have a rotation of drones performing sweeps, three satellites permanently tasked on the city, and a team of fifty plainclothes operatives in the field. But it's a large, densely-populated urban area. It'll be pure luck if we spot him."

"We're sure he's here?"

"He *was* here. We picked up chatter from an interested group, naming him. We monitored them negotiating terms for a handover to another party."

"They were selling him?"

"As far as we can tell. We were triangulating their location from their comms, although we were hampered by some high-grade encryption: they were tracking him, we were tracking them... but then he vanished."

Truman raised his eyebrows. "How did these people find him in the first place when our systems haven't?"

"They probably just got lucky. But things didn't work out as they expected. The locals found two sets of dead bodies: one was clearly a bunch of amateurs, but the second included some men we have to suppose are ex-special forces."

"How do they know of Faraday's significance? Do we have a leak?"

"As far as we can tell they just knew he had a price on his head."

Truman sighed. "Is he alone?"

"Our best guess is 'no'. Three of the dead operatives were shot from a distance."

Truman shook his head. "Why would he be here? What's in Peru that he could need?"

Jeffers glanced at the other men standing around the table. "It's hard to guess when we don't even know what he is supposed to have stolen from us. Given the scale of mobilisation I've got to wonder if he took a nuke."

Truman shook his head. "If only."

Jeffers eyes widened. "Do my men need to be wearing protective gear?"

"The risk is low, but protective gear will either be not necessary or... irrelevant."

There was a shout from the other side of the table. A man working at a laptop waved them over. "We have a hit. Network traffic with similar signatures to yesterday."

"Network traffic?" Truman asked. "He has tactical backup?"

Jeffers shrugged. "We don't know. But whatever he *was* doing, he's doing it again." He looked at the analyst. "Do we have a drone nearby?"

"Yes. And I'm seeing two figures entering a second floor apartment in a supposedly unoccupied building."

"Send a team in," Truman said. "This is our chance to tidy up this mess. Let's make sure we do."

THIRTY-NINE

TOM AND ALEX WALKED FOR five minutes, then she led him up two flights of stairs and opened a plain wooden door. Tom found himself in a small apartment furnished only with a metal bed, a table and two chairs.

"Make yourself at home." She took the backpack from him.

"Been here long?" he asked.

"A few days. Same as you. I find it best to stay off-grid. You'll identify with that, I'm sure."

"How did you know I was here?"

"I told you: I can feel you, Tom. I can sense exactly where you are. I just didn't need you until now." She pulled out the laptop and set it on the table. "Now show me."

"If I do this, I want you to show me what you can do as well."

"So *now* you want to learn?" She reached forward and kissed him on the cheek.

Tom felt his skin prickle where her lips had touched, unnerving in a way he couldn't quite define. He shivered and powered up the laptop. "Where did you find this thing? It's ancient."

"It works, doesn't it? Just do your thing."

He closed his eyes and concentrated, but the ice was still

there, making him shudder.

"What's the matter?"

"Something they did to me. I can still use my abilities, but it... hurts... a great deal."

"Try to calm your thoughts. Slow your breathing. That always helps with any pain."

"Oh sure. I'll just do..." But she was right. The icy cold was there, but not as overwhelming and he immediately felt the computer's system. His nanites, refuelled by the food, made the connection. He quickly launched some applications on screen.

Alex whistled. "Excellent. Now run some searches on the following--"

"We're not online here."

"Then connect us." She gripped his shoulder so sharply it made him flinch. "I know you can."

He concentrated, finding an accessible network. It was some distance away, but with effort he made the connection and re-routed the data path. In seconds the laptop was on the net.

"There you go," Alex said. "Now run a web search for me. For anything. I just need to see it working."

He blinked rapidly and a search-engine page filled the screen.

Assassin.

"Very funny," she said, looking hard at the screen. "Wait, that lists me? How can that be?"

Tom smiled. "I shaped the search. Added my own parameters."

"And how do you do that?"

"I just... kind of reach out to the computer. In my mind. If I think hard enough I can almost feel it."

She closed her eyes. "I'm not feeling anything."

"It isn't something you can master in a moment. I didn't find it at all straightforward."

She opened her eyes. "Then what solved it?"

"I guess there came a moment when I had a need."

"Well *I* have a need."

"Perhaps your brain doesn't believe it. As I said, I can't promise I can help you."

She ground her teeth. "You're going to have to do better than--"

"Look! This is from a confidential Scotland Yard briefing." He flicked a collection of headlines up on screen: 'Bern Escapes House Arrest', 'Serious Crime Squad Baffled by Billionaire Disappearance', 'William Bern Vanishes Again'. His jaw grew hard. "Did you know?"

"Why do you think I'm here?" She glared at Tom. "Did you help him?"

"You are kidding? Why would I be involved? How *could* I be involved?"

"He's your father."

"After what his company did to me? After what *he* did to me?"

"OK, fair point. Bern's release was the trigger for why I came to find you - and since then he actually escaped. He needs to be brought to justice. And for that I'm going to need your help with a special project." She gave a smile. "Rescuing *my* father."

He glared at her. "Let me make this really clear for you: if there's one person in this world I have reason to hate more than my father, it's *your* father. Why would I do anything that might assist in getting him out of prison?"

"Because your father needs to be stopped."

"Isn't Marron in some specially designed, super-security prison?"

"That's *why* I need your help."

Tom closed his eyes and reached out to the net. Within seconds images were streaming across the screen of the laptop.

"This is Northwell A, where you father is being held. If Fort Knox were a prison, Northwell A would be laughing at it." He looked at her. "Breaking into CERUS Tower last year was a piece of cake compared to this."

"Don't underestimate what I can do. What you can do." She placed a hand on his cheek.

Tom's skin prickled again, but something stopped him from pulling away.

She smiled. "And don't underestimate what your father will do if someone doesn't stop him. Did you really think that Tantalus was the only dangerous project Bern was involved with? There is more. So much more."

FORTY

GERALDINE SAT AT HER DINING room table in her Wapping apartment, her laptop open in front of her, feeling the buzz of her third glass of red wine. She glanced at the bottle, considering whether to have a fourth. Right now she wasn't clear if she wanted more or fewer of her wits about her.

It had not been a good week. Four days ago the *Business Week News* Board had informed her that she was going to get replaced: 'a new strategic direction,' they'd said. According to them, stories were found by working connections and relationships, not by forensic analysis of reports, so BWN needed somebody more in-tune with the way business was changing: more plugged into the digital world. 'So you'll be hiring Tom Faraday,' she'd wanted to say. But they would have missed the irony.

Tom's story should have changed her world, but that ship had sailed, and nobody had been on board. Without an inside track in the form of Kate's unique knowledge, she had only been able to come up with the same angles as a hundred other journalists. If you weren't exclusive, you weren't anything. And if you didn't have proof, you were just spouting speculation.

Of course she couldn't blame Kate for the path she had chosen. Geraldine was sure she would have done the same - it was such a unique opportunity. And she knew how the world worked - Kate had new masters, and new confidentialities to respect. So Geraldine simply hadn't asked. But then she had received the news of her replacement at BWN. Then she'd been prepared to try anything.

And, inevitably, the meeting in Kate's office had been a total failure. She had received a string of messages from Kate since. They suggested Kate wanted to apologise, which was perhaps a little gratifying. But an apology wasn't what Geraldine needed. She needed a miracle.

There was a knock at the door. She glanced at her watch. It was past 11pm and she wasn't expecting anyone. She shrugged and went to pick up her wine glass. Another knock. Muttering, she got up and padded to the front door of her apartment.

A third knock.

"Who is it?"

"Federal Express. Courier package."

"Bit late for a delivery?"

"Problems with the system. We're running behind."

She looked through the spy hole and saw a short, uniformed man. Muttering again, she opened the door on the latch. "Can I see some ID?"

He held up a photo card. She blinked and opened the door. The man nodded and held out a brown card envelope with a printed label. "Sorry about this."

He was very short, she noticed, as she took it from him. He held himself with poise. Too much poise. Suddenly she felt alone and vulnerable. Exposed. "Thanks." She stepped back and began to close the door.

He moved forward, his foot inside the frame. "I need you to sign," he said, producing a clipboard. Like when he had showed the ID card, the movement was fluid. Too fluid.

Her breath caught in her throat. "Take your foot out of my door."

"I think we know," he said, "that I'm not going to do that." The voice was calm and polite, the eyes intense.

Geraldine put her weight on the door, trying to force it closed, but he moved forwards, catching her arm, twisting and forcing her off balance. She stumbled back, screaming as he entered the apartment, closing the door behind him. Then he struck her in the stomach and she collapsed, gasping for breath.

"That's better," he said.

"I don't have any money," she groaned, folding over in pain.

He pressed a button on his belt. The Federal Express uniform shimmered and became a black jumpsuit. His features blurred and changed.

Geraldine gasped. "What the hell--"

The man reached into his pocket and produced a silenced pistol. "I'm not here to rob you."

Geraldine shrank back, the air rushing from her lungs. "Why are you here?"

"Because you are on my list. I work for Andrei Leskov, in relation to the death of his father."

"What does that have to do with me?"

"You were linked to the plot against Viktor. Mr Leskov is casting the net wide."

"This is ridiculous. I want to speak to him."

"I have no way to arrange that and it's not part of my instructions. This is simply about broadcasting a message, which I'm sure you understand. You do it for a living." He raised the gun. "Any last words?"

She thought quickly. "A last drink." In the next room was her mobile phone and the panic button for the burglar alarm. If she could keep him talking, maybe she could find a way to use one or even both.

He tipped his head to one side. "That would seem fair, but it wasn't in my brief."

She saw his finger clenching on the trigger. "There's information I can share. About my investigations into Bern. Mr Leskov would find it very valuable."

"My instructions tell me you know very little: that it's my next target who warrants detailed interrogation before termination." He paused. "I believe you know Kate Turner."

"No!" cried Geraldine. And she did the only thing she could do: she lunged at Sharp, hoping to distract his aim, hoping he would miss and she could grab the gun.

Sharp pulled the trigger. He did not miss.

FORTY-ONE

TOM LOOKED AT ALEX SUSPICIOUSLY. "What do you mean 'there was so much more'?"

She stood up and walked over to one of the windows, glancing down at the street below. "Bern had another location where CERUS experiments were conducted."

"An off-books laboratory?"

"Something more significant than just a lab: a fully-equipped and serviced beta site. Somewhere with a full research capability, where they could carry out experiments too sensitive to conduct within the jurisdiction of an observant government."

Tom frowned. "There was nothing in any of the company records. Believe me: I reviewed *all* of them."

"No records were ever kept. Bern was smarter than that. He might not have anticipated what you could do, but he certainly feared hackers. And you know Bern was siphoning off funds. He wasn't doing that for no reason. He never did anything for no reason."

"Wasn't the money reason enough?"

"Bern has always been driven by proving himself. My father wouldn't have stayed with him all these years if it was just about the money."

"So your father's been to this beta site?"

"It was where we were headed on the motor launch when you caught up to us and spoiled everything. I'm sure it's where Bern will have gone. Why would he go anywhere else?"

Tom took a deep breath. "Why do we care? How does that help your father?"

"Don't you want to make Bern pay for what he did? Don't you want revenge?"

"Can I make him atone? No. Can I make him pay for what he did? Can I make him suffer? Perhaps, but I'm no sadist. Doing that won't help me." He shook his head. "To be honest, I just never want to see him again."

"Unfortunately for you I don't think he's going to let things lie. My father said that Bern always had a backup plan. In fact his backup plan always had a backup plan. So if he's gone to the trouble of escaping, you can bet your life that he won't have done that just to sit on a desert island and drink cocktails. Plus he's the one who sent that team after you."

Tom raised an eyebrow. "How could you know that?"

"I've been here a few days. I captured one of them." She inclined her head. "We had a conversation."

Tom felt his flesh creep.

"The important thing is that Bern is on your trail. He wants to acquire you and he's not going to stop until he gets you. And it gets better: Leskov is mobilising too."

"He died. Or did you miss that?"

"Not Viktor. His son, Andrei. He will likely already have sent someone to wreak revenge. And get what he paid for." She looked at Tom pointedly. "I'm suggesting it would be better to take the fight to them, rather than sit and wait for someone to find you."

"So what's your plan?"

"We rescue my father. We find where Bern is, assault the beta site and kill him. Then everyone's happy." She gave a smile. "Well, except Bern."

"And forgetting the hundred problems with that, you don't think that Bern will be ready and waiting for us?"

"It won't make a difference. Not against the two of us combined."

"You really think that will be enough...?" He trailed off, frowning. "Something changed in my connection."

"What do you mean?"

"Something is using up bandwidth. A lot of bandwidth." He hesitated. "Broad-frequency comms. Video streaming."

Alex walked over to the window, then swore. "A team is deploying around us."

"Your people?" asked Tom.

"Of course not," she replied tersely. "I don't have any *people*. You?"

He shook his head. "Did you sweep this place for bugs?"

"I did the best I could with the equipment I had. And most people think I'm dead."

"Well, if it's me they're tracking, how have they managed it?"

She looked around sharply. "I found you because of our link. They cannot do the same. I don't like this."

"A minute ago you were talking about taking on Bern and his personal army. Now you look nervous about a bunch of men."

"If we approach Bern on our terms, with the benefit of careful planning and the element of surprise, that's one thing. Currently we have none of those advantages. We have a poor environment to fight in - which will swing any fight - and rest assured, if they're good, they will use it against us. Plus I'm carrying dead weight."

"Me? Thanks a lot."

"Then prove me wrong. Come up with a plan."

"They'll be using a closed comms loop. If I could get one of their earpieces, it's possible I could overload them. It *might* take them all out, but there are so many, I can't guarantee it. And obviously they're unlikely to just hand one over."

"A lot of 'ifs' and 'maybe's'."

Tom grimaced, feeling the cold in his veins again. He needed an idea, any idea: something to keep them alive, something that would move them forward. "Give me the gun."

"What?"

"You heard me. In fact, I'm sure you have several. Give me *all* your guns."

"Do you even know how to fire one?"

"Can we shoot our way out of here?"

"Extremely unlikely."

"Then it doesn't matter whether I know how. Just do as I say." He stared at her.

She hesitated, narrowing her eyes, then she passed across a pistol and a submachine gun. "The sniper rifle is under the bed. I dropped it off before meeting you at the cafe."

Tom nodded. "How long before they're here?"

"Any moment now. Are you going to do something with your... powers?"

"There's too many of them for it to be reliable. No, I'm going to try something counter-intuitive. So just play along. All you need to remember is that I'm the 'bad guy'--"

There was a bang and the door exploded inwards.

FORTY-TWO

IT WAS THE KIND OF street you only got to live on with serious money, or serious connections. Possibly both. Dominique Lentz had only been there once before and she'd disliked it almost as much that time. But she needed to hold the kind of conversation that could only work face to face, so she had no choice.

Lentz knocked lightly on the apartment door. It was opened immediately by Reems, who waved her inside. "Sorry to keep you up," Lentz said.

"I was working," Reems replied, leading them to her study, an oak and leather-trimmed room with a huge slab of a desk. "I usually am. Now I assume we'll be needing a drink, because if it was something less serious it could wait until business hours."

"I won't say no."

Reems poured two large glasses of cognac from a chipped decanter, then they eased into leather armchairs either side of an antique coffee table. "Aren't we a pair," Reems said. "Wedded to our jobs these days. I'm not sure if I ever pictured life this way."

"I certainly didn't picture myself as a suit," Lentz said. "Wish I'd stayed in the lab."

"Or the field?"

Lentz shook her head. "The intelligence game was always too disingenuous for my tastes."

"You never married." Reems paused. "I mean when you were younger."

"Never thought of it as a real option. I couldn't face the thought of lying to a husband every day about who I was – given that I expected most days I would be pretending to be someone else."

Reems tapped her nose. "Most marriages are built on carefully economical truth. I had to lie to my husband every day about what I did. Some lies are necessary."

"I was sorry to hear about Gavin's passing."

Reems looked at her drink. "Yes, well, ironically he was lying to me. He managed to hide his condition until almost the end."

"It must be hard."

"Everyone has their time. Gavin's was too soon by many a measure, but he never really got over our son; when they found the cancer, I think he just let it take him." Her eyes moistened. "You know, Bern once said that CERUS might have some nano-related treatment options to explore but, thanks to government rules, he couldn't go any further with the research. I expect he just said it to hurt me." She lifted her glass and took a slow sip. "So, what did you want to discuss?"

"Actually it's about Bern." Lentz sat up straighter. "Some information came into my possession. It suggested you were behind Bern's release on bail."

Reems sucked in her top lip. "Who told you this?"

"I'd rather not say. I also heard there was a murder at Bern's mansion – his assistant, Eli Quinn. Is that connected?"

"Are you expecting me to comment?"

"In the privacy of this room? Yes, I am." Lentz folded her arms.

Reems put her glass on the table. "I don't report to you, Dominique. Aside from our friendship, our relationship is not one of equals."

"I don't report to you either, despite what you think," Lentz said, her voice quiet. "Dammit, if this is nonsense, just say so."

Reems drummed her fingers on the arm of her chair. "As much nonsense as the fact that you have uncovered a secret cache of research at CERUS," she said eventually.

Lentz felt her breath catch in her throat. "We don't really know what we've found. I prefer to present answers, not questions."

"That's not your call. With anything connected to CERUS, I need to know as soon as you know."

"I still want to know about Bern's release. After everything last year, I *deserve* to know. Was Quinn murdered because he knew what was going on?"

Reems looked at her. "I don't have time for this. Now do you have any intelligence to share with me? Anything that will help us locate Bern?"

"Seriously? That's your response?"

"I'll take that as a 'no'. And you should go home and forget that we even spoke."

Lentz stood, sticking her hands in her pockets. "Not hard given that, in every meaningful sense, we didn't."

Reems shook her head. "Goodnight Dominique."

FORTY-THREE

KATE STEPPED FROM THE BUS onto Wapping High Street and looked at her phone again. Still no reply to her text messages, still her calls went straight to voicemail. Was Geraldine ignoring her?

Up ahead Kate saw the blue and red pulse of emergency lights, but this was London and it was hardly out of the ordinary. She needed to discuss what she'd found out about Tom's mother and see what else Geraldine might know about Bern, now that he had escaped. The fact of his escape had swamped old and new media for the last 24 hours.

Nobody knew how Bern had engineered his plan, but one thing was clear: he would seek to track down Tom. It was all too much for her to process on her own and she wanted the benefit of Geraldine's experience and judgement. Perhaps, at the same time, she could give her a gift: something she now knew Geraldine needed. She'd called Geraldine's PA to see if he would pass a message to her. First he'd said he didn't know where Geraldine was or when she would next be in the office, but after some gentle persuasion she had learned that Geraldine was being replaced at BWN and had known about it for a few days: since before their meeting at CERUS Tower.

Why hadn't Geraldine said anything?

Kate approached Geraldine's apartment block, suddenly aware that the red and blue pulses came from three police vehicles parked directly outside. Yellow police tape was up, marking off the entrance, and a crowd had gathered, whispering in urgent tones. A chill began to creep over her. "What's going on?" she asked a woman in a pink dressing gown.

"There's been a shooting." The woman shook her head. "Terrible business."

Kate felt herself shiver. "Is someone hurt?"

"Shot in the head, I heard," said a man standing next to them, flicking his fingers open, as if that illustrated the outcome. "Didn't stand a chance."

An ambulance pulled up quietly next to the police cars. Two paramedics got out. They did not look to be hurrying.

"Professional hit," continued the man. "Woman in apartment 35. Gang-related most likely."

Kate raised her hand to her mouth. Before she knew what she was doing, she had ducked under the yellow tape. A policeman immediately moved to intercept her.

"Please step back, Ma'am, unless you're a resident."

"I'm visiting my friend. In apartment 35." She said it forcefully, as if by doing so she could make everything OK. The policeman's reaction told Kate everything she needed to know.

"I'm sorry, Ma'am. I can't let you--"

But Kate had already turned away. There was nothing she could do that would change anything.

*

Kate flagged the first cab she could find, letting it whisk her back to north London. Inside she felt numb: why would someone want to kill Geraldine? She was just a journalist and most of her work had been covering major corporates: the risks were legal, not physical. The most questionable characters Geraldine had had dealings with were probably from CERUS. And they were all behind bars... *except Bern.* But why would he go after Geraldine? Her links to the Tantalus incident were tenuous at best. If revenge was the aim, there were far more obvious targets. Like Lentz or Reems. Or Tom. *Or Kate herself.*

Before Kate realised it, the taxi had pulled up outside her apartment. She paid the driver and got out, feeling the chill night air on her face, but feeling far more chilled within. What could Geraldine have done against someone with a gun? Kate was a trained martial artist and she would have stood little chance. At least after last year, Kate had upgraded her home alarm system against break-ins, but she was still vulnerable. And because the extra security locks took so long to activate, she usually didn't bother. She would from now on.

Kate walked up the stairs and reached the door, sliding her key into the lock. It opened smoothly. Inside all was dark and quiet, and she pushed the door quietly closed. How would the killer have got in to attack Geraldine? Did they bluff their way at the doorstep? Easy to do, with enough confidence, even against someone as naturally suspicious as Geraldine. But easier still to break in while she was out...

Kate froze and listened intently. Along with the faint rumble of the building ventilation, could she hear breathing? She started to edge back towards the door, her hand reaching for the handle, when the lights snapped on. A compact man, dressed in a black jump suit, stood watching her.

"You're observant," he said. "What gave me away?"

"Circumstance." She measured the distance between them in her head: four metres – a little too far. "Did you kill my friend?"

"So that's where you went." He pulled a pistol from his pocket. "Stay where you are."

Her eyes took in the weapon, noting it was fitted with a silencer. "Did Bern send you?"

"I work for Andrei Leskov."

Kate blinked. "What?"

"You work for the company that double-crossed his father."

"That was Bern and Marron. I didn't work for CERUS then."

"Not a significant detail."

She swung her eyes around the room. She had to find an advantage. "All details are significant, as you should know, in your line of work."

"Oh?"

"My silent panic alarm was triggered thirty seconds after walking in, when I didn't deactivate it. The police will be here in three minutes."

The man's eyes narrowed. "The Queen would be lucky to get that kind of response time."

"Look at the control box over there." She pointed to the corner of the room where a blue LED was flashing rapidly.

He frowned, then edged towards it, bending down to look. "That's just a cable modem. There isn't--"

But Kate didn't hear what he said next because she had already pulled the front door open, stepped through and was slamming it shut again. Blood banging in her veins, she fumbled for her electronic key. If the man had immediately tried to open the door he might have caught her, but he did not. Instead he fired his weapon three times. Kate felt the painful shock of the impacts, but the armoured panel held. She heard swearing then he started to turn the door handle. The extended locking mechanism activated, bolts firing into place around the frame and the handle froze in place. The door would now only open with the key. Without professional cutting equipment, he was not getting through it. She had no doubt he'd find another way out, but it would give her long enough to escape.

She ran.

*

Sharp put his gun away and gave the door a prod with his fingers. It held firm. He'd missed the extra security features when he broke in because they had not been activated, but he should have been more thorough. Now he had alerted the target and she would be doing everything she could to make his task more difficult. Experience told him it was best to give such a target some time to wear themselves out. Then, once they thought they were safe and they lowered their guard, he could easily mop things up. Next time he would ensure there were no surprises. But for now, he needed a new target.

He would move to the next name on the list.

FORTY-FOUR

TOM WATCHED THE DOOR BURST open. Two heavily-armed men, clad in black ops gear, moved into the room, pointing rifles and shouting *'Drop your weapons!'*

Alex stepped away from Tom, raising her hands. "He was going to kill me."

Tom looked at her, then in an exaggerated manner lowered his guns to the floor. Two more soldiers followed the first pair into the room. They advanced on Tom and Alex, kicked away the loose guns, and placed plastic cuffs on their wrists, hands behind their backs.

The first soldier touched the earpiece in his helmet. "We have Faraday. Plus an unidentified female."

"Why am I being cuffed? Who are you?" Alex looked at the man speaking into his earpiece. "Will somebody please tell me what is going on?"

The soldier spoke to his colleagues. "We're to bring them both."

"Where are you taking us?" asked Tom.

The soldier stared at him, then raised an eyebrow. "To our leader, would you believe?"

They were driven away in a plain, unmarked van. From the

level of equipment and technology in evidence, it was clear to Tom that their captors were not just another band of mercenaries. None of the four men would engage in conversation.

After a while, the van slowed and stopped at what sounded – from the muffled conversations Tom could hear - like a checkpoint, then it was driven onwards and inside a building. He and Alex were guided out and into separate rooms. Tom was shown to a small cell, perhaps ten feet square, which contained a small table and two chairs. Moments later a suited man in his early fifties walked in, carrying a tablet computer. He sat down, staring with unblinking eyes. He steepled his fingers but said nothing. A clock ticked in one corner. Otherwise there was silence.

After several long moments Tom gave up waiting. "Why am I here? What do you want?"

The man in the suit nodded. "Where is it, Mr Faraday? Where is the Accumulator? Did you think we would simply let you take it from us?"

"I don't know what you are talking about."

"You were identified at the scene. I suggest you start talking."

Tom frowned. "I still have no idea what you're talking about. Who are you?"

"My name is Connor Truman, and I am--"

"Deputy Director of the CIA. Yes, I've heard your name. How were you able to find me?"

"Mr Faraday, you will answer my question."

"For the third time, I don't know. But I do know I want a lawyer. Given that I'm a British citizen, why am I even here?"

"Because of a crime committed on US soil." Truman tapped his tablet computer, then turned it to Tom as video started playing. It showed a series of shots of a grey metal warehouse.

"This was taken ten days ago at a US government facility that was robbed."

Tom saw a figure moving low and fast in the shadows up to the front door. Clad in black it waited for a patrol of armed guards to move past, then walked up to the camera, removing something from its belt, and then the image cut out. The man's face looked up at the CCTV for the briefest of moments. Tom tapped the screen, rewinding the footage, then he zoomed in on the face. It was *his* face. Slightly blurry, but undeniably him. "I've not been in the US in months. The footage must have been altered."

"Nobody can hack our security cameras."

"Give me ten minutes and I could..." He trailed off, realising what he was saying.

Truman raised an eyebrow. "Is that an admission of guilt? We've had the footage analysed multiple times. It has not been tampered with."

Tom leaned closer to the tablet. "Why didn't you catch the thief?"

"All the building's systems were deactivated. You escaped in the confusion. The 'Accumulator': where is it, Tom?"

Tom sat back in his chair, folding his arms. "If I was capable of breaking into that warehouse, why would I simply show my face? Wouldn't I have worn a mask?"

"You tell me. Look, before this incident you were already a person of interest to us, but this theft has put you at the top of our most wanted list."

"I'm not your guy. And why were you looking for me before that?"

Truman narrowed his eyes. "We know about the Interface that CERUS was developing."

"You know what, exactly?"

"Did you somehow use it to help execute the theft? Did you adapt the helicopter control protocols to do something else."

Tom shook his head. "Listen to me: I did not do this."

"I have direct orders from the President; I'm authorised to take any steps necessary to recover the item."

"And what do my government have to say about your abducting me?" Tom sighed. "Why don't you humour me and tell me what it is that you believe I've taken? Given that you think I have it anyway, what do you have to lose?"

Truman narrowed his eyes. "An experimental high-capacity power-cell. It's based on a form of room-temperature fusion."

"Then you have a serious problem. But it's got nothing to do with me."

"Used incorrectly the fusion cell could overload. We could have what is effectively a stray nuke on our hands." Truman's expression hardened. "We believe you're working with your father."

Tom gave a snort. "He and I are not on speaking terms."

"A convenient misdirection, no doubt. And, given that your father has escaped custody, perhaps more likely than ever."

"You need to understand that we're on the same side here. I have no argument with you people."

"This is getting us nowhere. Should I just send in the interrogation team?"

Tom's jaw twitched. "You know, I only really came here as a courtesy."

"I'm sure the heavily-armed soldiers had something to do with it."

"What did you do with the woman who was with me? I need to speak with her."

Truman shook his head. "She's not your concern anymore."

"Then I have nothing more to say."

"Have it your way. But this is not over."

Tom smiled. "That's the first thing you've said that I agree with."

FORTY-FIVE

JUST AFTER MIDNIGHT, STEPHANIE REEMS closed her computer, notified her security detail that she was retiring for the evening and switched off all but one light. All completely normal for her.

However, she then deviated from her usual routine. She activated an ambient-noise generator in her bedroom, mimicking the sounds of her breathing in her sleep. Then she changed into a black jump-suit, shouldered a small backpack and left the apartment via her emergency-exit chute. It was one-way only unless you had both the code to open the chute and climbing gear, so her security team did not view it as an access risk.

She slid out of a hidden flap and landed on the pavement in a tiny side street. Reems walked two blocks then flagged a taxi. She glanced at her watch, noting that she was perfectly on schedule. She allowed herself a brief moment of doubt: was she really doing the right thing? Should she be managing this through official channels, as her deputy director would have insisted? But she knew the answer: too much was at stake and, if she allowed the situation to continue, then the consequences would be serious. For her. For her department. For everyone.

She thought again about her visit from Dominique Lentz.

The woman was, as always, an agent of change, always inserting herself at the very heart of a difficult situation. Now she had introduced a complication. But, hopefully, that complication would very shortly be gone.

*

Twenty miles west of London, Reems' taxi dropped her at a bus station, though she didn't enter it but, instead, walked in the opposite direction. Half a mile away, she located the vehicle that had been placed ready for her: a plain red Ford Focus hatchback. It was an off-book MI5 asset and would be completely untraceable by anyone without the highest levels of clearance.

She removed the keys from a hidden compartment within the rear-wheel arch, then drove to the M4 and cruised west, keeping almost exactly at the speed limit: there was no need to draw unnecessary attention or risk being stopped. Two hours later, she crossed the River Severn via the suspension bridge and drove into Wales. Half an hour after that, she was pulling up at a quiet little harbour. A man in grubby overalls appeared from a small hut.

"Ma'am," said the man. "We're ready."

"Do you have a signal?" Reems asked.

"Heading to the Caribbean. Course steady."

"We have a satellite tasked to follow him?"

"Two, Ma'am. Just in case." The man pulled a communicator from his pocket and spoke into it briefly. Almost immediately a sleek motor-launch appeared round the headland. It powered in to shore, pulling up alongside them at the quay. The man in overalls held onto a rope while Reems jumped aboard, then he pushed them away and returned to his hut.

Reems steadied herself on deck as the craft began powering

towards the open ocean. George Croft appeared on deck and nodded.

"Evening, Stephanie."

Reems looked at her watch. "Morning might be more accurate."

"Still sure you want to attend in person? We could always send a private team to monitor the vessel."

"Never been more sure."

"We'd best go below and strap in. The skipper is keen to get under way."

"How long until we catch up?

Croft gestured to a narrow set of stairs downwards. "If we maintain optimum speed, approximately twenty-four hours. The weather could add some variables."

Reems nodded then began descending. "And he doesn't know we're following?"

"The tracer is passive and was planted subcutaneously: it's impossible to detect unless you know exactly where it is and what to look for."

Reems entered the lower cabin. "Let's hope so because if he escapes it'll be more than our jobs on the line."

"Was Lentz a problem?" asked Croft, following her inside and pointing to an oversized seat with a harness mechanism. "I heard she came to visit you after-hours."

"Dominique has a knack for ending up with information that's disturbingly accurate. But I don't think she'll be a problem. I'm more worried about Truman."

"Because he flew to South America?"

Reems took the seat and began fastening the harness. "Yes. Why would he do that?"

Croft took his own seat. "Could be something completely separate. I'm sure he has other matters within his purview."

Reems shrugged her shoulders. "Sometimes it feels like I don't."

FORTY-SIX

TOM SAT IN THE CELL, considering his options. He was starting to regret surrendering; it had seemed like a good alternative to getting shot, but, given what had happened since, perhaps getting shot would have been preferable. Truman hadn't yet brought in the interrogators. Maybe it was just a bluff, but maybe not.

Tom turned his thoughts to the camera footage. Assuming it had not been altered, how had it been possible for his face to appear on the face of the intruder? Did he have a doppleganger? A long-lost identical twin? That was lunacy. Could it be a mask or a projection? Even if true, why would someone attempt to place him at the scene of the crime? Why pick his face out of billions?

There was one thing he could do something about: his father's escape. Just not from here. He needed to get out. While he was now captive in a hi-tech facility, and they thought they had isolated him in this cell, they were wrong. There was no shielding, just physical separation and thick walls. It was not nearly enough.

He closed his eyes, forced his mind to be calm, and reached out. He felt the networks around him and he opened his mind to the data, felt it start to wash over him. Perhaps he could deactivate some specific sections of the system: CCTV, door locks. But as he tried to focus, he felt the increasingly familiar chill inside, the buzz of the dark nano, and his grasp slipped... An alarm went off. He heard footsteps outside. A guard burst into the room, automatic rifle raised.

"What have you done?"

Tom forced himself to look puzzled. "What do you mean? I haven't done anything--"

"How did you trigger the alarm?" The guard turned as there was a shrieking and groaning from down the corridor. "Stay here," he shouted, stepping from the room. There was another noise: a scuffle, then silence.

Alex stuck her head into the room. "That alarm was the signal, yes?"

Tom smiled. "They wouldn't let me use the phone."

"We'd better hurry. I elected not to kill them, but the downside is they'll probably wake up shortly." She paused. "And then I *will* have to kill them."

"Let's keep that up our sleeve for now. Just follow me."

"Where are we going?"

"Home. To see some old friends."

"And how are we going to get there?"

"We're on a military base. I'm sure there's something useful we can *borrow*."

FORTY-SEVEN

IT WAS LATE WHEN DOMINIQUE Lentz nudged her Citroen 2CV through the gates of her home in Herefordshire, but the journey had passed in a blur as she thought over her meeting with Reems. She parked next to her house: a tumbledown property set in forty acres of orchards and untamed gardens, it was a haven, away from the world. With the money that came from her new role, she had been able to pay for a full programme of renovations and improvements: new heating and lighting, additional storage and a new underground workshop for her private tinkering. She oversaw the installation of a reliable and diversely-routed power-supply, a back-up generator that would kick-in automatically if the mains failed, and two *fat pipes* to the net. Finally, there was a sophisticated intruder alarm-system patched directly into the police. Hallstein had helped her install the majority of the tech and even she had been impressed by the set up. Reems had been less effusive when she made her formal Security Service inspection. Lentz was pretty sure MI5 also kept a watchful eye on her, although Reems had never admitted to it.

Lentz made herself a pot of herbal tea. She was still much too alert to sleep. Why had Reems blanked her? Was it just an intelligence matter that Reems could not share? That didn't ring true. Involuntarily Lentz glanced around her. Could she be in danger? She'd been targeted by a killer once before and had only just managed to escape. She shivered at the very idea that it could all be happening again.

Feeling a burst of adrenalin, she hurried down the stairs to her underground workshop and placed her palm on the lock of a heavy steel cabinet. There was a soft beep and the reinforced door hissed open. Inside was a pump-action shot gun: a light-weight military model with laser sight. There were also two tasers. She grabbed all three weapons, loaded the shotgun, and moved back upstairs to her study. The room was equipped with numerous computers, mostly plugged into CERUS' systems, but a couple were set up for her own purposes. She would run a systems scan to see if...

A draft blew across her neck. That only happened if she left the front door open, and she never did that. She grabbed the shotgun and walked to the front door. It was closed and the draft had stopped. She listened carefully. Nothing but the sound of the wind. No, wait, there was a soft thumping noise, though not that close.

A helicopter? There was a military base not far away, so it could be heading there. She tapped her finger on a section of wall and a panel slid back to reveal a large touch-screen. She activated it and called up a real-time parse of each of the many motion sensors. Nothing was showing. She let out her breath, only then realising that she had been holding it. She tapped commands to display historic data over the last ten minutes. And she gasped. Somebody had followed a near-invisible route to get into the house. Their path led to a ground floor window, which meant...

Cold steel pressed against her neck, a blade that felt sharp enough to cut molecules. A voice said, almost politely, "Lower the weapon to the floor, Ms Lentz. Take your time."

She swallowed and did as she was asked, setting the shotgun down.

"Now turn around. Slowly."

Lentz turned and found herself looking at a small, compact man with grey eyes.

"Any other weapons?" he asked, hefting the knife with clear intent.

She shook her head and cursed. She really should have listened to her instincts. "Did Reems send you?"

He frowned. "I'm sorry, I don't know that name."

"If we're going to do this, at least do me the courtesy of being honest."

"I think, perhaps, you were expecting somebody else. I represent Andrei Leskov."

Lentz felt the ground shift. "Viktor's son? What does he want?"

"He wants you dead. Why don't we go into the kitchen and discuss the specifics?"

FORTY-EIGHT

THE MI5 BOAT REACHED ITS destination in a little over twenty hours. Reems had been jarred roughly throughout all of them.

"You know you didn't have to come in person," Croft said, rubbing his arms. "We could have kept you informed."

Reems shook her head. "I'm not going to have this mission compromised by an errant broadcast. We've stayed dark the entire time for good reason." She pointed at a display screen, which showed that their target was only two kilometres ahead.

"How did you know he would manage to escape?" Croft asked.

"Because of who he is, and what he wants to do. I didn't expect the bracelet would prove a barrier."

"And your alternate tracking solution – the subcutaneous transmitter – you're sure he won't be able to detect it?"

"Not likely."

"What did Lentz say to you borrowing CERUS tech?"

"I didn't give her the opportunity to argue. It might have revealed what I was doing."

"You're sure Bern won't anticipate his own tech being used against him?"

"What choice did I have? We have to find where this beta site is. If he does work out what we're up to, then we just cart him back to prison."

Croft frowned down at the screen. "He's stopped moving. Engine troubles?"

"I don't like it. Can we run a scan?"

"We can. But they might detect us."

"Then bring us closer. Quietly."

Croft radioed an order and the boat glided forward on quarter power. The sea was calm, but mist limited visibility. They went up on deck.

"It's a motor yacht," the captain said, from his position at the helm. "Ten years old, no identifying marks. There are lights on, but I can't see anyone moving on board."

Reems shook her head. "This feels wrong."

"What if..." Croft trailed off. "There's another boat."

To starboard, the silhouette of another craft appeared from the mists, perhaps twice the size of their own launch. It slowed and matched their course.

"Why didn't we detect it sooner?" Reems asked.

"It's US registered," Croft said. "No military markings."

"Transmit our government override code. Tell them to back off."

Croft activated a control panel and reviewed the display. "They've received it. But they don't appear to be standing down. In fact, they're sending us their own code back." He paused, then swore. "The vessel is CIA."

"What would they be doing out here?"

"It could just be an odd coincidence. I'll ask them to clarify--" Something flashed red on the control panel. "They're arming weapons."

"The CIA boat? What is going on?"

"No, Bern's vessel."

"It has weapons? That seems pretty unlikely."

"Spearfish torpedoes," Croft replied, "and it's launching at both of us." He turned to the captain. "Move us!" The captain immediately slammed the throttle down and the boat lurched backwards, turning tightly away. Croft slapped his hand on the control panel. "Launching counter measures." Tiny globes spat from clusters on the front of the boat. Reems looked across the water and saw the CIA craft undertaking similar measures. The two torpedoes detonated short of their targets.

"What is Bern thinking?" Reems said.

"That he doesn't want to be captured?" Croft replied, reading the display. "No hull damage."

"It makes no sense. Bern isn't this stupid."

"They're preparing to fire again. And the CIA boat is targeting its own missile."

"No! Order them to stop--"

But it was too late. There was a flare on the CIA vessel's deck. The missile lit up the night sky, as it travelled the short distance to its target. Then Bern's boat exploded.

FORTY-NINE

THE MAN TIED LENTZ SECURELY to one of her kitchen chairs, using a number of plastic cable-ties. Every move was practised and unhurried.

"Perhaps you could tell me who you are?" Lentz asked, forcing herself to keep calm. "It would be polite."

The man set the knife down on the table, eyes reflecting in the blade. "My name is Sharp. Andrei Leskov asked me to enlist your help with the Tantalus Project: the one that his father paid one billion dollars for."

"As I recall, delivery was made."

"I'm not here to argue the past: I'm here to talk about the future. You are the CEO of CERUS, the company that developed this project. Mr Leskov seems to think he could do business with you." He pointed the knife at her face. "However, my instinct is that you are not someone to be trusted. A woman who can hide from the world for twenty-five years, who can persuade a hired killer from doing his job – is dangerous."

"I was lucky."

"Luck usually comes from focus and training. You will need to work very hard to convince me you will be of use. Am I making myself clear?"

"Completely."

"Out of purely professional curiosity, what did you say to the last man hired to kill you to persuade him not to carry out his contract?"

"I negotiated. And he was clearly less committed to his cause than you are." Lentz looked at him carefully. "You know what I think? I think the whole story about Leskov wanting my ongoing help is rubbish. If you were going to abduct me, you'd have more people with you. And it's not really your skill set, is it? You're more the torture-and-kill type."

Sharp moved forward faster than she could follow, bringing the knife to her neck. She felt the blade against her throat. "My brief," he said, "is to help my client draw a line under this sorry business. Part of that involves locating Tom Faraday. I will do what I need to get that information."

"I don't know where he is. You should ask Marron or Bern."

"Bern isn't on my list. I will be visiting Marron later, but for now I'm asking you." Sharp pushed the knife harder against her throat. "Where is Faraday?"

Lentz felt the blade break the surface of her skin, an awful hot, wet touch. She coughed, trying to pull away, but the cable ties bit into her wrists. She turned back to face him, ready to curse and spit. Then her eyes widened. "I'll tell you."

Sharp raised his eyebrows. "If you lie I will know."

"Look at the screen behind you."

Sharp pulled the knife away from her, turned around, and they both stared at the screen. There was an image of Tom Faraday. He was standing next to Lentz's car, waving. His voice emerged from the speakers. "Dominique. Are you in there? I don't want to just wander in and startle you."

Sharp turned back to her. "What is this? Some kind of trick?" He looked at her uncertainly, then tucked the knife into his belt, next to a couple of rounded cubes. "Wait here." He stepped from the room.

Lentz watched him go, wondering if she was doing the right thing. She hoped Tom knew what was going on. And that he had a plan.

FIFTY

KATE LEFT THE ROAD AND pushed her bicycle through the trees, glancing over her shoulder as she went. The road behind her was deserted: as best as she could tell, she had not been followed. For now, the assassin had lost her trail. She could have gone to the police, but that hadn't worked very well twelve months ago. First she would get herself safe, then she could consider her options. The most likely being to call Lentz.

She left her car, work mobile and tablet behind so she couldn't be tracked. After a tortuous journey on buses and trains, she found an old bicycle in a station carpark secured with only a broken padlock by an owner who doubtless thought no thief would bother with such a decrepit old thing. The tyres were firm and it was perfectly good enough for her purposes. She rode west out of London with only her wallet, a prepaid mobile she had never even fitted with a SIM card, and a torch. The cycle ride took nearly three hours, but she remembered the route well. At last she reached the small woodland on the outskirts of Windsor, that marked the edge of the farm property. Now she emerged from the trees into a clearing. Ahead was the old barn.

Lentz's barn, her secret hideout, where she had taken Tom twelve months ago.

Nobody was in sight. Kate moved forward, slipping the heavy key from her pocket, and opening the padlock. Inside were several items of farm equipment, covered in dust sheets. She ignored them, kicking sawdust from the middle of the floor to reveal the trapdoor. Running her fingers along the edge, she found the concealed handle and lifted it up. LEDs immediately lit up, showing metal stairs descending. She smiled. Lentz had made a few upgrades.

Ten minutes later, Kate sat in front of one of Lentz's computers, nursing a hot cup of tea and trying to get her thoughts in order. A man hired by Andrei Leskov had tried to kill her. He had already killed Geraldine. She skipped quickly past that thought. Why now: why wait a whole year? A question for later. She had to presume the assassin would not give up, but maybe she wasn't the second and last person on his list. Who else could Leskov be after?

Tom. *Good luck finding him*, she thought.

But Lentz also had to be on that list and Lentz could easily be found. She had to be warned. Kate ripped open the package containing the new SIM card and plugged it into the cheapest, ugliest mobile phone she had seen in five years. When she called, Lentz's phone was not answered. Getting voicemail, she growled with frustration. "Protocol Alpha. Call me, dammit," she hissed into the receiver before she hung up. Then she turned to the computer and sent the same message by three different communications apps.

Should she also call Reems? The Head of MI5 was probably at the top of the assassin's list, but with her security she would be no easy target. Kate shrugged: she had no choice. She dialled and again got a voicemail. She left a message for Reems to call her back, then she took a long drink from her tea.

Could Bern's escape be linked with Leskov's actions? The

assassin hadn't asked where Bern was. Did that mean anything? She hadn't given him very long to talk, of course. She didn't know how to go about getting answers about a hired killer. He was almost certainly a ghost as far as public records were concerned and she didn't even have a name. She could try looking into Leskov, where she would at least have some material to work with. But she still doubted the published data would be that helpful. No, there was only one person to focus on. It was time to look into Bern. He had revealed his hand by escaping. And that meant he had received help. She would find whoever had provided it.

FIFTY-ONE

SHARP MOVED QUICKLY. HE HAD a single firearm and a couple of emergency options, but his weapon of preference was always the knife. However, this was an encounter on which he had not been briefed. Leskov had not thought he would happen upon Faraday. In the absence of instructions, Sharp knew he would have to capture the target alive. Although as long as Faraday was breathing, anything else was a detail.

He stepped from the house. Faraday stood ten metres away, watching him, holding no weapon, not hiding.

Which meant it was a trap.

Sharp felt rather than saw the movement. Somebody fast. He flexed backwards, rapidly adjusting his assessment: somebody *very* fast. An open hand struck where his neck had been: a blow that would have broken his spine if it had connected. Form and power showed in the movement. His attacker was clearly an expert.

But then so was he. He extended the backward flex into a roll, flipping over and bringing the knife up in a thrust, catching sight of a slender figure almost on top of him. She swung suddenly away to avoid his blade. Her eyes flashed, but did she did not appear worried.

The look on her face said she expected to beat him.

Now *he* was surprised.

"You look familiar," she said, regaining her balance. "I've seen your photo."

Sharp stepped sideways so he had one eye on Faraday, who had both eyes on him. Very few people had ever seen his photo. Of those, even fewer had remained alive for long. He grunted and lunged forward. A stutter jab. A feint then a thrust. But she read it and deflected his arm effortlessly. He altered the movement and crunched his elbow into her jaw. She fell back, hissing, her eyes angry emeralds.

"You're good," she said. "But I don't have time for games tonight." She ducked then thrust herself directly at him. No attempt to evade, no hesitation, despite him holding a blade. Her hand swung, as if to hit him in the chest, but then it twisted sharply and cracked his right hand: the one holding the knife.

Her open palm felt like hardened steel. With a shriek, he watched the weapon fly away to one side, vanishing into the undergrowth. Smiling, she coiled to lunge again. He was in trouble.

He activated the suit.

Its panels shifted, matching the dark of the terrain around him.

She stopped, looking quickly about her.

Sharp stepped cautiously backwards, the camouflage-suit hiding him in the low light. She was impossibly quick. But he had regained the advantage. He positioned himself for a strike. Still she was blind to him. Just one step closer...

"I can see him," said Faraday. Sharp looked up and saw him close his eyes. Then he felt the jolt. The suit he was wearing, the gift from Leskov, had caught fire.

At least that was how it felt. He wheezed and groaned at

shocks of pain, scalding white heat. He looked up in anger and saw Faraday spasm and collapse. The fire in the suit seemed to go out. His momentary relief was dashed as he saw the woman closing on him. The suit must have stopped working. His advantage was gone. She smiled a smile that put ice in his veins: for the first time in a very long time, Sharp saw an opponent he was not sure he could defeat.

At least not if he fought fairly.

His fingers flickered to his belt. Plucking out one of the two rounded cubes, he threw it at her. There was a hiss of gas and an ear-slamming percussive crack. In the confusion, he turned and ran. As he put distance between them, Sharp shook his head. He needed to re-evaluate. There was no shame in that. There was only success or a lack of it. And he was old and battle-worn enough to know you truly could not win them all. He would simply switch targets again.

And he knew just the one to set him back on the path to success.

FIFTY-TWO

TOM AWOKE WITH A START and found himself looking into two pairs of concerned eyes. Of those, one pair was also casting nervous glances at the other.

"Welcome back, Tom," Alex said. "No time to sleep on the job, you know."

"Indeed," Lentz said, turning to a cluster of medical equipment that he seemed to be connected to. "You had us worried."

Tom looked around. He was in a room filled with computers and screens. It was completely devoid of windows. "How did I get here?"

"I carried you inside," Alex said. "You blacked out."

"What did he do to me?" Tom asked, his head throbbing.

"If by *he*," replied Lentz, "you mean the man with the knife, then not very much. We think you did that to yourself."

Alex folded her arms. "Did *you* try and do something to *him*?"

"He had this... camouflage suit on. Hi-tech. I was trying to help. I tried to interface with it, then everything went..." Tom reached up to rub the bridge of his nose and found his arm weighed down by tubes. "Who did all this to me?"

"I had the equipment," Lentz said, "but *she*," Lentz nodded at

Alex, "hooked you up to it. Incidentally, what is *she* doing here? How is *she* even alive?" Her expression turned to a glare. "And is she going to kill us both?"

"I don't think so," Tom said. "It's complicated."

"Uncomplicate it for me."

"She found me in Peru. She saved me."

"What were you doing in Peru?" Lentz shook her head. "After everything, how can you possibly trust her? She killed your best friend."

"*She* is standing right here," said Alex, looking at the fingernails on one hand. "And actually that was my colleague."

"Who was that man outside?" Tom asked.

"Hired assassin," Lentz replied. "His name is Sharp. Sent by Leskov's son Andrei to clean house."

Alex nodded. "Sharp. My father spoke with him in the past."

"Yes, well, Marron always moved in dark circles."

"He was here to kill you?" Tom asked.

"Eventually. It was fortunate you got here when you did." She hesitated. "Did you know what was going on?"

Tom frowned. "Kind of. I tapped briefly into your security system and saw the footage of him arriving. But we're here because we needed your help. Plus you're one of the few people I know with a field large enough to land a helicopter in."

"Who did you steal one from this time?"

"The US government. Actually, it was a military transport plane I stole. We refuelled twice at mercenary bases Alex knew about. Then we traded the plane for a helicopter."

"It was lucky we turned up," said Alex, "to save your sorry hide." She, rather too casually, walked over to Lentz, then drew a long knife. Lentz's eyes widened as it glinted in the artificial light. "Now we need your help. And I'm guessing you don't want to give it."

Tom started to step forward but Alex pointed the knife at Lentz and raised her eyebrows. "Stay where you are."

"Alex, there's no need for this," he said.

"She's always been a problem. If she hadn't come back, if she'd stayed dead, everything would have been fine."

"If Dominique hadn't come back," Tom said, "I would never have got the Interface working. Which would have rather frustrated your plans. And let's not forget, your father sent a killer after her."

"He didn't succeed, so that doesn't count. Besides, it's no thanks to her that you got the Interface. She tried to stop Project Tantalus."

Lentz folded her arms. "You think I shouldn't have? Most of your subjects died."

"I didn't," Alex said. "*Tom* didn't." The tip of the blade weaved an intricate pattern in the air. But she stepped back, re-sheathing her knife. "Let's put a pin in this discussion for now."

Lentz took a long step away from Alex. "So, Tom, not that I'm not pleased to see *you*, but why are you here?"

"To discuss Bern." Tom replied. "How could they let him escape?"

"He is *very* resourceful. He had clearly laid plans long ago. We think it may be linked to the rumours of a beta site. We think he may be there." Lentz hesitated. "We just have no idea where *there* is. We've pored over the CERUS records and there isn't a single reference anywhere. Maybe it's a complete work of fiction and he's just messing with us."

"It is real," Alex said. "We were headed there last year when boy wonder here got in our way."

Lentz turned to her expectantly. "So you know where it is?"

"No. But I know a man who does."

FIFTY-THREE

"YOU'D BETTER NOT MEAN WHAT I think you mean," Lentz said.

Alex shrugged. "My father knows the location of the beta site, which makes it clear what we have to do."

"I tell you what we do: we leave him to rot," Lentz said.

"Dominique," Tom said, "we have to consider the bigger picture."

"Marron is a murdering psychopath." She looked at Alex. "Not that you aren't, of course."

"Don't waste your flattery on me."

Lentz turned to Tom. "Forgetting the supreme idiocy of the whole idea for a moment, I presume you know where Marron is so you also know it's impossible. Northwell A is one of the most secure prisons ever built. You'll never get inside without being detected."

"It's not like either of us is a regular Joe," Alex said. "We'll find a way."

"Either of you?" Lentz stared at her and her face went white. "She's got nanites? Tantalus nanites?" She pointed at Tom. "*Your* nanites? How is that possible?"

"She had the sample that they took from me back at the

Tower."

"And they haven't killed her?"

"It would seem not."

"Well, that's a pity." Lentz gave a frown. "So can she do what you can do?"

"My abilities," Alex said, "seem to be different from Tom's. We're still comparing notes."

"Mine, however," Tom said, "are proving problematic. Someone got to me and injected me with some dark liquid that's causing... difficulties."

"The CIA?"

Alex shook her head. "I'm pretty sure they were Bern's men. The CIA encounter came later."

"The CIA wanted to talk to you about Tantalus?"

Tom shook his head. "Not really. Truman was there. He thinks I stole something from them. Some sort of experimental power source."

"So that was why he was in London," Lentz muttered. "Why do they think you took it?"

"They have CCTV footage of me at the site, which is interesting, because I was never there."

Lentz narrowed her eyes. "So it was tampered with?"

"They say not."

"A disguise?"

"If so, an impossibly good one." He grimaced again as he felt the edge of ice in his veins.

"Actually, I think I know the answer. I think someone could have been wearing the same type of suit that Sharp was wearing. But that can wait. Right now we should be checking out what has happened to you." She walked over to a metal cabinet and opened it. "Let's see if we can run some diagnostics."

*

It took just over an hour. Tom saw Lentz reviewing her computer with a worried face.

"What?" he asked. "Is it a narcotic? Or some sort of virus?"

"It's not a drug, or anything biological." She paused. "It's nanites."

Tom peered at the screen, trying to make sense of the data streaming across it. "Like mine?"

"Not like yours. I mean, based on the same CERUS technology, but programmed to interfere with and counter the nanites you already have."

"Bad nanites?" Alex asked. "Dark nano?"

"If you like. That will, rather obviously, explain the pain and discomfort he is feeling."

Tom frowned. "Will they deactivate or assimilate or something?"

"I don't think so. This could be serious. From my initial analysis they have been designed specifically to attack you. They're spreading through your system, fighting you from within."

"So if they win I'll just be back to normal?"

"I'm not sure that these... dark nanites are actually deactivating yours or whether they're modifying them – evolving them into something else."

"So stop them," Alex said. "We need Tom to have his abilities."

"I don't know if I can."

"But you're a scientist. You're in charge of CERUS. You have massive resources."

Lentz put her hands on her hips. "Yeah, I'll just divert CERUS money and staff to working on illegal nano projects again. Nobody will raise an eyebrow." She paused. "Even if I could, I have no idea how long it might take. Or if it can even be done. Not without the original specifications."

"What original specifications?"

"Someone engineered this dark nano. With the source code I might be able to reverse things. Without it, it's near impossible."

Tom turned away. "For now I can cope."

"Oh sure," Alex said. "You may just faint whenever you do anything."

"What choice do I have? I'll just have to deal with it. I need to find the scientists who did this, which means I need to find Bern and the beta site. Our only lead is Marron, so there is no option." He placed a hand on her shoulder. "Will you help us?"

Lentz sighed. "What do you need? Tech? Weapons?"

Alex smiled. "You know, I'm starting to think we can be friends after all."

FIFTY-FOUR

AFTER AN HOUR OF FURIOUS computer work, Kate leant back in her chair and smiled, her cup of tea cold and forgotten. Following a number of internet searches, and a couple of well-placed calls, she had built an extensive file. She had been looking at everyone who had visited with Bern. He had no living relatives, no apparent friends outside business. His late wife's family had taken sides against him. As a result, his only visitors were from his legal team. One lawyer, who looked like she was probably in her late twenties, seemed to have visited once or twice a week. Her name was Fiona Farrow.

Kate had found a nicely professional profile and picture on the law firm's website. Something about her looked familiar, but she couldn't place it. A law firm surely couldn't be party to Bern's escape, but perhaps off-the-record Farrow would be prepared to share a few clues picked up in her dealings with Bern.

Kate needed to speak to her face-to-face. She quickly made a note of the law firm's address, then started gathering her things.

Three hours later, having travelled by bike, train and the Tube, Kate strolled through the door of Kravats, Solicitors, located just near Liverpool Street in the City.

The perfectly preened receptionist looked up, with a mixture of warmth and condescension. "Can I help you?"

"I hope so," Kate said, trying to sound important. "I'd like to speak with Ms Farrow." Kate was ready with a complicated ruse, but the receptionist's reply was unexpected.

"I'm sorry, we have nobody of that name here."

Kate frowned. "Of course you do."

The woman's smile stiffened. "We only have thirty staff. I know them all."

Kate shook her head. "She's on your website."

The receptionist raised an eyebrow and turned to her computer. She quickly called up Kravats' website and typed in the name Farrow. The profile came up.

"Well I don't understand it," said the receptionist, peering closer with a frown. "Clearly there's an error."

"This woman has been visiting one of your clients in prison."

"I don't see how that would be possible. Who exactly are you?"

Kate drew herself up to her full height. "I was hoping to speak with her."

"Yes, but what about? Let me call one of the partners."

Kate rolled her eyes. "Never mind. I'll show myself out."

As she hurried away, she discounted the possibility that the receptionist knew what was going on. Perhaps someone in the firm did, but whatever the case, Farrow had gone to a great deal of trouble to fake her identity in order to speak with William Bern. Whatever the reason, whatever the truth of the firm's involvement, she didn't just have a name. She had a face.

FIFTY-FIVE

AT NORTHWELL A, SOMETHING WAS very wrong. A delivery van, with all the right credentials, had negotiated the nest of gates and drawn up in front of the guard house. Then suddenly the site's limited connections to the net were shut down, its automated systems deactivated. The guards hastily grabbed their radios to call for support, but they were much too slow. Thus, with minimal fuss and bother, the United Kingdom's most secure detention facility was compromised.

Peter Marron was unaware of any of this until he heard the sound of a brief scuffle in the corridor outside his prison cell. He looked up from his book at a sharp groan followed by a thud. Then there was silence.

"Come in," he said in a tired voice. "You'll forgive me if I don't offer you refreshments. I wasn't expecting guests."

The door to his cell slid back. A man dressed in black appeared, pulling up a face mask. "You don't seem surprised to see me. Do you know why I'm here?"

"Of course I do," Marron said, staring at the table in front of him, then he turned and gave a weary smile. "I also know *who* you are."

"I sincerely doubt--"

"You go by the name Sharp." He smiled. "I once had you on the shortlist for a job I was setting up."

Sharp raised an eyebrow. "Why didn't I get the call?"

"Your CV spoke for itself, but I ended up recruiting internally."

"Ah yes, your daughter."

Marron's expression fell. "Anyway," he waved his hand around the room, "I'm tired of all this. It's never going to change and I really don't care anymore. Why don't you just do what you've come here for?"

Sharp stepped into the room, looking around cautiously. "Are you attempting to play me? Because I'm on a deadline here."

"I have no intention of doing anything of the sort. I'd appreciate it if you do this quick and clean."

"Mr Leskov has instructed me to follow certain guidelines."

"Ah. Of course. Andrei, I presume. I suppose that's to be expected. I don't really care anymore."

Sharp gave a snort. "Your daughter was nowhere near so cooperative. Quite a handful, in fact."

Marron narrowed his eyes. "What do you mean?"

"Your daughter, Alex." Sharp tipped his head. "You didn't know she was alive?"

Marron's jaw grew hard, his eyes suddenly alive. "Where is she?"

The assassin moved behind Marron. "It doesn't matter. You won't be seeing her again. And when *I* do, I'll do the job properly. No more surprises."

"Actually, one more," Marron said, bending low over the table.

"It doesn't matter. Now do you have any last--?"

Sharp didn't finish the sentence. He had seen many things. He had fought many opponents. But he had not dealt with anyone with the primal purpose that Peter Marron had at that moment, driven by the realisation that his daughter was both alive and in danger. In a single motion, Marron was rising out of his chair, throwing his head back into Sharp's jaw. The assassin staggered back as Marron twisted, driving his palm up into Sharp's chin. There was a splintering of bone, a sputtering of blood, and Sharp collapsed back, inert.

Marron paused, breathing hard. He listened carefully. Nobody came running. He wasn't sure how many of the guards his would-be murderer had taken out. He hoped it was a lot. If he was to escape, he would never have a better opportunity than now.

His eyes flickered down to Sharp's body. The man was wearing a close-fitting black fabric outfit. Something about it looked familiar. Marron felt behind the collar and read the tag. A formatted code. He didn't know exactly what it meant, but it was clearly an experimental CERUS issue product - one that seemed familiar, now he thought about it: *Project Resurface*. Why would Sharp be wearing it? Did Leskov's reach extend further than he expected? Or was something else going on?

It didn't matter. The suit was his now.

FIFTY-SIX

REEMS COULD STILL SEE THE explosion like it had just happened, the flash burned into her mind. Debris had continued falling onto the ocean for more than a minute. There was no trace of survivors, nor anything much larger than an egg box. The subcutaneous transmitter had ceased to send a signal. Reems stared out at where the boat had been. After everything they had gone through with CERUS and Bern, had their last best lead just blown up before them? Had Bern just flipped at the thought of being recaptured?

No. Reems knew better. She knew it had to be a lie.

The CIA craft had pulled alongside and they had conducted a rather terse conversation. Reems had demanded that the other captain contact someone higher in his organisation, someone who would have the authority, if not the inclination, to answer her questions fully. To her surprise they told her someone would arrive in a few hours. She sent Croft back to London ahead of her to get matters moving at headquarters; the cruiser carried a smaller powerboat that was far faster than the larger craft. He would take that some of the way and then be met by a sea-plane.

A few hours later she watched a military tilt-rotor aircraft land on the CIA vessel. Then she was invited aboard, where she was shown to a secure conference room. In it, Connor Truman was waiting. "We need to talk," he said simply.

"That would be an understatement."

"You're not the only one with a grievance."

"You just destroyed my operation."

Truman leaned forward, knitting his fingers together. "I knew nothing of your op because you didn't share it with us. We're in international waters. We were fired upon. Our response was proportionate." He frowned. "We *were* surprised by the magnitude of the blast. There was something volatile on his boat."

"You were following Bern. For some reason. I want to know more."

"If you didn't want him followed, why did you authorise his release?"

"Only to home detention. I will admit we expected him to try and escape. Clearly, however, you had your own plan. The whole black ops raid was a distraction, wasn't it, while you got him out some other way."

Truman spread his hands. "We provided the distraction, but we're still not clear exactly how he got out."

"You had some kind of deal with him."

"I can't say--"

"He's been playing us off against each other. It's what he does."

"I wouldn't say the deal's been that successful for him seeing as he's gone and gotten himself killed."

Reems paused and smiled. "It certainly *looks* that way."

Truman narrowed his eyes. "You're suggesting he isn't dead? How would that be possible?"

"With considerable planning and near-infinite resources. It wouldn't be the first time, as you know. Look, humour me. Let's assume he's alive. We can work out later how. It may well explain how he stole whatever he took from you. For that to work, it's time we started cooperating. And by that I mean *actually* cooperating."

He stared at her, then walked over to a cabinet and removed a bottle of bourbon and two glasses. He set them on the table.

Reems picked up one of the drinks. "Does this mean 'yes'?"

Truman raised his own glass. "What do you want to know?"

FIFTY-SEVEN

THE FIFTY METRE LONG, ZAT class 78 submarine headed north, making a steady twenty knots. It was cruising at a depth of thirty metres, a thousand kilometres off the coast of the United States, no other craft within range of their radar. The submarine's modified German design meant that, due to its considerable stealth-related enhancements, even if something was much closer, it was very unlikely they would be detected. But you could never be too careful.

The captain monitored his instruments, aware that he wasn't really in charge of the vessel. All the important decisions were made by the woman.

"I want the cargo brought onboard," she said, in her soft french accent. Most of the crew were turned to butter by that voice. But he knew there was a malicious steel in it. In him, it induced chills.

"Are you sure you want us to surface?" he said.

She raised an eyebrow. "Do you have a way of bringing it on board without surfacing?"

He preferred not to risk exposure and they would lose valuable time. But there had been no sign of pursuit or that anyone was trying to monitor them, so what could he say? He forced a smile and gave the order. She nodded and folded her arms.

Five minutes later they were opening the hatch and stepping out onto the main viewing platform, rivulets of salt water streaming back into the Atlantic Ocean all around them. Grey clouds streaked the sky and light wind made the water choppy. Three of his crew busied themselves detaching a large metallic pod that had been clamped to a rear cargo-mount. With great care, they winched it up to the platform. The woman walked over to the steel keypad and pressed in a long sequence of numbers. The pod beeped loudly, hissing as it began venting. Then the top hinged up.

"Six hours?" croaked a voice from inside. "Did you have to leave me in there for six hours?"

"Our primary objective was escaping unnoticed," said the woman, waving a finger at him, then smiling. "You were lucky. The captain wanted to leave you in there another six." She blew him a kiss. "Welcome on board, William."

Bern sat up and embraced her. "Should I call you Fabienne, Felicia or Fiona today?"

"Fabienne, my darling. And can I stop pretending to be a lawyer now?"

He nodded as he stood up stiffly and looked around. "Where are we?"

The captain stepped forward. "North Atlantic, Mr Bern. Twenty hours from our destination. More if we don't get back under way. And since you are expected, we really should..."

Bern nodded, clambering out of the pod. "A man who keeps to a deadline. I respect that." He held out his elbow to Fabienne. "Shall we go below?"

"You used the device I placed in the pod? To neutralise the subcutaneous transmitter?"

He rubbed his shoulder. "Of course. It would rather frustrate the plan if they could follow me that easily. Is there anything to eat? There was nothing but emergency rations in the escape pod."

"It got you off that boat in one piece," she replied, "so don't knock it. But I'm sure we can find you something more befitting your status."

"You know," he said, "this is the second time I've died."

"On this occasion, hopefully you can stay that way."

FIFTY-EIGHT

IT WAS MIDNIGHT, BUT LENTZ, who was working in her underground workshop, was not in the least tired. After Tom and Alex had left, she triple-checked her security and changed all the access codes, just in case: the assassin would not surprise her again. That issue dealt with, it had been time to get back to work, particularly given what she had witnessed that evening.

Lentz held up the square of fabric she had just dipped in a vat of fluorescing liquid and prepared to start the next test: the eleventh of the night. Seeing Sharp use the suit had confirmed that progress was being made. But it also showed the gap that had yet to be closed: it was one thing to be able to make yourself difficult to spot, when the conditions were already helpful, like at night. It was another thing entirely to become impossible to see in any situation. The designer had progressed matters to a point. But they had not gone all the way. The suit still only offered advanced camouflage.

Could she do better?

If she could get the maths right, with the level of resolution provided by these suits, coated in the new nano-particles, in theory it could be done using a two-way system. At the moment, the nanocells made a reading of the colour and light levels around them, then varied their own properties accordingly: crude but effective. What she needed was some way of conveying a perfect image of the space around the material. If that could be copied and projected onto its surface, then the entire suit would appear to disappear.

She held up the fabric square and frowned. She was thinking about this wrong. She couldn't test it on a flat piece of cloth. She had to test it on the suit, to make it work wrapped around an object in three dimensions. The trick was connectivity: the different nano-particles had to transfer data from point to point. She would have to write a program so that the image from the back of the object covered by the fabric could be passed through to the object's front.

Lentz smiled. She could model it on her computer, simulating the particle-to-particle communication. If she got it right, it should happen so quickly the effect would appear instantaneous to the human eye.

It took two hours to design the routine, culling work from other projects with technical overlap. The main programming framework already existed, but the new code had to interlock perfectly. Her first two attempts produced streams of error messages and caused dangerous overloads in the modelled version of the coating. If it had been real, it would have caught fire.

But the third attempt seemed to mesh. She held her breath, watching a virtual suit on the screen. There was a soft chime indicating no errors produced. Then there was a slight ripple on the screen and the suit vanished.

It was invisible.

Of course this was just a simulation, but, presuming they could manufacture the nanite-covering correctly, it would work. She almost rang Hallstein at home to tell her the good news. It was a huge moment. The first significant technological advance she had made since the Tantalus incident. She permitted herself a brief, luxurious moment of pride. It was broken by a sound that was slightly out of place.

Lentz knew the rhythm of all her computers. She knew when they were running efficiently. And she could also tell when they were overloaded and in need of maintenance or when the cooling systems were providing insufficient heat extraction. Right now, the vibrations were wrong. The fan was spun to max, which meant something was overdriving the processor. She frowned, running her finger over its surface. There was the smell of excessive heat.

Why had she not noticed this before? Had she been that distracted? Lentz called up a diagnostic tool and quickly saw the issue had only presented three minutes previously. She leaned back and thought. That was when she had finished running the simulation. Was it merely the increased load of running the new program? It seemed unlikely. A coincidence then? Frowning, she looked around the outside of the machine. And then she saw it. A tiny black capsule, plugged into one of the spare ports. She had no idea what it was.

Cursing she reached forward and pulled it out. Her computer protested with a myriad of error messages. She held the device in her hand. It was some sort of transmitter and it felt hot in her palm. But what had it been transmitting and where? Lentz called up the network logs and saw a huge burst of data sent three minutes ago. It had ignored the outwards firewall, something that should have been impossible. She tracked the transmission to a relay and then the trace was lost. Was Reems spying on her? Or someone else?

She wasn't sure which would be worse.

FIFTY-NINE

TRUMAN'S VTOL AIRCRAFT WAS A Bell Boeing V-25 Osprey, a tiltrotor design. It flew eastwards at 370 knots: more than six times faster than Reems' boat, and considerably smoother, but for Reems it was not nearly fast enough.

"Why didn't you tell us about the details of the theft sooner?" she said through her headset; normal conversation would have been impossible above the noise of the rotors.

"You know how this works," Truman replied. "I'm told what I can share in the interests of national security. I have no latitude."

"You were just embarrassed having someone walk out with your top tech."

"It wasn't just someone. It was Tom Faraday."

"That still doesn't add up for me. Not if Bern's organisation is behind it. Faraday hates his father. Are you sure of your footage?"

"Beyond reasonable doubt."

"Anything else you haven't told me?"

Truman shifted in his seat, looking uncomfortable. "We found Faraday."

Reems' eyes bulged. "Why didn't you say so sooner?"

"We picked him up in Lima." Truman paused. "He denied

the theft allegations."

"You didn't torture him?"

"The US government does not condone torture of any form."

"Of course not. Did you *question* him *rigorously* then?"

"We didn't have a chance. He escaped."

Reems ground her teeth. "What were you holding him in? A tent?"

"A cell at our Air Force base in Lima. We don't know how he got out, but he stole one of our aircraft."

Reems shook her head. "Yes, he does that. Consider yourself lucky."

"Oh?"

"He took five of ours."

"There was a woman with him. She hospitalised five of my men during their escape. We didn't identify her until afterwards. It was quite a surprise when we did, since Alex Marron's supposed to be dead."

Reems almost choked. "Impossible."

"Apparently not. I'm hoping it will be leverage over Marron. From what I hear, the only time he ever speaks is to ask after his daughter. If he knew she was alive--"

"Why would he believe you?"

"I have footage. Quite a lot. I'm sure he'll recognise her fighting style." He blinked, as if in pain. "It was brutal."

"The apple didn't fall far from the tree there." A light started flashing inside Reems' helmet. She heard the pilot's voice cutting in, telling her she had a priority call from London. She listened carefully to the short message, confirmed she had understood, then turned back to Truman. "There's been an incident at Northwell A, where Marron is being held."

"What sort of incident? An escape?"

"We don't know. The whole place has gone offline. It could be a hardware fault. We're sending in emergency teams. They'll be on site in thirty minutes and I've re-routed Croft to attend."

"We'll be there in less than two hours."

Reems shook her head. "Let's hope that it's soon enough."

SIXTY

TOM AND ALEX CROUCHED IN the cover of bushes, looking at the external gate of Northwell A. It was hanging open, the padlock lying in the dust. "You know, I may not be an expert in prison security," said Tom, "but I don't think it should be like that."

"We need to move," Alex said, hefting the shotgun that Lentz had given her.

Tom tapped the metal barrel. "Did you have to bring this? I thought *you* were a deadly weapon?"

"Sometimes nothing says 'I'm about to kill you like a loaded shotgun. If I just wave my fists people don't always get the message." Alex coughed. "And then I actually have to kill them."

"I suppose, when you put it like that..."

She raised her eyebrows. "OK, android boy, what does the security system tell you?"

Tom closed his eyes and concentrated. "It tells me... nothing." He grimaced with the strain. "It's off-line." He pointed at the open gate. "I don't like this. Perhaps we should reassess."

"You know what's at stake here, for you as much as anyone. Now follow me."

They sprinted between the front gates then along the lane,

and through a series of further gates. All hung open. All were unguarded. After the last gate they found themselves outside a huge glass wall. Three guards lay on the floor.

"Glass walls?" Tom asked. "Is that usual?"

"I haven't spent much time inside prisons," Alex replied, "but I imagine a transparent wall is pretty hard to hide behind." She stepped over the body of one of the guards and inside the compound. "Let's keep moving."

They crossed the courtyard, making their way towards one of the central buildings.

"The whole place is empty," Tom said, looking around.

"It was still under construction. They brought the completion date forward just for my father." They reached a junction and she pointed to the left. "This way."

"How do you know where to go? I couldn't find any plans of this place. And I'm good at finding stuff like that."

"Before I tracked you down, I found a guard and persuaded him to brief me."

Tom swallowed. "That's your standard MO, isn't it?"

"I do what I need to do." They reached a cell with the glass doors standing open. They entered the room. A man's body lay slumped on the floor. He was clearly dead, and he had clearly died in pain.

Alex knelt and rolled him over, revealing a bloody, smashed face. "It's Sharp. I guess he upset my father."

"Your father did that?"

"Just because he delegates the fighting, doesn't mean he can't fight. He taught me everything I know." She paused. "Well, everything I used to know."

"So where is he now?"

"I don't--"

The lighting in the room flared on, and the door slid shut.

Tom turned to Alex. "The building systems are coming back online."

She ran to the door, trying to slide it back, but it did not move. "There's not even a handle. You need to persuade it to open."

Tom closed his eyes and extended his perception. He felt the network flowing around him. He opened his mind to it, started issuing commands automatically. He would have this door open in... Something was wrong. It would not let him in. It was like there was a steel wall between him and the flows of data, for all he could access them. He opened his eyes. "This isn't good."

She put her hand around his throat. "Don't think for a moment that I won't kill you if I even suspect you are trying to double cross me."

Tom tried to breathe. He felt the anger in her face, the flow of electricity in her skin. He could almost touch it, but he could do nothing to weaken her grip.

"I'm... not..."

She tightened her hand. "I need you to take me seriously, Tom."

He reached his hand down, resting the palm on her bare skin. He focused his thoughts. And he felt electricity flow.

Her hand opened and flew backwards. He collapsed to the ground.

She held her arm, as if she'd been stung. "What the hell was that?"

They were interrupted by a knocking on the glass. They turned and saw four heavily-armed special-forces soldiers. One was gesturing to them to get on the ground.

Alex growled. "Only four. Is that all they sent?"

"I don't think they plan on coming in," Tom said, pointing to air vents on the ceiling. A cloudy gas was coming through.

Alex whirled like a cornered animal, then launched herself at the glass door, her shoulder striking it. She just bounced off.

"It's reinforced crystal. You won't mark it," Tom said. "Save your energy."

She glared at him, drew a deep breath, then exploded forward, this time leading with a heavy boot. Tom reflexively stepped back, aghast at the power in her motion. It was inhuman. Her boot connected with the glass door.

There was a loud crack.

Alex grunted and looked ready to launch herself again. The four men raised their weapons, calmly pointing at her.

But then the gas started billowing into the room. Tom felt it take him. He saw Alex collapse to her knees.

Everything went black.

SIXTY-ONE

CARL BRODY, GENERAL MANAGER OF the Dome, sat in the cafeteria, inhaling strong black coffee. He'd had barely two hours of sleep. He was just about to tuck into a much-needed cooked breakfast when the message echoed over the tannoy. Gulping a few mouthfuls of food, he pushed his tray aside, picked up the coffee cup, and marched to the nearest bank of lifts. Eight levels down, he swiped his card and accessed the lab. There were no technicians inside – he'd given them a few well-deserved hours to sleep – but a display-screen indicator was flashing. He touched his thumb to the scanner and a face appeared, slightly grainy from compressed transmission. It was Fox.

She smiled. "You've solved the transparency issue for the suits."

Brody nodded. "I had the team working on the update all night." He gestured to a dummy standing near to him dressed in a bodysuit. "Seeing is believing." He tapped some keys on a computer and there was a hum of power transferring. "Or, in this case, not seeing." The suit seemed to ripple, shimmer, then vanish.

"You're either manipulating the video feed," Fox said, "or that is seriously impressive. How is it done?"

Brody reached out tentatively, his fingers brushing across the surface of a suit that his eyes told him was not there. He could make out a ghost of an outline. Then it too was gone. "Not quick to explain without getting into the science and a lot of diagrams. It does require a great deal of power. I have it running off the main generator, but if we want to make it mobile, then with a powerful battery we can get perhaps seven minutes of functionality. The exact time will depend on a number of variables."

She nodded, not looking concerned. "What was the breakthrough?"

"I'd like to claim credit, but the answer was sent to us, transferred to our servers. When I logged on yesterday morning, a new particle-interrelation protocol was ready for inclusion."

"All that matters is that the breakthrough has been made. You've recoated one suit already. What's the schedule for the others?"

"It's better than that. We can perform a wifi update and patch the suits' systems remotely. They're all designed to poll every hour."

"Like a software upgrade?"

"Exactly like that." Brody hit the computer key again and the suit reappeared. "We should have it ready later this morning."

"Our boss will be delighted. And he'll be there to thank you in person very shortly."

"Things are moving that fast?"

"Expect us within twenty-four hours."

"That's... We won't have time to make any special preparations."

"Just focus on the work."

The screen switched off. Brody stared at it for several long seconds. He'd been waiting for the notification for a very long time. Now the moment had finally come he would have to hurry to put the rest of the pieces of the plan into action. He had to hope it would all be completed in time. People were going to die, but it would be a pity if there were more deaths than was strictly necessary.

SIXTY-TWO

TOM AWOKE TO FIND HIMSELF still in the same cell. He was tied securely to one of the chairs. Alex was not in sight. Instead a man in a suit stood, hands in pockets, staring at him.

"What's going on?" Tom asked. He looked around. Sharp's body had been removed.

"I might ask you the same question, Mr Faraday," said the man. He was holding a tablet computer in his hand, idly scrolling through a document. "Where is Peter Marron?"

"I know you." Tom frowned. "Croft, right? We met last year, on the roof of CERUS Tower."

Croft shrugged. "A lot seems to have happened in a year. Did you kill the man we found here?"

"He was dead when we arrived. He was here to kill Marron."

"How would you know that?"

"Because if he was here to conduct a rescue, Marron wouldn't have killed him. Look, why am I tied up?" He flexed against his restraints.

"You did just break into a prison," replied Croft. "And William Bern escaped. What do you know about that?"

"Less than I'd like to."

"And yet here you are, clearly trying to free Peter Marron."

"What would I do that for? You know he tried to kill me."

"Why else would you be here?"

"Because Marron had information we needed: Bern's location."

"That sounds unlikely. And you're here with Marron's daughter. You can't tell me she wasn't here to rescue him."

"Look at the CCTV footage. It will show Marron was gone when we got here."

"The system was taken offline, presumably by you, since that is your talent. This doesn't look good for you, Mr Faraday."

Tom ground his teeth. "We're on the same team here, Mr Croft, but I don't think you're seeing it."

"Nothing that has happened would support that argument. You came here with Alex. You were working with her."

"We were cooperating out of necessity. And, as I said, Marron knows Bern's location."

Croft raised an eyebrow. "Is it possible his daughter told you that in order to elicit your help?"

"Of course it's possible, but... Look, why don't you ask her?"

"She's gone. Broke through her cell door, killed three of my men." Croft opened a small bag and reached inside. "Another example of why this ridiculous technology has to be controlled. How are you feeling, Tom? Any headaches?"

Tom frowned. "Some, since you ask. Why would you care?" He froze. Croft had produced a syringe within which bubbled a liquid. A dark liquid.

"I think I can help with that." Croft tapped the small instrument with his finger.

"What are you doing?"

Croft reached forward and pushed the needle into Tom's neck. This time the feeling of cold was overwhelming.

"You?" whispered Tom. He felt his brain numbing, slowing

down. "What have you done?"

Croft's expression turned sad. "I'm sorry. It's not about you, really. It's about what you've become." He paused. "And it's about what they've promised me."

"Who?" gasped Tom, as darkness gathered. "Who promised you what?"

Croft placed the syringe back in the bag. "Don't try to fight it, Tom. You'd only be fighting yourself."

Tom tried to reply, but ice lanced through his brain.

SIXTY-THREE

ALEX MOVED SWIFTLY AWAY FROM Northwell A. There was no sound of pursuit, but she took nothing for granted. She carried a single automatic rifle, taken from one of the guards. Escape had been easier than she had expected. They really had not been prepared for her: they had not predicted that she would kick her cell door from its hinges. They hadn't even had time to raise an alarm.

She stopped on top of a rise near a cluster of trees and looked back at the prison, not because she needed rest, but because she needed to reassess. There was no way she could have rescued Tom. Most of the guards were watching him: more than twenty, all heavily armed. But they were not going to kill him, so she would wait until another opportunity presented to re-acquire him.

There was the sound of a throat clearing behind her.

Alex spun, poised and balanced, yet confused that anyone could have got so close to her. There was nobody in sight. Had she imagined the sound? She fell into a crouch, raising her weapon, wishing she had night-vision goggles at her disposal. All she could see was darkness and shadows. The voice came from her left.

"I'd prefer it if you didn't shoot me."

She twisted her weapon, finger on the trigger, ready to fire, even as she felt the voice touch her heart. A figure seemed to step from the night.

Her father.

Alex threw her rifle down and embraced him, gripping him hard, saying nothing.

He pushed her back. "You took your time."

"There were things I needed to do first. I thought you were safe here. Not that you needed my help dealing with Sharp."

"He wasn't as *motivated* as I was." Marron held her face in his hands. "And he made the mistake of telling me you were still alive. I've always known you were a survivor, but when I didn't hear anything for so long, even I had doubts."

"It's a long story."

"Did you manage to use the--"

Her eyes sparked. "Yes. Oh yes."

"And?"

"They've made me... more than before, but different from Tom. Although even with my abilities, I struggled with that assassin. He had this special suit--"

"I know." Marron tapped his chest. "I have it now. Quite a useful piece of kit. It's from CERUS's labs: part of a project they called Resurface."

She reached out and ran her hand over the fabric. "How did he get it?"

"An excellent question. I suspect the young Mr Leskov is the answer. We must remember to ask him for the details."

"We're going after Leskov?"

Marron smiled. "We're going after everyone."

She looked back at the prison. "What about Tom? He's being held in there."

"He is an acceptable loss."

"With his abilities he could be an asset."

"But why would he use them to help us?"

"He thinks there's nobody he can trust anymore. We could show him that he's wrong."

Marron sighed. "You feel some sense of kinship with him, but it's just in your head. We have to return to our plan. We have to go to the beta site and find Bern."

"You know he escaped?"

"I was questioned about it. They wanted to know if I knew anything. There are actually rumours that he's dead, killed in an altercation at sea. But, as we well know, with Bern it's best not to believe anything until you see it with your own eyes. And maybe not even then."

"And what will we do when we find Bern?"

"I'm going to let him explain why he threw me to the wolves."

SIXTY-FOUR

TRUMAN'S VTOL AIRCRAFT SWEPT IN to land in the field by Northwell A. An MI5 agent stood at attention, waiting next to a metallic black Range Rover.

"Where is Agent Croft?" shouted Reems above the sound of the decelerating rotors.

"He's on site, questioning Faraday."

"What about Marron?" Truman asked, stepping from the aircraft. "And his daughter?"

The agent's expression grew stiff. "Marron escaped before my team arrived. His daughter... She surprised us."

"By being alive?" Reems asked.

"No. You should see the video footage. I've never seen anything like it."

"What about the dead man?" Truman asked. "The one found in Marron's cell?"

"We've no ID as yet."

"Sent to free Marron or to kill him?" Truman asked.

"Either way we figure Marron wasn't happy about it. The man's neck was broken."

They reached the car and the agent pulled open the rear door.

"It's been quite a night here," Reems said. "I want additional resources called in."

The agent was about to answer when, behind him, the world exploded.

*

Lentz drove her 2CV at somewhat over its safe maximum speed. The engine, suspension and tyres all wailed in protest as she pushed on through the night, heading for the prison.

After discovering the device plugged into her computer, she knew someone other than the assassin had infiltrated her house and defeated the security. It was no simple task and would mean spying on her both at the office and at home. Her first thought was that it could only be Reems, but MI5 would not have hired a resource like Sharp: his story about Leskov was probably true. She tried to get hold of Reems but couldn't reach her. Lentz muttered, noting she had several messages from Kate. They would have to wait. A flag in her newsfeed had mentioned a murder in London. Lentz had gasped when she saw the victim was Kate's former boss at *Business Week News*. Whatever else was going on, Tom needed to be warned. Thankfully, Northwell A was only an hour's drive away and she was now fifty-eight minutes into that hour.

She was perhaps two kilometres away from Northwell A, when she saw the explosion.

Then she felt it.

*

Reems stood, looking at where the prison had been. A giant fireball was rising into the night sky, lighting up the countryside around them like midday. She felt the searing heat stinging her face, but somehow she couldn't avert her eyes.

Truman stood beside her, similarly transfixed. "What the hell was that? Last ditch security measure?"

"It wasn't us." She turned to the agent. "Any word from the site?"

He shook his head. "Nothing yet, but I'm getting orders to move you away from the scene."

"The hell I will. I'm staying to assess the situation."

"I'm sorry, Ma'am, but I have protocol to follow and emergency services are inbound. You'll only get in their way."

Her phone rang and she answered it on reflex.

"Stephanie, what just happened?" said Dominique Lentz. "I saw the explosion."

Reems frowned. "How could you possibly--?"

"I was on my way to find Tom. Was he inside?"

Reems froze. "How could you know that Tom was here?"

"Answer the damn question."

"We don't know. I thought you had no idea where he was?"

"And I guess you wouldn't know anything about the bomb. Just like you knew nothing about Bern's release from prison."

"Tread carefully, Dominique. Very carefully."

"Was Tom in there or not?"

Reems paused. "He might have been. Along with a lot of my team. I've got a situation to manage here. I'm ordering you to go home. Report to my office in the morning. We'll talk then. At length." Reems clicked the phone off. The field agent was looking at her with a serious expression.

"Ma'am, I've just heard by radio from Agent Croft's second in command. Croft discovered an explosive device in the cell where they were holding Faraday. He ordered everyone to evacuate." The field agent hesitated. "The device was connected to the door of the cell. Both he and Faraday were inside. He said he was going to attempt to disarm it."

"He didn't call for the bomb squad?"

The field agent looked pale. "Perhaps he had reason to believe there was no time."

"So he didn't get out?"

"His team were speaking on the radio right up until..." He hung his head. "I don't believe so."

Reems closed her eyes and shook her head. "Thank you for notifying me." Then she turned away and stared back at the red glow of the aftermath, the sound of emergency sirens rising in the night.

SIXTY-FIVE

LENTZ DROVE BACK TO HER home without stopping, the image of the fire burning in her mind. She could not believe that Tom had been inside the prison. Not because of any piece of actual evidence, but because, after everything that he had been through, for him to die so pointlessly seemed impossible.

As soon as she got home, she would use her computer to force a message through. She wasn't supposed to contact him unless he had contacted her first, but right now she didn't care.

Lentz parked in front of her house, quickly checking the security system. It reported that she was alone. She ran down to the underground workshop, not even pausing to make coffee. Within two minutes she was logged on, through several layers of security, and placing the call. She sent the system ping and waited.

There was no reply.

Hands shaking, she checked her settings. Everything was connected. Everything should work. She re-booted the program and re-sent the system ping.

Still no reply.

A trickle of sweat beaded on her forehead. Then something clicked. She looked again at the screen. The call *was* partially connected, though no comms had been transmitted. And it couldn't connect if nothing was there to receive it. That meant he was alive. He might be unconscious or in a deep sleep or even just ignoring it to avoid using his abilities. Maybe the dark nano had taken more of a hold on him. Maybe he had got out, but his Interface was damaged. She couldn't locate him from this system, but at least she knew he was alive.

So where was he?

Lentz fell back onto her sofa and put her head in her hands. Who had decided to plant the bomb and why? To kill Marron or Tom? Would Sharp or someone else be visiting her again shortly? She looked again at her weapons cupboard and wondered if it would be enough. Almost certainly not against a suitably motivated opponent.

There was a loud knock at her front door.

Could it be Tom? If he ran anywhere, he might run here. She was about to sprint up the stairs when she caught herself. When she spoke to Reems no mention had been made of Alex. Could it be her? Or the assassin, Sharp? But why would they knock? Lentz glanced at her security system; it had tagged a single figure who had walked straight up to the house and knocked on the door. She leaned closer.

It was Kate.

Lentz started to move towards the door, then hesitated as a thought struck her. There was only one other person who had been in her underground workshop, and she was waiting outside the house. Could Kate really be the one who had planted the bug?

Lentz swore. She just didn't know anymore: she didn't feel she could trust anyone. She grabbed her taser and a rifle; not a good weapon at close quarters, but it looked menacing.

Then she climbed the stairs.

SIXTY-SIX

THE BATTERED VAN HAD TURNED off the M5 motorway more than an hour back and was navigating its way assuredly northwest, toward the North Devon Atlantic coast. Scratched paintwork and a grime-laden windscreen suggested a vehicle that had not seen much love, but its engine belied that, purring smoothly as it covered the miles. Eventually the van turned down an unmarked side road, bouncing awkwardly on the unsealed surface until it reached its destination: a small cove. Steep cliffs rose on either side of the little rocky beach. A powerful motorboat was pulled up, outboard motor raised. Two men stood next to it, wearing military garb. The side door of the van opened and George Croft climbed out. His gaze swept the beach, then swung to the two men. "Everything in order?"

"Yes, Sir," said the first man. "All fuelled up. The equipment you specified is on board."

"Good. You can leave now." In his coat pocket, Croft felt the heft of his automatic pistol.

The second man frowned. "Sir, surely you're not going out alone? Protocol states that--"

"The mission is classified, soldier. I can't tell you any more."

"If that's the case," said the first man, "we'd still expect confirmation of orders from our CO."

Croft held his breath, his fingers brushing the stock of the pistol. "Why don't we get Director Reems on the line, so you can tell her why you're defying my direct order." He watched as they considered this. Had he played it too strong? He just needed them out of the way, so he could load his cargo onto the boat. He felt a trickle of sweat on his scalp, and his fingers tightened on his weapon.

"That's OK, Sir," said the first man. "I'm just going to note this conversation in my report. I trust that will be in order."

"I'd expect nothing less," Croft replied.

The two men glanced at each other, gave a quick salute, then moved away.

Croft watched them run to a Jeep and drive off. He waited five minutes, but they did not return. Nodding to himself, he turned back to the van. Inside, bound securely, was the heavily sedated form of his cargo.

Tom Faraday.

SIXTY-SEVEN

LENTZ PUSHED OPEN THE DOOR, holding the rifle prominently. "Are you alone?"

Kate put her hands on her hips. "What the hell is that for? And of course I'm alone. I need to speak to you."

"I've had the kind of twenty-four hours where I'm questioning a lot of things. Like why not speak to me at the office?"

"Because it couldn't wait. Geraldine was murdered." Kate blinked rapidly, her voice oddly uneven. "Then the same guy came after me."

"You mean Sharp? He was here too." Lentz shook her head. "I'm so sorry about Geraldine. Completely senseless."

"I agree. But I don't think it's over."

Lentz dropped the rifle to her side. "You'd better come in."

They descended to her workshop. Kate collapsed onto the sofa, rubbing her legs.

"How did you get here?" Lentz asked. "I didn't see your car."

"I've been doing my best to lie low. I took the train, then a cab to the village. From there I walked." She rubbed her feet. "It took nearly two hours."

"Have you heard from Tom?"

"No." Kate narrowed her eyes. "Why? Have you?"

"I saw him yesterday." Lentz hesitated. "He was here with Alex."

"He was what? I thought that bitch was dead."

"No, she's very much alive. And they were working together."

Kate screwed up her face. "That makes absolutely zero sense. She tried to kill him! More than once! And she murdered Jo."

"Technically it was another henchman that killed Jo... Look, I didn't believe it either, but they left together to rescue Marron."

Kate appeared to choke. "And you didn't try to stop them?"

"Alex said he had information they needed about the location of the CERUS beta site. Where we believe Bern has gone."

"And did they get to Marron?"

"Things got... complicated. While Tom was at Northwell A this evening, the site was destroyed by an explosion."

Kate's eyes widened. "You're not saying that he...."

"Is dead? Reems thinks so."

"I'm hoping there's a 'but'."

Lentz gave a faint smile. "I know he's alive. I have a way of contacting him. A one-to-one comms channel that uses his Interface." Before Kate could speak, she raised a hand. "He made me swear to keep it secret."

"So where is he?"

"I can't get a reply – probably because he's unconscious. The system doesn't tell me his location."

"You mean someone has him."

"That would be my guess. I just have no idea who. And, unfortunately, I have no leads."

Kate looked at her fingernails. "Maybe I do."

*

Lentz listened as Kate told of her discovery about Bern's lawyer.

"What are MI5 these days?" she said, after Kate had finished. "A bunch of amateurs?"

"To be fair, Fiona Farrow checked out on the law firm website – but they obviously didn't take the trouble to actually go to her firm, like I did. She presumably never tried to smuggle anything to him, nor did anything else to raise suspicion."

"So who is she?"

"That's why I came to you. I thought you might come up with some clever way of finding her."

"From what? Do you have a photo?"

"A splendid profile from the website."

Lentz gave a muted laugh. "It's not exactly a lot to search on."

"Hey, you're supposed to be the genius. My job is simply to dig up interesting facts. Then you can work some magic."

SIXTY-EIGHT

THEY HAD PASSED THE FIRST of the ice floes several hours back, the submarine slowing to negotiate them. Its hull was strengthened to navigate such waters, but cruising underwater at anything approaching full speed would still have been a risk. Its passenger may have been frustrated, but then it was a journey he had waited twelve months to make: even so, Bern knew he would have to put up with waiting a little longer.

The captain was relying entirely on his instruments as he tracked the coast of North East Canada. The sun had risen several hours ago, but remained low on the horizon, fiery red but weak. They passed Newfoundland and finally made progress up the Davis Strait, with Greenland far to the east. They had seen no other vessels, but then they were way off regular routes – which was exactly why the location had been chosen. If they had surfaced, they would have seen a humpback whale breaking the surface two hundred metres to starboard. Tourists travelled from all over the world to see such a sight, but the vessel's passengers were focused purely on their destination.

Eventually the captain located the beacon: a single, low frequency pulse, faint and highly directional. They were only five kilometres out. They surfaced. The coast looked white and featureless, rocky crags covered with ice and snow, the dock hidden from sight. The captain made a last course adjustment, then announced their imminent arrival over the intercom.

*

Bern, wrapped in cold-weather gear, emerged onto the viewing deck and stared towards the approaching cliffs. Last year so much had gone right, and then everything had gone wrong. He had failed to plan for two things – that Dominique Lentz was still alive, and that his son would prove so... capable. But now he had a second chance. Whatever happened, whatever the complications, he would not fail.

His thoughts turned to Fabienne, who was completing her preparations below decks. Smart and wise beyond her years, resourceful, and incredibly persuasive: he couldn't have done this without her, nor would he be able to complete the crucial final stages. He almost felt he could trust her.

The cliffs steadily drew nearer, but still nothing was visible. Nobody was going to find this place unless he wanted them to. They rounded a cliff and a small harbour was revealed; on one side a small metal jetty ended in a set of metal steps, leading up to a tunnel opening. No technology had been used to hide it: Mother Nature had done the job well enough.

The submarine powered its thrusters and manoeuvred alongside the dock. Two men appeared from the cave and began tying the vessel up. Bern smiled and made his way to the gang plank. Waiting was a familiar face, almost hidden in the hood of a parker jacket.

"Good to see you, Mr Bern," Brody said. "It's been a while."

"Longer than I'd anticipated." Bern stepped ashore. "How are our plans progressing?"

"The labs are in overdrive analysing the item." Brody motioned that they should start walking. "And we are making preparations for our various guests."

"What about the suits?"

Brody reached the metal steps and paused. "The operating system update has been broadcast, so they're already significantly enhanced. But the possibility of solving the power-consumption issue is getting the development team quite excited."

"What about security?"

"The usual systems are in place, plus we have a team of six in suits at all times. This site is almost impossible to find and incredibly difficult to reach. We're not going to be taken by surprise."

Bern stopped walking and turned to him. "The worst dangers usually come from within. Nevertheless, if someone does find us, then we need to be ready. And, as history has shown us, it's always a mistake to rely too much on automated systems."

"So you're concerned about..." Brody trailed off and looked over Bern's shoulder. "Good to see you, Ms Fox."

Fabienne was stepping ashore. She walked over and slid an arm through Bern's. "Exciting times, Mr Brody. I trust we are ready for William's arrival?"

Brody nodded, lowering his gaze.

"Good, because I..." She frowned and pointed behind them.

Bern turned and saw six men at the top of the metal stairs. Five of them were huge and muscular. They all raised handguns and pointed them at Bern.

"What is going on?" he asked.

The smallest man smiled, and spoke in a thick Russian accent: "I never thought I'd see the day." He hurried down the stairs, followed by his men, and jabbed Bern in the chest with his handgun. "Do you know who I am?"

"Someone with an overstated idea of his own importance."

The man swung sharply and punched Bern in the stomach. It was the easy swing of a man used to hitting people and not getting hit back. Bern doubled over in pain. The man kicked him hard, then again. Bern gasped.

"That is not for my father," growled the man. "That is just my way of introduction. Vengeance for my father will come later. But, first, we have something for you to do. Because my name is Andrei Leskov. And you are not in charge anymore."

SIXTY-NINE

LENTZ HAD TAKEN THE PHOTO of Fiona Farrow and run it through a suite of image processors and enhancers. Then she had co-opted MI5's databases and started running an analysis. So far no match had been found.

"How long is this going to take?" Kate asked.

"We have to be patient."

"But it will find her?"

Lentz shrugged. "This only shows people with criminal records or those suspected of criminal activity. She may not be on it."

Kate rubbed her eyes, staring at the screen as image after image flickered by. "Can we search more broadly?"

"A worldwide database of faces doesn't exist, whatever the media might have you believe. Or at least, the British government don't have one." Lentz paused. "You know, I can't get over how she looks a little familiar."

"I thought that. But maybe that's just a look some people have." Kate puffed out her cheeks. "I saw Tom a week ago. In London."

"You never said."

"He didn't look well. A year of living with the Interface has taken its toll. I felt like I didn't know him."

"Things have got a lot worse in a week. He's been injected with... we're calling it dark nano. Nanites hostile to his, designed to counter the Tantalus nanites." Lentz stood up and walked over to a centrifuge, pulling a test tube out and holding it up. "I took a sample of his blood, but I'm not making much headway analysing it."

"Who would have...?" Kate blinked rapidly, then held up her hand, rippling her fingers. "Did you feel that?"

"What?"

"A buzz of static."

"Where? In the air?"

"I... I don't know. You were saying?"

Lentz held out the test tube. "Whoever designed this had full access to--"

Kate closed her eyes. "There it is again."

Lentz frowned, looking at the test tube. Then she took a step towards Kate, holding the test tube in front of her.

"Again," Kate said. "Am I going crazy?"

Lentz shook her head. "No. I think this is craziness on a much larger scale."

*

Lentz ran a number of tests. "You can sense the dark nano," she said finally.

Kate shook her head. "I'm not just imagining it?"

"We've tried it enough times to be sure. The reaction is specific."

"But how?"

"I don't know. Have you felt like this before today?"

"When I met with Tom, I felt *something*. It wasn't as

pronounced, but when I touched his hand, I got a static shock. Was I detecting something in him?" Her face fell. "Or did he do something to me?"

"The latter is very unlikely." Lentz hesitated. "At least, I don't think he would have done anything intentionally."

"Could it have anything to do with the truth nano that Marron injected me with?"

"At this stage, I'm not ruling anything out--"

The computer chimed, distracting them both. It displayed a 'NO MATCH FOUND' message.

"What if she showed up on CCTV footage?" Kate said. "Near the law firm. Or where Bern was being detained?"

Lentz shook her head. "If I'd known in advance, maybe I could have traced her. But now the digital trail will be pretty cold. Even if we found her, what would we do?"

"Track her movements?"

"Perhaps. It wouldn't give us what we're hoping for. It would be easier to trace her mobile. Although of course we don't have it."

Kate snapped her fingers. "Or maybe we do. Her details were listed on the law firm website."

Lentz raised an eyebrow. "You think she'd list her actual phone there."

"She would need to be contactable. Even if she didn't have it on her all the time, she'd have to have used it while coming and going from the jail."

"You know that's just dumb enough that it might actually work." Lentz slid over to the nearest computer and pulled up a browser. Her fingers flew over the keyboard. "Come on, Fiona. Let's see who you really are."

*

They tracked the cell phone. Lentz discovered the woman had spent half an hour before each meeting at a cafe a short walk from the jail. Scanning the area identified there were three CCTV cameras to choose from and, using an MI5 hack, Lentz accessed footage from all of them. She got a much clearer photo, including one with the woman vanishing into a bathroom, where she apparently removed a wig, turning a mid-length blonde bob into dark hair that fell over her shoulders. The change was dramatic.

"This should have a much better chance of a match..." Lentz stared at the image. "*Felicia Hallstein*," muttered Kate.

"She's been at CERUS for most of the past year. God knows what she's been doing."

"I presume you ran background checks?"

"Clearly they were flawed. We have to find her."

"She'll be long gone. With Bern, I assume."

"Maybe that's exactly what we want."

"I don't follow."

Lentz rewound the CCTV footage. "Look at that." On screen a man in a suit came and sat next to Hallstein, spoke to her for a few moments, then handed over two phones, while taking hers. "One of them is a sat phone. Maybe I can run a trace."

"You can track a sat phone?"

"If it's used to make calls and you have direct access to a satellite." Lentz smiled. "Which we do."

"Don't you need to have its number?"

"Most sat phones aren't military - they run on a commercial service. But very few people use them. All I need to do is get into a few systems and find which sat phones were used at that time and place. Not entirely straightforward. But entirely doable."

Kate raised her eyebrows. "I wouldn't want to get in your

way."

"It's best not to try."

SEVENTY

REEMS, NOW DRESSED IN PROTECTIVE overalls, stepped through the charred ruins of Northwell A. There were minor injuries amongst the MI5 team, who had fled the site at the last minute, but they had all got out alive. All except for Croft and Faraday.

Truman walked over to where she stood, wearing similar protective clothing. "I'm sorry about the loss of your people," he said, his expression flat. "Someone's obviously trying to clean house."

"I agree. But who? Bern? Leskov?"

"I have no intel on that."

"Then, what we do have, we should share." Reems reached into the small backpack she was carrying. She removed a tablet computer and handed it to Truman. "It's a short brief on Project Tantalus. I've been authorised to disclose it as a gesture of cooperation."

Truman scrolled through the document. "My information just said it was an implant to control a helicopter. But this goes fundamentally further."

"We've not been able to verify whether it works because every test subject except one died. That survivor has spent the last twelve months avoiding us."

"Obviously Tom Faraday."

"He demonstrated some extraordinary abilities in the brief time we could observe him, but it seems now Marron's daughter may also have the tech in her. We're not clear how."

"Can she do the same things he could?"

"I'd love to ask her. I have teams searching in every direction but we've found nothing."

"So why did the assassin plant a bomb? There are cleaner ways to kill."

"Maybe he didn't? Maybe Alex brought it with her." Reems shook her head. "Your people have picked up nothing further of Bern?"

"You want us to trawl the ocean to see if we can find his body?"

Reems looked at him. "You won't find him there. Because he's not dead."

"You're convinced of that?"

"You would have had satellites overhead? What did they show?"

"Nothing. We've already reviewed the footage."

"What about for the hours before and after the explosion?"

"What are you thinking happened? Are you suggesting he had some sort of submersible waiting for him?"

"I don't know. But somewhere there's a clue. We just haven't found it yet."

Truman narrowed his eyes. "I'll make some calls." He stepped away.

Reems walked on between the embers and rubble. The smell of ash and dust was almost nauseating, but she ignored it. Her phone rang.

"Ms Reems, I'm sorry to disturb you." It was one of her tech analysts. "The CERUS security system – the covert one you had installed three months ago – has raised a flag for improper use of the network. It came from Dominique Lentz's account."

"What did they do?"

"Accessed various MI5 databases, ran searches on Bern's lawyer, Fiona Farrow: the one he dealt with on a day to day basis. Came up with nothing. But then they ran the same searches for a CERUS employee."

"Who?"

"Felicia Hallstein. After which they pinged a satellite for the ID code for a sat-phone."

A smile crept across Reems' face. "Good work. Leave this with me."

SEVENTY-ONE

THE THREE TOYOTA LAND CRUISERS negotiated the rutted snow-covered track at a cautious pace. Leskov sat in the front seat of the middle vehicle, looking ahead, a smile on his face. The sun, low on the horizon, was shining on the building that had just come into view: the silver-white structure of the Dome, CERUS's fabled beta site.

His father would be proud. Instead of brute force, he had applied his intellect. He had discovered his opponent's most secret plans, and he had used them against him. Now he would take what should rightfully have been his father's. Only one part of the plan had gone awry: the assassin, Sharp, had been killed while assaulting the prison where Marron had been held. Leskov shook his head: perhaps he had underestimated Marron. Then again, perhaps he had simply overestimated Sharp. It was a loose end to tie up, but the old man couldn't hide forever - not with the type of technology Leskov would soon have at his disposal.

Although if someone were trying to hide, there were few places more remote than this one. This area of north-east Canada was as far off the beaten track as you could get, lost in the vast snow-covered terrain. There was only one way in: the jetty. Scouting the coastline both north and south had revealed two large caves at sea level, but entry to them was mostly blocked by ice floes and, once inside, the only way out would be the way you came in. You could always fly to the Dome by helicopter, but the distance involved and the conditions made it challenging. All of this meant Leskov could now execute his plans in splendid isolation.

The three vehicles reached the Dome and drew up outside the front entrance. Leskov stepped out onto the snow, wrapping himself in his parker and fur-lined hat. He was used to Moscow winters, but they had nothing on this place.

Bern was being firmly ushered from his own car.

"How long have you waited to get here, Mr Bern?" Leskov said, pleasantly.

"You are spoiling the moment."

"I can spoil it more if you like. Fabienne, come here."

The French woman walked smoothly over to Leskov and wrapped her arms around him. Her lips found his and they shared a slow, lingering kiss. Bern's face grew hard.

"Sorry, William," she said. "Andrei made me one of those offers... You know."

Leskov turned to Brody. "Are you ready to give us the tour?"

Brody nodded. "We have a number of things to show you."

"Excellent. We'll all go." He jabbed Bern in the chest with a finger. "Assuming you have some availability?"

Bern glared at him. "Why bother bringing me all the way here? Why not just do whatever you wanted to do back in England?"

"You warrant special treatment. Plus there is one task I need you to perform for me."

SEVENTY-TWO

THREE HOURS LATER LENTZ'S COMPUTER chimed softly. She stood up from her workbench and walked over to the screen. "Felicia Hallstein is in north-east Canada. *Way* north. Or at least her phone is."

"What's up there?" Kate asked as she used a pair of tongs to lift a bodysuit from a vat of fluorescent liquid.

"Very little except polar bears and penguins."

"There are no penguins in Canada, or almost anywhere else north of the equator. I thought you knew everything?"

Lentz smiled. "Almost everything."

Kate placed the suit over a drying rack on the far side of the room, next to another already drying. "Is it me or does this seem a little too easy? There's just enough of a trail of breadcrumbs that we can follow."

"You mean the suits? That I solved them so fast? I suppose it looks that way. But if I'm honest, I had most of the answers already - Resurface is something I've been mulling over in my head for years. Once I had the project materials, it was just a case of putting things together."

"Partly it was that. But mostly I meant Felicia."

"You're suggesting she wants to be followed? That Bern wants to be found? Why go to all this trouble to hide, only to give it up?"

"Perhaps someone needs you there?"

"To do what? You're joining dots that aren't there. In any case, we haven't got much of a choice if we want to go after Tom."

"We're going to get shot at, aren't we?"

"Ah, but we're taking a few surprises of our own." Lentz nodded at the suits.

"You still haven't explained what they do."

"They will change the rules. Enough that we'll have a chance, now that I've used new technology to realise our original vision."

Kate snorted. "Yeah, because that worked out so well last time."

Lentz shrugged. "What are the chances that something will go horribly wrong twice in a row?"

"Probably better than even. Look, I'm not saying 'no'. I want to rescue Tom and I want to stop Bern, but how are we even going to get there? It's five thousand miles away and it's hardly on a commercial air route. Unless these suits fly, what are we going to do?"

"I see flight as a feature in the third generation suits."

"Very funny. I'll assume that response means you don't know."

Lentz folded her arms. "Never make that assumption."

*

Lentz pulled on her headset and activated a program on her computer. The software made an external call to a number not merely unlisted, but that most phones simply could not dial. It belonged to an SAS base five miles from her house.

The call connected instantly. "Yes," said a curt male voice.

"Colonel," Lentz replied. The voice that travelled through her headset was no longer her own. She sounded exactly like a particularly senior member of MI5.

"Ms Reems," the Colonel said immediately.

"I need transportation. For two agents on a black op, no questions asked."

"Where to?"

"Drop-off will be North America, max. range 5,000 miles. I want the fastest transport you have available," Lentz said. "I'll give the pilot the exact coordinates once we're over the Atlantic."

"Will we be landing?"

"No."

"That will save fuel. How soon?"

"One hour. I'll owe you one."

She heard the Colonel exhale slowly. "You already do."

"Are we a go?"

"Send your agents through service entrance E. I'll tell my men not to shoot them."

"Thank you."

The Colonel paused. "Ms Reems you sound overly polite tonight. Is something wrong?"

"Problems at another site. I'm sure you'll hear about it on the wire."

Lentz disconnected the call, let out a breath and smiled at Kate. "There you go."

Kate frowned. "I could hear his voice. What do you mean we won't be landing?"

SEVENTY-THREE

TOM DRIFTED INTO CONSCIOUSNESS TO find himself lying on a hard, metal-framed bed. The only illumination in the room was provided by a plastic light-fitting set in a metal ceiling. The smell of oil and salt-water filled the room and he could feel the floor swaying.

"How are you feeling?" said a voice from nearby.

Tom looked up and saw Croft standing looking out of a small, circular window. The pane of glass was misty with condensation.

"Betrayed," Tom said. "Among other things."

"Actually I saved you."

"You don't think *abducted* better describes the situation?"

"I had to get you out of there."

"By drugging me?"

"The injection was to make sure your... talents were contained. And to sedate you."

"So who are you working for? It clearly isn't MI5."

"I need to make a trade with your father."

Tom closed his eyes. In his mind all he could feel was cold and dark. The Interface was gone. "You're giving me to my father? What exactly do you think he's going to do with me?"

"He wants to help you."

"He wants to help himself."

"Those two things may be more aligned than you realise." Croft walked over to Tom and crouched down next to him. "Is your plan just to keep running forever?"

"I don't know, but it should be my decision. What are you trading me for?"

"My daughter has leukaemia. And CERUS has developed a number of technologies with medical applications as part of its nanotech research."

"Those were all stopped."

"Not so. The CERUS beta site has been developing what might be described as intelligent drugs: nanologicals. They can be tailored to treat my daughter's condition."

"So you deliver me and they give you some miracle cure?"

"That's pretty much the deal."

"Does it actually work? Because, unless you missed that part, CERUS test subjects have a habit of winding up dead."

"They're going to cure her." He rubbed his eyes. "And if not... Well, she's out of options." He returned to the window. "We're nearly there."

Tom stood up and walked over to stand next to Croft. He saw ice floating in the dark blue water, but the greater cold came from inside his head. He had thought he was lost before. But now he was disconnected from anyone and anything.

Without the Interface he was utterly alone.

*

Tom and Croft stood on deck as the boat was tied off at the jetty. On either side, vertical rocky cliffs vanished into the distance, at least two hundred metres high, perhaps more. On the other side of the jetty, Tom saw the sleek, black shape of a military submarine.

He closed his eyes and tried to feel for a network, but there was nothing. No sensation remained. It wasn't that he couldn't break the encryption or that there was no network. He simply couldn't feel anything. He had been neutralised.

A group of four armed guards approached, wrapped in heavy coats and woollen hats. They stopped opposite Croft and Tom.

"Your weapon, please," said the first guard.

Croft frowned at him, then unshouldered his holster and handed it over. "I'm to report to Bern. You should have been briefed."

The man shrugged. "I don't know anything about that."

"Then perhaps you should do your job and call him."

"Bern's not in charge anymore." The man raised his weapon. "Now come with us. And no sudden movements." He nodded at Tom. "You're the only one I've been told not to harm."

Tom glanced at Croft and smiled. "So, how is this going for you so far?"

SEVENTY-FOUR

LESKOV WATCHED THE LIFT DOORS slide back, then he followed Brody, Bern and four guards out onto Sub Level 8. Brody walked ahead to a security door and held a pass card up to the access panel.

"My team won't accept this," Bern said, as the door hissed and swung inwards. "They won't let you just take over."

"We've had few problems," Leskov replied. "Take Mr Brody here. He's been exceptionally cooperative."

"Probably because he thought you'd kill him and his family if he didn't. You can't just make innovation happen by pointing a gun."

"On the contrary, the research team have been very productive." They entered a room to find three scientists waiting. "We're here to view the latest suits."

"Suits?" Bern looked around the room. "What suits?"

Leskov snapped his fingers loudly. The air in front of them shimmered, then two men appeared out of nowhere. Bern took a step back. Leskov smiled. "Impressive, isn't it."

Bern watched as the two figures shimmered and vanished again. "You've solved the translucency issue for Resurface."

"We got help from an old friend of yours."

"There's only one person who..." Bern frowned. "Lentz did that willingly?"

"Unwittingly might be a better description, but she's widely known for not being able to refuse a challenge."

The two figures shimmered back into view.

"Power usage still limits the suits," Brody said. "We're fine-tuning the load requirements, but we still get at most ten minutes of concealment from a full charge."

"I always knew we could make it work," Bern said. "But this wasn't what Viktor contracted for."

"Let's move next door," Leskov said.

In the next room they gathered around a sealed inner chamber: carbon steel framing with thirty-centimetre-thick crystal-coated glass. Two scientists stood inside, each holding scanners out towards a black cube covered in indicator lights.

"Why the protective chamber?" Bern asked.

"It's the housing for a room-temperature fusion power cell," replied Leskov. "Which should come as no surprise because you arranged for its acquisition."

Bern glared at Brody. "So you've shared everything?"

Brody shrugged.

"Don't blame him." Leskov patted Bern on the shoulder. "As for the theft – an audacious move – I applaud you for killing two birds with one stone and simultaneously using it to bring the CIA into play: near genius to have them as unwitting contributors to your escape."

"I'm not expecting a round of applause."

"Still, you could have involved them in a less risky way." Leskov tapped his finger on the glass. "You must have had a particular goal in making it look like the thief was your son."

"I wanted to test the suit."

"But why Tom? The Americans still think it really was him."

Bern folded his arms. "You might have persuaded everyone else here to tell you everything. You haven't persuaded me."

Leskov raised his hands. "No matter. My goal is the project my father paid for: Tantalus."

"You can't have it. No one can, unless you've managed to capture my son. And the whole world has been failing at that for the last twelve months."

Leskov coughed and gave a signal to one of his guards. They walked over to a television monitor and switched it on. Bern swore. The image showed Tom sitting on a metal chair, hands tied behind his back. "He's on the floor above us," said Leskov, with a smile.

SEVENTY-FIVE

THE TWO PARACHUTES OPENED WITH a rush of flapping and shrieking, and the roaring wall of air reduced to a mere gale. Lentz groaned as the harness pulled tight. "I swear this hurt less last time I did it," she said over her headset radio. Above them, the military transport was gently turning away in the dark grey sky.

"At least you've done it before," Kate's voice replied in her ears.

"You sounded calm as we suited up."

"Rigid with fear, more like. And not just about the jump."

Lentz looked down at her feet, dangling towards the ice and snow. The landscape was so vast and featureless the ground could have been a hundred metres away, but her instruments stated it was just over twelve hundred. "I thought you'd see this as an adventure." Lentz tapped some controls on the wrist panel of her suit. She ran a systems check, confirming the location of their equipment pod, which was suspended from its own parachute. It was making micro adjustments to track their own descent and would land within a hundred metres of where they touched down.

"I had my crazy phase when I was twenty and backpacking,"

Kate said. "You're sure they won't have detected us?"

"Plenty of planes fly high in this airspace. Ours did nothing to make it stand out."

"And what about the pilot? Will he reveal where we've gone?"

"His orders were to drop us off and reveal the location to nobody, even under direct order of his commanding officer. By the time they work out anything is up, if they ever do, we'll be long gone." She paused. "Or we'll have failed. Either way it makes no difference."

"So, basically, nobody knows where we are."

"Exactly," Lentz said.

"The downside being that we are completely on our own."

"But with the element of surprise."

"Let's hope that will count."

They touched down gently four minutes later and began gathering up their parachutes, boots crunching in the snow. LED lights in their helmets scattered an eerie green glow on the ground. Lentz stuffed the parachutes into a sack and dug it into the snow, then she pointed to the black sphere, which had landed a short distance away. "Everything we need is in that capsule." They began walking over to it.

Kate cleared her throat pointedly. "You seem to be taking this all in your stride."

Lentz shrugged. "Remember, I used to be a field agent."

"No offence, but that was twenty-five years ago. Perhaps we should have called Reems."

"We've chosen our path. I just don't think we could trust her. Not to do the right thing for Tom, anyway." They reached the capsule and Lentz typed in an access code. A hatch sprang open.

"You are kidding," Kate said, peering inside.

"It's over fifty kilometres. Would you rather walk?"

"I didn't say that."

"Good. Let's get it assembled."

*

A hundred kilometres to the north, and with an air speed of three hundred knots, the military transport completed a large radius turn and began heading back east. The pilot had been told to follow whatever instructions the two agents had given him. They had seemed a little off-type for field agents undertaking a covert air-drop – one too old, one too nervous – but it wasn't his place to ask questions.

However, just as he completed the turn, he received a coded message on a system he had not even known existed. The message overrode his earlier instructions. It gave details of a call he was to make to confirm the agents and their package had deployed. An operator came on line immediately. He confirmed the location of the drop off and the equipment that had been provided. The operator thanked him and disconnected.

The pilot glanced to the south. They were down there, lost in the cold white expanse, heading to goodness knows where, to do goodness knows what. Whatever it was, some very important people wanted to know about it. He shook his head. Sometimes life was simpler just being disconnected from that kind of knowledge.

He checked his instruments and flew home.

*

Lentz and Kate sat strapped within the confines of a metal cage. The skeletal structure was ultra-light, designed for rigidity, supporting four over-sized bubble tyres and a single mast with a semi-rigid sail. It was similar to an ice yacht, but with wheels instead of blades it was designed to cover broken terrain – a wind-powered four-wheel drive. They bounced hard over a rock on the route the navigation system had chosen.

"That hurt!" Kate shouted.

"The satellite resolution is only so good," Lentz replied.

"Couldn't we have been dropped within walking distance? Or with a proper four-wheel drive?"

"Landing closer would have meant risking detection. As for an actual vehicle, did you think we'd have dropped a Land Rover out by parachute? Anyway, because this thing has no power, it makes almost no sound. They won't see or hear us coming."

"If we're still alive to travel that far. What if the wind drops?"

"Then we'll travel more slowly, but trust me, I've read the weather reports for this region: it never drops." Lentz peered at something on the navigation display. "Have you run your suit diagnostic?"

"Twice. Is it actually going to work? You haven't tested half this stuff properly."

"I did what I could with the time we had." Lentz tapped the screen. "At this speed we should be there in ninety minutes. Presuming we don't hit a boulder on route."

"The good news just keeps on coming--"

"Or a polar bear," Lentz said with a smile. "And then of course there could be a blizzard--"

"Let's just stop the speculation, shall well?" Kate hissed. "Before you can think of anything worse."

SEVENTY-SIX

THE GROUND CREW AT CAPE Cod Air Force Base opened the hood of the modified F-15 Eagle and helped Reems clamber out of the rear seat. She nodded a quick thanks to the pilot, although she was fairly sure he'd taken a few liberties with the flight parameters in the interests of getting them here in the shortest possible time. She'd travelled in many different aircraft in her time, but not one that exceeded Mach Three. The acceleration had been brutal, almost suffocating – but then the need was great. Heat radiated from the fuselage as she climbed down the metal gantry. Connor Truman stood waiting. He did not extend his hand.

"This had better not be some kind of joke," he said.

"Is there somewhere we can talk?"

He walked them over to a nearby building. They were waved into a small conference room. There was coffee waiting.

"You checked this place?" Reems asked.

"I had it swept two hours ago." He paused. "And again ten minutes ago. Now start talking."

Reems poured herself a large cup of coffee. "We may only get one chance to contain this situation. I know where they are." She added three sugars to her cup. "Bern. Faraday. Maybe your stolen tech. The intel comes from Dominique Lentz. She had recent contact with Tom Faraday and Alex Marron, without reporting it. She also made technical discoveries relating to another CERUS legacy project, codenamed Resurface. Discoveries we believe were transmitted out of the country. And she was in the vicinity of Northwell A around the time of the explosion. She then left the UK via a black ops flight. She thought she was untraceable." Reems paused, stirring her coffee. "But I know where she is."

"Don't be coy."

"It's an extremely remote location in Northern Canada. It can only be the CERUS beta site."

Truman took a deep breath. "Perhaps you should have watched her more closely. She had been off the grid for twenty-five years. Did you ever really know what happened to her in that time?"

"At this point all I know is that she's not reporting her actions."

Truman shrugged. "A corporate role can have more impact on national security than an intelligence position these days."

"We can get in to the finger-pointing later."

"You told me to pull together a task force. I have two destroyers and a couple of smaller craft in the North Atlantic." He paused. "Plus an aircraft carrier. I'm also moving one of our submarines to the area, but you're just going to have to take my word for that."

"Air support?"

"From the carrier. Plus long range bombers standing by."

"Will you need to involve the Canadians?"

"Director Banetti is managing that. I note you haven't brought anything to the table."

"Other than *all* the intel. And it's hardly on our doorstep –

our forces aren't in the right location."

"And where is that location *exactly*?"

Reems leaned towards him, tapping him in the chest with a slender finger. "Give me your word you're not simply going to launch a bunch of cruise missiles at the site. Lentz may have made a bad decision, but she is a friend: I don't want to see her die. And Faraday may well be there. We definitely don't want to see him die."

"We just want our technology back."

"More than you want to risk it being used by someone else?"

"You have my word."

"Yes, I believe I do. Do you trust Banetti?"

"He asked me the same question about you. I guess we're both going to have to take a leap of faith."

SEVENTY-SEVEN

TOM WATCHED THE LIFT DESCEND to Sub Level 8. He was surrounded by guards, all heavily armed. George Croft stood next to him, handcuffed. They were pushed roughly out of the lift, along a long corridor, then inside a spacious room, lined with equipment and display screens. The air was filled with the hum of electricity and the cold wet smell of something that was not quite organic, but not quite inorganic. In the middle of the room were five huge vats, heavy cables connecting them to a bank of computer servers. It was a nanite production facility based on the methodology used for Tantalus nanites. The technology in this room would, in the past, have been the motherlode for him: a point to which his Interface could connect with impunity. But now he could feel nothing, and once again Tom was aware of how completely alone he was.

He took it all in, then his attention moved to the group that had followed them into the room. A young man stood at the front. He had chiselled features, an almost regal bearing and a familiar look. Behind him was another, older, man.

His father.

Tom felt a tightening in his chest. He had hoped never to see his father again, and now that he did, he had nothing to say.

Bern glanced at him, and made the barest of nods. His eyes gave nothing away, his expression remaining blank.

It was the young man who spoke first. "Mr Faraday, my name is Andrei Leskov. You met my father a year ago."

"Only briefly."

"So I understand. I'd like to ask a question about him."

Tom blinked. "Ask away."

"How did he die?"

"I was in a helicopter with him. Something messed with our weapons systems so that we opened fire. The government simply responded."

"And you didn't think to save him as you made your own escape?"

"I was his prisoner, so I wasn't really in a position to save anyone. I'm still not sure exactly how I got out."

"Or perhaps you committed the sabotage using your abilities."

"I never asked to be part of this nonsense. And now I've been injected *again*, with some sort of *dark nano*. So don't talk to me like I'm the one who had any choice in anything."

Leskov shrugged. "What's happened has happened, but you *will* help me with what happens next. As will your father."

"And what exactly," Bern asked, "do you think I'm going to help you with?"

"Fabienne, can talk you through it."

The slender woman stepped forward, adjusting her glasses. "We're going to re-establish Project Tantalus."

Bern laughed. "And how do you plan on doing that given that everything was destroyed and all the scientists are dead, with the possible exception of Dominique Lentz. And she must be several thousand miles from here."

"As you well know," Fabienne said, "a complete set of files

were stored here a week before the events of last year, as part of the plan to move development to this site. Mr Brody has shared everything."

"So what? It didn't work. The subjects all died, remember."

"One of them lived," Leskov said. "One worked out extremely well."

"Tom's situation is not replicable."

"We know about the earlier experiments. We know about the overheating," Fabienne said. "And we know that for some reason combining the two meant Tom survived. We think we have a solution."

Bern shrugged. "I don't know why you're telling me. You can screw things up on your own."

Fabienne cleared her throat. "We just need your authorisation to activate the nanite replication suite." She walked over to one of the computers.

"Not been able to work around the security?"

"If we get the code wrong three times, the system will wipe."

Bern raised an eyebrow. "How *precarious* for you."

"Don't get any ideas, Mr Bern," Leskov said.

"You're obviously going to kill me. What do I have to gain?"

Leskov snapped his fingers again and one of the bodyguards passed over his handgun. Leskov stepped forward, pushing the barrel against Bern's forehead.

"If you kill me, you won't get the code. I feel dumb even having to point that out."

"Old habits. I usually only shoot people once." Leskov moved the barrel and jammed it against Bern's knee. "But in your case we can try many times. You have two knees, two hands. Maybe then I'll switch to a knife or pliers. Now I'm going to give you ten seconds." Leskov pushed the gun harder against his knee. "Can someone get some cloth? We don't want him bleeding out--"

"OK," Bern shouted, "there's no need for that. I'll do it if you promise you won't just shoot me anyway."

Tom stared at Leskov. "I can't believe either of you would trust the other."

"Concern yourself with your own fate, Mr Faraday. You feature in my plans as well."

"I won't help you."

Leskov gave a snort and nodded to his men. "Unlike your father, you truly have no choice." Two of the men grabbed him firmly, while Fabienne approached with a large syringe, jabbing it into his upper arm.

"Sorry about this," she said.

Tom gritted his teeth as Fabienne pulled back on the syringe, drawing out his blood. He saw Bern walk over to the computer and type in a long code.

"I'm sorry, son. It looks like I have no choice."

Fabienne stepped back, holding up the syringe. "That should be enough to run a first parse."

Leskov clapped his hands. "Excellent. Now put them both in the detention block while we check if there are any complications."

"I did what you asked," Bern said.

"Did you?" Leskov replied. "That's what I intend to confirm. Trusting you was my father's mistake. It won't be mine."

SEVENTY-EIGHT

THE BUILDING HAD SHOWN UP as a faint blip on their scanner when they were a kilometre distant. Lentz quickly turned it off, even as a blizzard moved in. Visibility was barely ten metres.

Kate frowned at her. "You don't think we'll need the scanner to help find it?"

"It's a big target and I know which direction to head. We don't want them detecting our equipment as we approach. We're going to need to lose this vehicle as well."

Kate shrugged and adjusted her clothing. "Let's hope these super suits pull their weight."

"I'm hoping for more than that."

They clambered out of the vehicle's metal cage and shouldered slim but heavy backpacks, then trudged forward through the snow, as fresh flurries blew around them. The terrain rose steadily then fell away. Lentz dropped to the ground and shuffled forwards on her elbows until she was looking over the lip of the ridge. The huge silver-white dome lay before them, dusted with fresh snow. There were several outbuildings and two parked four-wheel drives, but no sign of any people.

"Impressive," Lentz said. "Especially for something built

without anybody knowing about it.

"Another oversized CERUS structure," Kate said, shuffling up next to her. "Although I suppose we should give them credit for mixing it up and not going with another tower." She shivered visibly.

"Cold?" Lentz asked.

"I'm dealing with it, but it would be good to get inside. What's your plan?"

"We have to get a security pass. We'll wing it from there."

Kate rubbed a gloved hand over her face. "That's your plan?"

"I don't know what's inside. CERUS Tower had publicly available blueprints and I'd been studying them for years. This place, as far as anyone is concerned, does not exist. Of course we have one big advantage. They don't know what's *outside*."

"Us? I bet they'd be quaking if they knew." Kate pointed at the Dome. "So, shall we walk up and knock?"

"No. We watch and wait. An opportunity will present itself."

"If we don't freeze first."

"Among your suit's more basic functions is a thermal booster. Use it."

Kate glared. "Now you tell me..."

SEVENTY-NINE

THE DETENTION ROOM WAS PURPOSE built. It had prison-like metal-framed beds with foam mattresses, a metal toilet and very little else. There was no physical lock: it was electronic, with no panel on this side. Not that he could do anything about that any more, thought Tom. Nor could he do anything about the person sitting on the bed opposite him.

"Kind of ironic that we should end up in here together," Bern said, scratching his chin.

"Ironic how?"

"You wanted to put me in prison. But you ended up in here with me."

"You built a prison cell in your research facility," Tom said. "And you wonder why I don't admire you."

Bern shrugged. "Sometimes people need to be dealt with."

"By which you mean 'murdered'."

"If I meant *murdered*, we wouldn't need a prison."

"I don't know why I'm talking to you. And for that matter I don't know *how* I'm talking to you. I heard you were supposed to be dead. *Again*."

Bern raised his hands. "Another of my convoluted attempts to escape justice. My plan was always to vanish, with the world thinking I was dead. But I've had time to reflect on things since then. I've realised I can't just run away from my mistakes."

"Getting captured by Leskov has certainly flushed out your regrets."

"An understandable conclusion. But that's not it."

"Really? And what about that Fabienne? Aren't you mad with her for betraying you?"

"I've treated a lot of people badly. Some might call it Karma."

Tom laughed. "So you've finally seen the light? Was that before or after you had me injected with that dark stuff?"

"You misunderstand. That was to protect you."

"It's done nothing but cause me pain. I don't believe you've changed at all. You agreed to help Leskov far too quickly. I'm sure you have some other trick up your sleeve."

Bern shrugged. "I'm sorry for what we did to you last year."

"You're suggesting we go for coffee or something? That we hug and make up?"

"That might be a bit of a leap, but I can take a step in the right direction by getting us out of here."

Tom gave a snort. "And you have the key to this room in your pocket? Excuse my scepticism that you'd want to help me."

"I've already helped you. I've made you useless to them. That dark nano is changing you, destroying your nanites."

Tom's jaw hardened. "All I've noticed is pain."

"I know a year ago you told me you wanted to keep the Interface. But hasn't the last twelve months changed your perspective? Don't you want to be normal again? Isn't that the best gift I can give you? The pain you're feeling now is an unfortunate side effect, but the fact that it is hurting means it is working. Anyway, we can talk about that later. For now, I need you to trust me." Bern walked over to one of the walls and tapped the panel in the bottom right corner five times. With a hiss, it slid back. He reached in and produced two plastic pods, handing one to Tom.

"What is it?" Tom asked, turning it over in his hands.

"An advantage," Bern said. "This is *my* base. Leskov only *thinks* he is in charge."

EIGHTY

"JUST TELL ME WHAT IT means," Leskov said, as Fabienne finished her explanation of the on-screen test results.

"It means," she said, "that the new nano particles introduced into Faraday's blood stream – I quite like the name *dark nano* – are working as intended. Faraday's abilities have been locked down. He is no threat to anyone."

"But is he still a useful subject?"

"*If* we can get the dark nano out. There are no guarantees."

"We can progress that soon, but, for now, do we have all the information we require? Do we still need Bern?"

"I suppose not," Fabienne said.

"You're having second thoughts?"

"I'm just wary. He plans so far ahead."

"You think he planned for *me*?"

"Of course not, but it might be wise to keep him around in case he has a secret or two in this base."

Leskov shook his head. "Brody searched thoroughly all the way down to Sub Level 12. He found nothing."

"Then I guess we can--"

An alarm sounded. Fabienne reached over to her computer and called up a different screen. "It's the detention block. The cell door has been forced open."

Leskov turned to four guards who were standing quietly to one side of the room. "With me. Now!"

*

Leskov ran down the Sub Level 6 corridor followed by his four bodyguards and Fabienne. Two more guards stood outside the cell, standing at attention. They looked at him, puzzled.

"Sir?" asked the first.

"How did they get out? You were supposed to be guarding them," shouted Leskov.

"We've not moved, Mr Leskov," said the second. "Door hasn't opened. No one's gone anywhere."

Fabienne held up a tablet computer. "The system shows the door was opened."

"Open it again," Leskov said. "And let's find out."

The first guard nodded, waved his card over the lock and pushed the door open. They all rushed into the room.

It was empty.

"Well?" Leskov shouted.

"It's impossible," said the second guard.

"Really? Perhaps you were asleep?" Leskov snapped his fingers. One of his four bodyguards handed him a pistol. He turned to the first guard and pulled the trigger. The bullet hit the man in the chest. He fell back with a jerk, collapsing against the wall. Leskov turned to the second guard and fired again. The crack reverberated around the room and Leskov slapped his ears in frustration. "Remind me to use a silencer next time," he said, handing the pistol back to its owner. The bodyguard nodded in silence, glancing warily at the two bodies.

Fabienne blinked, then looked again at her tablet. "One of

the lifts is moving up from this floor. It could be them." She tapped a quick command. "I'll hold it on Sub Level 2 until we can get there."

Leskov nodded. "Good. Bern would have been trying to get to the surface. Where is Brody?"

"He's showing as on Sub Level 1."

"I want all our people there. We have to contain whatever is going on. If they've gone outside, we'll go after them." He paused, allowing himself a smile. "Not that they've got anywhere they can realistically go."

*

The sound of footsteps receded from the cell, the door hanging open. Tom let out a breath from his position under one of the beds. Under the other, the form of William Bern shimmered into view.

"Deactivate the translucency," Bern said. "Don't waste the suit's power."

Tom reached out and tapped the control panel on his wrist. His body rippled back into sight. "What if they'd reached under the beds to check?"

"What ifs won't get us out of here. We need to move."

They both eased out and stood up. Tom tried not to look at the bodies of the two guards. "Leskov is a bastard, isn't he?"

Bern shrugged. "He doesn't tolerate failure."

Tom shook his head. "So, where to?"

"The comms room. There's a message we need to send."

EIGHTY-ONE

OUTSIDE THE CERUS DOME, THE two guards were at the northern most part of their patrol route when a flashing green light appeared briefly on the snowy ridge surrounding the building, then vanished.

"Did you see that?" asked the first. "Up the slope?"

"I saw something blinking," said the second. "It might have been a reflection off the dome."

"We should check it out."

"There's equipment all over the place up there. Could be that."

"What sort of equipment?"

"Heavy drilling gear, I think. Brody said it was off limits." The second guard adjusted his goggles, wiping snow from them. "I'd rather get back. We're due to go on our break."

"It won't matter if we're a few minutes late. It might be important. Look, there it is again!" said the first guard, starting to run up the hill.

The second guard muttered under his breath and followed. They crested the rise and found a silver torch lying in the snow.

"It must have been this," said the first guard, bending to pick it up. "Why would someone leave it out here?"

"Grab it and we'll head back in--"

Neither of them saw the two figures approaching. But then in fairness, nobody would have done so.

*

Lentz and Kate stood over the two unconscious guards.

"Nice moves," Lentz said.

"Not exactly a fair fight," Kate replied. "Couldn't we have zapped them with something?"

"Zapped?"

"You didn't mention weapons, but I presume you've brought something hi-tech."

"I have one automatic rifle coated with Resurface nanites, but these are just people doing a job. I'd rather we didn't hurt them unnecessarily."

"Speaking of which, what are we going to do with them? If we leave them out here, they'll freeze to death."

"About two hundred metres to the north is an insulated storage barn. We can leave them there."

"Did you bring anything to sedate them?"

Lentz raised an eyebrow. "Tying them up should be enough. Sedation, really? Ever considered a career in intelligence?"

"Would you recommend it?"

"Life expectancy can be short. And there's a lot more paperwork than they'd like to have you believe."

"Maybe I'll pass."

Lentz pulled a camera-like device from her pack and held it over the face of the first guard. After several seconds, she nodded and clicked the camera onto an attachment on the belt of her suit. There was a soft beep, and then her suit shimmered.

Kate gave a gasp.

Lentz smiled. "So, what do you think?"
"I think," she said, "that you really aren't looking yourself."
"Now it's your turn."

EIGHTY-TWO

THE CORRIDORS WERE DESERTED AS Tom and Bern made their way from the detention area; they took a staircase down, ignoring the lifts. The comms room was located on Sub Level 7; it was a cramped space filled with monitors displaying views from around the base.

Bern walked over to a large microphone and keyboard. "I need to contact Stephanie Reems."

"Very funny."

"It's no joke. Do you think we're going to escape without some serious assistance? Leskov has at least sixty armed men. And I'm pretty sure he has a *lot* of weaponry here as well."

"That may be true, but what makes you think you can get through to--"

Bern tapped a code into the keyboard and a series of clicks came through speakers. Then a voice spoke: "Who the hell is this? And how did you get this number?"

Bern smiled. "Stephanie, would you believe it's good to hear your voice?"

There was a moment's silence, then a muffled curse. "Bern? I knew you were alive!"

"Did you ever really doubt it?"

"You're too rich to die it seems."

"Unfortunately I doubt it. In fact, my life is rather at risk at the moment. To that end I thought I'd tell you where we are."

"I already know where you are. I said we would find your Beta Site."

Bern paused. "That is excellent news."

"You don't want to know how I know?"

"Right now I'm more worried about us getting out of here safely."

"Why am I immediately suspicious that you're up to something? And what do you mean by 'us'?"

"Suspicion is in your nature. And I'm here with Tom Faraday." He motioned to Tom to speak.

"That's right," said Tom. "And we really need your help."

There was a lengthy pause. "Also not dead, I see. What is your situation?"

"The facility," replied Bern, "is under the control of Andrei Leskov."

There was the muted sound of a conversation between Reems and someone else, then Reems' angry voice. "You keep pleasant company these days."

"To be honest, we're doing our best to avoid him, but I don't know how much longer we'll be able to do that."

"We're close. Perhaps only an hour away."

"I hope you brought some serious resources."

"We've come prepared."

"Be careful. Leskov will do anything to defend himself."

"I have a... friend here who is asking if the stolen power source is on site. He suggests complete transparency would be the best approach."

"I agree. And I've seen it in one of the labs."

"Good. We'll be with you soon, William."

Tom watched as Bern terminated the call. "The power source? You mean the Accumulator? The one you made it look like I stole. Wait, does that mean Reems is with US forces?"

"A Navy task force, I expect. I had to find you Tom. I couldn't do it alone, so I made sure that someone else had a really strong reason to find you."

"But why tell Reems all that? Are you just giving up?"

"I'm trying to protect you," Bern said. "I want you to trust me."

"You think that's possible?"

"I have to try. Now let's go."

"Where?"

"First, we're going to collect the Accumulator before someone else thinks to grab it. If we're going to have any leverage with the US, we'll need it in our possession."

"And after that?"

"We'll head the last place Leskov will expect: down."

EIGHTY-THREE

ON SUB LEVEL 2, LESKOV and his team approached the lift. The indicator showed the lift-car was there, but the doors remained closed. "What are you waiting for?" Leskov said. "Open it."

Fabienne tapped her tablet and the doors slid back. The lift was empty. She frowned. "I don't understand. Nobody else in the facility was anywhere near. It had to be them."

Leskov's voice became a growl. "What is going on--?"

"Someone has taken over the lifts. Possibly other systems, too. Look, I'm a scientist, not a security expert. Brody would know better."

"Then let's go speak with him."

One of the bodyguards held the staircase door open and they sprinted up the heavy metal steps. Emerging onto Sub Level 1 they saw the room was full of Leskov's men: more than sixty of them.

"Where are the scientists?" Fabienne asked, looking around. "They should be here."

Leskov's eyes bulged. "Somebody had better explain things fast."

Two more guards walked in, slightly shorter than the others.

They brushed snow from their uniforms.

"You," Leskov said. "What's happening outside?"

One of them cleared their throat and spoke in a gruff voice. "All... fine, Sir. We didn't see anything unusual."

"No civilians trying to run away across the snow?"

The guard hesitated. "No, Sir."

Leskov clenched and unclenched his hands. "Anyone got any ideas?"

Fabienne swallowed. "Maybe they're all wearing suits."

"Just how many did we make?"

"Over a hundred. I thought you'd requisitioned them."

Leskov scowled. "You're saying they might still be in the building, but we can't detect them?"

"They might be. Either with translucency or camouflage activated. The power sources won't last long, though. They can't hide for long."

"I'll start conducting a sweep," said one of the short guards, heading to the stairwell, their partner following.

"Some initiative: excellent," Leskov said. "This is our *only* priority."

The two guards nodded and disappeared down the stairs.

"I don't know if it's the only priority," Fabienne said. "We have another problem." She tapped on her tablet again and turned to a large display screen hanging in the cafeteria. It flashed up a map of the Dome and the surrounding terrain, extending out to the sea to the east. Three large red dots were blinking in the bottom right of the display.

"What are those?" asked Leskov, his voice rising. "Fishing vessels? Cargo?"

"From their signatures, they're military." A bigger dot appeared, blinking angrily. Fabienne swore. "And that, from its size, is an aircraft carrier."

"Heading here?"

"Based on their course I don't think there's any doubt." Two green triangles appeared and started moving much more quickly. "Jets," Fabienne said. "From the carrier, I'm guessing."

Leskov snorted loudly. "So it's shock and awe, then. I'm sure they'll be on the ground here within the hour. We should prepare a welcome party."

"You're not really suggesting you can outgun them?"

"Not in a fair fight." His eyes gleamed. "But we won't be fighting fair."

EIGHTY-FOUR

THE TWO SHORT GUARDS RAN down three flights of stairs, then stepped into the main corridor of Sub Level 3. The first one touched a control on their belt. Instantly, the male features blurred, changing to those of Lentz. The other morphed into Kate.

"We aren't being followed," Kate said, listening at the stairwell. "I can't believe that worked."

"They seemed distracted," Lentz replied. "Which is good, because I forgot the suit only changes your appearance, not your voice."

"Oh I don't know. You sounded like a very convincing man."

"Must be my MI5 field training. Or a sore throat."

"Well, considering they're untested, the suits have held out pretty well."

Lentz shrugged. "We haven't really touched on the untested functionality yet, but let's cross that bridge when we come to it." She felt her phone buzz in her pocket. She pulled it out and saw a familiar name on the caller ID: Reems.

"You have reception here?" Kate asked, frowning.

Lentz snorted. "My phone has reception anywhere."

"OK, but why would Reems be calling you now?"

"Maybe she's found out I've gone missing. Well it's too late for her to do anything about it." Lentz put the phone back in her pocket. "I'm certainly not going to waste time talking to her now."

"How are we going to find Tom? I thought we'd be hacking into the building systems like at CERUS, but if the building can't track him we have a problem."

Lentz pulled out a scanner and started adjusting it. She frowned. "I'm detecting an odd signal. Traces of radiation."

"Could it be the Accumulator thing Tom mentioned?"

"Probably. I'm guessing the theft was conducted by someone wearing one of the suits even if it doesn't explain *why* they would want to look like Tom."

"Where's the signal coming from?"

"It's not really directional. And all this metal isn't helping, but it's stronger below us so I guess we head down."

Kate looked around the corridor. "How far down do you think it goes?"

"Now that," said Lentz, "is an excellent question. Why don't we find out?"

EIGHTY-FIVE

THE *USS INIMITABLE*, A 9,000 ton destroyer-class ship, was a kilometre off the coast, making ten knots through icy waters. The coastline was a near unbroken line of high cliffs apart from a single point where a tunnel had been cut through and a short jetty constructed.

Stephanie Reems stood on the bridge, staring at their target. "They'll know we're coming."

"I don't doubt it," Truman replied, looking through a pair of binoculars. "I hope they do the sensible thing and surrender." Two jets screamed overhead, returning from their sweep. "I'm told we're not seeing any activity on the ground."

"And what if they don't acquiesce?"

Truman lowered his binoculars. "They are not keeping that power cell. We'll do what we have to."

Reems leaned close to him. "Faraday and Bern are in that building and I had your word they wouldn't be harmed. I also have reason to believe Dominique Lentz and Kate Turner are there too. Any action you are planning needs to make their safety a prime consideration."

"Assuming you're right about all this. I know what Bern said, but can we really believe him? Look, we'll send in a team and evaluate when we have more information. Just be patient."

*

Three small reconnaissance drones flew overlapping patterns, providing different views to a set of display screens in the ship's communications centre. Reems and Truman, accompanied by the ship's First Officer, watched as two squads of twenty US commandos used small, powerful boats to cover the kilometre to the jetty. They were clad in white thermal jackets, wore special variable-enhancement goggles, and carried powerful small arms.

The boats approached the dock. A submarine was positioned there, and they drew alongside, jumping onto the jetty. Nobody else was in sight.

Reems pointed at the submarine, triumphantly. "I'm guessing that's how Bern made his escape from the explosion."

Truman coughed. "Does it matter now?"

A voice broke over the speakers, the Lieutenant in charge of the operation. "The sub's sealed up. Can't tell if there's anyone on board. Do you want to send over cutting gear?"

"Negative," Truman replied. "It's not a priority. Leave two men to watch it and proceed. Just remember Leskov's background. He may have brought some of his merchandise with him."

"No sign of anyone at this point, but we'll stay frosty." The Lieutenant hesitated. "That's no reference to the conditions."

Reems and Truman watched as the two squads advanced quickly up the metal staircase and through the rocky tunnel. The drone footage then showed them appear at the far end, a single four-wheel drive vehicle sat empty. Their scanners showed no movement ahead, so they proceeded down the heavily-rutted ice road, towards the target location.

Ten cautious minutes later they approached the huge dome structure. At a signal from the Lieutenant the men split into four smaller groups and sought cover.

"I'm still seeing no movement," said the Lieutenant.

"Two squads proceed," replied Truman. "Two provide cover. Blow the door if you have to."

"Yes, Sir." The Lieutenant raised his hand to give the signal. As he did, a voice broke out from a hidden public address system.

"What was that?" Reems asked.

"I'm focusing the sound for you," the Lieutenant replied. The message repeated:

"YOU ARE TRESPASSING ON PRIVATE PROPERTY. LEAVE NOW AND YOU WILL NOT BE HARMED."

"Orders?" the Lieutenant asked.

"Proceed," Truman replied. "The drones show nothing outside the Dome."

"Yes, Sir." On screen the lieutenant raised his hand again. "Squad A, follow me, and--"

In front of them the air shimmered and warped. From nowhere, weapons fired. There were screams.

Truman turned, swearing. "What the hell just happened?"

The First Officer stood, white-faced, staring at a real-time satellite image on the main screen. "I don't understand. Were they using some form of camouflage?"

Reems frowned. "Could this be the same tech that Bern used to escape from his home?"

Truman ran a hand through his hair. "How many casualties?

"I'm not getting any telemetry," replied the First Officer.

The Lieutenant's voice broke over the speakers, harsh and urgent. "Do you copy?"

"What happened?" Truman shouted. "What's your status?"

"Hit bad," he gasped. "Never saw them. Don't know how..."

He trailed off.

"We're sending in the chopper." Truman gave a sharp hand signal to the First Officer. "Stand by."

"Negative. They may have ground-to-air. I'll make my way--" There was the sound of gunfire, then the comms went silent.

Truman smashed his fist onto the desk.

"Orders, Sir?" asked the First Officer. "Are we sending a second strike force?"

"Hold that action. I need to make a call."

Reems gripped his arm. "We need to speak to the Dome: see if we can negotiate."

"They just killed forty of my men. The only person I need to talk to is not in that Dome." Truman walked from the Bridge.

EIGHTY-SIX

TOM EMERGED ONTO SUB LEVEL 12, noting that the stairs didn't go any lower. Bern followed him, carrying the Accumulator in a backpack. Five minutes earlier they had retrieved it from the lab.

"Are you sure that thing is safe?" Tom asked. "I presume it was in that containment chamber for a reason."

"That was for running tests," Bern replied. "As long as we don't activate it, we'll be fine."

"So what are we doing?" Tom asked, feeling his suit itch. "Hiding down here until the cavalry arrive?"

"Something like that. This way."

Tom followed as Bern wound his way through a system of corridors. "You seem awfully sure of yourself."

Bern shrugged. "I'm good at making decisions." He stopped outside an unmarked door. "And you know me, I always have a plan." The room looked like a storeroom. It was filled with several mismatched items of furniture, stacked on top of each other.

"Your decision-making led us to a cupboard."

"They certainly won't look here first. It even has a lock on the door."

"A mechanical one? With a key?"

Bern stepped forward and turned it. "If anyone follows, it will slow them down a bit." He switched on a screen embedded in one wall. A menu appeared and he tapped through layers of icons. A map flashed up, filling the screen, showing the Dome and its surroundings. In the sea to the East there were four red dots, one much larger than the rest.

"What are those?"

"Our friends from the US Navy. Reems said they were close. For once she wasn't lying." Two green triangles appeared and began moving rapidly away from the large red dot, in a sweeping arc around the Dome.

"Jets?" asked Tom.

Bet nodded. "The US will try and force their way in. Leskov will fight back, because that's who he is. At least, he'll fight back for a bit as a precursor to negotiating a way out of the situation. But it doesn't matter. The moment he kills anyone, the US are going to decide they have only one option: to make sure that nobody makes it out of here with this." He patted the backpack. "They think it can be turned into a bomb."

"So they're going to kill us all?"

Bern shrugged.

"You don't seem that bothered."

Bern walked over to a plain section of wall and tapped the top right corner five times. There was a groan and the panel slid back. Inside was a metal cage, similar to a construction lift. It could probably hold five or six people at a squeeze. "We had something very much like this at CERUS Tower. I think you used it."

"An escape route?" Tom asked. "To where?"

"The real question is 'to *what?*' And the answer is 'to something that Leskov knows nothing about'. He didn't infiltrate my organisation quite as well as he thinks." Bern pointed to the cage. "After you, if you want to live."

Tom climbed in, gripping the metal. It felt warm. The air in the lift shaft was thick with the smell of electric motors and grease. "This has been used recently."

Bern nodded. "Several times today. Now let's get the hell out of here."

EIGHTY-SEVEN

TRUMAN WALKED ALONG THE CORRIDOR then down two decks, arriving at a secure conference suite. He closed the door behind him then placed his palm on a desktop reader. When it verified his ID, he placed the call.

An image of CIA Director, Lazlo Banetti, appeared on the large screen, his shaven head gleaming. "We agreed no communications during the operation. This had better be good."

"The situation has... I needed to consult with you."

"Were the President's orders not clear? Recover the tech, or make the situation safe."

Truman shifted in his seat. "I sent a team of forty SEALs in to take control of the facility. They were all killed. We were taken by surprise: they used some form of advanced personal camouflage. It may be the same technology that was used to acquire the Accumulator, and that Bern used to leave his mansion."

"So who is running things?"

"Andrei Leskov, who I'm sure needs no introduction."

"Do you think you can negotiate with him?"

"Not to a deal we'll find palatable."

"And have you verified the presence of the device?"

"Our scanners are detecting trace signatures of the radiation.

We have a 98% certainty."

"I'm not hearing anything that impacts your orders. If it's not safe to go onsite, then use the TW."

"Bern and Faraday are there. And, according to Reems, Dominique Lentz as well."

Banetti's brow creased. "Reports said Bern and Faraday were both dead?"

"Reems received a call from Bern, asking for assistance for Faraday and himself. Lentz is here on some mission of her own: Reems seems to have lost control."

"None of them are blameless in this situation. Continue with your orders."

Truman puffed out his cheeks. "Even assuming that Bern, Faraday, and whoever else is there are less important than destroying the Accumulator, maybe we should consider whether this is what Bern wants us to do."

"I don't follow."

"Maybe he wants us to erase the site - don't ask me why. All I can say is that he has a history of forcing extreme courses of action."

"That's absurd. He has no way out - why would he prompt his own death?"

"As I said, I don't know. Even leaving all that aside, Reems won't be easy to contain."

"I'll manage Reems. I'll go over her head to the British Home Secretary. You need to see this through. Call me when it's done."

EIGHTY-EIGHT

LENTZ AND KATE EXITED THE stairwell on Sub Level 8. The corridor was deserted. Lentz pointed to the right and they moved along, their boots clanging on the metal walkway floor. Kate pointed at a series of flashing red lights. "What do they mean?"

"Some sort of alarm or warning. Maybe triggered by Bern and Tom." Lentz held up the scanner. "I'm getting a much stronger signal."

"Isn't it odd that they aren't sending more guards to sweep the floors? Did they really think we'd cover the whole building?"

"Maybe they're just moving slowly. Let's not get distracted." Lentz pushed through a set of large metal doors into a technical laboratory. In the centre were five huge vats made of some type of glass: they were connected to each other and various computers by heavy cabling.

"Are those what I think they are?" Kate asked.

Lentz nodded. "Nano vats are inevitable given they've been manufacturing these suits in bulk. It's Resurface technology."

"Not Tantalus?"

Lentz shook her head. "Different type of nanite, different type of vat." Lentz walked over to the nearest computer and logged into the records.

"You can access the computers?" asked Kate.

"Standard CERUS protocols. Clearly they didn't expect me to be on site." She read something on screen and her eyes narrowed. "Goddammit. They *did* get me to do their work for them."

"What do you mean?"

"We found old records of Resurface in a hidden second safe in Bern's office. Of course, I leapt at the chance to use new technology to solve the problems that stumped us originally, but it was a set up. Someone – probably Hallstein, or whatever her real name is – planted a device on my computer that transmitted the data out to them. The minute I solved the transparency problem, they had the answers too."

"So anyone could be here, in this room, and we wouldn't see them?" Kate swung her head around, eyes wide. "Do you have an infrared camera or something?"

"I could rig one up, but it wouldn't help. Infrared is just another form of electromagnetic radiation - the suits would still be all but invisible." Lentz shook her head. "The key words being 'all but' - it's not perfect. If you looked hard enough you'd see the ghost of a reflection. So there's no one else here, Kate." She held out her scanner again and turned to a door in the far side of the room. "Come on. The readings are strongest over there."

In the next room they found a self-contained inner chamber, with steel framing and thick, glittering glass. An access panel hung open. "Whatever I'm reading was in there," Lentz said, holding out her scanner. "The radiation levels are peaking. It's a very strange wave form. Something experimental: I'm guessing the power cell that Tom was supposed to have stolen."

"What?"

"The CIA have Tom down as public enemy number one. It's

why Truman came to London to talk to me and Reems, not that he admitted it when he saw us."

"Why would the CIA think Tom had stolen something?"

"Because they have video footage of him taking it. Except it wasn't him. It was almost certainly someone in one of these suits. They didn't have translucency then, but camouflage would have worked. Like when we copied the guards, they copied Tom."

"But why Tom?"

"Why indeed," Lentz said. "There's a hand behind all of this, guiding it."

"Bern?"

"That's what I would have said, but things seem to be going badly for him right now."

"I guess you can't plan for everything."

Lentz felt her phone buzz again. She pulled it out and saw there were ten messages, all from Reems. Lentz blinked and read them: *If you are where I think you are, you need to get out. Call me.* Lentz coughed and pressed dial.

"You're making a call?" asked Kate. "How on earth are you getting a signal down here?"

"I'm extending off their internal wireless. As I said, I can get a signal anywhere--"

Reems voice crackled out of the phone. "Tell me you're not in the Beta site."

Lentz froze and stared at Kate.

"You think," Reems continued, "you can borrow an SAS plane without me knowing? I tracked you here. I'm on board a US destroyer, just off the coast. I think they're about to drop a bomb on you. A very big bomb."

"What?" Lentz felt her mouth go dry. "We're eight levels down. And Leskov has armed guards all over the upper levels. If we start running past them, they're going to ask questions."

"You need to try."

"There's no way. And Tom is in here. We're trying to find him." Lentz paused. "We're all pretty deep underground. Maybe we'll be OK."

"I wouldn't count on it. I'm sorry, Dominique."

"Truman is doing this to destroy the power cell, isn't he?"

"He says it could be reconfigured as a bomb."

"It *was* here. I'm in the lab where they were working on it, but it's not here anymore."

"I'm not sure he's going to take your word for it."

"How long do we have?"

"It could only be a few minutes."

"Then I intend to use them." Lentz clicked the phone off.

"They're going to bomb us?" Kate shouted.

"To try and contain their secrets," Lentz said. "Although I don't think it's going to work. In fact, I'm counting on it."

"So we're *not* going to die?"

Lentz grabbed Kate by the shoulder and marched her back in the direction of the stairwell.

"We're going back up? To try to get out?"

They arrived at the stair-access door. "We'd never make it."

"Then what?"

"We're going down."

EIGHTY-NINE

TOM CLUNG TO THE SAFETY bar as the metal cage screamed down the tracks. He tried to focus instead on the fact that his suit continued to itch.

The tunnel bored through cold, wet rock. It descended at nearly forty-five degrees, twisting occasionally in the near darkness. The cage turned a sharp corner and they burst into light: not daylight, but illumination from what Tom saw were banks of powerful spotlights. The track levelled out and they slowed down.

They were in a huge cavern, the size of several football pitches: natural from the looks of the walls and roof. Half of the floor was smooth rock, the other half was not floor at all but a vast pool of what, from the pervading tang in the air, must be seawater. A wide channel led away down a tunnel. People wearing different-coloured overalls moved purposefully around the cavern, checking and packing hi-tech equipment. It looked like an evacuation.

Tom noticed this only in passing. Filling the pool - which was really more like a lake - one thing dominated the cavern. It was enormous - a dull grey-white, and constructed of steel. If an article he'd read once was right, it must gross over thirty thousand tonnes.

An *aircraft carrier*.

"You have to be kidding," Tom said. "Where did you get that?"

"It's an old Russian model," Bern replied. "I stole it from Leskov while it was being sent for a refit. Now it's our way out of here: not just for you and me, of course, but for the whole base staff. With the obvious exception of anyone affiliated with Leskov."

"Are you just going to sail it out?"

"This cavern leads directly to the sea."

"But the Americans will see it."

"We'll negotiate our way past."

A man rushed up. "Mr Bern, you're the last. We have Croft on board."

"Thanks, Brody," Bern said. "What about Fabienne?"

"She's still with Leskov. There was nothing we could do."

Bern shook his head. "Unfortunate, but we are where we are. Now, has our Russian friend sufficiently pissed off our American friends?"

"We believe so."

"Excellent. We should get under way before the bombing starts."

"Bombing?" Tom asked. "What do you mean?"

Brody frowned at him. "Get on board if you don't want to find out first hand."

Bern nodded. "Tom, I said I'd get you out of here and I meant it. Just do what my men say and everything will be fine."

NINETY

REEMS WATCHED AS TRUMAN WALKED back onto the bridge. "Tell me you're not going to do something stupid."

His eyes didn't meet hers. Instead he turned to the First Officer. "Please have someone escort Director Reems to her quarters."

She stabbed a finger in Truman's direction. "You wouldn't even be here if it wasn't for me."

"Then I'll politely ask you to shut up," Truman said. "I have orders." He turned back to the First Officer. "Ready the TWs."

"A thermobaric weapon?" Reems gasped.

"It's the biggest non-nuke missile we have."

"Two aircraft loaded and standing by, two packages per aircraft," replied the First Officer. "Ready to launch on your order."

"This is mass murder," Reems shouted.

"We're making the world safer."

"It's only in danger because of something you created."

Truman wiped sweat from his brow. "This is not a decision that was reached easily. But it is necessary."

"I managed to speak with Lentz. She said that the Accumulator may not even be on site any longer. This could all be for nothing."

"Our data says differently."

"Maybe you should check again."

Truman shook his head, then nodded to the First Officer. "Launch when ready." The man started giving orders into a headset.

"Did you tell Banetti this was lunacy?" Reems said. "I never liked him. Never understood how he rose so far and so fast."

"Sir," said the First Officer, "we're being hailed by the Dome."

"Put them on."

"Hello, US Navy." It was a man's voice with a Russian accent.

"This is Deputy Director Truman. Why do you want to talk *now*, Leskov?"

There was an intake of breath and a short pause. *"We wish to negotiate terms. We have things you want. You have things we want. So we negotiate."*

"After what you did to my team? Negotiation is based on trust."

"You sent an armed team to storm this base. We defended ourselves. Also I have hostages, including William Bern and Tom Faraday."

"Both more dangerous alive than dead."

"You need to calm down, Deputy Director, because I believe--"

"I have only one thing to say: you have three minutes until I bomb your dome." Truman signalled that the call be cut.

"What are you playing at?" Reems asked.

"I'm giving them a chance." He cleared his throat. "Launch the jets. Have them fly directly overhead, but do not drop the TWs. Wait for my order."

"Very good, Sir."

Reems shook her head. "He doesn't believe you. And Bern, Faraday and Lentz are too deep in the base: they'll never get out, even if they get the warning."

"If they all evacuate in a hurry, maybe we won't have to drop the bombs." Truman folded his arms. "We might flush them out, unprepared and disorganised. Then we'll use tear gas and flash bangs to mop them up, camouflaged or not."

A flicker of a smile crossed Reems' face. "You think it will work?"

"Let's hope." He pointed across the water to the aircraft carrier, stationed half a mile from their position. Support crews were swarming away from two aircraft on the flight deck. Sixty seconds later both jets screamed into the air. They banked sharply and flew directly towards the Dome.

Reems nodded and pulled out her phone. "I'm going to try and contact Lentz again, see if I can--"

A huge flash lit up the horizon. Reems clamped her eyes shut. The sound wave hit them a moment later: a sharp, deep, jarring roar.

"I said not to drop!" screamed Truman. "What did they do?"

The First Officer's face was white with confusion. "The jets are confirming a direct hit in accordance with your verbal order."

"What verbal order? Pull them back. Abort!"

"They're not responding. They're circling again for a second strike."

NINETY-ONE

LENTZ AND KATE ARRIVED ON Sub Level 12, having taken the stairs at least two at a time for several flights. They sprinted down the main corridor, Lentz holding out her scanner. "I'm still getting traces of that radiation down here," she wheezed.

"Meaning what?" Kate gasped.

"That the Accumulator was probably moved down here."

"To protect it?"

"I don't think a few extra floors will help."

"Will the explosion really hit us down this deep?"

"They're not going to mess around. Probably some type of fuel-air bomb. The real trouble is that a surface strike will shut down the air systems. Without them, we won't be able to breathe down here. Nor will we be able to climb out."

"So we die in an explosion or we suffocate?"

"Let's hope it doesn't come to that." Lentz stopped outside a door. "The reading is strongest here." She reached for the handle. "It's locked. Of course it is."

"Looks like a storage cupboard."

"You might be right." Lentz crouched. "I can see the end of a key still in the lock, meaning it's been locked from the *inside.*"

"Someone went in there and didn't come out?"

"That would be my thinking."

"Stand back," Kate said, lunging forward with a perfect kick. Her boot struck the door, but it held firm. Kate fell away, swearing.

"It's steel reinforced," Lentz said. "That's not going to work unless you have a lot more firepower." She pulled a small black cube off of her belt and stepped away. "We should get clear." They ran back down the corridor and Lentz pulled out her phone. "They've got an app for everything these days." She touched the screen and the door exploded inwards.

They ran into the small room, guns raised. Apart from old furniture, it was empty.

"Someone was in here and locked the door, so they *must* have got out some other way. We just have to find it."

The floor shook violently. Kate looked around. "What was that?"

"I'm guessing the first of the bombs. Time's up."

"Is one of these walls hollow?" Kate asked, hitting the nearest with her fist. It rang dully, as if solid concrete were behind it.

Lentz joined her, moving around the room. Kate kicked out with her boot. A panel burst inwards and she stumbled forward, only just catching herself on the sides of the opening. She looked down and gave a whistle.

Lentz peered down. "It's a shaft for an escape lift."

The floor shook again, this time more violently.

"So where is the lift?"

"At the bottom?" The room shook a third time. The walls started to creak and groan. "There's a cable," Kate said.

Lentz tapped the controls on her belt. Her suit seemed to vibrate as the surface recalibrated. She ran her fingers over the surface and smiled, then nearly slipped over. She caught herself and beckoned to Kate. "Come here and get ready to grab something." Lentz made the same adjustments to Kate's belt.

Kate felt her feet start to slip out from under her. "What did you just do?"

"Reduced the friction coefficient on the entire exterior of your suit. Significantly."

"Why?"

"We're going to need to slide. And fast." The ceiling of the room started to buckle. Lentz stepped up to the gap in the wall. "Lock your arms around the cable and hope."

NINETY-TWO

LESKOV HEARD THE CALL DISCONNECT in bewilderment. He was not used to being cut off. What kind of a tactic was it to say you were going to bomb your opponent? It made no sense. He turned to Fabienne. "This man is an idiot. Does he think he can call my bluff...?"

She stared back at him, an odd look in her eyes. "He's not bluffing. We need to get out of here."

"What? You don't believe--"

She grabbed his arm and pulled. "*Now*!"

There was surprising steel in her grip, inevitability in her tone. And he let himself be led.

They sprinted up the staircase to ground level, then ran through the lobby, snatching at thick coats hanging on a row of hooks. Bemused staff watched them run past. Leskov slapped the emergency release on the airlock and they burst outside, the cold hitting them like shattered glass. Three four-wheel-drive vehicles stood waiting. Leskov jumped into the first and, hardly waiting for Fabienne to climb in next to him, gunned the engine and pulled away.

"It still could be a trick," he said.

"It's not. Believe me."

Above them the noise of jet engines obliterated all else. Two aircraft tore the skies apart. Leskov slammed his foot on the accelerator, barely keeping the car on the ice track. Then the planes were gone.

He slowed. "See! I told you they wouldn't--"

Fabienne's voice was urgent. "They're coming back. Drive!"

And then the world erupted behind them. The blast wave shunted the car forward, slewing it sideways. Leskov gripped the wheel, fighting for control. The rear windscreen cracked and splintered. One of the tyres burst, but the car stayed on the track and kept moving.

Leskov's eyes widened. "You were right. Oh my God, you were right. Why are they doing this?"

"Bern," she replied. "Maybe they followed him here? Or the Accumulator? Does it matter?"

A second bomb struck behind them.

"All this for that device?" Leskov saw their destination ahead. "It's ridiculous."

"You were outplayed. Deal with it."

He frowned. "Perhaps. But Bern is the one who is not going to escape." Leskov pulled the car to a halt next to the ice tunnel. "We, however, will." He glanced over his shoulder, towards the Dome.

Fabienne leapt from the car and he followed. They ran down the tunnel, slowing to descend the metal staircase. At the dock the submarine sat waiting.

"There should be three crew on board," Leskov said. "It will be enough. We'll sail right under the Americans." He pushed ahead of Fabienne, who suddenly seemed distracted. He climbed on deck and half-jumped down the hatch. "Get in here! We're leaving immediately--"

His words caught in his throat. Three uniformed bodies lay

on the floor.

"I wasn't able to persuade them to my cause," said a voice from the air behind them.

Leskov spun to see the air shimmering and a figure warping into view. It was the man who had murdered his father.

Peter Marron.

Leskov instinctively reached for the automatic pistol in his belt. Marron was only holding a knife. The old man had misjudged--

Something gripped his wrist. Steel-like fingers twisted his hand away from the gun, then he felt another hand remove the weapon. The air shimmered again and Marron's daughter, Alex, was suddenly standing in front of him, holding his pistol.

Leskov felt the air sucked from his lungs.

Marron cleared his throat, hefting the blade in his hand. "This was one of the knives Sharp was carrying. He won't be needing it any more. I thought you'd like it."

Leskov raised his hands. "Peter, we can negotiate."

"No," Marron replied, stabbing fast and hard, "we can't."

*

Marron wiped the blade clean on Leskov's clothes. "Seems our timing was impeccable."

Alex secured the hatch above them. "I'm loving these suits. There was a certain symmetry in using them against Leskov."

"Before we spend too much time congratulating ourselves, we should remember we still have work to do. And what happened to the woman that was with him? She didn't follow him inside?"

Alex peered at a monitor showing a feed outside the submarine. "No sign. Maybe she fell in the sea? Or maybe she has one of the suits as well?"

"It doesn't matter. She was just a lackey. Either she'll die out here, or the US will scoop her up."

"They didn't mess around with those bombs - the Dome has been obliterated. Do you think Bern will have made it out?"

"He's reliable in that respect. How quickly can we be under way?"

Alex moved to the helm and began tapping instructions. "Three minutes. Where are we heading?"

"After Bern, naturally."

"But how are we going to find him?"

"In all the clever trickery he's come up with, he's overlooked one thing: he's still using CERUS nanites. In their uncorrupted state, we can track them."

She frowned. "Sorry, what is he using CERUS nanites in?"

"In the Accumulator, for one thing. And if there is one item that Bern will have made sure he escaped with, it will be the Accumulator."

"The thing that he had stolen from the US? I don't understand, how does that contain CERUS nanites?"

"That's quite a long story, so I'll explain on the way." Marron stood and walked over to a silver flight case. He popped it open to reveal a black cube, pulsing with red and green LEDs. "And when we get there, do remind me that I have a present to drop off."

NINETY-THREE

TOM STOOD ON THE DECK of the aircraft carrier, watching the final crates being secured. Far above there was the sound of a deep rumble.

"It's started," Brody said. He pointed up at the cavern roof, where spirals of rock dust were falling. "We have to hurry."

"We won't even get a hundred metres outside," Tom said. "If we don't surrender, they'll sink us on sight."

"We'll see," Bern said. Above them another huge rumble shook the cavern. "Why don't you go below decks and leave this to those of us who are running things?"

Tom shook his head and made his way to the nearest steps down. On the lower levels there was a steady hum of activity. Men and women in overalls flowed around him, bearing equipment and serious expressions, but nobody was panicking. A security guard recognised him and pointed him to a cabin. George Croft was there, waiting.

"So he did keep his promise to you," Tom said.

"So it seems. I'm sorry about how I brought you here, but, as I think you'll find, William Bern really has changed."

"Doesn't he seem a bit too prepared for this situation? Those tunnels. This ship."

"However well-hidden this base, having an escape route was just common sense."

"The US Navy are just off-shore: we either surrender or get sunk. Unless this thing is equipped with missiles."

"It's equipped with a lot of things. It pretty much *is* the beta site now. It's why he chose an aircraft carrier. Well, and the fact that it has a nuclear power source: important when you can't risk regular fuel stops."

Tom walked over to the porthole. "I guess we won't have long to wait to see how this works out." The staff from the base were untying the ship's moorings. His eye was caught by a sudden movement on the tracks where the tunnel emerged from above. He thought he saw two black objects shoot out of its maw, but as he tracked where they would be, he could see nothing. He rubbed his eyes, realising he felt strange: distracted by an itch he couldn't scratch. Actually, as he thought about it, he was feeling an actual itch. Lots of them. He'd been feeling them off and on for a while, but now the suit was itching all over.

"Something wrong?" Croft asked.

"It's this suit. It feels like it has ants inside it."

"Maybe you're allergic to the fabric?"

Tom reached behind his neck for the zip fastener, but it was stuck. "Can you help undo it?"

"I'm not sure if there's a change of clothes here--"

"There'll be a spare set of overalls somewhere. I need to get it off."

Croft walked up to him and tugged on the zip. "It's jammed."

Tom pushed him away. "I could have told you that."

Croft reached behind his own neck. "You know, mine won't move either." The ship started throbbing. A voice broke over the ship's tannoy system: *'DEPARTING IN SIXTY SECONDS. SECURE FRAGILE ITEMS AND PREPARE FOR RUN-QUIET*

OPERATION.'

"We'll have to sort these suits later," Croft said.

"What's 'run-quiet'?"

"No movement, action or conversation louder than a whisper."

"But what difference will that make? How can they possibly think we can sneak away without being noticed?"

NINETY-FOUR

BERN STOOD ON THE BRIDGE, watching as the aircraft carrier, *Phoenix Reborn*, began to move. Behind them cracks were forming in the cavern ceiling, spirals of dust and fragments of rock falling faster and faster.

Brody cleared his throat. "Time to see if everything was worth the effort."

Bern nodded. "The reactors are online?"

"They're running at 80%. It should be more than enough."

"And the circuits are ready to engage?"

"We only tested it yesterday for the first time, and we only had limited power available, but--"

"I guess we'll find out pretty quickly. What about the Dome?"

Brody pointed at a monitor showing a wide angle view of the dome in ruins. "We won't be going back there."

"I never go back. Anything salvageable?"

"It's possible."

"Then you know what the plan calls for."

Brody took a deep breath. "I do." He leaned forward to the keyboard and brought up a new screen. "If you could confirm your code."

Bern leaned forward and typed in a ten-digit sequence.

Brody tapped a further sequence. A red button lit up on the screen. "It should seem like a secondary explosion, but it will wipe the lower levels. Would you like to do the honours?"

Bern nodded and clicked on the button. Above them came a deep boom, resonating more loudly than before. The *Phoenix Reborn* moved into the tunnel and towards the sea.

"We'll be clear of the cave in thirty seconds," Brody said. "Holding speed at seven knots. Standing ready to activate circuits."

Bern slapped Brody on the back. "Let's get out of here."

*

Thirty thousand tonnes of steel, painted grey-white, approached the exit to the cave system and the cold waters of the Davis Strait. The *Phoenix Reborn* was not a modern design, but it had received a number of modifications in recent weeks, one of which came online as they emerged, its powerful computer drawing power from the nuclear power plants. It fed a complicated matrix of commands into the billions of tiny particles contained in the newly applied paint covering the ship's surface.

The *Phoenix Reborn* rippled, shimmered and vanished from sight.

NINETY-FIVE

TOM STARED OUT OF THE porthole, looking at the huge grey forms of the three destroyers and the accompanying aircraft carrier: a vessel that, at over eighty thousand tonnes, would dwarf them if they were closer. The *Phoenix Reborn*, at least two kilometres away, was sailing slowly but surely for the open waters of the North Atlantic.

And it was being ignored.

"Are they blind?" Tom said in a whisper.

Croft stood next to him. "Can you not guess what is happening?"

Suddenly, it was obvious. "Project Resurface. Somehow they've made a suit on a super-sized scale." He hesitated. "This ship is... *invisible*."

"Effectively."

Tom frowned. "But... what about radar? Won't that pick it up?"

Croft shook his head. "That's just a different wavelength of electromagnetic radiation."

"And the displaced water?"

"The Resurface field displays what is behind the entire vessel - just more sea water. It can't hide the ship's wake, but we're travelling slowly and we're a good distance away from the US fleet. Plus the ocean isn't calm today."

"So they have no way of detecting us?"

"I'm told a secondary effect also absorbs sonar, but obviously it won't block outgoing sound."

"Hence the run quiet instruction," said Bern, appearing at the door.

Tom span to look at him. "This is audacious, even by your standards."

"In fairness, they are a bit distracted." Bern pointed at a grey cloud in the sky. "It was a pretty big explosion."

"Hang on. From the conversations I heard, you literally only just got the invisibility working. Your whole exit plan depended on it?"

Bern shook his head. "The full translucency was a major upgrade, but we were confident we could get it working. And if we hadn't, static camouflage would have given us a very good chance."

Tom shrugged. "So where are we going?"

"That's what I wanted to talk to you about. Follow me. And, just in case our American friends are listening, please do it quietly."

*

A tarpaulin covering one of the lifeboats at the rear of the *Phoenix Reborn* lifted and two pairs of eyes peered out, trying to make sense of what they were seeing.

"You know, it could have been worse," Lentz said.

"How?" replied Kate, rubbing her elbow. "I think you landed on me after we came out of that tunnel."

"Well, excuse me. I was distracted by trying to switch the suits from low-friction mode to translucent."

"It's a bit of a flaw that they can only do one thing at once."

Lentz raised an eyebrow. "One *incredible* thing. But, sure, if that's how you want to view it. It meant we got on board without Bern or his men seeing us. It means we still have the element of surprise."

"To do what?"

"First we find out if Tom is on board. After that, we'll come up with something."

Kate pointed at the navy vessels off to the south. "Why aren't they reacting to us?"

Lentz pulled out her scanner and activated it. Every LED lit up. "It's because they can't see us. Bern's people must have coated the ship in the nanite particles, then activated translucency."

"But wouldn't that take a lot of power?"

"This ship will have a nuclear reactor."

Kate shook her head. "Shouldn't we do something?"

"Like what?"

"Attempt to contact those ships: reveal what is going on?"

"We'd give ourselves away to Bern's crew, who might shoot first, ask questions later. I think we need to find Tom before we try that."

"Then what do we do?"

Lentz looked at an indicator on her belt. "I've tweaked the power consumption, so we've got another twenty minutes of translucency. Let's take a look around."

NINETY-SIX

THE LABORATORY WAS LOCATED TWO decks down. It was filled with equipment. Three technicians were busy working on computers, but one look at Bern and Tom and they quickly left the room.

Bern ran a hand through his hair. "Can I speak candidly?"

"It's your ship."

He nodded. "I wanted to say that I'm sorry about what happened last year."

"You're sorry?" Tom almost choked. "You have to be kidding. Do you think *sorry* really covers it?"

Bern sighed. "Please keep your voice down. And it was a difficult time. I wasn't thinking clearly."

"You oversaw projects that messed with my brain. *Twice*. I think you knew exactly what you were doing."

Bern shook his head. "You were such an incredible success story, you have to admit. The things you could do were... well, we never anticipated how the Interface would develop, but on a scale of 1 to 10, I'd say you were a 14."

"You never asked me. You just did it."

"And I'm sorry. I've had a lot of time to think over the last year: to reflect on what I've done. There are so many things I want to talk to you about. I want you to trust me."

"And you thought sending Croft to abduct me was a good way of achieving that?"

"I needed to save you."

"By injecting me with dark nano. And again you didn't ask."

Bern raised an eyebrow. "Wherever did you get that name?"

"Lentz ran some tests on me when my abilities started going... wrong." Tom hesitated. "The first time I was injected was back in Peru. That was your team there too, I guess."

"We were trying to acquire you before the CIA could."

"They didn't seem like they had my interests at heart."

"When you hire mercenaries in South America, the people with the right field skills don't always have the right people skills. We had to move fast and you've been pretty difficult to find, you know."

"I was threatened at gun point several times."

"If they'd told you the truth, would you have believed them?"

"I don't know who to believe any more. There's no one I can trust."

"Then let me tell you what the dark nanites do. They actively seek out intelligent nano particles, and attach themselves, then they neutralise them. It's not unlike how a virus works."

"That's kind of what Dominique said."

Bern gave a snort. "To the extent she could possibly have understood it. This is technology she has not been involved with, although she does have a habit of refusing to admit she doesn't understand something."

"She might be the smartest person I've ever met."

"Perhaps, but are you really sure you can trust her? She does work for Stephanie Reems. And I think we're in agreement that we can't trust *her*."

"What gives you the remotest idea that I trust *you*?"

"Fair point. And I need to prove myself by permanently removing your problem."

"We had this conversation a year ago. I told you I didn't want it out."

"Yes, but then you didn't know it was going to kill you."

Tom blinked. "What?"

"I'm sure you haven't been feeling well. That's because your Tantalus nanites haven't stopped evolving." Bern closed his eyes. "We've been able to apply a temporary fix, but we don't know what will happen longer term. The dark nano, as you call it, could become detached from the Tantalus nano or degrade in performance. Or it could start to malfunction."

"So I'd get my abilities back?"

"Not like you knew them. There would be side effects that we couldn't predict. Almost certainly harmful ones."

"So you've just made things worse."

"No, it's just we've only done half the treatment. We can cure you, but we have to take the nanites out - and the dark nano makes it possible. We need to transfuse your blood, while applying a targeted filter. We have to draw them all out."

"You think that will work?"

"It's our best shot."

"And it won't hurt me?"

"We don't know, but we have to try."

"Dominique said my nervous system might struggle with the sudden removal of the nanites."

"You know, she used to be a great scientist, but these days I think she's just making things up as she goes along. That is, at best, a wild guess."

"And I'll really be free?"

"That's the plan." Bern placed his hands on Tom's shoulders. "I need things to end differently this time. Give me a chance to save my only son."

Tom stared at his father, trying to decide what to do. He couldn't feel anything - electronic or human. But as he searched inside himself for some kind of sign, he swore he could feel the dark nano eating him away. And the only thing he did somehow know, with absolute certainty, was that if he wasn't treated, he was going to die.

"OK," he said finally. "I'm going to trust you. Let's do this."

NINETY-SEVEN

THE TECHNICIANS RETURNED, AND WERE joined by a doctor. A hospital bed was wheeled in and Tom lay down on it. "Can I get this suit off?" he asked. "It itches like anything."

Bern smiled as he leaned over Tom to help, but the zip refused to budge. "It's stuck. Let's get this done, then we'll cut you out of it and find you a fine new set of clothes."

Tom was about to reply, but a technician used a knife to quickly cut a hole in his sleeve, then jabbed an IV needle into his arm, smiling as she did it. "Mr Faraday, it's important that you relax." She inserted a second needle in his arm, no less roughly, then placed an unconvincing hand on his forehead. "Try to visualise the nanites leaving your system."

Tom raised an eyebrow. "I'm sorry, what?"

"You mustn't exert any residual control over the nanites or they will fight to remain in you."

"But I thought they were neutralised."

"Restrained is a better term. They're still linked to your neural network. If you try to fight this procedure, it won't work."

There was the sound of a table being hit and a set of pliers clattered to the floor. Everyone spun at the noise, but there was nothing to explain it.

"The boat must have shifted," said the technician, stooping to pick the tools up. "I think we're ready to start."

Out of the corner of his eye, Tom saw one of the computer screens scrolling through some data. There was nobody in front of it. Then he blinked. Was there a slight shimmer in the air? He was distracted by Bern's hand resting gently on his shoulder.

"This will change everything," Bern said. "I promise."

"You'll let me leave?"

"If that's what you want."

"And you'll trust me not to turn you in?"

"I've asked you to trust me and trust should always go both ways."

"Then let's do this."

Bern nodded to the technician, who pressed a button. Blood started to cycle through the tubing attached to the IV.

Tom leaned back and cleared his thoughts. "This is an impressive set up you have here. An invisible, movable research facility. They'll never find you again."

"That's the plan."

"But why take the Accumulator when this ship already has a nuclear reactor."

"It has two, but neither is what you'd call portable. Some of our experimental technology needs that functionality. It's *all* about mobile these days."

Tom nodded. Everyone was watching him. Nobody was noticing the computer screen flicking between files behind them. "Well, you certainly plan ahead."

"I've had my fair share of luck," Bern said. "Although the more I plan, the luckier I seem to get."

The screen flickered and showed a technical document, headed 'Nanite Augmentation'.

"Is it working?" asked Bern, turning to the technician.

She looked at her laptop. "38% complete."

"Everything you've done," Tom said, "has been for a reason. Once you set your mind to something, you don't let anything get in your way."

"Right now," Bern said, "I'm setting my mind on getting these nanites out of you and making sure you're OK."

"Ah, but that's only half-right," said a woman's voice. Everybody turned to see Dominique Lentz materialising in front of the computer screen. She wore a grey bodysuit that shimmered in the artificial light. In her hand she held a sophisticated automatic rifle.

"You!" Bern said, stepping backwards.

"William," she smiled, aiming the rifle at him. "It's been a while."

NINETY-EIGHT

TOM WATCHED THE BLOOD STILL cycling through the tubing in his arm. Other than the soft beep from the medical equipment, and the distant rumble of the turbines, everything was silent.

"What do you want, Dominique?" Bern said.

"I want you to stop this process before you kill Tom." Lentz nodded at the screen. "I've just been reading the specifications of your dark nano."

"We're trying to help him."

Lentz hefted the rifle. "It's clear from this that the main purpose--"

"Do it!" Bern shouted. Two guards burst into the room, holding handguns.

She glanced at them warily. "How did you warn them?"

"Concealed comms system in my suit," Bern said. He nodded and both guards fired.

Lentz blinked in surprise as the bullets hit her. But she continued standing. The guards looked at her, dumbfounded, and fired again. There was a dull, flat sound like the bullets had hit concrete. The two men looked at their guns as if they had been deceived.

"OK, my turn now," Lentz let go of her gun, which was slung round her neck on a strap. She pulled two tasers from her belt and fired at the guards. They jerked backwards and collapsed. The technicians shrunk as far back as the wall would allow, but Bern strode towards Lentz. Smoothly, she grabbed and raised her gun again. He stopped.

"My suit has some features that yours doesn't," she said.

"You'll never get off this ship."

"Let me worry about that. Now shut off the filtration."

Bern shook his head. "It's saving his life."

"No, it's killing him. You're not neutralising the nanites: you're stealing them." Lentz nodded at the screen. "It's all in the specs. The dark nano are some form of communication and control mechanism, taking over the existing nanites, boosting their output."

"To do what?"

"I don't know that part," Lentz said. "But they are not designed to shut your original nanites off. Quite the reverse."

"Then why can't I feel my nanites anymore?"

"Because the control part is holding them frozen. I'd wager that the pain you feel is their increased power output."

Tom looked at the blood flowing in and out of his arm. "But don't I want to get them out of me even more now?"

Lentz tapped the screen and a medical risks analysis was displayed. It showed his name. In red, bold text it stated: 'CONSIDERABLE HEALTH RISK TO SUBJECT. NEURAL FAILURE HIGHLY LIKELY.' "It's obvious," she said, "that even if Tom lives, you won't be letting him go. You've gone to so much trouble to hide the fact that you're still alive, there's no way you would take the risk."

"But why," Tom asked, "would he bother with this whole charade about helping me if he was just going to take what he needed and dump me?"

"You remember they asked you to cooperate with the process," Lentz said. "If you resist, they can't remove the nanites. As you once said, they're *your* nanites Tom." She turned to the technician. "How far are we progressed?"

The woman edged closer to the screen, glancing warily at Lentz. "76%."

Tom looked at Bern. "Is what she's saying true? Is what's in that report true?"

"I asked you to trust me, Tom. If I'd wanted you dead, I could have killed you long ago. The only thing that is sure is that you need these awful things out of you. That's what you should focus on."

"83%," muttered the technician.

Tom ground his teeth.

"You need to decide who you believe in a hurry, Tom," Lentz said. "Once that reaches 100% I don't think there's any going back."

Tom closed his eyes. He could faintly feel the nanites: the deserting army that he had ordered away. But, other than that base level of awareness, he was getting nothing from them. He needed something to change. His eyes flicked open. "I'm not angry enough. I know I should be, but after everything that's happened, I'm just too tired."

"You have to fight, Tom. Or you're lost."

"89%," said the technician.

Bern laughed. "Give up, Dominique. This is over."

Lentz pointed at Bern. "You can't let him win. The father who abandoned you, then nearly killed you. And it wasn't just you he wronged. I'm sure there are things about your mother he didn't tell you."

Tom blinked. "Like what?"

"Kate did what you asked. And she uncovered files in the archives. Amelia used to work at CERUS. Then she was fired, just before you were born."

"They got rid of her?" Tom jerked. "Because she was pregnant?"

"Your mother had her own agenda," Bern replied. "The real reason she was..." he cut himself off. "It doesn't matter."

Tom's jaw grew hard. "What do you mean?"

"I don't mean anything. She worked at CERUS. It was how we met. So what?"

Lentz banged her hand on the desk. "It was far more than that. Kate found that your mother changed her identity. A full professional set-up. It could only have been done by a government agency."

Bern shrugged. "You're making this up. But even if you aren't, whatever else Amelia did, I don't know anything about it."

Tom heard the words. And he knew they were a lie. He struggled to sit up. "What are you hiding, William?"

"94%," whispered the technician.

"What's in the past is gone. Live with it."

Behind them another large computer display flickered into life. An image of a computer folder appeared. On it was the name 'Amelia Faraday'.

Bern narrowed his eyes. "Is that you, Dominique? What are you playing at now?"

Lentz raised her hands. "Not guilty."

Tom sat further up. "That's the file I found when I hacked CERUS Tower last year. But it was empty."

The folder opened to reveal a document. It showed a detailed log of Amelia's movements: prior to, during, and after her time at CERUS.

Lentz moved closer, her eyes scanning the display. "She wasn't just an employee. You targeted her! What was this all about?"

"Lies," Bern shouted. "I don't know who put this here, but it's a complete fabrication--"

The document vanished and a video started playing. It showed Bern arriving at a restaurant. He was led to a table where a woman with grey-brown hair was already sitting. The woman took off her glasses. Her face looked old and tired. But there was no doubting who it was: Amelia, Tom's mother.

Bern's face darkened. "So we had dinner. So what--?"

"This wasn't when you were having the affair," Lentz cried. "Look at that newspaper on the table. This was less than four years ago."

"This has been doctored--" Bern shouted.

"No it hasn't," Tom cried. "Why did you meet?"

"She told me she was sick."

"Did she ask for your help?" Tom said with a glare. "Was that why she wanted to meet? Maybe to treat her cancer? Because I know you hold that out as a carrot."

"You need to trust me, Tom." Bern shrugged. "I said we had nothing that could help her."

Tom nodded. "I believe you said that. But was it correct?"

"Yes."

Tom heard the word, and he knew it was a lie. He growled. His eyes slammed shut and he reached out. He could feel the nanites. He could feel the block around them: an almost impenetrable barrier. *Almost.* It would need a great deal of effort to prise the nano apart. Tom shaped his thoughts like a chisel, channelling his anger, his frustration. Then he struck at the barrier.

"97%," said the technician, "Wait. Something's happening."

"Shut it off," Bern shouted. "97% will have to do."

Tom heard the words and he *knew*. Without any doubt. What

Bern really wanted was not to help him, but to help himself. His anger blossomed.

"83%," said the technician, sounding alarmed. "It's not responding to my commands to close the process."

Tom felt the rush as the nanites opened to him. They were familiar, yet different, as if their volume control had been turned up to eleven. Or more. They were telling him things, but it was almost too loud and painful to register. His mind reached out into the systems in the room, to the computer that had displayed the report and the video. It was a discrete system but encrypted, and yet his mind overwhelmed its defences in moments. Then he was reading reports and secure messages. The lights flickered repeatedly. Tom's eyes shot open. "You bastard. You just need the code from my nanites. That's all you ever wanted. Everything else you said was a lie."

"52%," said the technician. "And it's speeding up."

"Dammit, cut the cables," Bern shouted.

"Move and I shoot you," Lentz said. "In fact, why don't you back away from the computer, William, so neither of us gets tempted to do anything rash?"

Tom was filtering through the information, making connections. He was distracted by two more guards bursting into the room.

"Sir, we're reporting fluctuations in the reactor--" they froze as they saw Lentz, then brought their weapons up.

She turned to face them. "Tom, if you have any tricks up your sleeve, now would be the time to play them."

Tom looked up at Bern, suddenly knowing it was too late for any tricks, and knowing what was about to happen. His father held up a remote control and pressed something on it.

"They might be your nanites," Bern said, "but it's my suit. I didn't leave it on you without reason."

The itching changed as every part of his skin touching the suit exploded in pain. He grabbed his head and screamed.

NINETY-NINE

"OK, NOW WE CAN STOP the pretence that I've become nice," Bern said, turning to Lentz. He pointed the device at her and pressed a button.

She froze. Her suit felt like it was made out of concrete.

"Impressed?" Bern asked. "The same control routines that are in the dark nano are also in the Resurface code. I can control your suit, even with all the many *interesting* upgrades you've made to it."

"13%," said the technician.

"Whatever," Bern said. "We have what we need." He walked over to Tom, who was quivering and muttering, his eyes closed. "I might have been lying, son. But Dominique here was wrong. You did want those things out of you. Removing them *might* be fatal, but keeping them *will* kill you."

"What's happening to him?" Lentz asked, twisting to look at Tom. He lay rigid, his eyes staring.

"Neural overload. I'm sending a basic pain signal straight into his nervous system. It'll probably cause no lasting damage at this level of intensity, but it'll definitely prevent him doing anything for a while."

"You've been thinking about this since he beat you last year.

Your own son? Again?"

"Morality is a crutch on which the weak blame failure." Bern raised an eyebrow. "If you want to talk I'd be more interested in the new features you've developed for the suit."

"You think I'd share them with you?"

Bern smiled. "Like you have a choice." He pressed a button on his controller then started reviewing data on a screen. "I like the body armour. Very useful. And low-friction mode: intriguing." He scrolled down. "Some of these other things... Well, I doubt you've tested them. You wouldn't have had enough power available." He looked over her shoulder at one of the guards. "I need the Accumulator brought here immediately."

"You've been planning for this since before the government blocked nano development. How long, William?"

"I realised which way the wind was blowing. I took the necessary steps and, once that decision was made, other steps became necessary. A strong leader has to take control. Tantalus, for example, was all about control. But now my work is about the future. At least, controlling it."

"Not money?" Lentz gasped.

"When you have as much as I do, you have to define other goals. And now we've reached a milestone."

"Some chess-players sacrifice a piece to achieve a greater goal. You sacrifice an entire set, because you're always playing more than one game." Lentz paused for breath. "But you can't plan for everything. You can't plan for an irrational move."

"You? Irrational?" Bern laughed.

"I mean the half-crazed superhero you've created."

"Tom?" Bern glanced at Tom's figure. "As soon as I check that the next phase of my plan has worked I won't need him anymore."

The technician cleared her throat. "Mr Bern, I've completed

the process. With some duplication, the 13% we retained was enough. Your nanites are ready for upload."

Lentz blinked. "Wait, what now?"

Bern smiled. "What did you think this has all been about? They're for me."

Her eyes narrowed. "But they'll kill you."

"Oh, I'm not putting them directly in me - because you're right they probably would kill me - and if not that, then as Tom's experience has shown, there could be many side effects. No, I'm putting them in the suit. The one you helped perfect."

Lentz gasped. "You've built an Interface suit - just like we originally hypothesised."

Bern nodded. "We have the connectivity. The full body contact means the suit's wearer can control its systems - it detects impulses and signals in the skin, and interprets them. But it's only half of the solution."

"Which is why you need Tom's nanites."

"Quite so. I control the suit, and the suit controls the nanites." His smile broadened. "I've created an Interface 2.0. All those concerns about injections and brains overheating, actual brain surgery, that's all in the past."

"But what about when the suit runs flat in twenty minutes?"

"An excellent point." He placed the controller in one of his pockets as a guard came in carrying a container covered with hazard warning symbols.

The technician popped open the container and removed a black cube-like object with LED displays on each surface. "Ready for insertion," she said.

"No!" Lentz cried. "That's your power supply?"

Bern turned so that the technician could slide the cube into what she'd thought was a backpack, but was clearly a custom housing for the power source. He tapped a touch-screen on his wrist and there was a low-frequency hum as something engaged. His suit shimmered. "You wait until I've calibrated this. Then you'll see what nanites can do," he said.

"I've seen what nanites can do," replied Lentz. "And it rarely ends well."

Bern walked over to her, leaning close. She could feel the hum of power from his suit. "I'm the one who says when it ends."

Lentz tried to lean away, but her own suit held her fast. "You've got what you wanted. Now stop hurting Tom. There's no need for it. Let me help him."

Bern closed his eyes. "I knew you'd solve the problems, but you went so much further. Once his nanites connect with my suit's operating system, I'll have an interface of my own."

Lentz's eyes flickered over his shoulder. "You'll have a chance to test out that suit quite soon I think."

"Oh?"

"When I spoke about Tom as a half-crazed super hero, it turns out I wasn't only talking about *your* child."

Bern frowned as Lentz pointed at one of the monitors. It showed a view of the deck of the *Phoenix Reborn*. Several men lay motionless. A woman dressed in a black bodysuit stood over them, looking straight at the camera.

Alex.

Bern growled in anger.

Then he vanished.

ONE HUNDRED

KATE MADE A STEADY COUNT in her head, trying to keep the beat. With the suit working its invisibility magic, she couldn't see her watch or her wrist. By her count she had another seven minutes to locate the item of equipment Lentz had sent her to find. The problem was that there was equipment everywhere. Every corridor, every room was full of advanced tech, mostly stamped with the CERUS logo. She could imagine the firm's auditors having a fit about how many assets had somehow walked out the door. But that was not her concern right now. She needed to find an operational nexus, drawing a tremendous amount of power.

There were many personnel, lots of them scientists, moving quietly about their duties. There were also a few guards. None of them seemed to be looking for an invisible infiltrator. She finished searching one corridor. None of these systems were what she was looking for. She could almost feel the battery in her suit drawing its last breaths. There was no way she was going to have long enough. The vessel was simply too large.

If only she'd been able to borrow Lentz's phone with its scanners and detectors. Instead, all she had was her brain. She stopped and closed her eyes. How could she narrow down the options? How could she use what she knew to help her? She stretched and breathed deeply, as she would before practising karate. She felt the smooth fabric of the Resurface suit teasing over her skin and she imagined for a moment she could feel the tiny particles coating its surface.

She shivered.

Could she feel them? Maybe it *was* more than her imagination. The sensation was a little like when she had been close to the dark nano, but not as unpleasant. It had a certain character, a certain texture that she couldn't quite define. Wouldn't the Resurface generator for the ship share the same technology? Might it feel the same?

She held her breath and tried to detect it, but there was nothing. She swore and a crew member ten metres away glanced around, puzzled. She quickly closed her mouth and he shrugged and walked on. Her heart beat faster, her blood pounding.

And then she felt it.

She wasn't quite sure what *it* was: like a touch on her skin that was not a touch. It was below her and ahead somewhere. With a half-smile she made her way to the nearest staircase and descended.

Four minutes later, she found what she was looking for: a room next to one of the two reactors. Two scientists stood monitoring a bank of screens next to a large computer set up. Next to that stood several heavy, metal-coil arrays, plastered with warning symbols and vibrating ominously. Kate stepped aside to let an armed guard walk past her and up the stairs she had just descended. That left her and the two scientists.

How long did she have? In her excitement she had forgotten to count. What should she do? There had been no announcement on the tannoy system. Did that mean Lentz had failed? At the base of her spine, she felt a glow of warmth. Was that the suit's battery? Her heart pounding again, she stepped forward, between the blissfully unaware scientists. Behind a glass panel was a large red switch: EMERGENCY POWER CUT OFF. Kate shook her head and lifted the glass.

She threw the switch as the battery in her suit died. All around her, alarms shattered the air. The two scientists turned towards her.

The first froze where he stood.

The second tried to grab her, shouting: "What have you done?"

Kate stepped smoothly aside, gripping his arm and twisting it behind his back until he yelped. "I've saved us," she said, gritting her teeth.

"No," he hissed, "you've signed our death warrants." He nodded over at the metal coils. "As soon as those discharge, the system goes offline."

"I know."

He turned to look at her, his expression white. "And then we're all dead."

"We'll see."

"Exactly!" said the scientist. "The fleet out there will see us."

Kate pushed him away. "Doesn't mean they'll try to destroy us. We're worth more alive." She looked at the coils, which were vibrating at a lower frequency. "How long?"

"Five minutes." He rubbed his arm angrily. "Maybe less."

"And you're not going to try and turn it back on?" she said, her eyes narrowing.

"Can't be done: not until the capacitors have discharged and reset, by which time it will be too late." A phone rang on the wall. The first scientist picked it up, listened then, with a look of shock, held it towards Kate.

"Yes?" she said.

"It's for you."

ONE HUNDRED ONE

BERN MOVED LIKE A GHOST through the corridors of the ship. The Resurface nanites bound together to present a shimmering in the air and nothing more. He was, at last, beyond scrutiny, beyond oversight, beyond control. He was free.

The suit was the culmination of all his work. *He* had made this happen. *He* had brought the money, people and technology together, fighting off almost incalculable opposition. He wanted to savour the moment.

But first he had something to attend to. Or rather *someone*.

He had no idea how Alex was here: how she had found her way to the middle of nowhere and onto a vessel that was theoretically invisible. He had no idea how she was even still alive. But it didn't matter: no one could stand in his way now.

With a smile he climbed to the top of the stairs, and stepped onto the deck. A breeze wafted over him. In the suit, he couldn't feel the cold. Instead he felt so much more: the ripple of the webbing, the shimmer of the Resurface coating, and the flow of the nanites. Within its fabric he could tell the interface was forming. But even before it did, he had considerable capabilities at his disposal. And now he would get to test them.

To his surprise, Alex was not hiding. Nor was she standing,

ready to fight. Instead she sat, cross-legged, eyes closed as if in meditation. Around her lay the broken bodies of his guards. He could see she had not been merciful. He approached her. Invisible. Silent.

She placed her palms on the deck. "I thought I might have to rescue you. But clearly I should never have doubted your capabilities."

He froze. Held his breath.

"Although you do make more noise than a herd of water buffalo."

Bern controlled his breathing. She had to be guessing.

"I've waited a long time for this moment. For us to finally stop him. I'm sorry I had to leave you for a little while, but you always knew I'd find you again. Once I found my father." She paused. "But something's different." She tipped her head. "You seem... different?"

Bern began moving silently to one side. Something about her was unsettling him.

"Are we no longer friends?" She held her face up. "You can't hide from me. I can *smell* you."

She must have simply heard a noise and presumed it was him. He stepped quietly around her, standing directly behind, an arm raised to strike.

"You want to fight? I guess you have to learn somehow. But not bowing to me first, that really is rude."

Was she crazy? Or did she really know he was there?

"Where did you get your suit?" she said suddenly. "Did you steal one from your father?"

Bern shook his head. She *was* crazy. And she needed to die. He swung a blow at her head. She could not possibly see it coming. As he moved, her words echoed in his skull. *"Did you steal one from your father?"*

Alex moved like a flower opening, but so fast his eyes could not track it. Her legs slid out in a rotating motion and she swept him from his feet. He hit the deck hard, landing on something in his pocket; pain shot up his leg. The effect was shocking, disorienting. He was supposed to be in charge.

She stood and bowed formally to him, then eased into a stance. Balanced. Poised.

Ready.

He rolled quietly away to regain his breath. She seemed totally at ease. He wasn't sure whether to be more shocked that she knew he was there or that she wasn't surprised that he was invisible. Then something rippled through his suit. An unpleasant sensation. Something was wrong with his left arm. Frowning, he looked at it. He could see it. Even as he realised the suit must be damaged, he saw the rest of the Resurface field falter and he shimmered into view. He looked back at Alex and saw shock on her face. Of course an invisible person had just materialised in front of her. But as he looked at her expression he realised it wasn't that she was seeing *someone* materialise. It was that she was seeing *him* materialise.

"You?" Her expression was one of overwhelming confusion, like the moon had risen in place of the sun. Her voice was like boiling mercury. "Where is Tom? What have you done with him?"

Bern hesitated. "You thought I was Tom? Why?"

Her eyes hardened.

Bern knew he had been right to be unsettled, but wrong to ignore the feeling. He had made a mistake. He resolved not to make another.

ONE HUNDRED TWO

IN THE LABORATORY, LENTZ HAD been half-watching Tom, half-watching a live feed of Bern confronting Alex on deck, when her suit had unfrozen. Managing not to cry out, she had stretched cautiously, assessing the situation - the guards and technicians' attention still fixed on the fight playing out on the screen.

The two guards realised too late that something was wrong, turning just as Lentz fired her second pair of tasers, knocking them out. The scientists exchanged looks and ran from the room. With a quick motion, Lentz shut the door and started doing what she did best: taking control.

An alarm was sounding somewhere in the ship. Using the nearest computer terminal she quickly traced the problem to a room next to one of the nuclear reactors. She had no doubts who had set it off and quickly placed a call to the room.

Three minutes later, Kate hurried into the lab. Together, they pulled heavy equipment across the door, then turned to look at Tom. He was lying on the bed, his face a terrible shade of grey.

Kate rushed over. He was shivering. "What's happening to him? Is it what he was injected with in South America?"

"That was only a partial dose. Bern boosted it, then filtered it."

"Is it... contagious?"

"If it were, then we'd already be infected. This is personal: special nano designed to attack Tom, and Tom alone. And with a specific purpose."

"What purpose?"

"To capture the output of Project Tantalus so Bern could copy his abilities in a way that he could use for himself."

"I thought the nanites would simply kill a normal person, like all the original test subjects. Why would he risk that?"

"Because he's found a new way." She patted the fabric of her suit. "He's put the nanites in one of these. Once it starts working, he will control the suit, and the suit will control the nanites."

"Someone needs to give that man a permanent smacking. For all the awful stuff he's done." Kate placed her hand on Tom's forehead. "Why is he ill?"

"I think the leftover dark nano is poisoning him, but that's just a guess. Or it could be from when Bern jacked a burst of power into Tom's nervous system. That may well have changed the nano again."

"So, basically, you have no idea."

"I'm sorry."

Tom's eyes flickered open. "Kate?" A smile fluttered across his face before a grimace overtook it. "Dominique? How did you both get here?"

"Long story," Lentz said. "How do you feel?"

Tom screwed up his face. "Wrong, on so many levels."

"Let me see if I can help." Lentz held out her phone and started making adjustments to a calibration tool.

"Is it the nanites you stopped them removing from me?"

"I thought I was helping you." She frowned as she read the display. "This can't be right. You're definitely still in pain?"

"Are you kidding?" Tom said, through gritted teeth. "It's like there's acid in my veins. Acid that's on fire."

Kate gripped his shoulder, shivering as she did so.

"I need it to stop," he hissed.

"I don't know why it hasn't," Lentz replied. "According to my scan, there's no dark nano in your system. It's just your own nano, 100%."

"Then what's causing the pain?" Kate asked.

"It's different than before," Tom said. "Then I couldn't feel my abilities. Now I *wish* I couldn't."

Lentz shook her head. "The dark nano might be gone, but the nanites left behind have changed. They're malfunctioning, mutating randomly. If I could study them properly I might--"

Kate glared at her. "Spare us the theorising. Can you *do* anything about it?"

"Given more time, I might be able to find a way to get new code to propagate, maybe to shut them down. Of course that would--"

"What is going on there?" Tom sat up suddenly, staring at the display monitor. "Alex is here too?"

On the screen, Bern and Alex were warily circling each other.

"I don't know how she got here," Lentz replied, "but she's bought us some time."

Tom shook his head. "She always knows where I am. She can sense my nanites."

Lentz looked suddenly interested. "Bern used them in his suit."

Tom shook himself, rising up onto his elbows, gasping. "I don't care how much it hurts. I've got to stop him."

"You're in no fit state to go anywhere," Lentz said. "Besides, it's not like you even have your abilities. Whereas he has many."

"I have to try." He rolled forward on to his knees.

"Just let them kill each other," Kate said. "The world will be a better place if they do."

Tom shook his head. "I can't let that happen."

"You want to save your father?"

"I didn't say that." Tom slowly began standing. "Besides, he doesn't need saving."

Kate frowned. "You're trying to save *her*?"

Tom closed his eyes. "I have to help Alex. My father cannot be allowed to win."

"Dominique, you're not going to let him go, are you? He's clearly all messed up."

Lentz shook her head. "I don't think you should go, Tom." She sighed. "But it's your choice."

ONE HUNDRED THREE

"WHAT DO YOU WANT, ALEX?" Bern said, taking a cautious step away from her.

She stood, staring, her eyes dark pools of oblivion as she assessed him. "I want Tom." She dragged her boot across the deck, scraping an imaginary line between them. "And then I want retribution." She closed her eyes. "I'm not leaving without getting both."

Bern held his breath. He knew Alex was a capable resource. Marron had used her for many of his more difficult operations: the ones Bern had always preferred to know as little about as possible. But something about her had changed. She had always been confident, but now there was an air of invincibility. She didn't appear to be carrying a weapon, yet the bodies of seven of his guards lay around her.

"You weren't expecting me, were you?" he said. "You were certain I was Tom."

Her eyelids fluttered. "Tell me where he is. Now."

"Does he really deserve your wrath?"

Again she looked confused. Then she sighed and rolled her eyes. "I don't want retribution against Tom. I want it against you."

"You think you'll kill me?"

Alex shrugged. "It's what happens when I fight someone. And in the last twelve months I've fought a lot of people. You could call it a bit of a personal quest."

"Maybe I'll be different."

She gave a snort. "Because of your suit?"

Bern blinked. "What do you mean?"

"The CERUS tech you're wearing. It gives you certain advantages, like the erratic invisibility."

Bern swore. "How could you possibly know that?"

Alex folded her arms. "As I said, a lot of things about me might surprise you."

"I'm sure, but they won't be enough."

"Really? Did you bring some weapon that I haven't seen?"

Bern went to take another step back, but checked himself. "What makes you think I need one?"

"Against me you will, and I like everyone to have a fair chance." She looked around her then moved towards a rolled fire hose and a red handled axe behind glass. With a jab from her elbow, she shattered the glass and retrieved the axe. Then, with a smooth motion, she slid it across the deck towards Bern.

He stopped it with his foot. "You want me to use this?"

"Unless you have something better to hand."

Bern reached forward and picked up the axe. "You really are overconfident, aren't you?"

"It's only overconfidence if I'm wrong. Of course you wouldn't have come out here to take me on unless you thought you had a huge advantage." She pointed to the axe. "Shall we find out if you're right?"

ONE HUNDRED FOUR

WITH THE EFFORT OF WALKING, Tom was feeling far worse. He staggered up the metal stairs, tipping from side to side, his legs like heavy wet sacks. Around him people moved quickly out of the way, as if they'd rather not have seen him at all. They knew who he was and they knew he was trouble. He probably looked like he was dying. The pain was becoming almost unbearable, but he had to get to Alex. They had to stop Bern, if that was even possible.

Somehow it had come to this - his only chance to defeat his father was to collaborate with someone else who had tried to kill him. Someone to whom he now had the strangest of connections. He shivered.

Above him the artificial lights were flickering angrily. It made it hard to see and, as he turned a corner, his suit snagged on a broken strut in the handrail. Cursing, he pulled away and a long strip tore off. He looked at the artificial webbing underneath and shuddered as he remembered how Bern had used the suit against him: his salvation and his doom, like the nanites forced upon him a year ago. How could he ever have believed Bern had changed? At least Alex was true to who she was. No lies. No deception. Just an unstoppable force.

Except that would not be true against Bern. Not with him wearing the suit. Tom began to climb again, but even slower. *He* was still wearing a suit; if he emerged on deck wearing it, what was to stop Bern controlling him again? He had to get out of it.

Reaching behind his head, he found the zip, but it was still jammed. Bern had rigged it that way obviously. Yanking hard, he only succeeded in hurting his neck. Muttering, he looked around for something sharp. Another scientist appeared on the stairs, saw him, went pale and ran away before Tom could speak. The frustration was swept away by a wave of pain and Tom collapsed forward onto his knees. He screamed. At the same moment, all the lights went out.

He had to try and focus: to regain control. He stuck his hand out, feeling for the handrail, and hit something sharp and metallic: the broken railing.

He smiled inwardly then took a deep breath. With eerie timing the lights flickered back on. He nodded to himself and placed the broken strut of the railing against one of the seams of the suit. On the second attempt the strut flexed and snapped off; he picked it up and continued working. Three minutes later, he stepped out of the last shreds of fabric, wearing just undershorts and a t-shirt. He felt exposed, but free. He had removed at least one ace from Bern's deck.

He tucked the broken strut into his waistband, then wearily started climbing the final flights of stairs. At the top, the metal door hung open. He looked across the deck and saw two figures circling each other. He tried to call out but his voice was weak. His legs finally collapsed under him and he fell to his knees.

He fell forward, hitting his head on the deck.

ONE HUNDRED FIVE

BERN COULD SENSE THE NANITES in his suit configuring the Interface, but it was not yet complete. Still, Lentz had provided a great many feature upgrades. Most were untested. *He would soon change that.*

He hefted the axe and stepped towards Alex, swinging to get the feel of it: to see how she would react. She stepped aside smoothly. He quickly swung again, this time with more intent. He still hit nothing but air.

"Had much combat training?" she asked, looking utterly untroubled.

"A little." He swung a third time. She leaned back as the axe-head sailed inches from her face. "I was on a local fencing team, before I--"

"Got arrested? Not really the same thing, fighting with a cocktail stick. Although I'd have thought you would have learned about fighting in jail."

"They kept me in isolation at a special facility." He jabbed a fake blow, but she didn't even flinch.

"And you've never been one to do your own fighting, have you? Prefer to outsource it."

"I don't think there's any rule against paying someone to do something for you." With a cry he swung the axe in a high arc. It smashed into the deck where she had been a moment before, sparks flying. He struggled to hold onto it as the handle reverberated.

"You're not really trying," she said.

Bern gritted his teeth. "I could say the same. You haven't even struck back."

"I'm waiting for the right moment."

"You have some reason, I assume."

She smiled.

He moved forward again, but this time he activated the suit. Power flowed through the fabric, rippling from nanite particle to nanite particle, reinforcing the acceleration of his movement. The axe blurred and whistled, the blade grazing her arm. A few drops of blood flew onto the deck.

She stepped back and ran her finger along the cut, bringing the blood to her lips. Her eyelids flickered momentarily. "That's more like it," she said. "You have something in your suit that I don't."

"I do like to be on the bleeding edge." He nodded at the axe blade. "If you'll pardon the pun."

"Just do it again," she hissed.

Almost without thinking, the instructions reached into the suit and he felt his arms moving faster than was possible. The blade screamed as it made for her neck.

But Alex ducked under it and drove her shoulder into his stomach, launching him back. He fell across the deck, landing heavily, the axe flying from his grasp.

"You're fast," she said. "But there's no subtlety. It's like fighting a wounded bear."

Bern jumped to his feet, ready to fight back. She was already upon him, fists flying, striking his torso. He tried to twist away, but there was nothing he could do to avoid her. The suit hardened to her touch. She looked in irritation at his stomach.

"Apparently a wounded *armoured* bear. Still, you've no real technique. You're just fast and strong, with a tough shell."

"Qualities that are not undesirable in a fight."

She snorted. "You have nothing to teach me. There's no art to your moves."

"I didn't realise I was here to teach you."

"Everybody is. Until I've learned all I need to." She looked around her. "Now let's see just how impermeable that suit is."

And then Bern realised what she was looking for.

The axe.

Alex was already there. She hooked the weapon with her toe and flipped it into the air, catching it effortlessly and twirling it from one hand to the other. "I can feel you, William. I can feel your life in my hands." She stopped the axe, holding it still. "Do you feel it?"

"You really don't doubt yourself do you?"

"Not ever." And she swung, hard. Bern tried to fall away from the strike, but he was far too slow. The blade hit him square in the stomach. The blow should have cut him in two.

Instead the head of the axe crumpled like it had hit a granite wall. The handle split, the head falling to the ground.

Alex stared at the remains of the handle in her hands. "That's not fair."

Bern snorted. "And you fight fair?"

"Don't confuse me with my father. I take a bit more pride in my craft." She shook her head. "This is going to be tedious if I can't hurt you."

Bern looked at her. "You seem more irritated than surprised by my suit. How do you know so much about it?"

She smiled. "Because I'm wearing one." She ran her hands

over the smooth black fabric. "And I have to say it looks better on me." She began to advance on him.

In an instant, Bern knew what he had to do.

ONE HUNDRED SIX

REEMS STOOD ON THE DECK, staring out at the ocean, trying not to blink. She wasn't sure what she was hoping to see, just that she was looking for something.

Footsteps approached, and Truman handed her a cup of something that smelt a little like coffee. She took it, appreciating the warmth, but did not otherwise acknowledge him. She wasn't ready for that.

"I'm sorry about your people," he said finally.

"I haven't given up on them yet."

"If we were going to detect them, we would have done so by now." Truman sighed. "We've made an initial review of what happened with the jets. The pilots heard my voice: the cockpit recording confirms it. Except, of course, you were with me the whole time and you know I gave no such order."

"And yet how could someone impersonate you, given the level of encryption involved?"

"Not clear."

"But who would have known what was going on to the point that they could interject at exactly the right moment?"

"It's a very short list."

"What did Banetti say?"

Truman hesitated for several moments. "He asked if the situation was secure. I said all the evidence pointed to the destruction of the Accumulator at the site."

"Did you mention Lentz's warning that it had been removed?"

"There's nothing to support that claim."

Reems gripped the handrail tight. "Don't you get it? Once again, Bern showed us what he wanted us to see. With Bern there's always a way out. We just haven't thought of it yet."

"I'll believe it when I see it."

"That's the problem. Maybe you won't."

There was a shout across the deck. Two crewman stood pointing. Reems followed their gaze. In the distance there was a shimmer. And then a ripple. And then something unbelievable appeared out of thin air.

ONE HUNDRED SEVEN

"THIS IS *MY* SUIT NOW," Alex said, as she continued to advance on Bern.

He reached into his pocket and pulled out the remote control then pointed it and pressed. Alex froze where she stood. "Actually, it's very much still mine. Most convenient you should be wearing it."

The sinews in Alex's neck stood out as she strained against the now-rigid fabric. A roar emerged from between frustrated lips.

"I might ask where you got it," Bern said, "but it doesn't really matter."

"Coward," she hissed. "I will not be contained."

"Ah, but you will – just long enough anyway. Now where's another fire axe?" Bern looked around the deck and saw a figure lying near the stairwell. He marched over and crouched beside the slumped form, wearing only a pair of shorts and a t-shirt. With a gentle push, he flipped Tom onto his back, his fingers tingling slightly at the touch. "How the hell did you get up here?"

Tom groaned, his eyelids flickering. "Must stop..." He seemed to focus on Bern. "Am I too late?"

Bern gripped him by the shoulders. "You saw Alex was here? You came to help me?"

Tom blinked rapidly, shaking his head. "Have to stop..." He grimaced. "It hurts..."

Bern felt his son's forehead. He was running a fever, his skin a sickly grey colour. "It's OK, she's just over there. She's incapacitated: no threat to us. Soon to be no threat to anyone. Never mind that for now. Why isn't the Interface working?"

Tom looked at him, confusion on his face. He clutched his head. "After what you did--"

"Yes, yes. I'm sorry about that. But I'm talking about *my* Interface. I promise to do everything in my power to help you get well again, if you help me with this now."

Tom nodded slowly. "It's hard to describe. You kind of feel the electronics around you and extend your thoughts towards them."

"That's it? And then it just worked?"

"Not at first. I tried all sorts of things. Eventually, I had a moment of great need."

"Well, I need it now. I really want it to work."

Tom shook his head, gritting his teeth. "More than that. A matter of life or death."

Bern turned and glared at where Alex was still standing. "*She's* been trying to kill me for the last few minutes."

"Apparently you didn't believe it."

Bern swore. "Fine. I'll worry about it later. For now we need to deal with her."

Tom narrowed his eyes. "Why is she here?"

"She said she wanted to see you. Just as well I found her first. Now, would you like the chance to pay her back? Revenge would be sweet, wouldn't it?"

Tom seemed to consider this for several moments. "You mean I get to kill her?"

Bern nodded. He reached down and removed the metal strut

from Tom's waistband. "You could use this. It looks sharp enough."

"Are you just getting someone else to do your dirty work for you again?"

"This isn't about my dirty work, Tom. This is about your retribution."

"Why is she just standing there?"

"She got hold of one of my suits. So I froze it like I froze yours."

"It's holding her in place?"

Bern nodded. "No way she can take it off unaided."

"That control works on any of your suits?"

"Any except mine." Bern waved the metal strut. "Now, shall we?"

ONE HUNDRED EIGHT

TOM GRIMACED BUT NODDED. "I'M ready." He stood awkwardly, then walked towards where Alex was standing. Every step sent agony through him. He had none of his abilities and the pain made him all but helpless - and already the biting cold was cutting into his bones. The only factor in his favour was that Bern had made some incorrect assumptions. Tom looked down at Alex.

"Great timing," she said. "Here to rescue me?"

Tom glanced from Bern to her. "What does it look like?"

"It looks like none of us understands exactly what is going on."

Bern stepped forwards and handed Tom the metal strut. "Actually it's very simple. He's here to deal out some justice."

She laughed. "Not something you've ever been keen to face."

"But today is your day. Are you up to this, Tom?"

Tom gripped the metal strut. "Like I said, I'm ready."

Alex's eyes lowered to the strut. "Not exactly an honourable death."

"You're right," Tom said. "I certainly wouldn't do this if you weren't frozen in that suit. And there's no way you can take it off on your own. It would seem you're done for."

She blinked. "Yes, it would."

"You understand what I must do."

"I do."

Bern coughed. "At the edge of the face. It's the weakest point - where the face cover joins the rest of the suit."

Tom nodded. "I need to do this. To make things right."

He struck. The jagged metal tip caught in the collar of her suit, tearing the seam, and he ripped it down, making a great rend in the rubbery fabric. Tom ripped further, cutting down below Alex's waist as Bern lunged at him. Alex stepped from the remnants of her suit as Tom spun, raising the strut in defence. Bern's suit-clad hand gripped it like a vice and yanked it from him.

"Why would you do this?" Bern shouted. "You came up here to save me!"

"I came up here to *stop* you."

Bern's expression turned to one of rage. He raised the metal strut. Tom saw it crashing down towards him. Nothing was going to stop it.

Except there was a loud tearing sound and a booted foot hit Bern's wrist, knocking the improvised weapon from his hand. Before Bern could react, Alex had somersaulted over him and, gripping the arm that had been holding the metal strut, she continued the motion, flinging him away across the deck, where he sprawled heavily.

She turned to Tom. "Thank you."

"Thank me later. Worry about him first."

She nodded and moved herself between Tom and Bern.

The older man had rolled to his feet. "You can't win," Bern said, tilting his head to one side.

She smiled and leapt at him, twisting in the air, her movements almost impossible to follow. But he moved faster, catching her extended foot and throwing her over his shoulder. Alex landed with a roll and spun to face him. "OK, you're improving," she muttered. "That's a concern."

Bern snarled. "Let's just end this."

She swung her head around. "Do you know what one does when faced with an opponent who outmatches you in every way?"

"What?"

"Look for complications. Can you swim?"

"What?"

"Let's find out." She sprinted forward, diving low, and head-butted him. He staggered backwards, then her shoulder caught him in the stomach, and she picked him up like a sack of flour. Bern screamed in surprise, flailing, as she charged to the edge of the deck. He tried to hit her, to break free, but it was futile. Then she threw him over. He fell with a shriek that was lost in the wind.

Tom staggered towards her, tripping as he walked.

Alex smacked her hands together. "Can't believe I didn't think of it sooner. Sea temperature is about four degrees centigrade here. He'll be dead in two minutes." She looked over the side. "Always remember your environment in any fight."

"You think it'll be that easy?"

"What's he going to do? Fly back up? Now it's time we got out of here."

"How?"

"The same way I arrived. Trust me, we have a plan."

"*We*?"

"Let's keep that part a surprise."

ONE HUNDRED NINE

BERN FELL THROUGH THE COLD air. Alex's move had caught him completely off-guard. Such a simple idea, so quickly executed. Below him was an ocean of near freezing water and near-certain death. The suits had not been designed to work immersed in water. What would happen to the power supply? He had been guilty of a stupid mistake in assuming he was invincible.

He needed a solution. One of the upgrades Lentz had so unwittingly provided perhaps? Could he adjust the Resurface nanites to somehow produce a waterproof barrier? Could he signal his crew to rescue him? All of these thoughts rushed through his head, faster than he rushed through the air, but there was no time to do anything. He needed a miracle.

Deep inside the suit, something changed. There was the sense of a switch being thrown. It was as if the world was suddenly twisted into sharp, colourful focus. Suddenly he could feel the suit like it was part of him: its control systems, its architecture, its capabilities. The very idea that it could do only one thing at once was, he realised, laughable. All it needed was control and power.

And in his backpack was the Accumulator, all its near-limitless power at his disposal.

He could do *anything*.

*

Up on deck Tom watched as Alex tapped a code into a small communicator.

"Who are you calling?" he asked, staring around them.

"Our ride, but don't worry: it's a special paired communicator. No one can listen in."

"Does the ship feel different to you?"

"No, but it's about to look different." There was a heavy thump, as if something had hit the carrier. "What was that?"

Tom was about to say something when pain erupted in every part of him. He screamed in agony, falling to his knees. In front of him, a hand appeared over the edge of the deck. And then another. And then with the inevitability of a mountain, William Bern hauled himself back into view.

Alex stepped forward. "Not possible."

Bern stretched slowly, as if unkinking tired muscles. "I'm afraid it is. Tom will know what is going on, and I have him to thank for it. In more ways than one."

Tom closed his eyes. "The Interface."

"Now my control over the suit is truly sophisticated. Watch." He held out a hand and, across the deck, the broken metal strut twitched.

"Telekinesis?" Alex asked.

"No," Tom said, "magnetism. He's adjusting the properties in the suit's surface. It was one of Lentz's next-generation features." He coughed. "That was the loud thump: him clamping to the side of the ship."

Bern nodded. "Now I believe someone just tried to kill me. And that deserves a response." He ran at Alex.

Tom watched as she read his trajectory and began moving away, but then Bern's suit shimmered. He landed suddenly, his feet thudding down on the deck like they were vacuuming to it. Alex launched a blow, but Bern caught her arm and twisted sharply. There was a loud crack and Alex's face went white with fury. Bern extended his other hand away from her and the broken strut flew into it. He spun it in his hand then rammed it into Alex's shoulder.

She staggered backwards as Bern turned to Tom and closed his eyes.

Tom felt something inside him lurch. The damaged nanites within him were straining to the commands of a new master. He felt himself being forced into a kneeling position.

"Whose nanites are they now?" Bern asked.

"I don't care. I never wanted this."

"You have to play the hand you're dealt."

Tom looked up, trying to convey every drop of hatred he could muster over the overwhelming pain in his body. And then over Bern's shoulder he saw something. Something huge.

"Any final words?" Bern asked, his suit crackling with power. "Either of you?"

"Alex," Tom said, continuing to look behind Bern, "is that why you said we had to leave?"

Alex had her hand around the metal strut and was trying to pull it out. She gave a pained smile. With a hiss, she pulled the strut from her shoulder. The jet of blood that followed seemed to stop almost immediately.

"You really should look behind you," Tom told Bern.

Bern raised his hands. "What is this, a pantomime?"

A booming male voice reverberated around the deck. "*THIS IS THE* USS INIMITABLE *HAILING UNDESIGNATED RUSSIAN-CLASS AIRCRAFT CARRIER. YOU WILL*

SURRENDER IMMEDIATELY OR WE WILL--"

The voice was cut off suddenly to be replaced by a female one: *"BERN, YOU BASTARD. YOU HAVE A LOT OF EXPLAINING TO DO."*

Bern gave a final glare at Alex and Tom, then spun, a smile appearing on his face. "Stephanie? Is that you?" He slowly raised his hands. "I surrender. As always you are completely in control."

Alex staggered over to Tom. "We need to get out of here. Now."

Tom nodded to the approaching warship. "Isn't it too late for that?"

She shook her head. "Trust me. Which might be difficult given I just did this to your father."

"What--?"

With a sharp thrust, she pushed Tom over the side. He plummeted downwards, hitting the blue-black water with an explosion of cold. His chest and head screamed, as he plunged below the surface, vaguely aware of someone else entering the water next to him.

And then it got really cold.

ONE HUNDRED TEN

THREE ATTACK HELICOPTERS HOVERED OVER the *Phoenix Reborn*. Beneath them, William Bern sat cross-legged, waiting. A larger, transport helicopter landed on the deck. Eight heavily-armed navy SEALS emerged and surrounded him, shouting instructions. Another transport helicopter landed at the other end of the flight deck. Twelve more SEALs poured forth and ducked below decks.

Bern raised his hands as two SEALS rushed forward to search him. He was cuffed with plastic ziplocks and guided towards the first transport helicopter. Truman and Reems stepped from it.

"Welcome aboard," Bern said, with a smile. "Quite a show of force."

Two jets screamed overhead, as if reinforcing the point.

"We don't want you to be under any illusions as to who is in control here, Mr Bern," Truman said.

"Being in control means not having to say it," Bern replied. "Stephanie, lovely to see you again. How have you been?"

She glared at him.

"We had a deal, Mr Bern," Truman said. "You reneged, to say the least."

"I doubt you planned to honour your side of things. All you

wanted was free access to my tech." He nodded to Reems. "Governments are all the same."

"You stole something from us," Truman said. "The Accumulator. We know you used your chameleon suit to frame Tom Faraday. Now where is the device because I'm guessing it wasn't destroyed in the Dome."

Reems cleared her throat. "More importantly, where is Tom? Did you get him out of there?"

"Indeed I did," Bern replied. "He's right--" He turned and frowned. "He *was* right here." He took a step back.

"Stay where you are," Truman said.

Bern turned to Reems. "You seem to be here as a passenger."

"This isn't my operation."

"Frustrating for you. Well, I did not *steal* the Accumulator. You might say I recovered it seeing as the CIA stole it from CERUS in the first place. The power cell is based on our nanotech."

"That's ridiculous. If you had designed it, you would have built your own."

"Exactly. Admittedly it was not operational at the time. Still, it took an insider to get it."

Reems coughed. "Truman, is this true?"

"Of course not," Truman said. "He's deranged."

Bern smiled. "So you don't know. But now you hear it, you think it might be true, don't you?"

Reems raised an eyebrow. "Is this why Banetti has been so sensitive?"

"We'll explore the details back in DC," Truman said.

"I don't think I want to go there," Bern said.

"What you want is irrelevant. Now are you going to tell us where the Accumulator is, or do we have to tear this ship apart? I'm getting weary."

"You're weary?" shouted Bern. "I'm the one who has put in all the preparation and planning. I have taken incredible ideas and made them reality: ideas so far ahead of their time, most people wouldn't even believe they were possible."

"Many people lost their lives," Reems said, "because of your research. Thankfully, that's all over now."

"Did you really think I'd have given up that easily, Stephanie, if I didn't have some further plan in reserve?"

"Everyone runs out of ideas eventually."

"Cling to that hope." Bern closed his eyes. "What's the melting point of nylon?"

There was an acrid smell then Bern's plastic cuffs fell to the deck, lying warped and melted. He stretched his arms slowly. Around him the eight SEALS raised their rifles. Bern lifted a hand, pointing at one of the SEALs. With a wrenching sound, the rifle flew out of the man's hands, hurtling through the air. Bern caught it neatly.

Truman backed up quickly as Bern shouldered the weapon and aimed it directly at Truman's face. "I have the Accumulator right here. And with it powering my suit I think you'll concede that *I* am the one in control."

ONE HUNDRED ELEVEN

TOM AWOKE IN PAIN. HE was also, perhaps surprisingly, alive. He was strapped to a metal bed, electrodes attached to his chest. Above him were strip-lights and a panelled ceiling. There was the dull heavy creak of metal under pressure in the air.

"What is going on?" he croaked.

"We're on a submarine," said a familiar voice. "Although you're a smart kid so you'd probably worked that out already."

A face loomed over him. Ice ran through his veins.

"Hello, Tom," said Peter Marron. "It's been a while." He held up a large syringe and smiled.

Tom tried to shrink back. "You've got to be--" The lights flickered.

"I know we've had our differences, but that's in the past. I'm actually trying to help you."

"He's telling the truth," said Alex, appearing next to her father.

"Then why am I strapped down?"

There was an odd look on Alex's face – something he hadn't seen there before: sadness. "It's so you don't hurt yourself." She placed her hand on his brow and he felt a powerful tingling sensation.

Tom strained against the straps, but they held firm. "Why would I hurt myself?"

"Because," said Marron, "we're going to treat you. And it requires a delicately placed injection."

Tom stared at the syringe Marron was holding up. A milky liquid was swirling inside.

"This," said Alex, "is the antidote."

"To the dark nano?"

"To everything," Alex said.

"I knew all Bern's plans," Marron said. "He didn't want to leave anyone with your abilities permanently. You should know what he's like by now. This injection contains specific time-limited nanites that will locate and dismantle any nano material inside you."

"Will it hurt?"

Marron laughed. "These are going to fight what's in you, so, yes, it will hurt. Like death. Fortunately you don't need to be conscious during the process. Once it starts, we're going to place you in an induced coma. If everything goes to plan you'll wake up a new man. At least a normal one."

"And how long will it take?"

"It'll be done when it's done. But it could easily be a number of weeks."

"So I just go to sleep and wake up when it's over."

"By which time we'll have sailed somewhere rather warmer. There's an island in the Pacific that we'd like to show you. Lovely white sand, crystal blue waters."

"And if it doesn't work?"

"Then you don't wake up."

Tom saw the lights flicker again, hissing with static. "It sounds risky."

Alex shook her head. "Worse. After that you'll be normal

again."

Marron sighed. "If you don't get this treatment, you're going to die. The nanites inside you have mutated, glitched." He pointed at the lights. "You're doing that, Tom. It's like a random spasm: you can't control it. And it's going to get worse. It's started affecting our other equipment." He turned and tapped the display screen connected by wires to the electrodes on Tom's chest. "Above all, it's affecting you. You might not feel it yet, but your biochemical balance is off. Before long your brain will start to lose functional control of your body."

"I don't understand why you're helping me."

Marron leaned close. "It would be simpler just to shoot you, but my daughter seems to have become rather attached."

Alex pushed him away and placed her hand over Tom's heart. "I know the gift you gave me. I'm just so sorry that yours has been taken from you. If there were anything I could do to prevent you losing your Interface--"

"We've discussed this," Marron cut in. "Now we need to get this done and get out of here. We need to be safely out of range."

The lights turned off for nearly a full second. "Out of range of what?" Tom asked.

"You saw what Bern has become with that suit, your nanites and the Accumulator. He has to be stopped. So I left them a little parting gift, clamped to the outer hull."

Tom's eyes flared. "You mean another of your bombs."

"Fittingly, it's built around nanotechnology. We have to make sure Bern is eliminated. There can't be any possibility he survives."

"And to make sure you're going to kill everyone on that ship."

"Everyone on *all* the ships in the area, I expect. Can't be helped."

"But Lentz is there, and Kate and Reems." Tom looked at

Alex. "You're just going to let him do this?"

"Necessary collateral damage." Alex frowned. "Besides, who is this Kate to you? She seems pretty ordinary."

Tom jerked against his straps again. "You can't just kill them all."

"What's your alternative?" Marron said calmly. "Are you going to head back up there and kill your father? Even if you could, and I doubt it, what would you do afterwards? Negotiate with the US and UK intelligence services to leave you alone?"

"I have to try and stop him." Tom grimaced as a wave of pain shot through him.

"Tom, you're sedated. If not, you'd be unconscious."

Tom shook his head frantically, then suddenly stilled. A smile spread across his face. "What if you gave me more nanites? Tantalus nanites. Ones not infected with the dark nano."

"We don't have any."

Tom looked at Alex. "Yes, we do."

ONE HUNDRED TWELVE

REEMS WATCHED AS THE NAVY SEALs formed a circle around Bern, rifles aimed at him. Bern kept his own rifle aimed at Truman. Nobody moved.

"I'd like to speak with him," Reems said loudly, her voice echoing across the deck. "Before anyone does anything rash, I want to negotiate. Make him an offer that benefits everybody."

Bern nodded. "Lower your weapons and she can approach. I will do her no harm."

She walked up to him slowly, as an eerie silence descended on deck. The wind seemed to have died, as if they were in the eye of a storm. Reems patted her pocket.

"You're not just trying to stall?" Bern said.

"I thought you might want to explain the situation. I don't think our American friends have any idea, and I'd hate more people to die unnecessarily."

He tipped his head on one side. "All those times I 'died'. You never really believed it, did you?"

"It was less convincing after the first few occasions. Still, you did a good job of drawing other people into your web. Leskov Junior, for example."

"He wanted revenge. I was never going to persuade him

otherwise, so I used it against him."

"How did you coordinate your escape? How on earth did you get Tom out from Northwell A? And where is Tom?"

"Your man Croft was my asset once I found the right lever: his daughter. And it doesn't matter where Tom is. His abilities are gone. His nanites are destroyed. I took everything I needed from him."

"You did quite a job of hiding the beta site."

"And the moment you find it, you destroy it. Well done."

"Not my plan. Anyway, why did you turn off the cloaking device on this ship when you'd all but escaped?"

"It wasn't my idea. But here we are." He folded his arms. "So what now? You said you had an offer for me."

"I do. A choice." She pulled something from her pocket: a round metal object with a pin and lever. "Do you know what this is?"

His eyes flickered in alarm.

She pulled out the pin, gripping the lever firmly. "A good old-fashioned hand grenade."

"So my choice is what?"

"Take off that suit – I know it's what is giving you the abilities – or I let go."

Bern nodded. "And I'm supposed to believe you're ready to die, Stephanie?"

"I couldn't live with myself if I let you get away again. Something tells me the trouble you've already caused is only the start."

He reached forward and gripped her hands before she had time to move, prising one of her fingers from the lever.

Her eyes went wide. "You said you wouldn't harm me."

"You did this to yourself." He prised another finger away.

She turned and shouted, "Take cover!" But there was none

near enough for her.

The soldiers rushed several paces back. There was a shimmer of movement across the deck near Bern and Reems as her hand seemed to fly off the grenade.

Then an explosion ripped across the deck.

ONE HUNDRED THIRTEEN

"I NEED MY NANITES BACK," Tom said. "I need some of your blood."

Alex's eyes flickered. "Will it work?"

"Fundamentally, they're still my nanites. I can tell when you're close. I feel the connection."

She gripped his hand. "I used to be able to feel you. But everything that Bern has done must have changed things."

Marron coughed. "Let's get back to reality. Remember, you have no chip in your head now. The nanites are new to you. They could kill you, like they did all the other test subjects."

"I can control them."

"Can he use a suit, like Bern did?" Alex asked.

Marron shook his head. "There are spare first generation suits on this vessel, but Bern has the only functional suit of that specification."

"I want to do it," Tom said. "I don't care about the risks."

"Get a syringe," Alex said.

Marron gripped her arm. "We'll have to lower the sedation. It might kill him and even if it doesn't, the pain will be indescribable." He looked at Tom. "You may recover some abilities or you may be a chaotic mess."

"If it gives me a chance to save my friends, I'll do it."

Alex leaned forward, pressing her cheek against Tom's, and whispered: "It will give you a chance to be extraordinary again."

"Or die trying," Marron said.

Tom's skin burned where Alex touched him, and yet he did not pull away. "At least this time it's my choice."

*

Tom felt the needle in the base of his neck, felt the red liquid in the syringe, ready to become one with him. Alex's blood. The nanites. So much potential. So much danger.

"Hold very still," Marron said.

"Could you have chosen somewhere less risky?" Tom asked through gritted teeth.

"Shut up and let me finish."

"Blood for blood, *brother*," Alex said. "Are you ready for this?"

Tom closed his eyes.

His world exploded. The cabin lights went out and emergency sirens began sounding, but he was only barely aware. His head was hot. His body shook. Electricity started to flow through his nerves. At least that was what it felt like.

He screamed: a scream of pain so pure it was blinding. His mind reached out and he felt the systems around him on the craft at the same time as another urge told him he could break them with but a thought. He edged back from that feeling and let his thoughts extend further. An aircraft carrier floated on the surface above them. Clamped to its hull he sensed the point of impossible energy that was the nano bomb.

He knew where it was. He knew what he had to do.

And then he saw the second point of light. A singularity of a very similar nature. On the deck.

The Accumulator.

And he saw they were different facets of the same thing. And both would destroy everything within reach if he didn't stop them.

It was time to move.

His eyes flew open and he found himself standing, the heavy strapping lying in tatters around his feet. The pain was still there, but something stronger was shutting it out. Marron had an expression he had never seen before. Was he nervous?

Alex looked at Tom, her mouth hanging open, her pupils dilated. "Incredible."

"I have to go now."

Marron nodded. "When you face Bern, don't try and do too much. You don't have a power cell to draw on. You have to fight smart."

"I'll bear that in mind."

"Now I'm going to bring us close to the surface. I'd offer you one of the suits, but, as we know, Bern seems to have master control over those."

Tom's eyes flashed. "I don't need the suit. I am the suit. I am the nanites."

Alex reached forward and embraced him. "I will see you again, Thomas Faraday. I think there are things you can teach me."

Tom stared back at her, his eyes liquid darkness, and she flinched, pulling away.

"Something's changed," she whispered.

"No," he said, "*everything* has."

ONE HUNDRED FOURTEEN

BERN STOOD ON THE DECK, encased in whispers of flame, but protected by the suit. Reems lay on the deck, groaning...

Wait, he thought. *How could she have survived the explosion? It was impossible unless she was shielded.*

There was a crackling hiss and the shape of Lentz flickered into view, crouching over Reems. She looked up. "Even for you, that was a new low."

Bern took a step back, confused. "You jumped between us?"

"If I hadn't, she'd be dead. As it is, she's hardly breathing."

"How did you activate translucency and protection at the same time without Tom's nanites?"

"I shorted a few circuits. It wasn't very power efficient."

"I see. Looks like your suit is exhausted now." He raised the rifle, then realised it was useless, twisted out of shape by the grenade. Muttering, he threw it to one side and extended his hand, instructing the suit to channel energy directly from the Accumulator. His hand crackled with electricity.

"My suit may not have power," Lentz said, "but there's one thing you need to remember."

"What?"

"Not to get distracted."

Bern was about to reply when something hit him on the back of the head.

*

Lentz watched Bern fall to the deck, unconscious. Kate stood behind him, holding the broken handle of an axe.

"I won't pretend I didn't enjoy that," Kate said, "but why didn't his suit protect him?"

"Because he has to tell it to do so. He didn't know about the blow, so it didn't harden to protect him."

"That seems like a significant design flaw."

"Yeah, well maybe I'll fix it in the next version."

From behind them Truman cleared his throat loudly. "Will someone explain just what the hell is going on? Where did you get one of those suits?"

"It wasn't that difficult, given I designed them."

Truman shouted an order and the SEALs raised their weapons, targeting Lentz.

"What are you doing?" Lentz asked, incredulous. "Put those guns down."

"You just admitted to working with Bern."

"He stole the tech from me, you moron. Just like it seems you stole tech from him."

"I never said that--"

Kate banged the axe handle on the deck. "We just saved you. And if we hadn't disabled the invisibility on the carrier, you'd never even have known we were here."

"Of course," Lentz said, "it's no more than I would expect from the idiots who dropped a bomb on that dome. What were you thinking?"

"I..." Truman trailed off.

"That's what I thought. Now can we get a doctor over here to look at Stephanie? And can someone give me a hand to get Bern out of this suit before he wakes up and uses it to kill us all." She frowned. "The words you're looking for are 'right away' and 'thank you'."

Truman shouted an order and one of the SEALs radioed for medical support.

"No!" shouted a man's voice. Lentz turned and saw George Croft running across the deck. He reached Lentz, and stared for a moment at Reems. "Oh my God, is she OK?"

"I hope so."

He nodded and turned to the unconscious form of Bern. "What have you done?"

"What we had to," Lentz said.

"Goddammit." Croft lunged forward and slapped Bern on the face. "Where is my daughter's cure?"

"Stop him," Truman said. "We need Bern unharmed for interrogation." Two SEALs moved forward and lifted Croft away none too gently.

"Who gets to interrogate him still needs to be decided. He's not your prisoner," Lentz said. "You have no jurisdiction here. He is a British citizen."

"Let's not be stupid about this. Reems isn't even conscious."

"Because she was trying to force him to surrender. It's thanks to her the situation is under control. Are you really going to take advantage of her injuries?"

"I have my orders."

Kate coughed. "Did anyone feel that? I thought I..." She trailed off.

"He promised me the cure for my daughter," Croft said. "I just need him to tell me where it is."

Lentz turned and saw Bern's eyes flickering. "We need to

sedate him. Quickly."

"No," said a new voice, both familiar and strangely different. "You will do no such thing."

ONE HUNDRED FIFTEEN

LENTZ TURNED AND SAW TOM standing, staring at them, his eyes dark and unreadable. His skin had an unhealthy grey pallor.

Kate took a step towards him, then hesitated.

Tom ignored her and looked directly at Truman. "Are all your people wearing comms?"

"Yes. I'm very--"

"Remove yours. Right now." Tom adjusted the backpack he was wearing.

Truman pulled it from his ear. "Why?"

Tom blinked and all the US personnel clutched at their ears, screaming, and fell to the ground.

"What the--" Truman began, shocked.

"Your Interface is working again?" Lentz said, standing up.

"I can't let them take my father."

"I agree. We won't let--"

"I can't let you take him either. I need him."

"What's needed," Lentz said, "is to get that suit off of him before he regains consciousness." She moved towards Bern.

"No," Tom said quietly and held out his hand towards her.

Lentz's suit locked rigid. "What are you doing?"

"I said I need him. Now give me some space." He pointed and she took three steps back.

"Tom, you're not well. Just let me help you."

"I know what I'm doing." He crouched next to Bern, who was beginning to stir. "I'm going to take care of my father."

"Tom, stop it," Kate said. "You're not thinking straight."

He spun to face her. "Stay out of this. I don't want to hurt you."

"Why would you hurt me?" She screwed up her face. "I'm not wearing a suit, so you can't control me."

"I don't need to control you." He nodded in the direction of a deck gun. It spun up and pointed at Truman. "I can instruct the gun to fire at any target I choose. And I can keep doing that until I find someone who will help me."

"Help you do what?" Truman asked.

"I'm going to take Bern away from here. It's safer for everyone."

"What?" Kate hissed. "Why would you do this for him?"

"It's complicated. Just like when I worked with Director Reems last year at CERUS Tower. Isn't that right, Dominique?"

Lentz blinked. "As I recall that was very simple. Tom, you need help."

"You're right. I do. Mr Truman, I need something from you: a helicopter."

Truman frowned. "I suppose at least you asked this time. What if I refuse?"

The deck gun twitched.

Lentz shook her head. "Do what he asks. It's not worth the risk."

"I cannot let them leave this ship. Not with the Accumulator. Not now we've seen what Bern can do with it."

"Surely you can track them anywhere. Nobody needs to die

on this deck."

Bern's eyelids flickered, he groaned, then he went quiet again.

"Time's almost up," Tom said. "Do you really want him to stay?"

Kate stared at Tom, then cleared her throat. "Do it, Mr Truman."

Truman gave a glare. "I don't suppose we're going to see our aircraft again."

Tom shrugged. "You'll have bigger things to worry about."

*

Lentz watched as the helicopter receded, carrying Tom and Bern away, until the tiny speck vanished, heading south. Reems had been flown to the US aircraft carrier for urgent medical attention. She was in a serious but stable condition.

Truman stood next to Lentz, his earpiece plugged back in. "We're tracking them via two satellites, and I have other aircraft moving into position."

"Very thorough of you."

"I really hope this doesn't prove to be the worst career decision I've ever made."

"I think the bar has been set pretty high."

"Director Banetti is *en route*: he wants to assess the situation first hand."

"How delightful. Perhaps he can comment on Bern's allegations that you stole his tech."

There was a buzzing from Truman's earpiece and he listened intently. "What do you mean we've lost them?" He screwed up his eyes then turned back to Lentz. "Our satellites have been re-tasked."

"Have they?"

Truman stared at her. "You knew this was going to happen."

"I suspected something would."

"But Tom was right," Kate cut in. "There was danger in Bern staying here."

"Well, obviously, while he was in that suit--"

"No, something else. Something more."

Lentz frowned and pulled out a tablet computer. Her fingers danced over the surface. "While I was in the lab downstairs I accessed this vessel's CCTV. If I run a facial and bio-mechanical recognition search for Tom, we should be able to see if he was anywhere specific..." She stopped and tapped on a particular feed. "This is from a hull-mounted camera a few minutes before Tom appeared on deck." She turned the tablet to let Truman and Kate see a figure in scuba gear pulling a metal cube from the hull, then carefully placing it in a backpack.

"What was that object?" Truman leaned closer, re-winding then enlarging the image to peer at the cube. "It looks like the Accumulator."

Lentz zoomed the image in even further and shook her head. "It is CERUS tech, but I thought it was only theoretical."

"What is it?"

"A nano bomb. Significantly more powerful than the thermobaric weapon you dropped on the Dome. The tech is very similar to that used in the Accumulator – the one you deny stealing from CERUS. The bomb is fusion driven."

"So Bern had a bomb on board, like a self-destruct? And Tom was trying to get it off this ship?"

"Perhaps it couldn't be defused," Kate said softly. "And this rather re-frames his actions, wouldn't you say?"

Truman rubbed the bridge of his nose. "Where will they go with it?"

"I don't know," Lentz replied. "And, judging by what Tom did to your satellites, he doesn't want you to know either."

ONE HUNDRED SIXTEEN

TOM FLEW THE HELICOPTER SOUTH for more than three hours. The waters below had warmed considerably; Tom could feel them. He was different than before: the Interface had returned, if not as sophisticated as previously. It was like restoring from an old software backup; his abilities were at the level of sophistication he had passed on to Alex a year ago. But now there was something else: the adaptations in the nanites, put there by Alex and her experiences and, above all, her ability to learn. Yet for him it was manifesting differently.

He looked at Bern in his suit. Still unconscious, but impervious. He looked at the flow of particles on the suit's surface. He saw how it worked. And he sent a spark of electricity through it.

Bern flinched, then jerked upright, his eyes flying open. "What's going on?"

"I'm getting us to safety," Tom replied from his position in the flight seat.

"Someone hit me..." Bern's hands flew to run over his torso, checking to see that he was wearing his suit. "You have a helicopter?"

"I negotiated."

"How... are you flying?"

"It seems I've regained use of my Interface."

"Why are you doing this? I thought you were in league with Alex."

"It's become clear that I cannot trust her. Or Lentz. Or Reems. And certainly not the CIA. Maybe I *can* trust you. With the US there, the *Phoenix Reborn* is lost. We needed to get away and consider our options." Tom pointed out to their right. A small, rocky island had come into view. "I need to take a break."

*

Tom brought them low and set the helicopter down on a rocky beach. There were no trees, just some scrubby bushes and lots of rocks. They climbed out and stretched their legs.

"Do you ever plan on taking it off?" asked Tom. "The suit?"

Bern smiled. "Who'd want to be normal and vulnerable again?"

"Hopefully we're safe here," Tom said, stepping onto the smooth pebbles. "It's uninhabited."

"I should thank you for saving me back there. You could have let me be captured."

"I didn't think prison was the right place for you. The turf war for whether it would be a British or American prison was already starting."

"I have no doubt." Bern frowned. "Look, Tom, I'm sorry for how things have worked out. I know at times it looks like I've given no regard to your rights or feelings."

"You're a driven man. I understand that. Don't apologise for who you are."

"I never personally meant you harm. I was looking for a--"

"Way to change the world? Yes, I understand that too. And

you're never going to stop."

"It's not in my nature."

"I agree. And if the US or British had imprisoned you, I'm sure you'd have found a way to extricate yourself or buy your way out." Tom unshouldered his backpack and placed it on the ground between them. "You're impressively resourceful."

"The world isn't changed by eighty per cent effort."

"Given that they weren't going to deal with you, I had to take on that task." Tom unzipped the backpack and removed the black metal cube. There was a prolonged moment of silence as Tom watched Bern stare at it.

Finally his father spoke. "Where did you get that?"

"You're not going to ask what it is?"

"It's a CERUS prototype. Archived. Almost nobody had access. How did you--?"

"Peter Marron planted it on the *Phoenix Reborn* to kill you."

Bern reached his hand out, then withdrew it. "I upset him more than I realised."

"He said he was returning a favour."

"You spoke with him? Did the US capture him?"

"No, he kind of captured me."

"And then let you go?"

"He also gave me the codes." Tom flipped open a control panel on the cube to reveal a timer display. It read ten minutes, but the counter was static.

"Why would he do that?"

"I persuaded him that it was unfair to kill everybody on board, which is why I engineered things to bring the bomb on the helicopter, safely away from the fleet. Here there'll be no collateral damage."

Bern froze. "Why would there be any kind of damage?"

ONE HUNDRED SEVENTEEN

BERN SHOOK HIS HEAD. "YOU would commit suicide?"

Tom narrowed his eyes. "I'm dead already, after what you did to me. But now you're dead too. There's a kind of poetic justice to it."

"And that's your plan? To give up?"

"It's one of my options, but first I thought I'd ask you about my mother."

Bern swallowed. "You already know she was a CERUS employee: that's how we met. There's nothing else to tell."

"I want to know what *really* happened to her."

"And if I tell you?"

"Then I'll let you go. I give you my word. And I'm a lawyer."

"You're not really that any more."

"If that's right, it's your doing."

Bern frowned. "You can have the truth, but you might not like it. Your mother betrayed me. She joined CERUS with the sole intention of stealing our research and selling it to the highest bidder. And that's exactly what she did. She seduced me to get access to the technology. She got what she wanted and left."

"And what did she take?"

"Early-stage nano research: one of our most sensitive

projects."

"The Accumulator?"

"That's right."

"So you knew she took it and you had her arrested?"

Bern hesitated. "We made a judgement call to keep the theft confidential."

"I don't believe that's the full story for a second."

"It's the truth. I had some suspicions and had her followed. That was when we found out she was pregnant. What's the value in locking up a young mother?"

"You actually expect me to believe in your humanity? That you thought of her welfare or mine?" Tom shook his head. "You wanted her to take the tech."

"Why would I want that?"

"You needed someone to act as the go between, to unwittingly deliver the goods. I bet you chose her specifically - headhunted her to join CERUS. Just as you did with me. You wanted her to take something to them. How did that help you?"

"In my experience, the Americans only ever help themselves."

"So you made it look like they were helping themselves when really you were stuck. You had an item of tech with a problem that you couldn't solve, so you farmed it out to another research organisation: one that would be only too delighted to work on it, provided they didn't suspect they were being set up."

"Very clever." Bern ground his teeth. "So you wanted to bring me here to gloat?"

"I wanted to see if you would tell the truth. As usual, you came up short."

"Well, that's great. But you seem to be forgetting one thing: I also have an Interface and I have a lot more power behind mine. I also understand the inventions my company has built better than you ever could." Bern turned to the cube and closed his eyes. There was a popping hiss and a burning smell. The LED display turned brown. "I've deactivated the trigger circuits. The bomb cannot be detonated." Bern struck out hard, knocking Tom to the ground. "So this game is over."

ONE HUNDRED EIGHTEEN

TOM FELL TO THE GROUND, scrabbling among the rocks. With a growl he found his feet and lunged at Bern. He collided with Bern's chest, but it was like hitting steel and, with a crunch, Tom fell to one side. All he had to do was get close enough to make a connection. Somehow he had to find enough strength to do it.

"What are you trying to do?" Bern said, staring down at Tom, sprawled at his feet. "You must know you can't hurt me in this suit."

Tom rose, gripping Bern's shoulders. He closed his eyes and tried to reach out: to feel the suit that his father wore and the power source within its web.

Bern struck him with the flat of his hand

Tom fell back, gasping. "So what now?"

"I'm going to leave you here."

"Too much of a coward to kill me yourself, and nobody here to do it for you?"

Bern tipped his head to one side. "You're a fool. Just like your mother. That video shown in the lab was right - whoever the hell ran it, I have no idea - but Amelia came to me four years ago to ask for a cure? I said I couldn't help her."

"If she couldn't give you anything you wanted, why would you?"

"The thing is, she just laughed. She said she wanted to see if I'd changed. She said I wasn't the only person with experimental treatments under development and she would find a way." A smile flickered over his face. "That obviously worked out for her."

Tom lurched forward again, feigned a trip and staggered against Bern, holding onto him as if for balance, hoping not to get pushed away. The suit was like a firewall, protecting the Accumulator. He didn't have the strength to break through. He needed more power, but the only source was beyond the barrier.

"It's over. I don't know what you're trying, but it's futile. Accept this."

Tom slipped back to sit on the ground, next to the useless bomb. He needed to get more energy. There had to be a way.

And suddenly he knew that there *was* a way – if it didn't kill him.

All he had to do was force his opponent to act. Behind Bern he saw the helicopter and, with a thrust of his thoughts, he connected to its controls. Immediately the rotors started to spin.

Bern jerked around, alarmed. "Stop!" He lunged forward and placed a hand on Tom's chest, electricity crackling. Tom felt the energy flow into him, driven from the Accumulator, shaped by Bern's suit. His body fought and shook.

A normal person would have been paralysed, but instead the nanites drew the energy in hungrily. Tom reached out, following the flow back to its source. He could feel the incredible energy within the Accumulator. He placed his other hand on the bomb. Its energy was different and yet similar, designed to be channelled and controlled, then released in one terrible moment of destruction: derived from the same principles, built by the same process, just one tiny divergence in configuration, producing a hugely different outcome.

Tom felt the energy flow from the Accumulator. He didn't really need it. He just needed access. He felt the bomb. And he did what only he could do. He reached out and made a change. Then, with a sharp intake of breath, he made another, but the energy did not stop. Bern's hand was still on his chest. His heart was going to burst...

Shrieking, he flung himself backwards, his hair steaming.

Bern shook his head. "Goodbye, Tom."

Then he turned and climbed into the helicopter.

ONE HUNDRED NINETEEN

BERN CLIMBED ON BOARD THE helicopter and let his mind merge with the control systems. Already he was becoming more adept at working the Interface. In moments he was airborne, heading south west. There were many islands he could touch down on and refuel: islands where money would trump any theoretical formalities. After that, the world was his oyster.

Nothing could stand in his way.

His thoughts flickered briefly back to the island he had just left. Could he perhaps reactivate the nano bomb and leave not even a trace of Tom on this earth? He could feel the device in his mind as it sat on the boulder. Should he be humane and spare the boy some suffering, or should he let him die slowly? He was just weighing up the decision when something occurred to him.

Reactivating the bomb was possible, so why hadn't Tom done it? Bern had assumed his son's Interface wasn't working – at least fully, but the last moments of the island had shown otherwise. And if it was working, and Tom had wanted to blow them up, wouldn't he have done that, even after Bern had destroyed the detonator? It didn't add up. If Tom hadn't meant to die, what had been his plan?

And then he realised what Tom had done.

His mind shook in horror. It was such a delicate manoeuvre: a tweak here, and a tweak there. A masterful application of the Interface by somebody far more adept at manipulating it.

The nano bomb had become an Accumulator, repurposed into something intended to release energy far more slowly.

And the Accumulator housed in his suit had been through the reverse process.

It had become a bomb.

He could feel it all now. Once it reached a specified distance from Tom's newly created Accumulator it would detonate. The helicopter was turning as sharply as he could bring it round, even as he felt the trigger breach.

And he knew it was too late. There was nothing even he, with all his abilities, could do.

At the base of his spine he felt warmth turn to heat, turn to incandescent fury: so much energy – if only he could find some way to do something with it. If only he could guide the nanites appropriately, anything would be possible.

But there was no time. Suddenly everything was light and dark at once, and he was being gripped by something impossibly strong. Desperately he tried to resist, as around him reality tore apart.

And there was pain.

So much pain.

*

Tom lay on the rocks watching the helicopter fly away. Was this the right thing to do? Despite everything, he couldn't feel good about it.

Then the explosion blossomed: a white flare of purest light, almost blinding him before he could turn away. At last, a death his father could not have faked.

He thought of his mother. She had reached out to Bern and he had turned her away - her words about there being an alternative were surely just a futile, angry response. Tom could only imagine what it must have taken for her to approach the man she hated most in the world – and for nothing. Just as Croft's daughter would receive no miracle.

And he would die on this island. His father knew that and still he left him.

There was no food or water. He almost screamed at the irony. To have done so much, but to be foiled by a basic human need as old as time. No life without food or water, because without them there was no energy for life.

Then he felt a spark, and his eyes fell on the former bomb.

He had his own Accumulator filled with energy. So much energy.

Perhaps it was not over after all. He closed his eyes and let his mind reach out.

Far, far out.

ONE HUNDRED TWENTY

LENTZ SAT IN THE BRIEFING room on board the *USS Inimitable*, glaring at Truman. "I don't have anything more to tell you, Deputy Director."

He ran a tired hand through his greying hair. "Well, I suggest you try, Ms Lentz, because my instructions are to shake the tree until something falls out."

"I hear Bern's man Brody already defected to your team. Ask him."

"You know who we need to speak to. You know why."

"Tom saved you." Lentz slammed the table. "Or don't you remember?"

"Did he? Or did he deceive us? We have no way of knowing, seeing as how he disconnected the satellites. Look you can tell me or you can tell Director Banetti. He'll be here very shortly."

Lentz raised an eyebrow. "Is that supposed to intimidate me? I don't care if you wheel in your President, it won't make any difference to what information I have."

A loud phone ringtone rang around the room. Truman looked around, confused. "Do we have a phone in here?"

The ringing stopped and was replaced by a loud, slightly metallic voice. "Hello, Dominique. Hello, Mr Truman."

"Tom!" shouted Lentz, looking around. "Are you OK?"

Truman signalled to one of his aides. "Trace that, er, signal." He looked up at the air. "Tom, you're OK. Where are you? We need you to come back to us. Is Bern with you?"

"I can't come back to you or tell you where I am. I don't trust you. And even if I did, I don't trust the people with you. The world isn't ready for this tech."

"I'm not sure we can accept that. As I was just saying to Dr Lentz--"

"Let me be very clear, Deputy Director Truman, if you don't immediately let all my friends go, I'm going to notify the Canadian Government of what has been taking place in their territory. I have the Canadian Prime Minister's private number right here."

"How could you possibly--"

"I'm calling a US navy ship on a disavowed mission: not only that, I've called you in a room that doesn't even have a phone. And you think I can't get the Canadian PM's private number?"

Truman blinked rapidly. "Are you threatening me?"

"Yes, Deputy Director Truman, I *am* threatening you. Also, to be upfront about things, I'm afraid I can't return your helicopter. It was destroyed in a very large explosion, as your satellites will likely confirm in about forty-eight hours' time. Apologies but I've had to glitch their processing in case you try to work out where I am."

"What about Bern and the Accumulator?"

"They were *closely* involved with the very large explosion. Check the data when you receive it. It seems you were right to worry the Accumulator could be converted into a bomb."

Truman shook his head. "We're going to come out of this with nothing, aren't we?"

"That's for you to decide. Some would say coming out of this situation alive is something."

Truman slapped his hands on the desk, looking across at Lentz. "So what happens next, Tom?"

"After you've done what I've asked, then you never hear from me again."

"Banetti wants to talk to you."

There was a moment's silence, then Tom laughed. "Why would I do that?"

"I don't know. It's not like he shares anything with me. Except blame. And I probably mean 'passing' rather than 'sharing'."

"That's what I thought. In the time I have, he won't be a priority."

Lentz cleared her throat loudly. "Are you OK, Tom? Are you hurt?"

There was a pause. "I'm... There are some things I need to do. Some questions I need to answer." He paused for a moment. "Don't look for me. If you do, I can't promise what you will find."

ONE HUNDRED TWENTY-ONE

ONE WEEK LATER...

KATE SAT in her apartment in North London, a large glass of Rioja in hand, as she stared at the screen of her laptop. On it was her letter of resignation, giving the required one month's notice. She wasn't sure what she was going to do next, but whatever it was, she wouldn't be doing it at CERUS.

She stood up and walked over to the window, staring down at the street below - a light drizzle was falling, misting the glow from the street lamps. So many people had died, although there were few she would miss. Sharp, of course, killed in his prison cell - which had meant it was safe for her to return home. Leskov - who had hired the killer - cut to pieces and thrown on the jetty near the ruins of the CERUS beta site. Fabienne or Felicia or Fiona - or whatever her real name was - had not yet been found. Her body was most likely buried deep in the rubble of the Dome, probably never to be recovered - broken, like so much of everything touched by CERUS.

But the greatest of all those deaths - in terms of impact - was William Bern. Tom had confirmed it - or rather, she corrected herself, *Lentz* had confirmed that Tom had confirmed it. From Tom, Kate had heard nothing. She had risked her life to go and rescue him, and he hadn't cared. In fact, worse than that, he seemed to have some bizarre connection with Alex. It was clear that the Tom she had known a year ago didn't exist any more.

She shrugged, walked back to her laptop, and emailed her letter to Lentz. She didn't care any more. That episode of her life was over. She was moving on. She was fed up sitting in the shadows, and she was fed up with putting herself out for people who didn't care.

She wanted to do something for herself. Something that would make a difference. Even without knowledge of her resignation, she'd received a number of approaches from recruiters - one pushing a senior role at Glifzenko, the huge Pharma company. It was not where she saw herself going next. She felt the tingling in her palm, and permitted herself a small smile. She would persuade. She would change the world. Whatever she wanted, she was just going to ask for it.

Kate hesitated. There was a shift in the air. Or was that just subjective impression - was the shift in *her*. She could sense... she could sense...

She span to face the door.

Tom stood watching her. He brushed hair away from his face. He looked... different. Older. His voice, when he spoke, seemed to reverberate: "I wanted to apologise."

"For what?"

"For everything. For walking out when we had dinner. For never communicating. For being so... obtuse. I've not been myself. You and Lentz came to rescue me. That was no small thing."

"Just returning a favour. What happened to you? You looked like you were going to die. Now you seem... OK."

"I feel OK. I was in a pretty bad way. But I came back from the brink. I think I can keep things under control."

"That's good to hear."

He nodded. "And I've been less than gracious. After all the information you dug up."

"You were right, it's still my thing." She folded her arms. "Do you want to dig further?"

"I want to do something. There are so many things I could do. But I can't do them alone. I don't *want* to do them alone."

"You want my help?"

"I want to collaborate. I want to learn."

"From me?"

"I know I'm not the only one who's changed."

She held up her hand, rippling her fingers. "I'm still not sure where this will take me."

"Me neither. Nobody really understands nanotech. The only certainty is its *uncertainty*."

"And that means they're going to come after you. Because they want what you have."

Tom shrugged. "Let them try. We'll be waiting."

"So, while we wait, what are we going to do?"

"Some things that will make a difference." His eyes sparkled. "I have one for starters."

*

Lentz had read the message three times before destroying it with a blow torch. Written on a generic brown paper bag with wax crayons, it had appeared, neatly folded, in the wrong section of her household recycling. She didn't know *when* it had arrived, but on reading it she was pretty sure she knew *how*.

The words and paper were now ash, but the message was still burned into her mind.

My father really is dead, but this is not over. I'm going to do something with this 'gift'. I just haven't decided what yet. Maybe I'm beyond help, but maybe other people aren't. For starters, someone in particular needs your assistance. I could do this, but I wouldn't have your... people skills. Follow the link below for more detailed instructions. Then burn this note.

Now Lentz stood outside King's College Hospital, her hands in her pockets, one of them wrapped around the small padded envelope. The data she had been provided with detailed that the individual she needed to intercept would leave at a certain time: she was not surprised to find the information was accurate.

George Croft's ex-wife, Julia, walked out through a glass revolving door exactly on time, her face a mask, devoid of make-up and of hope. She glanced up at the grey sky, then shuffled slowly over to the designated smoking area, a metal-roofed area with scratched plastic windows. Inside, she placed a crooked cigarette between her lips then started patting her pockets. Lentz got to her before she found her lighter.

"You really shouldn't smoke those," she offered.

Julia looked up with a shrug. Her eyes narrowed. "Do I know you? You look... familiar."

"I work with your ex-husband. At least in a manner of speaking."

Julia's face darkened. "I haven't seen him in two weeks. What's this about?"

"He's been... It's complicated."

"It's always complicated. So where is he now, or is that classified?"

"Your ex-husband is in custody. I can't tell you any more than that, but it's why he hasn't visited."

"He could have sent me a message."

"I'm afraid he couldn't, which is why I'm here."

"Well, tell him I hope they throw away the key. And that he rots." She turned away.

"From my perspective, he's a good man who made a difficult choice." Lentz removed the padded envelope from her pocket and held it out. "He'd want you to have this."

"I don't want anything from him."

"It's not from him exactly. It's... the result of something he started."

Julia narrowed her eyes. "I *have* seen you before. On the news. You work at CERUS."

"I'm the CEO, at least until they fire me, which they might do for giving you this." She placed the envelope in Julia's hands.

"What is it?"

"It's not a promise, but it is hope. Currently I believe you have none."

Julia opened the envelope and removed a glass tube. Inside a green liquid sparkled. "What is this? Some type of drug?"

"Medical nanotech, specifically attuned to your daughter's condition. I can't guarantee it will work, but there's a chance."

"What do you mean, *work*?"

"It's a treatment."

"You have a cure for cancer?"

"As I said, it's merely a *hope*."

Julia stared at the tube. "If there's even a chance, why me? Why can't everyone have some of your 'hope'?"

"That's a very good question: one I intend to put to the people making all this cloak and dagger business necessary. But, for now, I have a group of scientists standing by to support your daughter's medical team." Lentz handed over her business card.

Julia stared at it for several long moments. Finally she placed both the glass tube and card in her pockets. Then she reached forward and hugged Lentz tight.

"I wish you and your daughter all the very best."

Lentz watched as Julia hurried back inside the hospital. Then she glanced down at her phone. As usual there were a stream of messages: from Kate attaching a letter; from Reems, even though she was still in hospital, and from Banetti, once again asking to meet her for lunch. She quickly deleted it.

There was nothing from Tom. But something told her that, today, he wasn't far away.

She saw a shimmer out of the corner of her eye, a ripple in the air.

Then it was gone.

THANK YOU'S

My thanks for choosing to read ***Resurface***. If you did enjoy it, do consider leaving a quick review on Amazon or Goodreads - as an author, reviews are absolutely critical in getting noticed, and are always hugely appreciated. As a thank you, you can also get a FREE short techno-thriller - use the following link: http://www.tonybatton.com/free-story-from-interface

I owe a great debt of gratitude to the many people who have encouraged and supported me through the long process of bringing *Resurface* to completion. A special thank you to my *beta team* who so willingly read (and re-read) the manuscript and provided feedback and criticism - it was invaluable in making the book better: *Jin Koo Niersbach, Chris Turner, Maurice Murphy, Elli Murphy, Alex Bott, Joshua Allarm, John Nicholson, Imogen Cleaver, Paul Cleaver, Johan van Wijgerden, Mary Seear, Chris Ward, Tania Williams, Patrick Wijngaarden and Judy Bott.*

If you have any comments, questions or feedback I'd love to hear from you. I can be reached via my website www.tonybatton.com.

Best regards

Tony Batton
London 2016

ABOUT THE AUTHOR

Tony Batton worked in international law firms, media companies and Formula One motorsport, before turning his hand to writing novels. He is passionate about great stories, gadgets and coffee, and probably consumes too much of each.

Tony's novels explore the possibilities and dangers of new technology, and how that can change lives. When not writing, or talking about gadgets, Tony likes to play basketball, guitar, and computer games with his two young sons. He lives in London with his family.

You can connect with Tony online at his website: www.tonybatton.com

on Facebook: https://www.facebook.com/tonybattonauthor/

and on Twitter: https://twitter.com/thetonybatton

Printed in Great Britain
by Amazon